FEELING FOR BONES

bethany pierce

FEELING FOR BONES

MOODY PUBLISHERS
CHICAGO

Editor: LB Norton
Interior Design: Smartt Guys design
Cover Design: John Hamilton Design
Cover Art: Constantini Michele—Getty

ISBN: 0-8024-6288-X
ISBN-13: 978-0-8024-6288-6

Library of Congress Cataloging-in-Publication Data

Pierce, Bethany, 1983-
Feeling for bones / Bethany Pierce.
p. cm.
ISBN 978-0-8024-6288-6
1. Teenage girls—Fiction. 2. Sisters—Fiction. 3. Anorexia nervosa—Fiction. 4. Domestic fiction. I. Title.

PS3616.I346F44 2007
813'.6—dc22

2006037790

We hope you enjoy this book from Moody Publishers. Our goal is to provide high-quality, thought-provoking books and products that connect truth to your real needs and challenges. For more information on other books and products written and produced from a biblical perspective, go to www.moodypublishers.com or write to:

Moody Publishers
820 N. LaSalle Boulevard
Chicago, IL 60610

1 3 5 7 9 10 8 6 4 2

Printed in the United States of America

To Mother and Father Dearest

part one

CHAPTER 1

at the age of sixteen, I suffered recurring nightmares. I was running as hard as I could while my destination on the horizon receded to a pinpoint and vanished like the white pop of an old television screen winking out. Awake, I lay in a trance at the bottom of a pool, suffocating beneath an invisible, silent weight: people's voices reached my ears across a great distance, and the reflection of my body was always before me, wavering in myriad and grotesque distortions.

It was the year Dad lost his job. He was given severance pay, but finding new work was only half the problem: part of his salary was our family's tenancy in the parsonage. I spent the first of those suspenseful weeks in a quiet circuit between school and the dinner table, navigating the maze of moving boxes to disappear into my bedroom each night.

To spare my little sister the final dismantling of our home, Dad arranged for both of us to leave for Great-aunt Margaret's a week before he and Mom would arrive with the moving vans. As a six-year-old, Callapher nursed anxieties about the move that were as imaginative as they were ridiculous. When she first learned we would be leaving the flatlands of southern Ohio for the Appalachian Mountains, she locked herself in the bathroom and cried for an hour because she was afraid she would fall off. Dad said, "We'll just tie a rope around your waist and secure it to the table." But Mom arched her eyebrow at him, so he stopped. Mom kept her eyebrows perfectly groomed, delicate and sharp like the moon crescents above the painted long-lashed eyes of Callapher's *Gone With the Wind* collector Barbie.

I envied my sister the naiveté of her fears. But after saying goodbye to my friends, I was surprised to realize there were none I would miss terribly. I felt a little ashamed of the fact, but at the same time strangely proud: proud that I didn't need anyone. When we boarded the bus for Great-aunt Margaret's, the sunrise was just a line of budding pink on the horizon. Taking my seat, I felt a flutter in my stomach, the kind you get when the crush you've had for a month walks into the room. A sense of anticipation.

It was the first of March, but unusually warm for spring. Callapher and I shared the bus with half a dozen other passengers. In a silent stupor, they swayed to the rhythm of the Greyhound as its engine roared against the Pennsylvania terrain. Twisting the heavy weight of my hair into a bun, I wiped the sweat from the nape of my neck. Callapher fidgeted in the seat beside me.

"How much longer?" she asked.

"We're almost there." I just wanted her to be quiet. "Sit up. It's too hot to be so close."

Sighing dramatically, she flopped back against the seat. Her legs were too short to reach the floor. She swayed them back and forth, watching the sunlight glint off the sparkles in her jelly slippers. She winked her eyes at them. First her right, then her left. Right, left, squinting.

"Something in your eye?" I asked.

"Look, when I do this it makes the colors change."

"I am looking."

"No, I mean try it." She covered her left eye with the palm of her hand so that she could only see from the right. She covered the right eye in turn. "See, everything looks different. Like more purple."

I said, "I see," but I was looking down at the book I'd brought. Callapher walked her finger people up and down my arm.

"Stop it," I murmured.

"Olivia?"

"Mmm."

"Olivia," she repeated.

"I said 'what.' "

She squirmed to her knees so that her face was level with mine. "Why do my eyes do that?"

"That's how they work together. One sees one set of colors and the other sees another set and then your brain puts the two together," I lied.

"I heard your eye flips things upside down and then your brain turns them around again." She projected her palm forward, like a policeman halting traffic, then turned her arm so that her fingers pointed down. "Like this." She repeated the gesture several times, rapidly.

"Where did you hear that?" I asked.

"On TV."

"Well, it's true."

She sucked on the zipper of her jacket meditatively. I told her not to be disgusting and to spit it out. She kicked the back of the empty seat in front of her. She slid around and sat backwards. She laid her head in my lap.

She asked, "Are we there yet?"

"Almost," I said. "Probably almost."

The road passed beneath the wheels of the bus, its path never-ending and monotonous as the slats of a treadmill. I stared out the window, excessively disappointed with the view. Nothing more than hills buried in blurred brush, brown and green. Bloated land. I closed my right eye to stare at the landscape with my left. I switched eyes, winking one then the other. The mountain jumped back and forth, shifting like an object in a room lit by strobe light.

I lift up my eyes to the hills—where does my help come from? The psalm occurred to me as clearly as if someone had whispered it in my ear. That's what you get as the daughter of a minister: a mind full of Scripture. My Sunday school teacher used to give us verses printed on thin scraps of paper the shape and size of the slips folded in fortune cookies. These printed papers littered my brain. The inside of my head, a ticker-tape parade.

We passed a bait shop, a gas station, and a spattering of white-washed houses, all sandwiched between city limits posted on leaning green signs. One after the other, these sparse islands of civilization gave way to greater and wider stretches of untamed land. Just seconds after passing the line of a little town named Cedarville, the engine of the bus roared up in protest, sending a shudder down the length of the floor that tingled the soles of my feet. We veered off the road slowly, coming to a complete stop at the curb.

The driver unlatched himself from his chair. It buoyed up in his absence. Standing at the front of the bus, he adjusted his belt beneath his overhanging belly. "Sorry, folks," he apologized. "Engine's overheated again. Gonna be a few minutes."

He stepped down from the bus, which, I imagined, lifted with a sigh like that of the chair in being released from the particular burden of that one man's excessive weight. In that same moment, a grouping of heavy-bellied clouds covered the sun. The darkness of a premature dusk raced over the land with all the speed of a heavy curtain drawn shut. Of their own accord, reading lights flickered to life along the perimeter of the bus's ceiling, creating green halos upon the heads of the passengers beneath who eyed the changing landscape with suspicion.

Callapher fussed to be free of her buckle. "I have to go to the bathroom," she announced.

I sent her to the toilet in the back. She returned with her face screwed tight in pain.

"I can't go; there's somebody in there." She did an impatient dance in the aisle.

"Hold on," I said, undoing my own seat belt. I remembered passing a gas station just at the city limits. "Get your jacket."

"But it's hot."

"I know—but it might rain while we're out."

At the front of the bus, I told a woman that we were going out for a second and not to let the driver pull away without us.

"Sweetheart, we're not going anywhere," she replied. "But I'll tell him."

The gas station was no longer visible from the road, but above the wall of trees an artificially white light glowed bright. We ran down the street in its direction.

"Slow down," Callapher demanded. She ran with the stilted gait of a one-legged man, her legs locked together at the knees.

"C'mon, it's not that far. You can hold it in; no one's looking."

She pinched her hand between her legs.

When we reached the station, a chime above the door announced our entrance.

"Bathroom?" I asked breathlessly.

Raising his eyebrows, the attendant pointed to the back. I helped Callapher pull her pants down as we ran. With her underwear around her ankles, she half tripped into the stall. I closed the door behind her.

"You make it?" I asked.

"Yeah," she managed.

Leaning against the door, I saw my own reflection looking back from the square mirror opposite. My skin was pale. The single light above the sink cast the bathroom in a yellowish hue, pulling deep shadows from beneath my eyes. I turned away.

The toilet flushed. A pair of twins about Callapher's age emerged from the handicapped stall. They wore matching pink dresses that fanned out, pleated and shaped like lampshades. Red curls kinked tight in the humidity had escaped from the once carefully arranged ballerina buns atop their heads. Together, they stood on tiptoe to lather their hands over the shared sink.

"You look very pretty," I told them.

"Thank you," they replied in unison.

"Were you in a wedding?" I asked, noting the stump of a withering bouquet on the edge of the sink.

"Yes," one of the twins answered with pride. "Our mother's."

They patted their hands with brown paper towels, and one wiped her palms against her dress for good measure. They skipped from the bathroom.

When Callapher emerged, looking better, I told her to wash her hands. "Use soap," I said. "Don't just rinse them off."

At the counter, I bought her a shrink-wrapped sub sandwich and a large soda. We sat for a moment at the single plastic booth situated between the coffeemaker and the row of candy machines.

Outside the window, parked beside the second gas pump, a blue minivan chugged in place. Pink and yellow streamers trailed the pavement behind it. White balloons hung from the side mirrors and the rear door. A sign had been duct taped to the back, just covering a hairline crack that cut the length of the glass. In handwritten cursive it read *Just Married*. I couldn't see the bride's face, but a cloud of white fabric and lace was visible just over the rim of the passenger side window. Occasionally, the great bundle moved as the bride readjusted herself; once, it trembled.

It was the groom who drew my attention: a man in a white tuxedo waiting beside the open van door, one hand behind his back, the other straight at his side. The twins ran the length of the parking lot, the second throwing herself into the groom's arms. He lifted her into the air and kissed her affectionately on the cheek before setting her in the van and closing the door behind her. It slid along its rusted hinges with the roll of a gentle thunder.

I was struck with a peculiar desire to study his face, but he got into the front seat without glancing back my way, and his features remain indefinite in my memory. The van drove away, white balloons bouncing with the eagerness of hands waving farewell.

"Come on," I urged Callapher, glancing at my watch. We'd been gone fifteen minutes. "You can eat the rest on the bus."

"I don't want anymore." She offered the remainder of her sandwich to me.

"I'm not hungry."

The rain began as soon as we started back. In seconds it was a torrential downpour. Lightning flashed on the horizon. Callapher screamed. When she was really scared, she grimaced with a deep and rigid downward turn of her bottom lip that made her chin jut forward and left her bottom row of teeth just visible. Her plastic shoes quickly filled with water. She tripped. I offered to give her a piggyback ride. Once on my back, she pitched her coat over her head and mine.

"You're choking me!" I called through the roar of rain on pavement. "Don't hold on so tight—it's only rain. It's nothing to be afraid of."

"I amn't scared," Callapher stated.

"You *aren't* scared," I corrected.

"Nope," she insisted. She grasped her arms tighter around my neck as a second peal of thunder shook the ground.

We arrived at the Greyhound dripping and panting. Through the narrow aisle, we managed our way back to our seats, avoiding the indignant grunts of passengers sprayed with rainwater by our passing. Callapher cradled her jumbo soda pop with both hands while I helped peel away her soggy shoes.

"Let me take off your shirt," I said.

"No. I don't want them to see me naked."

"You're soaked. No one will care."

She whispered, "They'll see my boobies."

I laughed. "You don't have anything to hide. Put your arms up."

Too tired to complain, she obediently raised her arms. The tight T-shirt pulled from her body with a wet slurp. Her skin was clammy and cool in the sallow yellow light. I took my own jacket down from the storage compartment where I'd left it neatly folded, and wrapped it around my sister's bare shoulders. We sat down. She laid her head on my shoulder and closed her eyes. In minutes, she was sleeping.

Half an hour later, the driver took his seat, and we began again up the road. This marked the second pit stop we'd been forced to make in two hours. It occurred to me too late that we should have called Margaret at the gas station so she wouldn't worry.

I tried to remember my great-aunt. The first years of my parents' marriage, they made an effort to keep in touch with that corner of my mother's childhood, but it had grown increasingly difficult to make time for a lone relative living so far from the rest. Margaret single-handedly maintained the old farmhouse and the great tract of land left to her by her late husband. The marriage was so long in the past that no one remembered it well or spoke of it often. Ten years ago Mom heard that Margaret had taken in a housemate, an unmarried friend by the name of Ruby Alcott. Together, she and Margaret were known in town as the Old Maids.

This permanent addition to Margaret's otherwise solitary life alleviated the burden on my mother's conscience. In the years that followed, each Christmas brought one excuse or another why we couldn't accept Margaret's annual invitation. We had never met Ms. Alcott. We knew her only by pictures and by the new signature adjoining Margaret's on each year's posted holiday greeting card, which we kept in a shoe box with the other rubber-band-bound Hallmark Christ childs that lay in beds of heavenly gold hay.

In anticipation of our arrival, Margaret had mailed us weekly installments of Bethsaida life: postcards, clippings from the local newspaper, church bulletins with all the exciting announcements circled in red. She sent me a help-wanted ad for a housepainter. The envelope had been addressed to "Miss Monahan," and the enclosed note said, "Possible employment opportunity. Thought you might be interested, since your mother says you are a talented artist." Mom scolded me for laughing at the note. "Humor her, Olivia," she'd said. "She's only trying to help."

I didn't need to be reminded of Margaret's help. You could praise my dad's credentials all you wanted, but I knew that she was the reason Bethsaida Christian Academy agreed to hire him for the coming year. No one would have overlooked the events of the past year without sufficient sway from a sympathetic party. And Margaret's was about the only sympathy we'd found so far; the rent she required for the cottage on her land was nothing less than outright charity.

The vision of the cottage as I had long since imagined it rose up before me. A picket fence lining a carpet of moist, spongy grass. Little shutters and yellow-checkered curtains blowing in the breeze. Tufted pollen of dandelion seeds bursting in a puff to become stars that spattered the air, soaring up in an explosion of gold . . .

My head banged against the window, and I woke up. Through the indistinct reflection of my face on the glass, the pavement wound, wound never ending, roadside weeds ripping through the shadowy half moon of my cheek. The cabin grew warmer as my head grew thicker. I lost concentrated vision to gathering splotches of brown. As if lifted from beneath, my seat tipped forward. I fell out completely, my body light and arms outstretched in abandon. Then I stood at a precipice beneath which churned a great swirling beauty. A red cloud shrank down from a pull at its center, as a stomach flushing, or a galaxy upon its axis spinning. There was a flashing sheet of an unbearable glory. I had to jump to live. Plunge to the bottom and spring up, reborn.

Lightning flashed. I blinked my eyes, grasping at consciousness. I tried to remember the bus and Callapher's heavy head against my arm. The road stretched without end toward the unknown. Another gas station passed, so exactly like the last that I expected to find the same minivan parked beneath its overhang. I wondered about the man and his bride. Now they were speeding in the opposite direction, streamers wavering behind as they rose up from the road to fly into the sky. Instantaneously, I found myself on the road. The bus had disappeared and I was running, desperately, my feet soaked from the puddles that mirrored the darkening sky, my lungs burning, my head on fire. I had to run after him. I had to find him. I had to run before that for which I ran shrank to nothing.

I stopped. Before me stood the man, a liveried servant dressed in a suit of white. He stood before an open door. A door, perhaps, to a carriage. Or a blue van or a chariot. His garments glowed with brilliant heat in the purple fog of rain. He stood at the open door, his open palm extending the invitation.

Would you come with me? I understood him to say. *You have to want something more.* With the eager abandon of a child, I ran to him.

Again, my head struck the windowpane. The rush of joy met its end and receded as a wave breaking. I woke to see the words *W lco e to Bethsaida* printed in fading letters on a fast-approaching sign.

CHAPTER 2

with my suitcase in one hand and Callapher's in the other, I stepped down from the bus. The fresh, cool air hit me like a clap of a hand to the face. I felt it cold at my armpits and my back where I was wet from sweating. Callapher stumbled in her fatigue. I squeezed her hand.

Across the street, two women sat waiting beneath the plastic yellow awning of the bus stop kiosk. Margaret, the taller of the two, stood at the sight of us. The flesh of her underarm jiggled as she waved.

"Oh, girls! I'm so happy to see you!" she declared as she hurried across the street. "How was your trip? Did you make it all right? Where's your bags . . . oh, let me get that, you shouldn't carry it, you look absolutely beat. No, really, it's no bother. Ruby, grab her other bag. There, that's better—hugs all around!"

Her breasts felt like feather pillows. She left my clothes with the aroma of apple blossom. Taking me by the shoulders, she looked my body up and down. "I was expecting children, but you're practically ladies." She winked at Callapher, who announced that she had just turned six.

"Six going on twenty," Margaret decided. "The last time I saw you, you practically fit in your daddy's palm. Ruby, aren't they grown up? Girls, this is Rosalyn Mae Alcott—just call her Ruby. Everybody does."

Ruby looked at us from a distance as if we were contagious. She wore bright lipstick that made the spittle at the corners of her mouth a milky pink. Her hair floated just above her scalp in a blurry auburn haze. She patted it gently, as if to make sure it hadn't gone anywhere.

"Margaret, we best get going," she said. "This rain is ruining my permanent."

"Right!" Margaret clapped her hands. "Out of the rain! Good idea. This way, girls, the car is this way. Mind you, watch the step. There's a little drop-off you can't see in the dark. Wouldn't do to get you here just to lose you on a step now, would it? I knew a woman once, busted her hip falling down two steps. Two steps! We're just so glad you girls made it all right. We had it in mind to call the police if you didn't get here in the next half hour, didn't we, Ruby?"

"Not likely," Ruby replied. She struggled to pull my suitcase against the sidewalk.

I offered to take it from her, but Margaret said, "Nonsense, she's fine. Callapher, dear, hold my hand. We're crossing the street. Anyway, like I said, we near gave in to calling help. We thought you might be lost up on the road somewhere. You hear terrible stories nowadays, girls getting taken off by complete strangers. Scares the living daylights out of me just to think it. You can't count on these public transportations. The bus schedule said arrival time: seven o'clock. Seven o'clock, my foot!"

I began to explain that the bus broke down twice, but Margaret interrupted me.

"How your mother got it in her head to let you come all this way without supervision, I'll never begin to understand. In my day and age a girl couldn't just get up and go off on her own. But then I suppose it was your father's doing, when it comes down to it. I do hope they can come soon. All that fuss and bother of moving. I've been unbearable homesick for your mother of late. Ever since she said you were coming, I've missed her something terrible. When she was little, your grandma and grandpa used to bring her down every year for a vacation in the summer and a weekend near Christmas. It was always so good to have those family visits. And I love a child in the house. That was when my husband had just died, you know. Now, I don't mean to say I'm lonely, because I'm not. Ruby here's all the company I can handle nowadays. She could talk the leg off a donkey, couldn't you, Ruby dear? Here we are. You can both sit in back. We had Beauregard clean it out last night. Callapher, are you all right? You look a little flushed."

A red splotch colored Callapher's cheek where she'd pressed it against my shoulder.

"She was sleeping when we got here," I explained.

"Sleeping?" Margaret said. "On that awful bus? With her little head banging on the window the whole way, no doubt. Well, we'll get you both back to warm beds. The sheets are all freshly washed and folded down, just waiting for you."

The Old Maids lived beyond the last intersection in town. A Dairy Mart stood to the left, bullied by the show lights of the neighboring used car lot. Triangle-cut circus flags hung between the light posts, swaying in the wind. Beneath them, shining with the gloss of rain and spotlight beams, the cars glowed in evanescent silhouettes of green, yellow, and red.

A mannequin sat on the hood of a convertible parked at the corner of the lot, her left hand raised with palm turned back in the manner of a waitress holding a serving platter. Her head was turned so that her blue jewel eyes stared vapidly just to the right of my window. She wore a red bikini, the top of which had been forced down to her waist by the onslaught of rain. Her breasts were bare, round and smooth and hard as pool balls. She taunted me with her cold stare and her empty hand. She offered me something. Or maybe she withheld it.

"That's the Bauers' car lot," Aunt Margaret explained. "Cameron Bauer runs it with her daughter, Mollie—she's your age, Olivia, or about. Comes to church every Sunday. Works in the nursery. You really ought to meet her, such a nice Christian girl, I'm sure you'd get along."

The light changed. We turned down the road, past a black wall of trees and into a secluded cove. Atop a small hill sat the Old Maids' farmhouse. Three plastic flamingoes stood guarding the steps to the porch. They had sunk into the earth made soft by rain and leaned into one another as if in private conference. Christmas lights lit the bushes that lined the perimeter of the house.

"Lovely, aren't they?" Margaret said when Callapher exclaimed at the sight. "Beauregard put those up for us this Christmas, and we forgot to take them down. But then we just didn't want to. They're so cheery. You can't see it now, but our land goes all the way back to the trailer park behind the trees. There's trails in the woods and a creek bed. And there's a family of little boys that lives in one of the trailers. The Speldman children. You'll have to invite them to play, Callapher."

The smells of the kitchen seemed vaguely familiar: nutmeg and dust and the moist breathing of plants. A radio above the refrigerator babbled the evening news. Aunt Margaret said she left it on so that if a burglar got near the house he would think someone was home and leave. You could never be too careful. You had to take precautions in this day and age. She, for one, never went anywhere without her safety money pouch.

"What's a money pouch?" Callapher asked.

Margaret lifted her blouse to reveal a white zipper pouch attached to her bra. It hung the way a pocket hangs from jeans turned inside out. Callapher was duly impressed.

It was so late, Margaret and Ruby didn't think to feed us. I felt a little guilty, knowing that Callapher would go to bed without dinner, but she was too tired to complain. Margaret took her by the hand and led her upstairs.

She pointed me to the bathroom, where a stack of folded towels and washcloths sat waiting on the counter, topped with a fresh bar of Ivory soap. I washed my face, rubbing the washcloth against my cheek in slow concentric circles. Standing sideways, I studied the profile of my figure in the mirror. I'd had oatmeal for breakfast that morning, a ball of cement that had hardened in my stomach during that awful bus ride. Now my stomach fell flat again.

Callapher and I were to sleep in separate bedrooms. My bed had a canopy suspended by wooden pillars as thick as saplings. The room was pink. Even the light switches were covered with rose print wallpaper. The sharp slant of the attic ceiling cut through the left side of the room. I was sleeping in a dollhouse.

Margaret came to say good night. She apologized for Ruby, who couldn't come up on account of the stairs being too hard for her legs. Their bedrooms were downstairs off the living room, should we need anything. I asked after Callapher.

"Sleeping," Margaret replied. Before closing the door she said: "Good night, sleep tight, wake up bright, in the morning light, to do what's right, with all your might."

I waited until she was gone to roll my eyes. Then I turned off the lamp and lay awake, waiting. It wasn't five minutes before the door cracked open and I heard the gentle pad of bare feet against the hardwood floor. I pretended to be asleep.

"Are you awake?" Callapher whispered.

I didn't answer. She lifted my hair and said into my ear: "Are you awake?"

"Stop it!" I turned to face her. I couldn't make out her expression in the dark. "Why don't you sleep in your own bed?"

The scold was only a formality. I always said it; she never listened.

"It's dark in there." She clambered onto the bed.

"It's dark in here," I retorted.

She wriggled under the covers and pressed her body against mine. I moved away, but she scooted closer.

"When's Mom coming?" she asked.

"Soon," I replied. Her hair smelled like sweat and sunshine. I moved over again and told her not to be so clingy.

"I can't sleep," she said.

"You haven't tried."

"I can't try. It makes my eyeballs roll back in my head and it hurts." She pinched at her eyelids. "It feels like somebody's pulling on them."

I said, "Just close your eyes and breathe slow. And think of something pleasant. If you try to sleep you won't. You have to think of something else."

She projected one leg straight up in the air, pitching the bedsheet into a teepee over her foot. "Like what?"

"I don't know. Imagine a story or something."

"I need Daddy to do that," she said, exasperated.

"Put your foot down. You're stealing my covers."

She sighed dramatically and flopped around to lie on her belly. "Will you imagine me something?"

I laughed. "I can't be in your head."

"No, I mean tell it."

"Go . . . to . . . *sleep*."

I curled up against my edge of the bed, but Callapher reached her foot until her big toe just brushed the skin of my leg. She couldn't sleep unless we were touching. Otherwise aliens might take my body away in the night and leave a fake in the bed without her knowing it. They'd leave a shape-shifter, who could take on my form.

I imagined I could change my shape by sheer willpower; if I closed my eyes tight and thought long and hard enough, I would feel the contour of my figure change.

Long after Callapher fell asleep, I lay staring at the curve of the white canopy hanging blue in the moonlight. My belly sank between the twin points of my pelvis the way the canopy sagged gently between the bedposts. I ran my fingers back and forth across my stomach, tracing with satisfaction the shape of the emptiness.

My watch alarm went off at seven. I dressed quickly and dug to the bottom of my suitcase for my tennis shoes. I would go out before anyone woke up so that no one would worry or miss me.

I didn't even make it to the door. At the bottom of the stairs, Margaret accosted me with a plate of bacon in one hand and a glass of orange juice in the other. From the kitchen, I smelled coffee and scrambled eggs. On the stove, grease popped and spat from the dozen sizzling link sausages frying in the skillet.

"I'm not very hungry this early," I explained.

"No such thing," Margaret said. "Everybody needs a good breakfast, hungry or not. I don't let a soul out of this house without a full belly in the morning—most important meal you eat all day, they say. I used to make a whole big spread of toast and eggs and coffee for my husband every morning before he left for work. He used to tell me, 'Woman, if you feed me any more you're going to have to roll me out the door!' He was only kidding, of course—about the 'woman' bit—always said endearingly. Have some eggs!"

"Sit down," Ruby insisted. "Margaret can make anybody hungry." She looked down at my tennis shoes in surprise. "Were you going somewhere?"

"Just out," I mumbled, blushing.

They got Callapher out of bed. She sat at the table with her eyes still shut and her hair rumpled straight up into a crown of static electricity.

"It's a beautiful day," Margaret said. "The birds have been making the most lovely racket all morning. Really makes it feel like spring."

She stood at the sink, elbow deep in suds. It seemed absurdly early to have pots and pans to clean. I moved the eggs around on my plate.

"I thought maybe later we could all go out for a picnic or something," Margaret continued. "We could show you around town, pick up some things from the farmers market. They've got the most gorgeous potted flowers over at that market, Olivia. You and Callapher can each pick one out, and we'll set them out on the porch of your new house before your parents get here—liven things up a bit. It's not an ugly house, I wouldn't say that, but it's in need of a little color . . .

oh, and Ruby thought you might want to see the school—"

The revving of a nearby car interrupted Margaret's train of thought. She pulled back the lace curtain from the window and leaned forward, squinting in the sunlight.

"Why, I do believe that's George McFanny. What on earth is he doing over here at this time of day—with his boat and all get out!"

There was a gut-wrenching turn of the engine. Margaret gasped, and her hand flew to her chest. "Lord Almighty!" she cried and ran out the door like the house was on fire, the screen door slapping-papping behind her. We followed her to the lawn, Ruby holding her coffee cup up in the air as if to keep it dry from a rising flood.

In the street, obstructing the little gravel road entirely, a black truck was backing a great white sailboat up the incline of the front lawn. The wheels beneath the boat's belly churned the grass into deep rivulets of mud. Margaret ran to the driver's side of the truck, waving her arms wildly and exclaiming: "George McFanny, you get this thing off my lawn this instant! You hear me?"

"Mercy," Ruby breathed softly, shaking her head. "Now he's done it."

I followed her eyes. A man sat in the sailboat, waving enthusiastically in our direction.

"Who's that in the boat?" I asked, but Ruby didn't hear me.

The sailboat stopped a mere foot away from Margaret's azalea patch. When the engine in the truck died, her voice became clear, like someone had turned her volume up.

". . . well, I never—Beauregard Lowett, you have done your fair share of damage in this household, and most graciously have I forgiven it, but this cuts the cake; this is absolutely unacceptable!"

As if he hadn't heard a word of this rebuke, the man in the sailboat stood and said a cheerful howdy do and good morning. He was lean and tall, with jeans that hugged the exact shape of his long legs. He wore a belt buckled with a golden medallion. Two plastic fishing lures dangled from the bill of his baseball cap.

"How are y'all this morning?" he asked.

Margaret put her hands on her hips. "Mr. Lowett, you have some serious explaining to do."

He threw a duffel bag down to the ground, followed shortly by a fishing rod, two tent poles, and a pillow.

Margaret raised her eyes to heaven and petitioned the Good Lord again.

" 'Morning, Ms. Margaret, ma'am," said the driver as he maneuvered his huge belly out from behind the steering wheel. He pushed his baseball cap back on his head and wiped his brow with a red-checkered handkerchief produced from his back pocket.

"Good morning, my foot," Margaret retorted. "George, I don't know what gives you these ideas. I don't care what Beauregard said to you; I don't ever want to see him pulling such a stunt again . . . riding around town in a boat. You know how these roads are—he might have flown right off! He might've been killed!"

"Don't you worry about it none, ma'am," Beauregard said as he hopped down to the ground. "Them seats have buckles: I locked myself in snug so I wouldn't fall out and bonk my head on the highway."

Margaret gaped at George. "You took him for a ride on the *highway*?"

"I did no such thing," George replied. He had bent over to unlatch the boat from the truck, so that his voice came muffled as if from a great distance. "I wasn't givin' nobody no ride. I's just deliverin' property."

"This is not our boat," Margaret said.

George stood and chuckled until his fat belly jiggled. "Is now."

Margaret followed him to the other side of the boat, talking too fast to catch a breath: "Well, I never . . . what on earth possessed the two of you . . . don't think you can just get away with this . . . poor azalea bushes, nearly wiped right off the face of the earth . . ."

"Where did you get the money?" Ruby asked Beauregard.

"Earned it shoving carts at Wal-Mart."

"Beauregard!" Margaret said. "That money was for your savings. We talked about that—remember? 'A penny saved is a penny earned'?"

"A boat sounded a mite more interesting," he replied.

"I told you not to let him handle his own money," Ruby said. "But look on the bright side: we'll have new lawn decor."

"We'll hose her down and paint her real nice." Beauregard ran his hand along the body of the boat. "Then we'll put her name right here. *The Ruby Mae*. In pretty choreography."

"Calligraphy," Margaret corrected.

Ruby said, "You name anything so ugly after me, I'll not speak to you again."

"She's not ugly," Beauregard said. "She jest needs a little cleaning up, that's all."

"Margaret, this isn't funny," Ruby protested. "Tell him he can't keep it."

"Of course he can't keep it. Beauregard, you have to give the boat back to George. Callapher! Get down from there."

Beauregard looked up to notice Callapher for the first time.

"Is she ours?" he asked.

"Oh, dear, I forgot," Margaret said. "Beauregard, these are my niece's children—Olivia and Callapher. Their family's renting the little white house beyond the bend."

Beauregard appraised us, lifting his cap from his head to hold it against his chest. His hair sprang up in an unleashed bush of tight ringlets. He gave a chivalrous bow. "Well, welcome to you both, I'm much obliged. Don't know what I'll do with four purties in the house."

He put his arm around my shoulder and squeezed. His breath smelled like he hadn't used a toothbrush five mornings running.

"Word of the wise: don't mind those two hens too much. You just tell them to keep their pots and pans to theirselves, and we'll all get along." He released me and winked at Ruby. "Ain't that right?"

"Olivia," she said, "tell that man if he has something in his eye he should go rinse it out in the bathroom."

"That's enough," Margaret said. "George, tell him—George?"

George had returned to the cab of his truck. Margaret realized it too late to stop him. He drove away, leaving us in a circle around the sailboat, splattered with freshly churned mud.

Margaret sat down on the porch steps, cradling her head in her hands.

Callapher leaned against the stairway railing. "Do you got a headache, Aunt Margaret?"

"Yes," Margaret replied. "He lives in my basement."

That afternoon, when the tumult over the boat had been sufficiently fussed over and nearly forgotten and Margaret and Ruby lost to their afternoon naps, Callapher and I followed the gravel path around the bend to see our new house. It was a depressing sight from any angle: a white box with three front windows framed in blunt black shutters. The window screens were stuck through with dust mites and dead flies. All around the little house, overgrown bushes bullied up against the walls, threatening to overtake the three-foot cement slab that constituted a porch. A single-car garage stood separate from the house, its white paint peeling in strips thin and curled back.

Callapher tiptoed through the bushes to examine the living room from the front window. Without warning, a squirrel leapt from an overhanging tree, snapping the branch from which it sprang. Startled, Callapher darted back, catching her pants on a protruding root and falling backwards into the grass. I laughed as I helped her up.

"I don't like this place," she said decidedly.

"It's just ugly, that's all," I said. "But it won't be bad. It's a shoe-box house."

Callapher picked a stick off the ground and flourished it in the air. "Remember when I was little and I used to play like I was a sword fighter?"

"You're little now."

"Yeah, but remember?" She pounded against the mud with the stick. "There was an old lady who lived in a shoe," she sang to herself. "She had so many children she didn't know what to do . . . and all the king's horses and all the king's men, didn't know what to do with them again."

"You're nuts," I said, taking her hand.

"You're nuts and a half," she retorted. We returned the way we came, Callapher singing happily about the Old Maids who lived in shoe-box houses.

Once my sister's fear of falling off mountains had been assuaged, her primary concern regarding the move had been whether or not we would be taking the bushes. Mom said no, we'd have new bushes. Would we be taking the cabinets? What about the books?

"Yes, honey," Mom said. "We'll take our books. And your bed and your toys. All the things we can pack up."

The Old Maids had three books: the Bible, a hymnal, and *Betty Crocker Teaches You Everything You Ever Wanted to Know about Cooking.*

Margaret didn't wear pants on account of personal conviction, and she looked about as good in a dress as a professional linebacker. She had broad swooping shoulders and the thickness of muscle and fat in her arms you usually see only in men accustomed to daily labor. Her one delicate feature was the wreath of tight gray ringlets that framed her forehead. They reminded me of late Grandmother Monahan's poodle.

Beyond the matter of modesty, Margaret was wholly unconcerned with her appearance. I never once saw her look in a mirror. She dressed and bundled her hair blindly, unaware of her figure but for what she saw when she looked down. Ruby, on the other hand, sought her own reflection everywhere: in the microwave door, in window-panes, in the bowl of her dinner spoon. She wore heels to compensate for the disappointment of her five-foot-two stature. In the house, she tied a scarf around her head to keep the ceiling fans from messing up her perm. After her nap, she sat at the kitchen table soaking her cuticles in a blue ceramic bowl filled with warm water, swishing her fingers back and forth the way children swing their feet in swimming pools.

She told me about Beauregard. He was thirty-one, an only child. His mother lived in the motel in town. During weekends he worked the Wal-Mart parking lot, shoving carts.

"How long has he lived here?" I asked.

"You ask Margaret," Ruby replied. "This is her business. I'll not say another word or she'll label me a gossip."

Beauregard joined us that evening for dinner. When he noticed Callapher gaping at him, he asked, "Got something in yer mouth?"

"No, sir."

"Then watcha doin' with it hanging open like that?"

Callapher watched him all night, sitting at the bedroom window to look down on the lawn where he worked tirelessly and ineffectively to erect a garage tent around his sailboat. The next day she moved closer to him by degrees, watching him first from the window, later from the porch. By midafternoon he'd recruited her to gather kindling for an evening bonfire. It was the dumbest fire I ever saw, just a tree stump in a nest of brush that smoked so bad I could hardly breathe. Beauregard hit the stump five times with the back of the shovel. It was a Boy Scout trick, he said. To make the flames higher.

I went inside for a glass of water. Watching my sister from the kitchen window, I asked Margaret, "Do you think it's all right to leave her with him?"

"Who? Beauregard?" She waved off the concern. "He's harmless."

"But he's not . . . he's not quite right, is he?" I didn't know how to say it.

"He hasn't the mind of an adult, no, if that's what you mean." She was using a dull butter knife to carve wax from used-up candle jars. "He's been that way for years. Ever since the accident."

"The accident?"

She stabbed at a bit of unrelenting wax. "When he was just a young man—not too many years beyond you, I'd say, well, late twenties, anyway—he was in a real bad car accident. It was just outside of town. Lord knows how treacherous these roads can be when you're alert. But he fell asleep at the wheel—went right through a red light as an oncoming car rushed through the other way. Beauregard and his mother, who was asleep on the passenger side as I understand it, both lived, but it was only fatalities in the other car: a young woman and her unborn baby were killed.

"Beauregard walked away from the accident. But his mother had a bad time. The impact severed her spine. It was two years of therapy before she could walk again. She lost her job and the house. And Beauregard, he was never the same again. Seeing his mom like that . . ." Aunt Margaret shook her head slowly. "He spent some time in therapy, but his mind was never the same. We can't know for certain. Some things are never explained."

She shook the newly cleaned jar free of dripping water and set it top down on the windowsill.

"How did he end up here?"

Margaret shifted her weight from one foot to the other. "He dropped out of school and left town. His mother—Barbara Lowett's the name—went away to stay with her sister, or at least that's what I heard. The Lowetts don't have much family. Not a soul came to their aid when it happened. But Mrs. Lowett returned, after her therapy. She's still in town—lives on the west end, across from the Dollar Mart. Came to us one night to say she'd found her son living in his van just outside town. She couldn't afford to take care of him, and he wouldn't have it anyway. Doesn't really acknowledge her as his mother.

"Well, there was nothing to do but go get him and bring him back. We thought about putting him up in the house where you'll be living. Thomas built it when we first married. Everyone says we should knock it down, but I know Thomas would want me to use it this way. Anyway, we thought about letting him rent the house, but I worried about him taking care of himself. So we just set him up downstairs with his own little apartment. He's got his own bathroom. Which you'd know is a good thing if you've ever had to wipe down the toilet of a grown man. It's like they're aiming for the window."

"How long has he been here?"

She raised her eyes to the ceiling and counted on her fingers. "Five . . . seven years? Could it be seven? Lord, time does fly. We never meant for him to stay so long. And did we ever have a time of it convincing our good friends in the Sunday school about keeping him on. They said you can only do so much and then you've got to get the person on his own two legs. Say you can't just spoon-feed them or they'll get dependant. But I don't think so." She swished her hand across the bottom of the sink to direct the soapsuds to the drain, but her eyes gazed out the window. "All I know is, Jesus said, 'Whatever you do unto the least of these, you do unto me.' I like to think of Beauregard as our own little Jesus, living in the basement."

CHAPTER 3

in the church where I grew up hung a painting of Christ standing in a garden at night, knocking gently on the wooden door of a cottage. A halo of light radiated from His face. His skin looked as soft as velvet, His eyes the glistening color of the chocolate we melted for dipping strawberries at Christmastime. The painting was nearly five feet high, framed by a thick weave of gold leaf.

In front of this painting, I asked Jesus would He please be so kind as to forgive me of my sins and come inside my heart, the accommodations of which I imagined to be exactly like the inside of Nick at Nite's Jeannie's bottle. My heart had red pulsating walls and a round pink couch. Jesus stood out in there, what with His white robes and lightbulb visage.

I don't remember anyone putting me up to the prayer, but Dad was with me. It was after church service, so he was wearing his Sunday suit and tie. He had to kneel down on one knee to be level with me. When I said *amen*, he cried.

Dad was never harsh with Callapher and me, though we were subject to what Mom called his "idiosyncrasies." For one, we didn't have a television until I was nine. He didn't trust them. In the years before Callapher, I was left entirely to my own devices. I played house, princess, intergalactic space war captain hero, and Barbies. I used the turkey baster as a microphone and sang to the adoring multitudes from my perch on the kitchen counter. After Mom mopped the floors, I would put on Dad's silk dress socks and ice skate on the linoleum. I was Kristi Yamaguchi and Brian Boitano interchangeably, because boys got the better jumps. Skating remained a favorite pastime until I triple-lutzed right into the hutch and had to get five stitches in the back of my scalp.

Mom blamed Dad for my overactive imagination. She said that if he didn't stop telling such cockamamie stories all the time, I'd have no sense of reality. But he maintained, "Never let the truth get in the way of a good story."

I grew up thinking there were little green men in radios. That if you swallowed watermelon seeds you'd grow an eight-pound melon in your belly until you looked pregnant. If you frowned too long, your face would freeze that way. Dad married Mom because she was the most beautiful mermaid he'd ever met during his stay on the Florida coast.

When I asked Mom to expound on life as a mermaid, she said, "Very wet. Now go brush your teeth. They're growing yellow scum."

She made me brush my teeth to an egg timer. When I got out of the bath, she thoroughly swiped my ears with Q-tips and clipped my soft fingernails to the quick. She kept a comb in her pocket for de-tangling my waist-length black hair and baby wipes in her purse for wiping Kool-aid stains from my lips.

I submitted to this routine out of adoration for my mother. Every Sunday morning I sat on my parents' bed, watching her lean into the mirror of the adjoining bathroom to apply her eyeliner and adjust her dangling pearl earrings. It transfixed me, this weekly transformation from bathrobed mother to red-lipped siren. At church I turned a critical eye on all the women, glorying secretly in the superiority of my mother's beauty.

Over the years her thin figure began to round out at the hips and belly, her bright smile grew dull beneath years of coffee stains. For the sake of fashion and convenience, she cut the long mermaid hair that had first attracted my father to a neat shoulder length. By the time I reached high school she was still an attractive woman, but in a carefully preserved, well-groomed way. I began to notice how the foundation she applied each morning lay thick upon her skin, giving definition to the fine lines gathering at the tips of her eyes.

As a Christian, my mother fought hard to suppress her worldliness, but there were things she couldn't help. She liked fashion magazines, for one. And she couldn't leave the house without lipstick. Our church choir director, Mrs. Jones, came to our house one evening to chastise Mom for caring too much about her appearance. Pastors' wives shouldn't get all dandied up in mascara and lipstick, she said. Mom cried that night while she threw her compacts away. They hit the bottom of the trash can with an echoing plunk. She resigned herself to a nude gloss on her lips. She gave up eye shadow entirely.

Until the day they took the vote.

The morning they kicked Dad out of the church, Mom walked into the sanctuary in the works: full-blown eye shadow, thick black eyeliner, bright, red lipstick. It satisfied me to see several of the women in the church stare as we filed by to the pew in front.

What features I was moderately proud of, I attributed to my mother. I had her dark hair and complexion, her deep-set green eyes. But I also had the long torso and short legs of the Monahan women. I had to purse my lips tight to get that shadow of a cheekbone in my profile.

Mom and Dad arrived with the moving van on Friday, Dad leading the way in the minivan, Mom bringing up the rear in the family pickup. When Callapher spotted them, she jumped up and down and waved the little American flag Beauregard had given her.

"What's this?" Mom asked when she saw the sailboat.

"It's Beauregard's," Callapher explained, breathless from her sprint to Mom's arms.

Mom frowned. "Whose?"

Dad stepped out from the truck. "Engine light's on again. Ought to let it cool down for a while . . . There's my angel." He took Callapher in his arms. She kissed the air in front of his puckered lips. "Have you been driving the Old Maids crazy?" he asked.

"No, sir."

The screen door banged open. Margaret appeared and called out, "Claire Louise, I thought you'd never get here. How are you? You hungry?"

Mom returned her aunt's embrace with the stiff economy of a mere acquaintance, but her expression softened as she held the older woman. My mother was never very good at showing affection.

"You've handled the years gracefully!" Margaret said.

Mom patted her sharp hip. "Not so gracefully, perhaps."

"Nonsense. You girls are all angles. Every one of you. If it weren't for your figure, I'd think Olivia makes herself skinny as she is. The child eats like a bird."

I looked away, pretending I hadn't heard, but I felt Mom's eyes on my body.

Margaret announced that dinner would be ready in ten minutes. Dad asked me to drive the van to the house so Mom could go inside and rest. He got back in the pickup, and I followed from behind, down the gravel road and around the bend to our new home. Together we stood on the lawn considering the situation. As if for effect, a shingle dangling from the roof caught in the breeze and clattered to the porch.

Dad smiled stiffly. He was sweating. It made the gray hair at his temples shimmer like silver. "Think we can suffer for Jesus here, don't you?"

I hoped he was joking. The flippancy of the statement was uncharacteristic of him. I said, "The Dairy Mart around the corner is hiring. I was thinking of getting some work."

He walked over and picked up the fallen shingle, turning it over in his palm. "Roof needs repairs." Then, as if just hearing me, he replied, "Work? Honey, there's no need for you to work. Not right away. Take some time to get situated in school first." He dropped the shingle. "Let's get back. I'm famished."

The Shoe Box had two bedrooms and one bath. The walls throughout were covered in wood paneling that grew moist in the humidity the way cold drinking glasses sweat in the sun. The adjoining living and dining areas suffered for light. There was one large window in the first, but its green curtains hung heavy beneath a film of cigarette smoke and dust. A breakfast counter complete with two mismatched stools separated the kitchen from the dining area. When we first walked into the house, a terrible odor permeated both. Mom opened the unplugged freezer to find its shelves overgrown with a green carpet of mold spreading from the leftover contents of a half-empty ice cream carton.

A miscommunication with the moving men left us with an empty house and a lawn full of furniture. That night we dragged two mattresses into the house and slept on them in sleeping bags. In the morning, I woke with Callapher's sweating body half on top of mine, her left knee kicking into my back.

Margaret said never you mind about the furniture. She knew some men from the church who could help.

Five men from her Sunday school class arrived at our doorstep that afternoon to help Dad carry the furniture into the house. It was the single largest gathering of people I'd seen since being in town, none in company younger than fifty. At three, Margaret arrived with triangle finger sandwiches and a Tupperware bowl of potato salad. After sitting down for refreshment, the men had trouble getting back up. They unbuttoned their trousers and sat heavy on the frayed ribbons of the lawn chairs, arguing about the new highway. Inside, their wives busied themselves with boxes, shuffling in and out of our bedrooms like a flock of doves bumping about. They shelved books, made our beds, stocked the kitchen cabinets, Mom working diligently behind them to reshelve the books alphabetically by author, strip the mattresses and put the sheets on the right beds, and rearrange all the pots and pans. When she found me "lollygagging about," she put me in front of the freezer mold with a scraper.

Dad entered the kitchen and raised his eyebrows at the overwhelming odor of Clorox. "Claire, come sit outside for a while. It's about toxic in here."

"I need to get the rest of these boxes emptied," Mom said from under the sink. She scrubbed at the corner of the cabinet with an old frayed toothbrush. "You go out and get some lunch. I'm fine."

"Let me help in here. What needs done?"

"No, no, it's fine. I've got it." She fell back on her knees and wiped her brow.

"Are you in here to unpack or are you just avoiding everyone?" Dad asked.

"Do you know how long it took me to reorganize this kitchen?" she demanded. "They put all the baking goods on the first shelf and all the pots and pans over the fridge."

"That's not where they go?"

"You can't put baking goods and pots and pans clear across from each another. They have to be near the oven . . . and the food goes on the shelves, so it's accessible anywhere."

"Naturally." He unwrapped a serving platter. "It looks like rain again," he continued. "We got the bedroom furniture inside, but the living room is something else. I don't know if the sofa's going to fit."

"Which sofa?"

"The little one. The what-do-you-call-it. Love seat."

"Maybe if you take the door off its hinges . . ."

Dad searched the cabinets for a place to put the platter. "I was thinking maybe we should sell it."

"Sell it?" Mom reappeared again from under the sink. "Why would we want to sell it?"

He looked at her with a distracted expression. "I was wondering why we'd want to keep it."

Mom stood and took the serving platter from his hands. She put it in the cupboard beside the refrigerator, but it stuck out three inches. She said, "You know, I don't think this is going to fit anywhere."

"Honey, I think you'll find that to be the situation throughout the house. I don't think half our living room furniture would fit in the living room and dining room combined."

Mom shuffled a stack of mixing bowls to make room for the platter. "Maybe I could keep some of these at Margaret's."

"I measured the living room," Dad said, "and I think we should sell the love seat and the coffee table or we won't be able to move once we get everything in."

"Do you think she'd care?"

Dad looked at her. "About the couch?"

"The bowls."

My parents had a talent for what my literature teacher called "indirect dialogue." This meant for all the words they fired at each other all day, they might as well be shooting blanks.

Callapher ran into the room. "Mom, they're putting my Barbies on Olivia's bookshelf."

"I'm sorry," Mom said. "They're elderly. They get a little confused. Why don't you go outside and get something to eat. Olivia—did you eat?"

I mumbled something.

"Da-ad!" Callapher shrieked.

He was wearing the salad bowl on his head like a bowler hat.

"Oh, for mercy's sake," Mom said. She took it off his head and sprayed it with Clorox.

Dad finally convinced Mom to join everyone outside and escape the fumes for a while. When they'd gone, I rummaged in the cabinets for the can of tuna I'd seen earlier. I drained the pink flesh of water, then spooned it from the can onto five white Saltine crackers. I ate slowly, savoring the strange tang on my tongue. When I'd finished, I swished my teeth clean with a glass of water. I drank a second to fill the empty space left in my stomach. Though I rinsed the can and sink thoroughly, the odor of fish lingered, coming up in pungent fumes from the drain.

In the bedroom, my first objective was to cover the atrocious wood paneling. I found the old shirt box in which I'd packed a stash of fashion magazines and clipped photographs. It took me a jar of glue to paste a collage across just the left corner of the bedroom, but the blank wall quickly became a hundred windows into separate worlds where people are beautiful and kisses are eternal.

Dad didn't approve of fashion magazines. He said they gave women the wrong ideas, made them feel inadequate. I didn't agree. Every page was another promise that life could become what it should, that I could be beautiful. In that world, strange men with golden chests clean beneath unbuttoned white Oxfords might rest their glorious faces against my breast, lay their lips against the flat of my stomach. The men and women in the magazines were ageless creatures drunk with desire. Bored with their own beauty, the women laid their elegant legs in golden light along the length of the centerfolds.

I didn't notice Callapher in the room until she said she was going to tell on me for gluing things to the wall.

"It's rubber cement. It peels off. Where have you been anyway? Mom was looking for you."

She ignored my question, crawling up onto the bed to shuffle through the pictures scattered everywhere. "Is she naked?" she exclaimed.

I snatched the photgraph from her hand. "No, she's not naked. She's got a bikini on, see. The material is tan, like her skin."

"But she doesn't have the top on," she retorted.

"Then she's half naked."

"You can't be half naked; you can only be whole naked."

"Well, she's half naked." I pressed my palms against a picture of Paris to push the bubbles out of the Eiffel Tower lights.

Propping her hands under her chin, Callapher considered the magazines. "Why do you like these?"

"Because they make me think of things. Each picture is like a story. Like a place I can go to in my head . . . they remind me of things I want to be."

She lay on her back and shot her leg upright in the air. "You want to be *naked*?"

"Stop doing that—you'll crumple them," I scolded, grabbing her ankles to pull her off the bed.

"Don't!" she cried, kicking her feet free.

I put my hands on my hips. "Get off."

She spread her arms and legs out across the bed, grasping the bed-spread tightly in her clenched fists. "Make me."

I lifted her shirt and blew a wet raspberry on her belly. She shrieked so loud, Mom came running into the room.

"Callapher, where on earth have you been!" she exclaimed. "I've been looking everywhere for you!"

"I was at the creek," Callapher answered. "Beauregard and me went digging for clay so we can make pots." She produced a plastic baggie of wet earth from her pocket. "I'm warming it up," she explained.

"You went with who?"

"Beauregard," Callapher repeated.

"That's what I thought you said. Let me see that clay."

Callapher obediently gave up the leaking bag.

"Did Aunt Margaret know where you were?"

Callapher shrugged.

"Or Ruby? Or me? Callapher, you cannot—do you hear me—*cannot* just go scampering off into the woods whenever you feel like it. And you most certainly may not ever, *ever* go *anywhere* alone with Beauregard. Is that clear? Young lady, acknowledge me. Is that clear?"

Callapher nodded.

"Thank you."

"Can I have my clay back?"

"I think maybe I should keep the clay for a while."

Callapher announced, "Mommy, look what Olivia did to the wall!"

I kicked her, not hard, but she cried, "Ow!"

"Girls, that's enough. Callapher, come with me." Mom extended her hand.

"I want to stay with Olivia."

"She doesn't need you bothering her all the time. Come on."

"But it's my room too."

"I said, come *here*."

Callapher scowled at me. "How come *I* always get in trouble?" she said under her breath.

When they'd left, I lay down on my bed. My stomach had begun to hurt, like there was a fist clenched beneath my skin just below my ribs. Every afternoon, my belly inflated uncomfortably when the food I had eaten began to roll up on itself. As a kid, I thought the food you swallowed just dropped down into the cavernous black space that was the inside of your torso. Then I accidentally swallowed a whole ice cube. I felt every move of the muscles in my throat as they massaged the iceberg down. Mom had to explain the esophagus to me.

Bodies are invisible until you know pain. Pain outlines the shape of your organs. You feel them working. You feel them fighting. You wonder how you never noticed them before.

I knew the time of day by the changes in my body. In the mornings my stomach growled with hunger. In the afternoons it was silent with air. I knew dinnertime by the dull aching bloat beneath my belly button, not by the smells coming from the kitchen. Mealtimes were a sanctified and compulsory affair in our home. You stayed until you were excused. You didn't read or sing. You kept your elbows off the table.

That evening was our first sit-down dinner in the new house. Mom sent me to call Dad to eat. I followed the orange extension cords from the hallway out the front door to where the living room lamps stood like sentries on opposite sides of our narrow driveway. Dad was busy rearranging the living room furniture beneath the twin pools of light.

"What are you doing?" I asked.

He replied, "Proving your mother wrong."

"He won't come in," I told Mom. "He says to start without him."

Mom sighed but didn't say anything. She put the casserole on the table.

"What's this?" Callapher asked.

"Hamburger Surprise," Mom said. "It's good for you. If you eat it all you can have ice cream later."

Callapher wrinkled her nose at me. I returned the grimace.

Mom said, "I saw that. Enough. Just eat some."

We were saved momentarily when Dad called us all out to the front lawn.

"Must we do this now?" Mom asked, crossing her arms across her breasts like she was cold. "It's damp."

Dad held up his hand. "A demonstration. Sit, if you please."

Mom rolled her eyes. We sat on the sofa. The plastic wrinkled underneath us, like the paper on a doctor's examining table.

"This"—Dad waved his hand to signify the little arrangement he'd produced on the drive—"is our living room furniture, situated as tight as I could manage. And these lines here represent the walls of the house." With a stick he had dragged a perforated line through the gravel to signify the perimeter of the cottage living room. It cut nearly two feet off the corners needed to fit all our furniture.

"Is it really that small?" Mom asked.

"I made a diagram," Dad explained. He set a piece of paper on the coffee table. On the paper he'd drawn the bird's-eye architectural diagram of the cottage. From his pocket he produced scraps of paper—squares and rectangles labeled *couch* and *table* and *love seat*, which he insisted he'd cut to scale. "Arrange it in as many variations as you like," he said. "You'll never get it all in."

Mom laughed when she saw the careful deliberation of his diagram. "Is this what you've been doing all night?" She sighed. "It seems such a waste to have brought it all this way just to sell it."

But Dad argued the matter with all the eloquence that had charmed church congregations for years. There wasn't a trick wasted: with Mom, even spontaneity had to be planned. And she hated to let go of more furniture. We'd already given away everything from our old office and den.

"Well, we're keeping the dining room table," she said. "I don't want to eat off the floor."

Dad said, "Angel, go back and unplug the extension cord for Daddy."

Mom interjected, "No, she can do it later. Let's eat dinner before it turns to paste."

Dad joined us at the table, where Mom began her customary critique of the meal she'd prepared. "I think I burnt it," she said. "And now it's cold."

Dad spooned a generous portion of casserole onto his plate. "Looks delicious," he said.

"I amn't hungry," Callapher stated.

"Well, you'll have some anyway. It's good for you," Mom replied curtly. "Eat up."

"It looks gross," she said. "It looks like monkey brains."

I gave Callapher a warning look.

"Beauregard says that some people eat monkey brains," she said anyway.

"Does Beauregard eat monkey brains?" Dad asked.

"Beauregard eats Spaghetti-O's."

"Beauregard eats what the Old Maids cook for him," Mom interjected. "And that's enough talk of monkey brains."

Callapher stared angrily at her plate and kicked her foot against her chair. "I don't want this!"

"If you don't want it, you can go to your room," Mom said. "Because that's what we're eating."

Staring Mom in the eyes, Callapher stood up from her chair.

Mom raised her eyebrows. "Well, go on then."

Callapher looked at me. I gave her an *I-told-you-so* with my eyes. She raised her chin, turned, and walked slowly to our room.

"I don't want her around that man. I am not joking," Mom said, "He took her off to the woods and who knows where else, and I didn't know where she was and Margaret didn't know. I'll never understand how she can just let him around her house like that."

"I'm sure Mr. Lowett's harmless," Dad said distractedly, watching Callapher's retreating back. "He's been there for years and hasn't caused them any trouble."

"How do we know that? All we know is what they tell us. They're old women, Benjamin. They don't have the energy to keep tabs on a younger man—and Margaret's kindness blinds her to every fault. She has no discretion."

"She doesn't have the prejudice against his disposition you have."

Dad didn't mean to be condescending, but Mom's voice hardened against him in response.

"She can do what she likes under her own roof, but I'll not let her threaten my daughter's safety. I want you to talk to her."

"Dear, I can't change Margaret's mind."

"Not Margaret," Mom said. "Callapher. I don't want her spending time with him. You have to talk to her; she listens to you."

"Now?" he asked, slightly exasperated.

"Not now. After we eat."

While they argued, I pressed the curds of ground beef on my plate into a flat pancake of gray paste. I teased out the kernels of corn and the bits of green beans, balancing them on the prongs of my fork. I chewed them slowly and individually to keep my mouth visibly busy for as long as it took my parents to finish. We ate in a silence broken only by the sound of forks scratching against china like fingernails on chalkboards.

I asked to be excused. They were so preoccupied with their own thoughts, they forgot to check my plate. I went to the bedroom. At the sound of the door creaking open, Callapher scampered from her circle of Barbie dolls to sit on the bed, rigid and expectant.

"It's just me," I said.

I'd situated myself at my desk to work on the wall collage when Dad knocked on our bedroom door. He sat down beside Callapher, leaning forward with a murmured groan to pick up a Barbie doll she'd discarded.

"What's her name?" he asked.

"Cordelia Jasmine," she answered.

"Nice hair. Does she come like that?"

"No, I braided it."

"I never did understand braiding." He examined the doll's head from all angles. "Do you just wrap it in knots?"

Callapher took the Barbie and planted its legs between her own. She undid its hair and patiently demonstrated the art of braiding. "She's going to a party," she explained.

"Mmm," Dad said. He rubbed his knee. "Your mother sent me in to talk to you. Seems like you've been spending a lot of time with Beauregard lately."

Callapher pushed her hair out of her eyes with the back of her hand. "We're probably best friends." She sighed.

"Angel, I'm afraid Beauregard's a little too old to be your best friend."

"Why?"

Dad glanced up at me. I shrugged.

"Does Beauregard ask you to go away with him to the creek?" he asked.

Callapher didn't answer.

"Does he ask you to take these walks with him?"

"He says I can come."

"Well, next time I want you to come to me or to Mommy and ask first. Okay? Because when you go off like that we get real worried about you. And you don't want to worry us; we're getting old." He paused, but she didn't look up. "You know, you get to start school soon. Maybe you'll find some new friends your own age. They can come over to the house if you want, and we can all go to the creek together . . ."

Callapher picked at a scab on her knee. Dad's voice trailed off as he watched this delicate operation. She asked if something was wrong.

He started, as if from a dream, then recovered with a smile. "Nothing, Angel."

"Dad, how come Mom doesn't like Beauregard?"

"That gets complicated."

Callapher frowned. "That's what Olivia said."

Dad hesitated a moment before asking, "Do you remember our soup kitchen in the old church?"

She nodded.

"We had all sorts of people come in who needed help. Some of them didn't have any homes, and some of them were like Beauregard. Some people have grown-up bodies, but inside they have minds like children."

Callapher petted her Barbie's hair. "Is that how Beauregard is?"

"Yes, in a way. Sometimes people like that can be dangerous without knowing it. Sometimes they break rules or do things they aren't supposed to, but they don't understand why it's wrong. When your mother looks at Beauregard it makes her think of Bill. You remember Bill? Who always wore the blue overalls?"

Callapher couldn't possibly understand the implications of what he was saying, but she nodded her head solemnly, as if Bill and his blue overalls explained everything.

Dad stared off into the distance again. "Well. I'd better go help your mother clean up." He stood and walked out the door. Remembering something, he peered back in moments later: "If you do run off again without telling us, I shall be forced to hang you by your ankles in the cellar for an hour until all the blood rushes to your head and erases all such rebellious notions from your brain."

He added that she could leave the room now if she wanted to.

She didn't. Subdued by the second reprimand of the day, she resigned herself to watching me work. We sat together Indian-style on the floor in silence.

"Dad says he's going to hang me by my ankles," she told me.

I raised my eyebrows. "Yes, I heard." But when I saw her expression, I added, "Nobody's going to hang you by your ankles. You know that."

"I know. But he said it."

I offered her the magazine. "Want to cut one up?"

She took this as an invitation to sit in my lap. I wrapped my arms around her little body, perching my chin on the top of her head. Hers was the easy beauty of children: hair so blonde it shone white in the sun, skin elastic and bright, as if lit up from within.

At night she liked to sleep in just a little T-shirt and her underwear. She put her underwear on backwards all the time, so that it sagged loose in the front and gave her the worst wedgie from behind. The sight made me want to laugh and cry at the same time. It made me want to cover her with kisses.

Dad used to make me walk around balancing books on my head to keep me from growing up. Holding Callapher, I understood why he feared the end of our childhood. I wanted to be my father's little princess again, prancing on rose-tipped toes, in legs strong for running games of tag and with eyes blind to mirrors.

CHAPTER 4

when the temptation to eat threatened to overpower me, I concentrated on the memory of Zachary Parker's face. Zachary Parker played for the boys' soccer team at my old high school. I'd had a crush on him since the seventh grade. I'd imagine that I was standing with Zachary on the beach. He looked over when I took off my towel and saw the fat folds bulging over the pinch of my swimsuit waistband.

Or this:

I lay on a metal table above which several suspended cameras fixed their blank stares on different sections of my figure. One camera for hips, one for thighs, one for stomach, one for breasts. The men sat in a separate room in front of computer screens that allowed them to mix and match bodies from the camera's live picture feed. One woman's breasts with another's hips. One set of thighs with another's breasts. I knew that none would pick all four parts of my body. I wondered if they would choose any. I was cold from the metal table. My skin purpled and pimpled with goose bumps. My legs were thick as elephant's knees. My stomach swelled like a woman with child.

Except that I hadn't bled in four months.

It was the fact that I hadn't had a period in so long that worried Mom. I told her maybe it was just one of those things. She said, "You don't eat enough."

My mom thought bleeding made you a woman. But the functions of my body or failures thereof were separate from me, things over which I had no control.

The first day of school, Callapher held on to me as if they were shipping her off to Thailand after breakfast. She straddled my waist and buried her head in my neck.

"Give her room to breathe," Mom scolded.

"I don't want her to go," Callapher said.

"You have to go too," I told her.

"I amn't."

Mom picked her up off my lap and set her in her own chair. She said, "Callapher, I'm serious now. Leave your sister alone."

Mom meant well, and it was childish of me, but I wanted Callapher in my lap. She sat at the table in sullen dejection, refusing her toast and orange juice. In the car, I let her sit in the middle and share my buckle.

"Love you," I said when we reached the high school. I kissed her cheek.

I hugged my books tight to my chest as I walked into the school. The hallways seemed to wind in a never-ending maze. The rooms smelled of dust and mold. I was terrified that I looked as strange as I felt, but everyone ignored me, and by fourth bell the nauseous anxiety in my stomach began to settle. I spent all of algebra making pictures of the water mark that spread through the ceiling tiles, an oblong blob brown and feathered at the fringes like the remnants of a tea stain.

At lunch, I sat at the corner of a crowded table. Occasionally I looked up in the direction of the five boys sitting just to my right. I laughed a little when they laughed so that if anyone passed by they wouldn't think I was sitting alone. One of the boys caught me smiling at something he'd said. He stared a moment before turning his back to me. Embarrassed by this rebuke, I looked down and concentrated on carefully dissecting my sandwich. I rolled the two slices of turkey individually, then ate the bread last, savoring the corner crusts for their thickness in my mouth. I chewed my apple to the quick, until I splintered bits of the core between my teeth. Though I ate slowly, I was finished twenty minutes before the lunch period ended. I spent the rest of the hour pacing the hallway that circled the library, studying the plastic football trophies in the display cases.

I made it to every class on time until eighth bell. My locker was clear across the building from the art studio. I stepped into the room all but panting from my sprint across the school, flying around the doorway so fast I ran right into a boy standing just inside.

"Whoa!" he declared, grabbing my shoulders to keep me from losing my balance.

"Sorry," I muttered.

"S'all right." He shrugged and let me go. He was so tall, I found myself staring into his shoulder.

There hadn't been any need to hurry. The teacher arrived ten minutes late. She marched into the room, already halfway through a scold: "How many times do I have to tell you to stop horsing around back there—get your work out, come on." She saw me, raised a finger for "just-a-minute," and continued to yell at the boys roughhousing in the back. She clapped her hands to the rhythm of her command. "I said get your things out. I'm not in the mood today. You want to kill each other, be my guest, but you can do it outside, not in my studio."

"She gets moody," the tall boy whispered in my ear.

I looked at him questioningly.

"Menopause," he explained knowingly. He walked away at the sight of her approach but raised his eyebrows at me in silent warning.

"I don't know what Matthew just told you," the instructor said, "but don't listen to him. Lori. Lori Kemnitz." She shook my hand. "And please call me Lori, no Mrs. This or Ms. That."

I could feel through her fingers to the delicate, perforated bones of a bird. She was a very small woman, short, with dainty features and a narrow face accentuated by the prominent line of a sharp nose. Her hair was white but an almost blonde-white, velvet soft as down; it betrayed no specific age. If not for the black-rimmed bifocals perched on her head and the word *menopause* whispered in my ear only moments before, I'd have thought her as young as thirty.

"So. How is it?" she asked.

I frowned.

"The first day. How is it?"

"Oh, fine," I lied.

"Of course it isn't," she retorted. "First days never are, but cheer up: we have a good time in here. You've come in a bit late in the semester, but you haven't missed much of the curriculum, really. They're doing still lifes now, but I have them working in a certain aesthetic. Are you familiar with impressionism?"

"Monet?" I asked, tentatively.

"Yes, precisely. Monet, the poster boy of impressionism. All right, so you know something."

She disappeared into the supply closet, gesturing for me to follow.

"I'll tell you what . . . they've only got another week to finish this project, and assuming you haven't worked in oils before—have you? Didn't think so—you'd be about crazy just trying to figure out the paint, and God forbid you'd have to make it all look like something." Her voice came muffled from inside a wooden cupboard.

She produced a fistful of brushes, handing them to me without removing her head from beneath the shelf. "So I'll just let you mess around with the paint for the week, get the feel of it, get to know where everything is. And they're a bunch of losers in this class, but you'll like them." She handed me a metal tin palette, a plastic quiver for the brushes, and two cups with rims small as quarters to fill with turpentine. "I thought I told them to clean this out. It's like they think I'm their mother."

"Lori," a student said from the doorway.

Lori bumped her head on the cupboard. "What? Jessica. Dragging your sorry flesh in late."

"I had to go to the bathroom." By way of peace offering, she produced a plastic pear from her book bag. "I got some fruit for my still life."

When Lori stood, her glasses fell on her head. She straightened them on her face to better examine the pear.

"It's plastic," she said.

"So," the girl replied.

Lori looked over her glasses. "I said if you brought food in, it had to be real."

"It looks real. It's even got brown spots."

Lori perched her hand on her hip. "You know what's wrong with a plastic pear? If you painted exactly what you saw here—I mean if you were striving for absolute realism and you painted precisely what you had in front of your face, do you know what you would have? A pear that looks like it was made of plastic."

"I can't paint that good!" the girl exclaimed. She turned her back to Lori and rolled her eyes for my benefit.

I smiled, as if in agreement, but immediately regretted the gesture: I liked Lori already.

"This way," Lori announced, unaware of Jessica's contempt. I followed.

Along the windows of the classroom, sixteen easels stood back to back, grouped in islands of four. Lori set me up in the corner with a spare canvas she'd rummaged up from her office.

"It's cheap," she said apologetically. "Later I'll show you how to stretch your own. But it'll do for now."

"What do I paint?" I asked.

"Nothing," Lori said. "Anything. You said you've never worked in oils before?"

I shook my head.

"Then all I want you to do is get the feel of them. Just cover the canvas with paint. Use your brushes, use your finger for all I care. See how the colors mix, how complementary colors work with each other. You know what I'm talking about? Complementary colors? Look at this wheel." She rapped her knuckles against the chalkboard, on which hung a poster of the color wheel. "Green with red, yellow with purple." She wriggled her fingers over a bunch of small print written across the base of the poster. "There's some blather down here to explain it."

Someone hollered her name. She patted me twice against the arm with more force than I'd have expected from a woman so small, then disappeared to answer the students' desperate protests against the general indignity of the project, that they didn't know how to paint, they were sick of this stupid assignment, and the bananas in the still life were rotting.

I squirted blobs of paint in rows on my palette as the other students had done. The colors were thick, the consistency of soft butter. I held a paintbrush awkwardly, staring at the blank canvas. I glanced up to find Matthew watching me. He brushed his long blond hair from his face and winked. I looked back at my canvas as if I hadn't seen him.

With the palette knife, I smashed a glob of blue against the surface. It left a satisfying streak across the white. I added a parallel swoop of red, then of yellow. With a brush, I swirled them together. In minutes I'd made mud, but it felt delicious to press the liquid paint against the sandpaper texture. I forgot myself completely in the mess of color.

Painting class was the first good thing that had happened to me since arriving in Bethsaida. At home I thought I'd lose my mind. Sharing a room with Callapher made for daily unpleasant discoveries. She left her dirty underwear in her pants and shoved both in the corner of the closet. When I crawled into bed, I scraped my legs against crumbs of dried-up clay. And she was on a mission to catch me naked. If I didn't lock the door, she'd barge in while I was undressing for bed.

It was the bra that fascinated her. She thought it was the most hilarious word. More than one night I fell asleep to the sound of her mumbling under her breath, making gibberish of the familiar sounds: *brabrabrabrabra*.

Mom spent the week scouring the bathroom and kitchen with bleach, and Dad made it his personal mission to sell half our furniture. We got rid of everything we'd voted out, except for a Pepto-Bismol-pink reading chair given to us by Grandma Monahan. Saturday morning, Dad got up from the breakfast table to announce theatrically that he was going to sit in his chair and read his paper. He then proceeded to walk right outside, still in his boxers and undershirt, and sit in the pink chair on the driveway. The light of the living room lamp glowed pale yellow in the gray of morning, shining through his thinning hair to lay a bright halo upon the balding curve of his scalp. Mom laughed and said it would be his fault if he caught his death of cold. Callapher didn't think it was funny. She crawled into his lap, laying her head on his chest with a forlorn sigh.

"Are we poor?" she asked.

"We're not poor," Dad replied. "We live creatively, that's all."

At school, while everyone else rushed to clean brushes and scrape pallets clean before the last bell, I lingered at my easel, reluctant to return to the narrow walls of the Shoe Box, to the naked Barbies Callapher left "sleeping" in my underwear drawer, and to my father sitting in the driveway in his underwear.

I'd never met anyone like Lori. She dressed in uniform black and swore with more frequency and eloquence than anyone I'd ever known. If she wasn't running around the room, she was tapping her foot on the floor or drumming her fingers on the table. She put her glasses on just to take them off again. During one class, she threw her arms out wide to demonstrate the gesture of Pollock's brushwork and accidentally winged the spectacles across the room where they smacked against the far wall and fell into thc Drawing I still life.

During the second week of school, she sidled up to me at my easel and asked quietly if she could see me in her office, please. Her "office" consisted of a renovated janitor's closet wedged between the two art rooms. Into this five-foot square she'd managed to crowd a desk, two bookshelves, one filing cabinet, and a real human skeleton hung behind a glass encasement like a winter coat in a closet.

"Sit down, sit down," she said, hastily clearing stacks of loose-leaf paper and books from the only chair in the room.

I sat obediently, scanning the titles of the book spines: *Painting with Watercolors, The Left Brain Crisis, My Dog Ate My Casework.* Lori rooted around the shelf beside her desk, producing a thick stack of drawings and an old, weathered sketchbook.

"My portfolio," I said. To join the class without prerequisites I'd been required to submit a showcase of work.

Lori set the drawings on her desk, tapping them twice with her forefinger. "I've wanted to talk to you about these." She crossed her arms. "School projects? Assignments? What?"

"No, not school," I said. "We only had three art classes at my old school. Art 1 and 2 and 3. It was really dumb, all crafty stuff, so I dropped out."

"And you did these . . . ?"

"At home," I supplied. "Well, some at school. During study hall."

She smiled. "Well, I can't say you've moved up far in the world"—she gestured to indicate her office—"but I do pride myself in this curriculum. For the limited resources we've got, I don't think we do a bad job. Now, let me see, there's a few I wanted to look at specifically . . ."

She shuffled through the drawings, absentmindedly knocking over a cup of pencils. They clattered across her desk, rolling noisily to the floor. She swore, then announced, "This isn't going to work. We need more room"

We carried the drawings to the adjoining classroom, spreading them out across one long empty table.

"Much better," Lori declared. "Now we can look at them more as one body of work. Are they in chronological order, as such?"

"Somewhat. I forgot to date them. This one's new, though." I picked up a pastel rendering of a sunset behind my house, purple-topped trees against the blazing sky. "The pencil ones are a lot older."

Lori took the pastel drawing from my hand. "Yes, this one! The subtle blend of color here, and the cross-hatching. It's well done. Do you know much of color theory?"

I shook my head.

"I think I mentioned it your first day. What you've done—unknowingly, then—is tone one color by blending it with its complement. You dulled the red with a bit of green, didn't you?"

"Yeah, exactly. It was an accident at first, but I noticed how it made the red less bright—more realistic, somehow. I didn't know there was a theory behind it."

Lori held the drawing an inch from her nose, squinting her eyes. "It's a principle of color. Where did I put my glasses?" She patted her pockets, felt the neck of her blouse, looked behind her on the floor. I thought about telling her the spectacles were on her head, but she'd stop searching. "When did you develop an interest in pastels?"

I didn't know. Since I was little, I'd been given art kits and paper for Christmas and birthdays. I couldn't remember the transition between coloring books and pastels.

Lori said, "I'm assuming this one is older?"

"It's not one of my better drawings. Kind of embarrassing, really."

"Of course not," she retorted. "You should never be embarrassed. That's the first rule. You have to approach this with a sort of abandonment. Just think of kids: they're never ashamed to pick up a marker and draw gibberish all over a page, are they? Do you know that most adults don't draw beyond a first-grade level?"

Silenced by the reprimand, I only shook my head.

"All their lives they never progress past the mind of a child," she continued, "and yet they lose that childhood freedom from inhibition. I have to say I enjoyed looking through this." She flipped through the pages of my last sketchbook. "There's a visible progression of your stylistic approach to drawing. In the beginning everything is line—strict line—and I can see eraser marks all over the page where you tried to correct perceived mistakes. But by the end, you're working with a more gestural, casual stroke. You're drawing with shadows and shapes and blocks of tone rather than line." She raised her eyebrows. "No erasers. And they look like they were done quickly."

I nodded with excitement. "I started making drawings like crazy, real fast. It's like they came out of the pencil themselves."

"Are these portraits from life?" she asked.

"No, from magazines mostly."

She slapped the book shut. "You'll want to get away from that. Firstly, magazine people are less interesting. No lines or wrinkles. No curves, for that matter. Secondly, you'll find that art schools value the ability to draw from life. When you draw a picture from a magazine, that image has already been flattened to two dimensions. The camera's already done half the work. In essence, you're cheating, not to mention plagiarizing: that picture was already someone else's idea. You wouldn't be able to put any of these in a show or competition . . ." She put her forefinger to her pursed lips, considering. "Except maybe the few landscapes. Of course, it's not a bad thing you've had all this practice. You've developed a good understanding of facial proportions, and you've got a decent grasp of human anatomy. Most students are intimidated by the body."

"It's my favorite thing to draw," I explained.

Lori scanned the tabletop of work one last time. She said, "I want you to work big. I want you to think outside the box. Which reminds me: hold on just a minute." She went to her office and returned moments later with a pocket-sized book in her hands.

She handed the booklet to me: *Design Language* by Tim McCreight.

"Some vocabulary to give you ways to talk about your work. To loosen that quiet tongue of yours. Well, you'd better get back in there and clean up; the bell's going to ring soon. You think about what I've said." She gestured toward my portfolio. "These are good, but they're not excellent. When you apply to school they're gong to want to see a solid body of work. You have to really put yourself to it. You have to want it, Olivia—really want it."

I left the room dizzy with excitement. This woman spoke of art schools and exhibitions: things I'd never dreamed of.

"What did she want?" Matthew asked when I returned to my easel.

"We were looking at my portfolio," I explained.

He opened his mouth to reply, but I heard nothing. His lips moved silently, blurred by the neon cloud closing in about his head. A sudden wave of nausea turned my stomach. Thinking I was about to throw up, I stepped away from my easel to escape toward the door, but then I'd gone in the wrong direction—there was the window. Which way should I turn? The floor rose up at an angle as a rush of wind or maybe blood roared in my ears. I felt a pleasant tingling in my fingers and legs, then I couldn't feel either at all. For a moment, I floated in a burning brown haze, everyone's voice in the distance, and my head so light I wanted to laugh. I flew up weightless.

The sound of chairs clattering to the floor woke me. I found myself looking up at the ceiling. Matthew's face floated over mine. Lori was patting me awake, the dry skin of her palm rough against my cheek.

Her voice gained clarity: ". . . You fainted, honey. Are you all right? Can you get up?"

The entire class had gathered to look down on me. I realized that I'd startled myself back to consciousness with the sound of my own fall. A set of arms reached beneath mine to lift me to my feet. When the dizziness overwhelmed me again, I leaned back into those arms, turning to discover that Matthew was holding me up.

"To the office," Lori commanded him.

"I'm all right," I insisted.

"We're going," she stated. "Everyone else, back to your easels."

I struggled once against Matthew but nearly fell in the attempt. I gave up and let him half-carry me toward the school office. The secretary directed us to the single cot wedged between the refrigerator and wall in the teachers' lounge.

In the doorway, Lori exclaimed, "Nothing like it! Just crumpled, right in front of everyone!"

The secretary laid a wet paper towel on my forehead. "Did you eat any lunch?" she asked.

I told her I had.

Lori appeared and shoved an ice-cold soda into my hand.

"Sugar," she said. "Drink some. Are you diabetic?"

I shook my head. I felt too nauseated to drink the Coke, but the cold, wet can felt good against my belly.

Lori sat right on the cot with me and held my hand. "It's nearly two," she said. "Do you have someone to pick you up from school?"

"My mom." I closed my eyes.

"Are you going to be sick?"

"No, I just need to lie here a minute."

"You just close your eyes and don't bother yourself with anything. Matthew—stay with her, I have to get back to the class. Honey, you just rest now." She patted my arm. "You tell your mother exactly what happened, and you see an internist, you got that? Matthew, don't let her walk off by herself. Carry her to the car if you have to."

I wanted to say that he shouldn't bother, but the moment she left Matthew assumed her position at my side, intent upon staying. My head ached terribly.

"Did I hit something?" I asked, reaching for my temple.

"You only landed headfirst against the window," he replied.

"It really hurts," I said.

He held my chin and turned my head. With his forefinger he touched my forehead. I jerked back in surprise. He said, "You're bleeding."

"Lord Almighty," said the secretary from the doorway. "Should I call an ambulance?"

Matthew leaned forward. He pinched the skin of my left temple slightly. "No, wait—do you have any tape?"

The secretary ran from the room.

"How many fingers am I holding up?" he asked.

"You can't be serious."

He asked, "What's today's date?"

I told him. I told him my name, my address, the name of the president, and I said he'd been holding up three fingers plus his thumb.

"There's a whole box in the storage closet if that runs out," the secretary said breathlessly, handing Matthew an entire box of Scotch tape.

"This is fine." To me, he said, "This might hurt a little."

His face leaned so close to mine, I blushed from embarrassment. I could feel his breath. If I turned my head, my lips would brush his cheek.

"What are you doing?" I asked.

"Hold still. I'm closing up the wound."

Giddiness had replaced my nausea. I laughed out loud when he said *wound*.

"What's so funny?" he asked. His fingers pressed hard against my forehead—there was a pinch, followed by a sharp pain.

"*Wound,*" I repeated. I made my voice low like a man's. "Doctor, we must suture the wound. Scalpel and Scotch tape, please."

He said fine, I could laugh if I wanted. I thought I heard a real sense of injury in his tone, so I shut up and tried not to think of his hands touching my skin. I was in a war camp being treated for injuries inflicted by a land mine. Shrapnel, right to the head. Lucky it missed the eye, but there were slivers splintered in my brain: potential permanent damage. There was no anesthesia, only alcohol, which they threw burning down my throat for the pain. "She's tough," the doctor said. "Amazing. Men, I think she's going to pull through." Outside the army tent, the billowing green clouds of an impending storm blew open the tarp to reveal an angry sky shot through with the bright flares of exploding artillery.

"There," Matthew said.

I traced the cool patch of tape now criss-crossed tightly at my right temple.

"It's a butterfly stitch. Boy Scouts," he added, ducking his head to hide his embarrassment.

He sat with me for the last half hour of school. The secretary was convinced I'd whacked my head good enough for some permanent damage: I'd lose consciousness and die or something, I suppose, she was so worked up about it—and then the whole school would be blamed.

Matthew insisted I didn't have a concussion. I wanted to ask Dr. Matthew if he'd learned that in Boy Scouts too. But considering he'd patched up my head, it seemed ungrateful to embarrass him more.

We waited until the after-school crowd emptied from the hallways before leaving the office. I said I was fine, but Matthew insisted on holding me up. He put his arm around my waist, saying, "Man! You're tiny."

Mom's car was one of two still waiting in the school driveway by the time we walked outside. She was angry for the delay until Matthew explained what had happened. He went into such detail I half expected him to reenact the whole thing right there in the parking lot.

"Olivia!" Mom exclaimed, looking at me in surprise, like I'd set fire to the art room. "Are you all right?"

"I'm fine, Mom," I said.

"Get in the car," she said. "Callapher, let her have the backseat. Lie down, Olivia—put your head between your knees."

"Mom," I answered through clenched teeth. "I'm all right."

Callapher crawled over the seat to sit up front while Matthew helped me into the car. Mom reached back to feel my forehead.

"How did this happen?" she demanded.

"She just sort of went," Matthew volunteered, leaning into the open passenger door window. "I've never seen anything like it. I mean, she just sort of crumpled." His hair fell around his face. He brushed it back behind his ears.

Mom considered him with silent equanimity. "Well, thank you," she said shortly. "We appreciate your help."

Matthew nodded. "Be careful," he admonished me.

Mom didn't say anything the whole ride home. Just studied me in the rearview mirror and pursed her lips so tight they peaked white at the tips. That evening she told Dad. He took a look at my head and said I should thank the boy.

"Saved you five stitches," he said.

Mom said, "Benjamin, take this seriously."

He said, "Claire, I *am* taking it seriously."

While they argued, I managed to escape to my room.

A lingering embarrassment rose hot in my cheeks each time I remembered waking up to find the class drawn around me like I was a car accident on the highway to be gawked at. I stayed in my room until dark, sitting in bed with my sketchbook in my lap. Drawing was the only way to quiet my thoughts.

I burned a row of candles on my desk. Their finger flames reflected in the glossy pages of the collage that now covered the entire wall. Beautiful women stared down at me, through me. The flecks of candlelight—emblems of my world—burrowed into theirs. I wanted to step into the magazine like Alice through the looking glass, like Mary Poppins into the magical world of a chalk drawing.

Someone knocked softly on the door.

"Come in," I said.

Mom entered. She sat on the edge of the bed.

"Be careful burning those candles." Wetting her fingertips, she pinched out the flames. "The wicks are too long. Its dangerous to leave them burning, especially if you're going to bed."

I rolled my eyes. "I know."

"I'm serious. They're a fire hazard."

"If you hear me screaming, you'll know something happened."

She picked up my sketchbook and began to page through it, ignoring my sarcasm. "Did that art teacher give you your portfolio back?" she asked.

I shook my head. "We looked at it together, though. She thought it was good."

"Make sure you get it back," Mom persisted. "Those were some of your best drawings." She stared at the dead candlewicks. She took a breath. "I made an appointment for you today."

I felt physically alarmed, as if someone had thrown a bucket of cold water over my chest. "An appointment?"

"His name is Dr. Palmer. Margaret recommended him. His office is out of town, but not far."

I traced the lining of the blanket with my fingertip.

"Remember, we talked about this," Mom said. There was an uncharacteristic gentleness to her tone that frightened me more than anything. "We said if your period didn't come back, we'd take you to the doctor and find out what's wrong." She pushed the hair from my face, then rested her hand against my arm. Feeling for bones. "I'm worried about you. You've been losing so much weight."

I shifted nervously.

"I know you don't see it, but you have," she continued, hastily. "Your cheeks are sunken in, and your arms are so thin."

"When's the appointment?" I asked coolly.

"Friday. I thought I could pick you up at lunch. You can have the afternoon off school."

As if this were some sort of prize.

"It might be something small," Mom reassured me. Or maybe she was trying to reassure herself. "But after today I think we should get you checked. They'll probably do some blood tests. You know, look for anemia, things like that."

I nodded silently. She kissed my forehead and left with a "good night."

I remembered the first time she looked at me with that awful expression of concern and mute surprise. I'd asked her to make my chicken without the marinade. When she asked if I was trying to lose weight, I looked up from shucking lettuce into a salad bowl and said no. It only occurred to me later that I'd lied.

CHAPTER 5

control

(kon TROL)

1. To exercise authority or a dominating influence over
2. To hold in restraint; to check
3. To verify or regulate by conducting a parallel experiment or by comparing with some other standard

the book of *Design Language* explains that surrendering control is different from losing control. When the Dada artists dropped torn fragments of paper onto larger blank sheets and glued them where they landed, they were relinquishing an element of control in order to unleash their subconscious.

Which is in control when you paint: the paint or the painter? Is the clay controlled by the potter's hands, or by the force of gravity and the spinning wheel?

In the waiting room the minute hand tick, tick, ticked loudly as it circled the face of the clock. On the television suspended from the ceiling, two blondes argued passionately. The volume had been muted, but you can tell a soap opera without the sound. The look is different: the people glisten.

Beside me, Mom leafed through *Home and Gardens* pretending to be interested in how to use your pasta maker as a paper shredder and how to get berry stains out of white T-shirts. She reached awkwardly across the armrest of the waiting chair to pat my knee. The gesture felt somehow patronizing. I smiled weakly.

Mom looked at the clock, then adjusted her own wristwatch with a frown. She set aside *Home and Gardens* to pick up another magazine. Twenty-five ways to take a vacation without packing a bag. Five easy moves to killer abs. How to trim those thighs. Instant antiaging, clinically proven, patent-bending formula . . . *Go through magazines and tear out pictures of women whose looks you admire,* says Laura Flannigan, director of Bailey studios.

"That looks good." Mom pointed to a picture for lemon-grilled chicken.

"It does," I replied.

Over our heads the clock tick, tick, ticked.

"Olivia?" asked the nurse. "Right this way. You too, Mom, if you'd like."

We followed the nurse through a maze of white hallways and closed doors. She stopped at a scale, directing me to take off my shoes and step up on the black rubber platform. My heart began to pound as she slid the weights of the scale to balance. Her red fingernails clicked against the metal. One hundred and four pounds. She noted the number on her clipboard without comment. I glanced at my mother, but she had turned away to rub at the corner of her eye with her pinky.

"This way, hon," said the nurse. In the next room, I sat obediently on the examination table while she took my pulse and checked my temperature with a quick and bored efficiency. She said to sit tight: the doctor would be in shortly.

I shifted my weight on the table. Mom sat on the stool beside the doctor's counter. It looked just like a kitchen cabinet, with its Formica top and blond wood cupboards, but it was stocked with canisters of cotton balls and swabs instead of sugar and flour. Beside the counter hung a pink-and-blue illustration of a uterus.

The paper wrinkling beneath my weight interrupted the silence that compounded between my mother and me. Her eyes were wet. They glistened like those of the women in the soap opera.

"Well," she laughed. "You *have* been losing weight, girl."

I laughed too. I didn't know why we were laughing. I felt relieved. One hundred and four pounds . . . so much less than I would have thought. If it weren't for my mother's anxiety, I'd have been proud. But with a deep and terrible dread, I began to realize that I'd done something wrong.

"I don't know," I blurted. "I mean, I don't know how . . . I just started eating healthy, Mom. I didn't mean to."

She put her hand on my knee and squeezed. "It's all right. It's all right. We'll figure it out."

Dr. Palmer entered abruptly, whacking the door against the foot of the stool Mom sat on. She stood and apologized profusely. He apologized in return, and she said it was nothing, that she really was sorry. He took the stool, and Mom moved to the corner chair, where she worried a tissue to shreds in her hands.

Dr. Palmer slid across the floor to the examination table, flipping through a chart of soft pink and yellow papers. He was balding but his beard was thick, crimped into reddish curls at the tips. The skin at his cheeks was wrinkled and pink, like he'd just come in from the cold.

"Two years since your last physical . . . no allergies, blood pressure good . . ." He clicked the end of his pen with his thumb. "Some significant weight loss. One hundred and twenty-three pounds to 104.

So. Olivia." He clapped the chart shut and held it to his chest against the white lab coat. "You're concerned with the cessation of your menstruation." He raised his eyebrows. "Your period had stopped."

I didn't need him to translate for me.

From the corner, Mom said, "Yes."

He acknowledged Mom with a nod but without a glance in her direction. "Could you tell me when your last period was?" he asked.

"I don't know for sure," I replied. "It was after Thanksgiving that I noticed." I looked to Mom. "Four months?"

"Almost five," Mom said.

"Five months," Dr. Palmer repeated. He scribbled on a notepad. "And there has been nothing: it has stopped completely?"

I nodded. "I didn't think it was anything at first. I just thought it would come back. When it didn't, I told Mom."

"I thought maybe—and I'm no expert on such things," Mom interjected, "but I thought maybe her cycle still had to work itself out. I know for a lot of young girls it takes a while for that sort of thing to get into pattern."

"Yes," Dr. Palmer nodded but appeared distracted. "Yes, sometimes there's a lapse, there are these"—he waved his hand—"irregularities. Olivia, how long had you been menstruating before the cycle stopped?"

"Since seventh grade. Three years."

"And it was regular, for the most part? By regular I don't mean by the calendar—but monthly, for the most part."

I hesitated. "Yes, I think so."

He paused and pursed his lips. He'd been sitting far back on his stool.

"Olivia," he began slowly. "Is there any chance you could be pregnant?"

The question startled me so much, I couldn't respond immediately. No boy had ever touched me like that. I remembered the pressure of Matthew's fingers on my forehead. I remembered paintings of the Virgin Mary: conception piercing her skin in beams of holy light as thin as surgical needles. I blinked and recollected myself. "No," I said. "I don't have a boyfriend."

"There is no way you could be pregnant?" he repeated without hesitation.

I stared into his steady, blue eyes in terror, as if his suspicion created the possibility, as if even now something inside me kicked to life.

I shook my head resolutely and assured him I was not—there was no way. "I'm a virgin," I said. The word fell out of my mouth, awkward and naked. I felt ashamed of it. Like no boy wanted me.

He sat back on his stool with reluctance. "As I noted before, you've suffered a considerable weight loss. Have you been trying to lose weight?"

"No . . . well, sort of. I don't know." I shifted on the crackling paper. "I'm not trying to lose weight. But I have to eat healthy."

He asked me about my activities. Did I exercise? Cycle? Run? Was I in sports at school? To Mom, he explained, "Oftentimes when females are involved in any sort of intense physical training, they exhaust their bodies and force menstruation into a sort of remission." He returned his eyes to me. "Have you been overly active in the last few months? More than usual?"

"I run sometimes," I offered meekly, hoping it would be enough. He seemed determined that I should be exhausting my body.

"For track? Soccer?"

"No. Just from home."

"How long?"

"Thirty minutes, maybe."

"How often?"

I shrugged. "Um . . . three times a week, I think. Sometimes more."

Mom looked at me in surprise. She didn't know I went running. I always told her I was walking to a friend's house or hiking through the woods. I never ran until I knew I'd gone far enough that she couldn't accidentally spot me outside a window.

"Is anyone pressuring you to lose weight?" Dr. Palmer asked.

The irony of his question almost made me laugh. For months everyone had been telling me to eat. Eat, you're so thin, they said. You're always cold because you don't have body fat, they said. Stand sideways and you'd disappear.

"She just started eating lots of fruits and vegetables," Mom intervened. "And she never will eat a bite of junk. I mean, I know that's good for her, she's better than the rest of us, but I don't think she eats enough. She never eats an ounce of fat. I think she eats in a very healthy way, but not enough fat."

Dr. Palmer looked at his charts. "Tell me what you eat, Olivia," he said.

"I eat three meals a day," I explained. "Even snacks after school, so I don't know how I'm losing weight."

"Yes, but honey," Mom interrupted, "you eat an apple for breakfast, and you barely touch your dinner."

Dr. Palmer stood. "Excuse me one moment, Mrs. Monahan. Could I have a word with you in private?" He opened the door and extended his open hand.

Mom's face went blank. She looked at me with an almost pleading expression but then immediately lowered her eyes, gathered her purse, and followed Dr. Palmer into the hallway. I sat alone in the silent room staring at the poster on the wall, tracing the pink fallopian tubes as they folded in on themselves. They looked like little rubber hoses. The uterus lay spliced in half like a melon: a fleshly inch of husk encasing the hollow center. This inside part was patterned with sinuous stripes of muscle tissue. With my forefinger, I poked my body beneath my belly button. This is what I was inside: pink tubes and vein-laced balloons.

But the real mess, I realized, was in my head. I felt as if I'd always known, as if the realization was only admitting a fact I'd been keeping secret from myself. I lived in two parts. The part everyone saw, and which I believed to be myself, then the inside part, where I lived in ugliness.

The revelation terrified me. There was a woman in our old church who suffered from severe depression. I knew her as the figure sitting silently in the back pew and imagined the rest of her life as a silent, black existence in a bedroom where the lights were always off and the television always on. Her misery was a thing you read about in the prayer requests, outlined neatly in print. You could read her like a character in a book, as if her suffering were not to be experienced but studied. I always felt relieved when we talked about her. Relieved that I wasn't her.

Dr. Palmer came back in. I pulled my finger from my side quickly.

"Don't be alarmed," he said as he reached between his legs to pull up the stool. "I only asked your mother to wait outside for a while so we can talk more freely. I want you to be perfectly honest with me."

I wanted to be angry with Dr. Palmer for making Mom leave, but

I felt grateful. Something in his steady eyes made me eager to trust him. I needed someone to explain to me what I'd done wrong so I could repent, fix it, run away from this place and never come back again. But his first question annoyed me.

"You're quite positive that you're not pregnant? There's no possibility?"

"No," I retorted impatiently. "I swear, I've never been with a guy at all." I bowed my head; I didn't want to see the pity in his blue eyes.

This time he accepted my answer. "Tell me about eating healthy," he said.

I tried to explain it:

There are good foods and there are bad. For example, white flour, meat fat, saturated fat, grease, pure sugar—these things are bad. Wheat bread is good. All fruits are good—just nutrition and no fat or simple sugars, and only sixty calories apiece. Too many calories is always, always bad, "too many" being any more than 1,100 a day at the absolute most. If you put the wrong foods in your body, you are contaminated and dirty and your stomach swells. Then the voice says, *Why did you do that? Don't you know better? Ugly and wicked, you are disgusting to me.*

Repetition makes things safe. You eat the same thing for breakfast and for lunch. Half a cup of raisin brain with a half a cup of skim milk. At twelve-thirty, approximately five and a half hours later, you have a slice of turkey between two pieces of wheat bread. Wheat is good, all that brown, to clean out your body. Items of food are parts of a puzzle that have to fit. At night, you lay your hand flat against your stomach and recount all the things you put in your mouth that day. Peppermint candies are bad, butter is bad, the pure sugar coating on half a handful of frosted flakes is bad. Things between meals are bad, a blaring wrong, wrong, wrong, a packet of calories you are not supposed to eat that now float around inside you looking for a flap of skin to burrow under and swell out to ugly fat.

I'd never tried to explain this to anybody. I didn't tell him everything. But even what I managed sounded absolutely absurd coming out of my mouth. If Dr. Palmer thought I was crazy, he didn't show it. He took little notes on his neat paper pad. I began to cry.

"It's all right," he said softly. He handed me a Kleenex, then wheeled away a safe distance from me to watch. When I'd settled down a little, he changed the subject. "Tell me about school."

"School?" I asked stupidly.

"How are things going? What classes are you in?"

"I've only been there like two weeks."

From this answer, he came up with a dozen other questions. When did we move? Why? He asked all about Dad's church, about our new house, about the friends I'd made. I just wanted to leave this place, to lock myself in my bedroom with my pictures. I answered all his questions immediately and unthinkingly, hoping that if I did so, he would let me go. I couldn't see what Dad's job or school or moving had to do with my weird body, with my stupid fallopian tube wiring clogging up.

I lay back on the examination table so he could press his palms against my belly and side. His hands were firm but gentle, rough at the fingertips like fine-grained sandpaper. I wondered what he felt in there, if he could trace the inside contours of my body like tracking a route on a map. When he finished, he stepped out of the room saying it would only be a moment, that he wished to speak to my mother privately.

I stayed back flat on the examination table exactly as he left me for what seemed an indefinite amount of time. When the door opened again, I sat up abruptly. Dr. Palmer nodded as if to reassure me. Mom entered the room behind him, her eyes to the ground.

"Olivia," he said a little too brightly, "thank you for waiting. Now." He sat down and began rubbing the knuckles of his left hand with the fingers of his right. "I've spoken with your mother about what we can do to supplement your diet and get you back to a healthy weight."

I glanced at my mother suspiciously.

"I would advise you to build up your portions," Dr. Palmer said. "Add some fat to your intake. Put a little butter on your toast, maybe some whole milk on your cereal. If you begin to care for your body, give it proper nutrition—as I said, larger portions, a bit of butter on the bread—your body will eventually find its own rhythm again. Menstruation will follow. I have, in the meantime, scheduled you for a blood test. We'll check for anemia and so forth—be sure there's nothing else to account for the fatigue. If that proves to be the case, I'll prescribe something that will, one could say, 'jump-start' your system. But I don't believe that's necessary just yet."

I nodded. I wanted to curl up tight beneath the covers of my bed, cradle my head, and cry, "Go away, go away." But I didn't know what I was hiding from.

". . . these thoughts you have about food," he was saying. "This need you feel to classify some foods as bad and others as good is an example of obsessive-compulsive behavior. So this is your prescription: whenever those thoughts come into your mind—the counting and the anxieties—I want you to get out and spend time with friends. Have a good time. When you wake up in the morning, don't make your bed."

It was very weird that he knew that: that I couldn't leave the room or eat breakfast until the covers of the bed had been straightened and tucked exactly so.

"And I want you to come back for a checkup in four weeks," he continued. "Maybe three. I've given your mother the contact information for some very good counselors. If nothing changes in the next month and you continue to lose weight, I strongly recommend you seek professional counseling." He turned to look knowingly at my mother, who nodded meekly. She stood in the corner of the room, silent in a way that seemed somehow obedient, the way chastised children stand by the wall at recess, watching.

It made me sick to see her that way. I felt dizzy. The room shrank away, its objects appearing to me as if from a great distance. Dr. Palmer and my mother were pink and orange distortions, their voices distant and blurred. It required a great deal of effort to surface from the heat and the exhaustion. Then they were saying good-bye. My mother and I were alone.

In the car, she forced a smile, glancing at me quickly, nervously, before returning her gaze to the road. She said, "It's not every day you go to the doctor and he tells you to gain weight!"

I hated her fake enthusiasm, but she was trying to make me feel better, so I just smiled as best I could. As we drove home the sun beat down hot and blinding against the window. My head ached terribly. Whatever that place I had just been—that place of guilt and shame—I would never go there again. Even if it meant butter on my bread and finishing a plate of food at dinner. But this resolution terrified me. What would I become?

It was evening by the time we got home. I found *To Kill a Mockingbird* and lay on the couch to read. Mom began cooking dinner while Callapher sat on the counter babbling about her day, slapping her heels against the cupboard doors. A suffocating blackness threatened to close in on me from the four corners of the room. I closed my eyes tight to will it away. I told myself that peace was possible. That normal was there in the kitchen with all the pleasant sounds and smells.

Later that night, Dad knocked on my door. He came in and perched on the edge of my bed. "Go okay?" he asked.

"I'm obsessive-compulsive," I told him with one of those fake reassuring smiles I was getting so good at. "That's the diagnosis."

"Yeah, well . . ." He rubbed his knee meditatively. "You get that from your mother."

I could tell that she had told him everything.

"So you're doing okay?" he said again. He stared at me intently, his eyes asking what he couldn't bring himself to mention aloud. Neither of us could say that awkward round word: period. It wasn't something you discussed with a father.

I nodded, perhaps too quickly. "I'm fine, Dad. Really."

"Because if something's wrong, you know you can tell me. I want you to tell me."

I nodded slowly this time, with a show of confidence I didn't feel.

"Okay, then." He rubbed his knee again and stood slowly.

"Your bad knee bothering you?" I asked.

He waved off my concern. "Getting old," he said. "That's all. This sitting around makes me stiff."

Though awkward, this brief interview with my father meant more to me than a thousand of my mother's practiced smiles. A pang of sympathy shot through my chest at the sight of his retreating back.

His shoulders hung low and heavy. I flattered myself that we shared an invisible tether, mind to mind, so that I only had to look at the way he sat in his chair to feel his thoughts exactly.

When everyone had gone to bed, I tiptoed to the kitchen and poured a handful of dry cereal into my palm. Back in the privacy of my bedroom, I ate each piece one at a time, savoring the taste on my tongue, hiding in the darkness with the wariness of a criminal.

part two

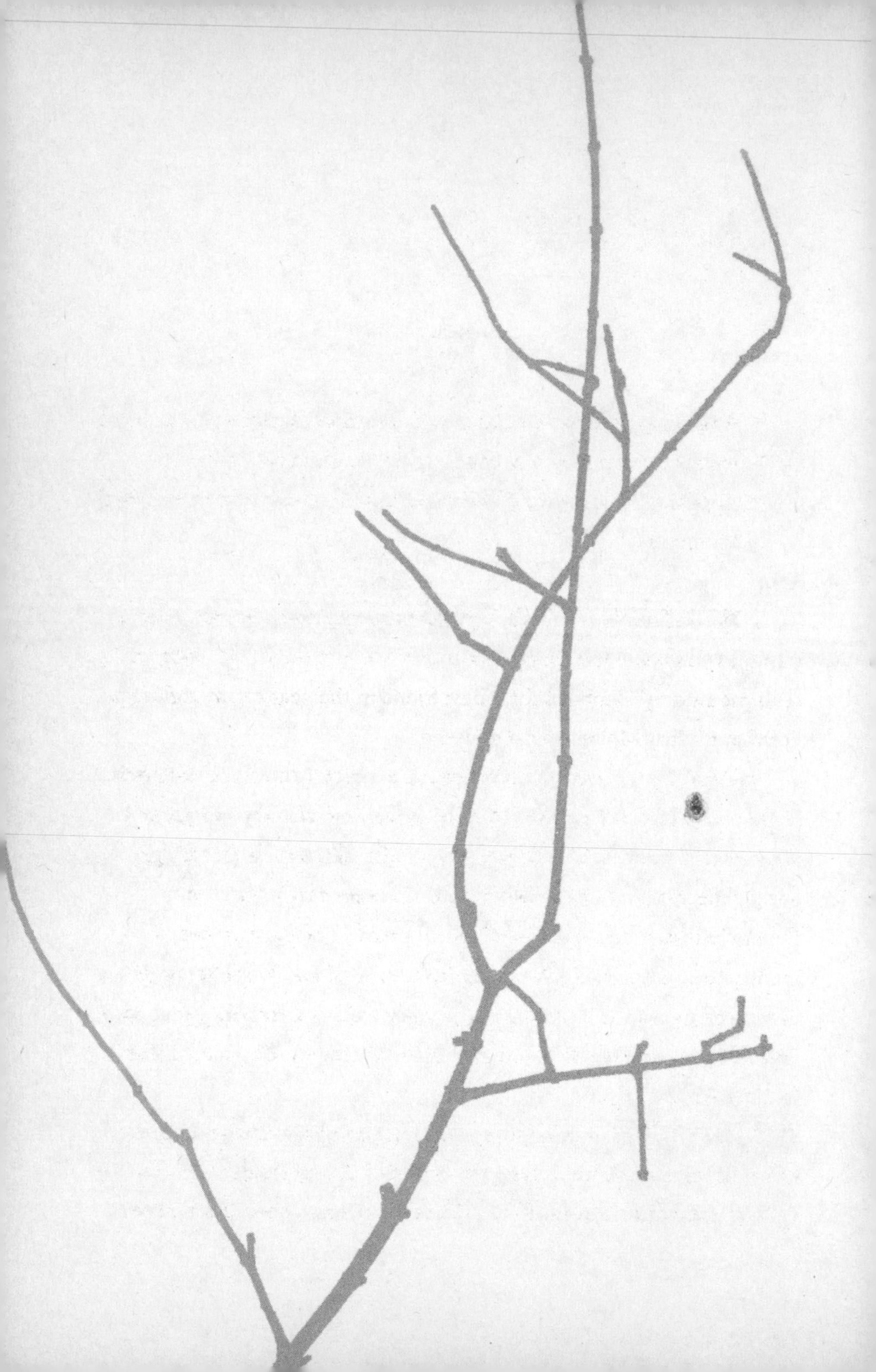

CHAPTER 6

beauty

(byoo te)

1. A pleasing quality associated with harmony, form, or color; excellence of craftsmanship, truthfulness, originality
2. Appearance or sound that arouses a strong, contemplative delight; loveliness

i maintain that God has a somewhat ironic sense of humor. I've asked Him many times what He was thinking, really, to send me Audrey Hepburn for a best friend in the year of my ugliness. For that is what Mollie was: a godsend.

In April we received the last severance check from the old church. Mom and Dad never talked to Callapher and me about money, but I could gauge the state of our finances by the contents of our fridge, and by the appearance of ninety-nine-cent paper towels cut into fourths and stacked on the back of the toilet for wiping. In bed, I made plans. We would sell more furniture. Dad and I would bag groceries side by side at FoodMart wearing matching neon orange aprons and white paper hats. When things got real bad, I'd sell my hair like Jo in *Little Women.*

Mom found part-time work as a secretary at the creepy dentist's office downtown. It used to be the home of a local resident. It was yellow with white shutters. Dr. Chenney, Mom's boss, paid a lawn service to keep up the flower beds on the perimeter of the white picket fence. A three-foot-wide poster of a woman's white smile hung on the veranda. It said: *Your Smile Is Our Reward.*

I tucked my lips up to my gums and bared my teeth at Callapher: "Your Smile Is Our Ree-Wardd," I said in our Stupid Voice. She laughed until she got the hiccups.

To save Mom one trip in the car and to give her some time in the afternoon to relax, Margaret picked Callapher up from school every day and kept her at the farmhouse until dinnertime. I still got a ride from Mom. The transmission in the truck was so bad, she wouldn't let me drive it to school. She offered to give me the van and have Margaret drive her to work each day, but I didn't want to drive the Cheese Wagon. Dad was on my side.

"She can't drive that thing," he said. "It's an eyesore."

"Well, then, I don't want to hear another word about it," Mom countered. "I'll drop her off, but I'm pulling up to the school. I'm not parking a block away so she can act like she doesn't belong to us."

Ruby offered to lend me her old Cadillac. I said no thanks, I didn't know how to navigate a boat. So Mom drove me to school and picked me up every afternoon, and at least, in that way, I retained some dignity. I could *ride* in the Cheese Wagon, so long as it didn't appear that I *owned* it.

It was the business of carpooling that began things with Mollie. I walked to the Old Maids' one afternoon to pick up Callapher and found Margaret standing on the driveway in animated conversation with a girl I'd never seen before. Seeing my approach from the road, Margaret called out, "Olivia! Come here, come here!"

Dutifully, I made a show of quickening my steps.

"What luck!" Margaret declared. "I was just telling Mollie here all about you, and she was just saying how very much she was dying to meet you."

Ashamed of Margaret's unbridled enthusiasm, I gave Mollie an apologetic smile. To my surprise she stepped forward and hugged me, crying, "Hey, girl! How *are* you?"

She was chewing a wad of pink bubblegum that made her breath sweet. Her auburn hair was streaked with three blonde highlights. She wore it cut just at her chin, gelled to curl up and out like pulled taffy. She looked and smelled like candy.

Margaret presided happily over our meeting. "It's Providence, your coming by just now," she told me. "Providence, that's what."

I explained that actually I'd just come by to get Callapher and that Mom wanted us home right away.

"Nonsense," Margaret replied. "There's no need to hurry. Mollie's just come by to drop off some extra clothes for the church charity drive."

"I have a rule," Mollie explained to me. "I never buy new clothes without giving a bag of old ones away."

"She used to drop them off at the Goodwill," Margaret said, "but we convinced her to give them to the church. Stuff at Goodwill just goes to high school kids now. They all like shopping at those places. It's fashionable, I suppose, but for the life of me I don't know why. It was a disgrace when I was a kid, but then things weren't the same back then. Mollie's in your grade," she continued, changing subjects without pause. "Works for her mom at the car lot just up the street—their house is just behind the garage. You're practically neighbors."

"That's nice," I said.

"Olivia's looking for someone to ride to school with," Margaret said to Mollie. "Their truck broke down this week, and she's had to get a ride from her mother every morning. I thought since you lived so close you might pick her up."

I wanted the burning sun to fall on my head, I was so mortified. But Mollie didn't act surprised or offended. On the contrary, she seemed almost eager.

"Sure, I can give you a ride," she said. "No big deal. Is seven okay? I usually leave my house at five till."

"Seven's fine," I said.

She arrived the next morning at 7:35.

"Sorry I'm late," she said, without looking at all concerned. "I totally thought it was six, not seven, and I was so proud of myself for getting up on time. Then I looked at my watch and saw it was quarter after and just freaked out. Here, breakfast."

She handed me an oatmeal cookie.

"Thanks," I said.

She held her cookie in her teeth while she backed the car up. She needed both hands, one for the wheel, the other for the stick shift. The words *FIVE EASY DOWN PAYMENTS* covered the windshield in puffy pink bubble letters outlined in neon lime paint.

"Is this yours?" I asked.

"Oh, no, I don't haf ma ow ca yet." She took the cookie out of her mouth and licked her full lips. "Mom lets me drive stuff off the lot."

"What about insurance?" I asked. I nibbled on a corner of the cookie, making sure to have it in my mouth when she looked in my direction.

"Insurance? Mom doesn't really worry about it. I mean, she's in so much trouble with the government anyway. She changed her name after my dad left, but she never did it like legally—just woke up one day and said her name was Kari now, not Cameron, and started signing all her papers 'Kari Landis' instead of 'Cameron Bauer.' Landis, that's her maiden name. Of course, sometimes she forgets and writes 'Cameron Landis,' and I think she even wrote 'Kari Bauer' on a few checks. Gordon—he works at the lot—keeps telling her that if she doesn't get it together, the IRS or somebody will come after her."

Mollie took a corner so hard, I had to grab on to the door handle to keep my balance.

"You work at the car lot?" I asked. When she turned away I slipped the oatmeal cookie inside my book bag.

"Every day after school." She rolled her eyes. "So boring sometimes I think I'll lose my mind. You should come over and bug me. It's only like a two-minute walk from your house."

At school, we stood in line together for a tardy slip. It was a whole new experience for me. I'd never been late for school in my life, what with my mother, the Patron Saint of Punctuality. The huge man who wrote up the slips looked miserable, as though he'd just stumbled out of bed to find someone had shot his dog. He grumbled at everyone except Mollie.

" 'Morning, dear," he said. "Was wondering when you'd show up."

"Don't do the X this time," she said, leaning across the fold-out table at which he sat and pointing out a spot on the slip. She had hot pink fingernails studded at the tips with sparkling gold star stickers. "Do the check mark in the little box; it looks so much nicer."

Without lifting his head, he eyed her sardonically. He made a quick little check mark. "This good enough, Ms. Bauer, ma'am?"

"That's fine," she said. "Have a splendid day, Mr. Berger."

He winked at her as we walked away.

"Where are you going?" she asked.

"Three thirty-six," I said. "Down that way."

"I'm the same way. What do you have? Algebra?"

"No, world history."

She stuck out her tongue. "You don't have Morris, do you?"

I began to ask what was so bad about Morris, but second bell rang to interrupt me. In moments, a mass of students packed the hallway. Two guys walking by shouted to Mollie. She ran to talk to them. I didn't know whether to follow or not, but I didn't want to look pathetic, so I walked away in the opposite direction toward my next class.

I didn't see Mollie at all the rest of the day. We'd planned to meet outside the office after last bell to drive home together. I decided that if she was with friends and looked busy I'd just turn around and call Mom to come get me.

I found her standing outside the office at the center of a small crowd, telling a story. She threw up her hands and said, *"Bam!* like that." Everyone laughed, but none as hard as Mollie, like she found her own punch line surprising. She had a brilliant, broad smile, exactly like the advertisement outside the dentist's office.

I turned to walk away, but someone shouted my name. Mollie was standing on tiptoe, waving rigorously.

"Olivia!" she hollered. *"Olivia!"*

I walked toward her.

"Where'd you go this morning?" she asked. "It was like I turned around for one second and you absolutely disappeared. Olivia, this is Mark, James, Lily, Ashley, Nolan—hey, moron." She slapped the tall boy beside me. "Look at me when I'm talking to you. This is my friend Olivia."

He looked down at me and sort of smirked. "Hey," he said.

I wanted to ask him what was so funny, but Mollie turned to me and said, "Anyway, did you get your stuff? Are you ready to go?"

"He looked at me funny," I said as we walked away.

"He looks at everyone funny," Mollie retorted. "Nolan's full of himself. Nice and very good looking but full of himself. I can't much like someone for being good looking if they *know* they're good looking, can you?"

When we got to my house, she asked what I was doing that night.

Maybe playing Uno with Callapher. Or singing hymns with the Old Maids. "I don't know," I said.

"Well, some of us were thinking of going to the movies. You want to go? It'd be an early show—like eight, so we wouldn't be out late."

"But I don't know anyone," I said.

"That doesn't matter. Nobody'll care. You'll be *my* date."

"Maybe," I said.

"Good. I'll pick you up at seven thirty."

That was it. I don't remember becoming friends with Mollie; I just remembering *being* friends with Mollie. The beginning of our friendship reminded me of making childhood playmates, when close proximity of backyards and age were reason enough.

Mollie and I carpooled to and from school every day. I made it to first bell three days out of five. In two weeks I had my first detention.

"What do I do?" I asked.

"What do you mean what do you do?" Mollie asked. "You sit in the cafeteria and sleep for an hour. It's incredibly stupid. It's supposed to teach you a lesson."

I raised my eyebrows.

"Trust me—it doesn't work," she said.

We served the detention together, the unhappy Mr. Berger presiding. I was seated alone at a round table near the doorway. Mollie sat with half a dozen kids placed three chairs apart from one another along the long fold-out lunch table bisecting the cafeteria. I noticed her gesturing toward the boy beside her. Moments later, in unison, the entire table broke out into spontaneous laughter. They roared for ten seconds, then fell abruptly silent. Five minutes later it happened again: unpredictable, unified hilarity that stopped with as little warning as it had begun. The third time it happened, everyone else in detention was laughing with them. Mr. Berger walked right to Mollie and escorted her to the hallway, where she remained the duration of the hour.

She explained the mechanics of it to me as we drove home: by an under-the-table note, she'd instructed everyone to laugh for precisely ten seconds at her signal (wink, yawn, nose pick) before stopping completely. This was a good game, she said, because by the end you weren't fake laughing anymore, you were for-real laughing. Mollie had a beautiful laugh. It came up from deep in her skinny belly, up through her bleach-white smile.

I've never known anyone who hated school more than Mollie; every day she thought up a hundred ways to escape the boredom. She had a criminal record with the school attendance office. By lunchtime the skin of her arms and hands would be buried beneath tattoos of roses and games of tic-tac-toe. Between classes, she passed me notes folded into origami triangles. Only "notes" is a deceptive word; they were more like war correspondence. I got one that was three pages long and included an illustrated story about a princess named Olivia trapped in a tower called Detention from which she escaped on a white stallion that looked very much like a bloated rat with sticks for legs.

To escape the claustrophobia of the Shoe Box, I spent most afternoons with Mollie at the car lot where she worked as secretary. Her duties included filing invoices, taking phone calls, ordering and/or delivering food for the mechanics, cleaning the kitchen, prank calling her own mother in the back office, and dressing the mannequin that sat on that week's show car.

The mannequin's name was Mani. She had her own wardrobe, made up of all the clothes Mollie had discarded since junior high. For the spring season, we dressed the doll in a yellow tube top, a Hawaiian print wraparound skirt, and a pair of hot pink sunglasses. Dismantling the mannequin made the costume change easier. Her hands and feet screwed off with a pop and twist to the right. The kitchen looked like Frankenstein's laboratory: disembodied legs and hands spread in a row upon the card table.

The head mechanic came into the kitchen for a soda. When he saw Mani's red bikini in a pile on the table, he asked, "Mollie, when you gonna come to work dressed in that little number?"

"Frank, I'd ask you kindly not to say things like that."

"What? You can't take a compliment? I think it's a compliment to say how nice you'd all look in little red bikinis like that one there."

Mollie just pursed her lips tight and turned her back to him.

When Frank left, she put Mani back together and set her naked on the single employee toilet. An hour later, Frank went into the bathroom with a newspaper in hand. He hollered so loud from fright I thought I'd pee my pants from laughing.

"There's nothing funny about it," he said, shaking his newspaper at us. "Nothing funny about scaring an old man half to death. What if my heart stopped, Mollie Bauer? When then? You think you'd be laughing? I don't think Jesus Christ would think very highly of your killing an old man."

Jesus Christ was a real point of contention between Frank and Mollie. The old man put it to her any time he caught her imitating the attendance man at school or complaining about how much work she had to do.

"Would the good Lord Jesus Christ approve of yer bellyachin'?" he would ask. Or, "I don't know, but I'd bet you money Jesus didn't talk slander 'bout people behind their back."

Mollie always conceded the rebuke and repented of the transgression: "You're right, Frank. I'm sorry; I shouldn't gossip." And that would be the last we'd hear about the football captain's sexual exploits or the principal's drinking habits.

Jesus Christ was about the only subject on which Mollie was entirely serious. She didn't speak of God often, but when she did, it was with an unnerving familiarity, as if she'd just gotten off the phone with Him that morning. As the daughter of a minister, I was used to people advertising their personal umbilical cord to God, but I'd never seen it in someone as otherwise sane and actually likable as Mollie.

She wasn't without company. The youngest employee at the car lot, aside from herself, was a man of twenty named Gordon Baker. He was the quietest of the mechanics and painfully shy. When you tried to speak to him, he averted his eyes, shifting his hands in and out of his uniform pockets. The fact that he drove with a big black Bible sunning on his dashboard didn't help matters. During lunch, when the other men propped themselves on the backs of truck beds with tin lunch pails, Gordon sat alone at the kitchen table behind the office, a cup of black coffee to his left, the open Bible to his right. His name badge boasted a carefully stitched *Gordon*, but in the garage and the office he was faithfully regarded as Preacher Boy.

Gordon had worked for the Bauers since Mollie was ten. They had a siblings' friendship, alternately affectionate and abusive. Mollie always greeted him with a hard punch to the arm. She'd jump on him for a piggyback ride when he walked through the kitchen for lunch, wrapping her arms so tight around his neck he complained he couldn't breathe.

Gordon was tall, with the well-built arms and shoulders of a man used to hard labor, but he carried himself with a certain sense of respectability the other men lacked. He always came to work with his broad cheeks ruddy red and clean-shaven, his fingernails perfectly trimmed and white, cleaned of the previous day's dirt. He spoke gently and he moved slowly, with a careful purpose that at first I mistook for grace and later recognized as exhaustion: his mother had only recently passed away after five years of battling cancer. Despite his polite smiles, a certain sorrow lingered in his eyes. The few times I stopped by the office and Mollie wasn't there to meet me, he lingered to make friendly conversation that, in its rehearsed and timid delivery, never failed to make me feel uncomfortable. I didn't like being alone with him. Having never buried a loved one, I tried to avoid the private company of the grieving. I feared that by brushing shoulders, sharing conversation and a room, I might step into their world. The world in which children outlive their parents and sisters bury sisters in the earth.

Gordon spoke of his mother only to Mollie. Their private talks usually featured none other than the Lord God Almighty. Mollie had intimated that Gordon was partly to blame for her joining the church, but the details of her conversion remained obscure. Whenever I caught them deep in one of their quiet, earnest conversations, I just kept silent and waited for them to finish. They could have their way, and I could have mine.

Mollie's mother, apparently, thought the same. Whatever conversation they may previously have had on matters of spirituality, it had been condensed into a single Saturday evening ritual: Mollie asking her mother would she like to go to church in the morning, her mother saying she'd rather have her cavities drilled with a jackhammer. Or something to that effect.

I saw where Mollie got her figure: not that Kari Bauer had a figure so much as a complete lack of one. She was skinny, board flat at the breasts and butt. She had the black, tangled straw hair of a witch and a firm, small bump protruding at the bridge of her nose. She cut a slight figure among the burly men of the garage, but she could cuss and fart with the best of them. Every day she wore the same blue mechanic's uniform, with—inexplicably—the name *Billy* sewn in red thread on the jumper's left breast.

Mollie and her mother lived in a dilapidated three-story farmhouse a hundred yards behind the car lot. Kari passed out on the futon in her office four nights of the week. Mollie never locked the doors to the house, in case her mother stumbled home late at night and couldn't find her keys. She was *always* forgetting her keys. Whenever I went to the Bauers' she was sleeping. At sixteen, I was still too naive to get it. I thought Kari was an absentminded narcoleptic.

"It's Committee Night," Kari said one Friday at close. "Come on, Frank—James. Get a move on. I don't want to be late."

I asked Mollie what committee they were all on.

"They're going to the bar," Mollie replied. "It's their way of saying they're all going to sit around Murphy's and get plastered."

She looked me in the eye. I felt I was supposed to understand something.

"There's no committee."

Mollie and her mother lived more like roommates than family: shared space, divided chores, and a mutual disinterest in each other's affairs. Mollie didn't want to know about Kari's committee. Kari didn't want to know about Mollie's religion. Kari paid the rent, bought the food, and supplied transportation. Mollie was responsible for housekeeping and laundry.

If there was one thing Mollie hated more than school it was housekeeping. I couldn't see their living room floor for all the dirty piles of neglected laundry gathered in soggy mountains around the couch and coffee table. I saw food as I'd never seen it before: discarded banana peels shriveled and crinkly dry like dead autumn leaves, cereal reduced to a coagulated mass of feathery brown pulp bloating in a bowl of curdled milk, petrified pizza crusts hard as dog bones.

Pleased that I was making progress in my inadequate social life, Mom insisted that I invite my new friend to join us for dinner. Mollie agreed readily. She talked with my parents the whole hour through and faithfully addressed Callapher as Cordelia Jasmine at her request. And she found all of Cordelia Jasmine's jokes hilarious:

"What's in common with bread and underwear? . . . They're both found in a store!"

Mollie's punch line was better: "They're both white and have brown crust." To which Dad covered his mouth with a napkin to keep from spitting his food, he laughed so hard.

After dinner we went into my room and locked the door. Callapher pounded against it.

"Oh, let her in," Mollie said.

"She'll just sit here and tell you more awful jokes."

"I think they're cute."

Mollie lay on her back on the bed, propping her long legs against the headboard. She studied my collage quietly. "You covered your whole wall," she stated.

"I can't stand the wood paneling," I said. I felt self-conscious, watching Mollie study the pictures. She opened her mouth to say something but seemed to change her mind.

"What happened with your dad?" she asked a few moments later. "If you don't mind me asking." Mollie seemed incurably fascinated by my family but by Dad in particular. I will never understand why Christians treat pastors like celebrities.

"Nothing happened with him," I replied.

"You know what I mean." She twirled a loose thread from the quilt in her fingers. "With the church. Why'd he leave?"

So I told her. "The church we were at was huge, real wealthy. We had a lot of families with a lot of money—corporate executives, company presidents, people like that. But the city itself had a lot of poverty, and our building was on the uglier side of town. Dad and Mom got their Bible study to start a soup kitchen. I guess it's been four years now since they first thought it up. In the beginning, it was just a thing they did once a month and at holidays. They opened up the foyer to serve hot meals and give away brown-bag lunches. It usually took up all of Saturday. Callapher and I spent all weekend at the church for it. She liked it, especially, even though she said the people smelled funny.

"After a while it got to be a bigger deal. More people got involved, and they started doing the brown-bag lunches every weekend, even taking vans out to parks to set up lunch lines. Then some ladies got the idea for a clothing and toy drive. The church was beginning renovations, and everyone was debating what to do with the old library in the basement. A lot of people wanted to just redo it, but Dad and the Mercy Corner—that's what they called it—argued that nobody ever used the library, anyway. So they made it into this walk-through thing, like a store, where people could come in and get assistance 'shopping' for clothes, toiletries, that kind of thing.

"There were a lot of homeless people that became regulars. Some of them even came to services on Sundays. But there was this one guy . . . I don't know. He wasn't quite right. They caught him in the church Christmas week. The pianist, Mrs. Bailey, came in to practice for the holiday cantata and found him sleeping in the choir loft. She absolutely freaked out. Her husband, who was the head of the church board, called a meeting. I don't know what people said, but Dad didn't come home that night, and Mom had to go looking for him. I guess things fizzled out for a while. They caught the guy in the church a couple more times, but Dad said we had to be kind with him—he didn't know any better."

I paused a moment, staring at a picture of Paris on the wall. I thought of how ugly the wood paneling was beneath. Of how Callapher and I had our own bedrooms in Moeller, both painted to suit us, hers yellow, mine blue.

"So what happened?" Mollie asked.

"They caught him in the bathroom with a little girl from Sunday school. I think she was eight. It was all over the church. I don't think anything happened with the first girl, but there was another girl, Samantha . . ."

Mollie shivered. The sheer physicality of her reaction surprised me.

"What happened?" she asked, almost in a whisper.

I shook my head. "I don't know exactly. People talked about how she had been molested, but Mom and Dad kept things quiet at our house, so I never knew the whole truth."

Mollie stared past me, to the distance. She blinked a few times, real fast.

"You all right?" I asked.

"Yeah," she said quickly. "It's just awful, that's all. But why'd your dad leave?"

"They were going to vote on whether to keep him as minister or let him go. So he turned in his resignation. They blamed him for his negligence—but it doesn't matter what they think; he was convinced it was his fault anyway. And it wasn't like it happened to just any little girl. Samantha was the daughter of my parents' best friends, James and Lily. My mom and Lily were real close—before, anyway."

"Did they blame him?" Mollie asked, frowning.

"I don't know." I shook my head. "It's more complicated than that."

Mollie was uncharacteristically quiet the remainder of the evening. After hearing the story her respect for my father seemed to grow, not wane. For a while, I worried she would fall in love with my family. I was afraid that they were the reason she spent time with me. The regard was certainly mutual. My parents liked Mollie immediately, especially Mom, who had the habit of forming unalterable judgments on people from very little information. The fact that Mollie covered her pretty legs modestly and worked in the church nursery made her instantly and unquestionably acceptable.

"She's lovely," Mom said as she watched Mollie leave. "She looks like a famous actress. I can't think of who. It's in the back of my mind."

The next day she was still trying to puzzle it out. "She so reminds me of someone. Maybe it was a picture I saw in a magazine once."

Mollie really was one of the most beautiful girls I had ever known. Her skin was fair, peaked pink at the cheeks, white against her thick heart-shaped lips. She had the impossible legs of a ballerina and a confident way of walking that said she knew she was lovely and that, frankly, she didn't care. In fact, I often suspected her of trying to hide her beauty. She made weird faces at the slightest thing—in response to a bad joke or to say hi in the hallway, contorting her lips, crossing her eyes, and pushing her nose up like a pig's snout with her forefinger. When eighth bell rang, she crouched low and crawled up the hallway with her book bag over her right shoulder like a hunchback. With her hands over her ears, she cried in a deep voice, "The bells! The bells!"

But eventually she'd have to stop making faces. She had to straighten up and walk normally. Then all the easy grace returned. She couldn't look bad if she tried. With her short hair and the mischievous glint of her eyes, she reminded me of fairies and sprites from children's books: strangely elegant creatures that were at once both impish and good.

CHAPTER 7

there was always music at the Old Maids' and always the smell of bread. In the kitchen, Margaret played the radio while she kneaded pillows of bread dough, flour powdering up and down her strong arms and puffing up to frost her gray curls. After supper, they spent the evenings practicing hymns for Sunday morning, Ruby on the organ, Margaret accompanying on the piano. Ruby practiced an extra hour each morning to perfect her playing. She claimed the extra work was for the glory of God, though I imagined her vanity was in part to blame. It sounded funny and even haunting to hear the chords of a hymn played without the melody.

Their piano wasn't just your usual run-of-the-mill piano. They couldn't be that normal. It was a player piano, the sort that you can open up and wind to create its own music, like a giant jewelry box. Margaret taught Callapher to load the scrolls and flick the golden switch inside the piano's cupboard. A deep-bellied grind churned over inside the instrument. The keys began to play of their own accord, music springing into the air as if conjured by magic. Callapher sat for hours singing the words from the scrolls as they rolled.

When I arrived at the farmhouse one evening to pick up Callapher for dinner, I found the house shaking from within. She was dancing with the Old Maids in the living room to the music of the player piano. Margaret was waving her dishrag like a hanky. Even Beauregard had joined them. I could smell the odor of his sweat from across the room.

"Come on!" Callapher called to me. "Dance, Olivia!"

I shook my head and watched from against the wall.

Callpher did a hard pirouette and collided with the footstool. She fell right on her butt but threw her hand in the air with a flourish, as if she'd choreographed tripping.

"Jitterbug!" Margaret declared, then proceeded to move her body in a way I'd have never thought possible for a woman of her age and size.

"It's a downright party!" Beauregard cried, clapping his hands twice, sharp.

Callapher laughed. She held his hands and stood on his boots. I used to dance that way with Dad when I was a little girl.

I left the room. Outside, I sat on the porch beneath the diamond-hard stars. Orange squares of light from the living room windows extended across the lawn, their shapes shifting with the shadows of the dancing figures inside. Beneath me, the deck shook each time Callapher performed one of her triple-lutz jumps. Without warning, I was overcome with a dreadful, aching homesickness for the way things had been before. I missed the privacy of my own bedroom, the unthinking way Mom threw things in our grocery cart. I missed seeing my dad come home from work in the evening.

We didn't know what Dad did in the Shoe Box all day. The way Mom put it, nobody wanted to know. He threw himself headlong, and still in his pajamas, into a myriad of time-consuming, elaborate, and useless projects. He repainted the living and dining rooms, accidentally cementing all the windows shut. That became a real problem when he took up lawn work and tracked fertilizer residue through the house with his boots. Callapher ran through the living room holding her breath and refused to eat any dinner. She said it smelled like a cow had pooped in our house.

Since Mom was working, Dad did the groceries and laundry. In an effort to acknowledge the unspoken fact of my "problems," he invited me to go grocery shopping with him.

"We could pick up some things you like," he said. "Some fruit and some cereal. Some salad maybe. Chicken—do you like chicken? We can get the non-fat kind. They have chicken without fat, don't they, Claire?"

I went with him and nodded dutiful assent to the things he held up for my approval: fat-free Jell-O pudding snacks, rice dinners, baked potato chips, light peanut butter. At the checkout lane, he watched the crowd, mumbling under his breath as his eyes darted back and forth. It was his system: he multiplied the number of shopping carts in a lane by the number of items in each respective cart, then divided that by the estimated proficiency of the cashier to determine which lane would move the quickest.

I don't know what he was in such a hurry for; it wasn't like he had a pressing agenda. Any time saved became more time to kill. I predicted it would end in either utter exhaustion or complete madness.

We went to the low-budget grocery on the edge of town where the city parked its dump trucks. The air reeked with the odor of exhaust and mashed trash. Across the street the neon pink letters of the Clairmont Motel sign advertising *CLE N ROOMS* cast an eerie light on the gray neighborhood of white box houses.

I sat in the car while Dad loaded the groceries, watching the *A* bulb on the motel sign fizzle on and off with the static noise of a bug zapper. A figure appeared beneath the sign, pulling a small carpetbag on wheels. She wore a flower-print skirt and a pair of white tennis shoes. I recognized her gait immediately.

"Hey, Dad," I said when he got inside the car, "isn't that Margaret over there?"

He clasped his seat buckle, then glanced in the direction I pointed. Leaning forward, he squinted his eyes. "Sure is," he replied. "Wonder what she's doing on this side of town."

Margaret parked her carpetbag in front of the first of the bright, blood-red motel doors. With methodical deliberation, she stacked a dozen cans from her bag into a small pyramid on the cement slab porch, buttressing the little construction on either side with a bag of flour and a bag of sugar. She set out a box of cereal and several smaller boxes, maybe of rice. Then she grabbed the handle of her carpetbag and rolled down to the third-to-last door to do the same all over again.

"Do people live there?" I asked.

"I wouldn't doubt it." He furrowed his brow. "I don't see Margaret's car—do you?"

"Offer her a ride, Dad."

We drove across the street to the motel parking lot.

"Good evening, Margaret," Dad called from his window.

Margaret turned to us with a start. "Oh my!" she exclaimed. "My, you surprised me, Reverend."

Dad ignored her customary way of addressing him. "It's kind of late to be out this far," he said. "Did you walk? We wouldn't mind giving you a lift."

She smiled and patted her palm against her chest as if catching the rhythm of her heartbeat. "No, no, that's not necessary," she replied. "It's a gorgeous evening, and I had myself in the mood all day for a walk."

"It's a long way home," Dad insisted. "We could wait for you if you have some errands to finish up."

"Now, Reverend, never you mind. I do this all the time. You go on; I'll be fine. Fresh air does me good."

"If you're certain."

"I'm certain." She nodded. Her cheeks were flushed rose-red like those of a child fresh from recess.

We drove away, but at the intersection I caught Dad studying Margaret in the reflection of the rearview mirror.

"Green light," I told him when the car behind us honked impatiently.

"Wait until your mother hears about this," he said.

"Leaving soup cans?" she asked when we told her. She stood on tiptoe to put the cereal Dad had bought in the top cupboard. "At the *motel*? Maybe it was someone else."

"Honey," Dad said, "we pulled right up and talked to her."

"Was she alone?"

"I didn't see Ruby anywhere. Didn't see their car, either. I believe she actually walked."

"What are we going to do with those two?" Mom asked. "Someday someone's going to come along and take advantage of their blind generosity. I'm just surprised they've gone this long without it happening. I ought to talk to Margaret. Do you think?"

I wanted to point out to my mother that Margaret might as well be leaving soup cans and cereal boxes on our porch. Then we wouldn't complain about blind generosity. But I kept my mouth shut. I didn't want to breach the unspoken truce that had developed between us: in just under a month, I'd gained six pounds.

Toward the end of April I had my first checkup with Dr. Palmer. At the scale, the nurse officially recorded my weight at 110. As if to reward me for this victory, Mom waited patiently in the hallway without being asked, letting me speak with the doctor alone. He asked about school and friends. He was especially pleased when I told him about Mollie. He recommended spending time with her whenever I felt overwhelmed; he seemed to think she'd be good medicine. I didn't tell him that Mollie had legs like stilts and a face fit for *Vogue*. I didn't tell him that sometimes when I washed my face at night, I stared at my reflection with hatred, repeating the word *ugly* to the face looking back.

On Sundays I attended the Old Maids' church with Mom and Callapher. Dad never joined us. He stayed in bed with the blinds pulled down over the window so that only a sliver of hot Sunday morning sun shone in. I envied him this silent rebellion.

With its white steeple and hard-candy-colored stained glass, the Old Maids' church looked like something straight off a postcard. The sign on the lawn read: *CH CH—WHAT'S MISSING? UR*. The sanctuary had orange grainy carpet and pews upholstered in deep crimson. The hymnals were red with pages tipped pink at the edges the way fancy Bible pages are painted gold along their sides. Up from the nursery came the smell of stale animal crackers and diapers, mingled with the sharp aroma of coffee from the basement kitchen where the senior citizens sat in a circle on metal folding chairs, balancing Styrofoam plates of crumb cake and donuts on top of their Bibles. For the most part, everyone in the congregation was older than fifty, including the minister, whose wrinkled hand trembled when he lifted his palms in worship.

We sat with Margaret and Ruby in the third pew to the front of the church. Callapher refused to go to children's church because she didn't know anybody. She sat in my lap. I entertained her by drawing cartoon men on the back of a tithing envelope. I made a picture of a fat man with his butt crack hanging out of his pants. She laughed and accidentally spit her peppermint on the floor. Mom whispered something vehement in her ear, and after that she sat obediently with her hands in her lap, only looking at me once to stick out her tongue.

Callapher accepted the rituals of church with a restless but uncomplaining acquiescence. Her only point of contention with the whole affair was the matter of wearing dresses. She told Mom that if God only cares about the inside then she shouldn't have to dress up for Him. Mom replied, "Wouldn't you want to look nice if the Queen of England was coming for a visit? Don't you think you could show God the same respect?"

Callapher said if the Queen of England was coming to church she'd arrive wearing her shorts, thank you very much. But she confessed to me later that she didn't want to hurt God's feelings. I thought about telling her that if there was a God He certainly couldn't be bothered with her wearing jeans or not. But kids grow up believing in Santa Claus and the Easter Bunny too. They figure things out in their own time.

I decided, though, that given the power, I'd spare Callapher some experiences. When I was eleven, for example, I stood in front of the church with twenty other girls my age and swore to remain a virgin until the day I married. It was not a vow that required a great deal of deliberation. At the time, I was loathe to touch a moron of the opposite sex for a game of tag, much less to engage in anything that even remotely resembled the forbidden act, the sordid details of which made me close my knees tight at the thought.

In this same church camp, we watched a movie about four teenagers who get in a fatal car accident on the way home from a party. Two die and are sentenced to eternal damnation. They are directed to hell by a man in a black tuxedo who stands behind a computer. You never see his face, you only hear his deep voice echoing through the cavernous black. The damned are taken to mesh prison cages smeared with the red of rust and of human blood. They are led by demons of this same red. Once locked away, the damned are lowered in the cages to the darkness of eternal suffering.

When I bring up these things—the promise rings and the receptionist God reserving rooms in hell—Mom denies the charges. She says I'm making things up. I'd like to know just where she and Dad were when these things were going on. Or maybe it didn't seem weird at the time that I sealed both my virginity and my eternal fate before I was old enough to wear a bra.

For a while, I tried not believing in God. I wasn't any good at it. I found that when I tried not to, I only ended up *telling* Him, "I don't believe in You," a statement which, directed at the very Thing I'd declared nonexistent, seemed to negate itself. The idea of God was inescapable to me—essential. Maybe because I had grown up as the daughter of a minister. Or, more likely, because the thought of a universe without order terrified me. Whatever the case, I couldn't quit the concept of a God. I quit the church instead.

I didn't stop going; I just stopped listening. I sat dutifully in the Old Maids' pew, staring past the pastor, the pulpit, and the hanging wooden cross. I went to appease my mother, not God. It's an understood fact in church that the state of your soul can be measured in direct proportion to the faithfulness of your Sunday morning service attendance. Sleeping in on Sunday felt as wrong as drunkenness or premarital sex in a parked car. By that account, Dad was quickly backsliding from righteousness to all-out depravity. Mom thought it was ungrateful of him to return the Old Maids' generosity with the Sunday morning lethargy of the unbeliever.

Margaret never failed to ask about Dad on Sunday mornings, but I don't think she worried the way Mom suspected she did. In fact, Margaret had only one thing to say about worry: don't. D-O-N-T, don't. "Worry's like a rocking chair," she said. "You use up a lot of energy going nowhere."

Among other things, Margaret served as president of the Society for the Awareness of Missionary Work Worldwide. Her main duty consisted of commandeering the evening service every second Sunday of the month to enlighten the congregation on just exactly what all was going on out there. This Missionary Night she'd prepared a slide presentation and coinciding skit she'd written and directed herself. And for the first time, they had the privilege of hearing from a real live missionary, a James Leroy on furlough from Africa.

Margaret planned to reenact the story of the separation of the sheep and the goats as told by Jesus in the twenty-fifth chapter of Matthew. The unruly flock comprised twenty children from children's church, the sheep wearing white T-shirts studded with hot-glued cotton balls, the goats in gray sweatpants with cardboard tails hanging from safety pins on their backsides. As narrator, Margaret dressed as the archangel of the Lord who would speak on Christ's behalf; she thought it ill fitting for a woman to dress as Jesus. She wore white wings left over from the Christmas pageant. They had been part of a child's costume and hung limp and dwarfed on her broad shoulders, knocked crooked by her extravagant gestures, so that one wing pointed up and the other down. Callapher gave her silver glitter to sprinkle in her hair.

I fought with Mom about going. In my mind, Sunday morning church was duty enough.

"Mom, please let me stay home."

"I said you're going. What part of 'no' don't you understand?"

I moaned softly and leaned my forehead against the frame of the bathroom door. Callapher spun around the corner, laden in cotton balls. She plucked Mom's red lipstick from the counter and smeared it across her lips.

"Callapher!" Mom exclaimed. "Wipe that off."

"I have to be dressed up," Callapher retorted.

"Sheep don't wear lipstick."

"Mom . . ." I said.

"Olivia, enough," Mom said. "I told you, you're going. We're all going."

"Dad's not," I muttered.

"Look," she said, "I know it's not the most amusing thing to do with an evening, but sometimes you just have to do things you don't want to do." Leaning toward the mirror, she pursed her lips together and colored them with the lipstick. Puckering like that accentuated her high cheekbones. She rubbed her bottom lip against her top to smear the color.

"Callapher," she said, "go get your shoes."

Callapher twirled around to give Dad the full benefit of her costume.

"Daddy, look. Look, Dad."

He peered at her over his reading glasses. The expression made his forehead wrinkle: it was the first time I ever considered him an old man.

"What do I look like?" Callapher asked.

"Like a child who's lost her stuffing," he replied.

Mom went out the door without saying anything to him, so I kissed him on the cheek to say good-bye. He seemed surprised by the gesture but grateful too. It made me angry with Mom to see that surprised look in his eyes.

At church I slouched in the Old Maids' pew and crossed my arms. I stared holes through everyone coming in from the foyer as if they were directly responsible for my misery. There were fewer than fifty people in the church, but they sat so far away from one another in the big sanctuary it seemed like even less. Those close enough to talk without yelling leaned over their respective pews, like neighbors conversing over shared fences. How's that arthritis treating you? When's that son of yours going to get married? And how do you make that chocolate pudding so thick? I scowled.

The missionary sat in the very first pew with his bald head bowed down in prayer. It glowed with the sheen of a newly waxed floor. Ruby sat beside him, manhandling the slide projector.

Margaret maintained that she'd been forced to take liberties with Scripture in writing her play. "As it says in Revelation," she'd told me, " 'I warn anyone who hears the words of prophecy in this book: if anyone adds anything to them, God will add to him the plagues described in this book.' " To prevent such a calamity, she'd assigned Ruby to flip through the original Bible verses on the slide projector as the skit progressed.

We sang a few halfhearted hymns directed by the grocer, who beat his hand up and down in the air like he was the majorette for a marching band. Pastor Evans led us in prayer. When he finished, a few scattered voices echoed murmured "Amens." Then the ushers dimmed the lights. Ruby flicked on the light of a reading lamp and directed the small halo onto the door to the choir loft. Margaret appeared in the doorway, flourishing the great white drapery hanging from her arms. She descended from the choir loft, undulating her arms up and down and swaying. I suppose this meant she was flying. Or descending. Whatever archangels do.

"At the end of all time," she said, "I, the archangel of the Lord, come before you to do His bidding, that the world may see and know the goodness and justice of the Lord" (flourish of the arms). "Amen."

She nodded toward the doorway. The sheep and goats filed in. The last sheep pushed a goat, who turned and slapped him upside the head. A little blonde sheep saw her mother in the crowd and screamed, "Hi!"

"All the nations are gathered to Him," Margaret continued, "that He might separate the people one from the other, dividing among the righteous and the unrighteous, between those sanctified for His glory and those living in darkness."

At the word "darkness," Ruby flipped on the slide projector. A blank white square lit the projector screen. Margaret raised her palm to shield her eyes. Seeing there were no words on the screen, she stalled, "And . . . this . . . holy light of heaven . . . in it we shall see all things as they are—for all things are revealed and brought to light, and 'if we walk in the light as he is in the light we have fellowship one with the other and the blood of Jesus purifies us of all sin' . . ."

Ruby flipped through the slides: three white screens and a picture of the watermelon seed-spitting contest from the previous spring picnic. Someone in the last pew laughed. Finally the text from Matthew appeared.

"First John 1:8," Margaret finished. She took a breath and continued, "The Lord says to you, His creation, that the sheep shall be divided unto the right and the goats unto the left."

The children separated.

Margaret addressed the sheep on behalf of the Lord: they were invited to the kingdom of God, for when Christ was hungry they fed Him, when He was thirsty they had given Him something to drink, when He was in prison they had visited Him.

"But when, Lord?" the sheep asked, more or less in unison.

"Whenever you did something to the least of these," Margaret replied, "you did it unto the Lord."

For failing to do the same, the goats were banned from His presence.

Ruby flipped the slide projector to a painting of Christ. He sat in the field teaching His disciples. They were all upside down. Ruby hesitated a moment before picking up the entire projector with her skinny little arms and flipping it over to aright the image.

I slouched down in my pew. Mom nudged me when I closed my eyes, so I fixed my gaze on the screen, staring through it, unthinking.

They served finger sandwiches and punch after service in honor of the visiting missionary. Mom stayed long enough to get a Styrofoam cup of coffee and tell Margaret how much she liked the skit.

"It did turn out rather well, didn't it?" Margaret asked, looking pleased. "The children always add a certain something." Taking Mom by the elbow as if afraid she would escape, Margaret said, "You must stay and meet our Mr. Leroy. His talk was so inspiring, wasn't it? He's from the area, you know. Called to the mission field in this very church when he was just a boy. A faithful servant in Africa these seven years . . ."

Mom followed Margaret across the room to shake hands with the missionary. He and Margaret fell into comfortable conversation immediately. Mom smiled and nodded her head at the appropriate moments, but as soon as she'd finished her coffee she announced that we had to be getting home.

On the drive back we sat wedged in the truck, Callapher picking cotton balls off her T-shirt to sop up her bleeding knee, the product of a quick brawl with a second-grade goat.

"What on earth did you do to make him push you like that?" Mom said, exasperated.

"I didn't do anything," Callapher said. "Just called him a nerd and stuck out my tongue."

"Is that all?" I muttered.

"Roll the window up," Callapher whined. "It hurts my knee!"

"It can't possibly hurt your knee."

"Does too—the wind stings it!"

"Girls!" Mom exclaimed. "Honestly, Callapher, you have been a handful this week. This episode tonight was totally uncalled for. Don't go around picking fights unless you're ready to accept the consequences."

I smirked. Callapher stuck her tongue out. Mom took a corner hard, and I accidentally fell into Callapher. When my hand brushed her knee she let out a piercing shriek.

"You're being a baby," I said.

"I amn't. It hurt."

"If I have to hear one more word," Mom interrupted, "I will pull this car over right now."

Callapher crossed her arms and sulked, "You're not the boss of me."

Mom stood on the brake. She parked the truck on the side of the road, killed the engine, and stepped out, slamming the door behind her. Callapher looked to me. I shrugged. Mom walked away from the truck a good thirty feet. Through the open window, we could hear her muttering. She shook her head back and forth, gesticulating with her hand.

"What's she doing?" Callapher asked.

"You drove her crazy," I said.

"Did not."

"Did."

We waited a good five minutes. Mom got too far away for us to hear her. It was quiet except for our breathing. Callapher looked so scared, I felt bad and offered to blow a little on her knee to help the sting.

When Mom returned to the truck, she buckled her seat belt without saying a word. Callapher informed her we'd made up.

"Glad to hear it," Mom said in a tone that clearly communicated she wasn't glad about anything. She turned the ignition. The lights flickered on, the churn of the engine vibrated the floor, then both cut off abruptly. She turned the key again. The engine grumbled but didn't turn over. The third time she tried, the truck plain died. She swore, slapping her palm flat against the steering wheel.

Callapher looked at her in wide-eyed amazement.

"Get out," Mom told us. "We're going to call Dad."

We walked a good half mile back toward the church and stopped at an all-night diner to use the pay phone. Mom bought a milkshake to break a ten for change. Callapher and I sat across from each other in a plastic yellow booth, the untouched milkshake between us, while Mom leaned on the pay phone in the back. Callapher pressed her forefinger and thumb into the frosted sides of the glass, leaving little ovals in the sweating fog on its surface.

"Mom said a cuss word," Callapher informed me.

"I was there, goofball."

"I amn't a goofball."

"I am not," I corrected. "*Amn't* isn't a real word."

"You just said it."

"I said it to quote you."

"What's *cwote*?"

"To repeat what someone said verbatim."

"What's *verbaytim*?"

"Word for word. Like copycat. You repeat something exactly."

"You repeat something exactly."

I gave her a warning look. "Don't," I said.

"Don't," she said, imitating my stern expression.

"I'm not playing that game," I said.

"I'm not playing that game," she repeated.

I said, "Callapher is a fart head."

"Olivia is a fart head."

Mom joined us at the table, so we both shut up. Beneath the garish light of the overhanging lamp, her skin took on a dull greenish pallor. Strands of hair had pulled loose from her ponytail. They twirled in the wind of the fan that spun above our heads. The smell of bacon grease was sticky in the air. I remembered what Mom said in the bathroom, about having to do things you don't want to do. It had never occurred to me that Mom disliked church as much as the rest of us. I felt a little embarrassed for her. Like the week before the move when I caught her in her bathrobe in the kitchen, greedily eating half a pot of cold spaghetti by the blue light of the fridge.

I asked her if she'd gotten hold of Dad.

"He didn't pick up. Margaret's coming. Finish up your shake, hon," she said to Callapher.

"I'm not hungry," Callapher murmured. She stood on the bench seat and pressed her face into Mom's arm. "My knee hurts."

"Come on." Mom picked her up. "Let's get you home. The Old Maids will be here soon."

They pulled up just as we reached the truck.

Margaret stepped out of her car already talking. ". . . pitch black on this curb. Can't see a thing. Claire, honey, you ought to keep your lights on so people know you're all parked over here." She traipsed over to our side, still wearing her white robe and angel wings. They glowed opalescent in the moonlight. "What happened?"

"I don't know." Mom sighed. "It was fine when we pulled over, but when I tried to start the engine again it wouldn't turn over."

"Good night," Margaret replied. "What were you doing on the side of the road?"

Mom didn't answer, and Margaret didn't press the issue. She lifted the hood of the truck to look inside. Glitter from her hair fell sparkling into the engine.

Ruby poked her head out of the Cadillac. "Did you leave your lights on?" she called. "Sometimes when I leave the lights on I come back and nothing in the car works."

"No," Margaret said. She put her hands on her hips. They left two black grease handprints on her white gown. "This is going to need a mechanic. We'll have to call someone to tow it to a shop in the morning. George McFanny owes me a favor. I'll just remind him I have a sailboat sitting over my azaleas, and he'll have a tow truck here first thing free of charge." She slammed the hood shut.

"You got your dress all dirty," Callapher said forlornly.

Margaret replied, "It's only a tablecloth—I've got plenty. Let's get you girls home. Looks like we've got a little knee that needs doctoring."

The problem with the truck was only the beginning. The next night when I tried to take a shower, spurts of brown gunk spat out the showerhead. I decided to run a bath instead, but nothing came out of the faucet. When I opened the door, I found my bathwater leaking beneath the hallway carpet, collecting like a massive ink spot on the living room floor. We had to push all the furniture against the walls and run fans to dry out the carpet. Callapher started wearing grocery bags on her feet, secured to her ankles with rubber bands.

Dad refused to call for a plumber. He maintained we had a car in the shop and rent to pay; we weren't making a fuss over a few leaky pipes. He'd fix it himself. The pipeline ran directly beneath the hallway. Peeling back the rug, he lifted a square of the floor to reveal a dusty cavern beneath. It looked like Batman's cave, with walls of crenulated dusty earth housing old pipes and a torpedo-shaped tank.

Mom was not silent about her reservations. She presided over the crater in our hallway with her arms crossed. "You'll throw out your back," she said.

Dad ignored her skepticism. "I can see the problem," he called up. "Shouldn't take but a minute."

The hole in the floor was right outside our bedroom door. Callapher lay on her belly to watch the operation with silent wonder. It was her job to hold the flashlight for Dad and kill spiders that came up out of the ground before Mom saw them and had a fit.

"If she sees a spider," Dad said, "she'll cement the hole shut and we'll live without water for the rest of our lives. Callapher, for heaven's sake, shine the light on what I'm doing; don't shine it in my eyes. . . . Yep, no water. We'll have to bathe in the creek."

Mom got Chinese takeout for dinner. She carried the bags of food into the kitchen, then went to check Dad's progress. "I stopped and talked to Margaret on my way home," she said. "She told us not to worry about the plumbing bill; she'd include it in the month's rent."

"It's all right," Dad insisted. "I've almost got it."

At the sight of food, Callapher abandoned her post. She followed Mom to the dining room, her cumbersome plastic booties *sop-sopping* on the carpet. We could hear Dad banging on pipes while we ate. There was a dull clang of metal followed by a sharp cry—of pain or anger, maybe both. Mom ran to the hallway. When she was sure Dad hadn't killed himself, she told him outright that he couldn't do it; he might as well give it a rest before he made things worse.

I finished half my Chinese rice. Rice was about 120 calories a half cup uncooked. But this was fried rice, which potentially tripled my numbers. I drank a second glass of water and counted again.

That night Callapher burst into our room shouting, "Hurry, hurry, Olivia—Dad's *fixed* something!"

I followed her to the kitchen, where Dad made a rather elaborate display of turning on the kitchen sink.

"Ladies," he said, "I give you the primary substance of *life—water.*"

A clear, hard stream of water shot out the faucet. It was ice cold, but we all clapped duly.

Mom laughed. She kissed him shortly on the lips. "I suppose you're fairly handy."

"I was about to quit," he said, "until you inspired me by saying I couldn't do it."

Dad came in the door with a grocery bag. "I'm home," he announced to us all. I was trying to read a book. Callapher sat in the dining room undoing a finished puzzle one piece at a time in order to reconstruct it again on the other side of the table. Mom sat on the floor with files and folders spread in a fan around her.

"You may all thank me," Dad said. "I brought us man's most necessary papers: the *Enquirer* and Cuddles Double Padded."

Mom cheered. We'd been using paper towels again for toilet paper. It might as well have been five-grit sandpaper the way Callapher complained.

"Claire, honey, why don't you sit at the table?" Dad asked.

"Callapher's using it."

"Callapher, get down and let Mom use the table."

"No, don't bother her," Mom insisted. "She's fine. Besides, I prefer working in the living room. It's more cozy."

"Sit in your chair at least."

"You sold my chair." She said it matter-of-factly, like a comment on the weather, but Dad grimaced. He told Callapher to help him unload the groceries.

"By the way," he added. "Thanks for filling up the gas tank."

"I didn't fill it up," Mom murmured around the pencil in her mouth.

"Olivia?"

"Not me, Dad," I said. "You know I don't drive the Cheese Wagon."

"Well, somebody filled it up."

Mom finally looked up at him. "You must have, dear."

"I don't remember." Dad cocked his head to the side and thought a moment. "No, I don't think so," he repeated with less conviction.

We attributed this mysterious manifestation of gas to Dad's absentmindedness until new apparitions occurred: fruit baskets, boxes of Kleenex, bottles of dish detergent, and rolls of toilet paper all deposited in crates on the doorstep. When we were all out of the house we'd return to find the lawn mowed in our absence.

Callapher asked who was bringing us food and cutting our grass. Dad told her to thank the good fairies of the North, who spread goodwill to mortals in need.

Callapher wrinkled her nose. "Fairies give away toilet paper?" She took up dancing around the house wearing her pink-and-yellow bathing suit. It was the closest she had to a tutu. She waved her baton around, casting spells on the house with fistfuls of fairy dust until silver glitter showed up in the cracks of the couch cushions, on the carpet under the table, and in the food on our plates.

In bed, she made me tell her stories about fairies. I thought up a bunch of nonsense about them living inside the streetlamps: when the lights came on at night it was the fairies waking up and their bodies glowing like the tails of fireflies. I caught her squinting at the amber orange streetlight that glared in our window from the dirt road. Waiting for magic.

And I told her about the two dearest fairies, who ran around the world at night doing good in resplendent robes made of tablecloths.

CHAPTER 8

invention

(in VEN shun)

1. A new device or process developed from study and experimentation
2. A mental fabrication; falsehood

Jesus said that the eyes are the windows into the body. If you open your eyes in wonder and belief, your body fills up with light, but if you walk around squinting in greed and distrust, your body is a dark cellar.

People told me I looked pale and tired, that I looked skinny. I did not see that. I saw a lot of white flesh and too much of it, bloating on my body in all the wrong places. My reflection followed me mercilessly in mirrors, car doors, shop windows. I lived in a world of circus mirrors, the grotesque distortion of my body looking back at me everywhere.

Food was the first thing I thought of when I woke up in the morning, the last thing to occupy my mind before sleep. But now that I had Mollie, things were better. I had a reason for getting out of bed in the morning other than basic survival; there was always the prospect that Mollie would make me laugh.

But I hated her too. I hated her for being beautiful, because her beauty wasn't mine. Because beside her I felt short and awkward and fat. Mollie ate oatmeal cookies and donuts for breakfast. Sometimes she just forgot to eat. I envied that more, the forgetting. For months I hadn't known a single moment when food was not in the forefront of my mind.

We still didn't have hot water. In the mornings I sat on the edge of the tub to give myself a sponge bath and tried not to look at my body. I felt my butt grow warm and spread on the cold porcelain. My skin rose up with goose bumps. You cannot eat too much today, I said. You cannot eat too much.

I needed a system. I had to break it down.

Without my period I was not a woman. If I ate, I would be a woman. I didn't understand this. I didn't understand that the body is an intricately connected thing, or even that the body and the soul are connected things. But I knew that something within me had gone wrong, and to fix it I had to gain weight. This prospect was too terrifying to face directly.

I needed a system.

In the food pyramid, all foods are categorized into six groups, the recommended portions of each rationed in specific numbers. You may have six to eleven servings of bread and two to three of fruit and two to three of vegetables and a spattering of "other." These numbers became guidelines for me, rules. I could eat the smallest portion recommended for each of the designated food groups. So I could have six servings of bread but never seven. I could have two servings of meat but never three.

At night I inventoried the things I had put in my mouth. If they fit inside the food pyramid, everything was all right. I began buttering my toast. I ate peanut butter on crackers instead of tuna. One hundred and seventy calories and seventeen grams of fat per two tablespoons of peanut butter, ninety calories and one gram of fat per five wafers, thus one tablespoon on ten crackers: one count protein, two counts bread.

Meals were a silent battle between my mother and me. She messed up my numbers. I caught her cooking pastas with heavy cream. She poured the extra two percent milk into the half-empty skim carton. Sometimes, to keep the numbers right, I spit chewed food into my napkin and threw it away. I chewed a long time so it looked like I ate during the whole meal. At dinner, Mom watched my plate and mouth with furtive glances, the way you watch a child playing near a busy street. At night, I lay my hand on my stomach. I counted.

Whenever Callapher and I complained about anything, Margaret said we were just looking at things all wrong. She liked to say it was all about perspective.

The book of design states: "*Perspecius* (Latin) = looking through." In Lori's class, I learned that perspective was invented during the Renaissance. In 1435, Leon Battista Alberti wrote the first known treatise on painting in which he introduced the first fully developed theory of perspective. He devised a mathematical formula by which an artist could calculate the placement of lines at specific angles and so, on a two-dimensional plane with two-dimensional shapes, create the illusion of depth.

Lori made us draw a chair. She placed it upside down on the drawing table and instructed us to stare at the negative space between its legs and parts until it was the empty air that gave the chair shape, and not the chair that shaped the air. I stared. It happened. The world inverted—the shapes popped forward, and I saw not the object but the thousand colors, curves, forms, and lines that made the visible world.

Lori explained that there is local color and then there is *color*. For me, local color meant cartoon color: in cartoons, apples are red and clouds are white. The color name you associate with an object. But the *color* of an apple is indescribably complex: deep amber, sour green, dappling yellow-browns, the bluish white tint of light reflecting in the dimple around the stem. Clouds are not white, but pale pinks bruised with soft grays and pale blues.

Color is white light shot through prisms. Sight, the world shot through the eye. You can go around just accepting everything. Or you can renegotiate the space between the eye and the brain; you can teach the two to communicate differently. Then the whole world changes. It's like the words from "Amazing Grace": I once was blind, but now I see. Suddenly I found myself walking around wide-eyed, in wonder, my body filling up with light.

Lori moved my easel so I would be closer to my classmates. I resented it; I'd preferred my solitary corner. It seemed a patronizing gesture on her part, a way of forcing me to make friends, something I didn't do easily. I met Mollie at her locker third bell and at the office after eighth. In between I kept to myself.

Matthew worked opposite me. Our easels stood back to back. Every day he asked me how I was doing and how was my painting coming. Every day I answered both with "fine."

He seemed eager to talk to me anyway. Each class, he interrupted my concentration to ask had I read any good books lately? Did I know it was supposed to snow early this year? Did I know how that first line of the song the Little Mermaid sings went, the one about hoping to someday be "a part of that world"?

"I don't know," I answered.

"Do you remember which part I'm talking about? When she's sitting on the rock looking up to the surface?"

"I remember."

He sang the end part: "Someday I'll be . . . part of that world."

When he found out we both had B lunch, he told me I should join his table.

"Okay, maybe," I replied. I had no intention of doing any such thing. But I forgot he was conversationally inept. He misunderstood "maybe" to mean "Yes, I'd love to; please escort me."

The next afternoon when I walked to the cafeteria, I found Matthew waiting for me at the door. Dutifully, I took my brown-bag lunch and sat beside him. It was a table of all guys.

One saw my sandwich and said, "What is that?"

"A turkey sandwich," I replied.

"That's not a sandwich; that's a piece of bread with meat in it."

I felt myself blush severely.

Matthew said, "Looks like a sandwich to me, moron."

And from that moment on, I liked him.

Joining someone's lunch table was like joining a club. Matthew's three friends acknowledged me in the hallway with a nod of the head or a moderate wave whenever we passed. And Matthew took it as an invitation to speak to me freely and openly on any subject that occurred to him. He even took the liberty of walking me to my locker after eighth bell.

"I've never seen him so chatty," Mollie said. We were walking to her car of the week, a Chevy Cavalier with green and yellow paint on the windshield that read *SAVE NOW*.

"What do you mean?"

"I had a few classes with Matthew last year. He's real quiet. The brooding artist type. He's a photographer, you know. Super talented. You should ask to see some of his work; it'll blow your mind. But he's painfully shy about people . . . especially girls. He must really like you."

I said, "He doesn't like me."

"Well, I've never seen him act so weird. I mean, weirder than usual."

Matthew was tall and skinny. His clothes hung loose on his lanky arms and big-boned elbows as T-shirts hang empty on wire hangers. Mollie was right about his reserve. He was forever the silent observer in the room, the figure leaning on the back chalkboard, watching with his arms crossed. There was something about the gentle intelligence of his eyes—pale and lucid, the color of smooth pebbles on the floor of a clear pond. A photographer's eyes, wide and quiet and vigilant.

I caught him watching me once while I knelt on the floor to varnish a finished painting. He didn't look away immediately when I returned the gaze, and I blushed beneath his scrutiny, standing abruptly to walk to the other side of my room and pretend to blow my nose. I didn't think he'd want to watch that.

My body never failed to embarrass me. I always felt like a naked person in a room of clothed people. I had closed up my mouth and shrunk my body in the hope that I might appeal to men. It was an end for which I lived. Suffered. Still, I was shocked to discover one wanted to look at me.

When Mom found me boiling water to make Callapher a warm bath, she got fed up and went to Margaret to complain about the broken water heater. Margaret promised to send someone right away. She was true to her word; the doorbell rang the very next day. When Mom saw Beauregard standing on the front porch with a toolbox in one hand and a plunger in the other, she made us lock the back door and hide in the bathroom with the lights off to pretend we weren't home.

The doorbell rang five times before finally falling silent. Mom told us to wait longer. We sat crowded on the floor around the toilet. Callapher turned and screamed. Beauregard stood looking through the window at us with his hands cupped around his eyes like goggles.

Mom said, "I suppose we have to let him in now. Yes, hi—" She waved at the window—a wave of hello. Or the wave used to shoo away a buzzing fly. "We see you; we're coming."

Beauregard entered our living room wearing overalls without a T-shirt. His upper arms were soft and surprisingly wide for such a thin man, with three tan sunspots floating beneath his white skin. A small patch of kinked black curls grew out from beneath his armpits.

"Sorry you ladies didn't hear me knock," he said. "You must have some mighty good insulation. Well, ma'am"—he tipped his baseball cap back and set his toolbox on the floor with a heavy clank—"Margaret says ya'll are having a problem with your water heater. If you'll be so kind as to show me the way . . ." He tapped his cap with the plunger, then snapped his teeth together twice in sharp succession.

He went right to the hallway and pulled back the rug. Mom couldn't stop him.

She telephoned Margaret. "But he's not qualified," I heard her say. Then a long pause. "No, Margaret, I understand, but I don't think . . . no, no, of course not. Yes, I know you *say* that . . ." Mom hung up. "I'm going to lie down," she said.

She stepped over the Bat Cave to her bedroom and stayed behind the closed door for a good two hours. I doubt she got any sleeping done. Beauregard made so much noise you'd have thought a dozen construction workers had taken to banging trash cans together under our house.

In the midst of the noise, I tried to finish my homework. As Beauregard had blockaded our bedroom, I had to sit at the dining room table to work while Callapher made a mess dipping Oreos in a bowl of milk. She shot jokes at me with her black teeth:

"How many dumb guys does it take to fix the water?" she asked.

"I don't know, how many?"

"Five. One to hold down the faucet and the other five . . . the other four to go swimming in it."

"That's completely not funny," I told her. "Why are you using a bowl? You should put that milk in a glass."

"But then I can't dip them all the way."

"You're making a mess."

She plopped another Oreo in the milk and shoved it around with a spoon. "Knock knock."

"Who's there?"

"Fino."

"Fino who?"

"How are you, I'm fino."

When Dad got home and heard all the commotion, he demanded to know what was going on.

"Margaret sent Beauregard to fix the water heater," I explained.

"I think he's breaking it, Dad," Callapher added.

Dad considered this with a furrowed brow but blinked the concern away quickly. He looked distracted. "Where's your mother?" he asked.

"Sleeping off a mibrain," Callapher said.

"Listen, girls, I need you to keep her occupied." For the first time, I noticed that Dad's face looked flushed and his eyes shone with a mischievous glint. "Don't let her leave the house for anything. And don't let her go outside until I get back—understood? Under no circumstances is she to open that door."

"What's up, Dad?" I asked.

"I've got something for her," he said. "Took me a week to find it." He hurried back toward the front door. "Just don't let her leave. I'll be back soon."

Mom got up an hour later. After splashing some cool water on her pink cheeks, she went to the kitchen and started fussing around with dinner. When she'd tripped on Callapher twice, she exclaimed, "For heaven's sake, Callapher, what are you trying to do, kill me? Go sit in the dining room. Mommy can't think with you in the kitchen."

Callapher complied, but laid her body across the floor to block the opening into the dining room.

When the doorbell rang, Mom told Callapher to get it.

"I think you should get it," Callapher replied.

Mom gave her the eye. "Excuse me?" She wiped her hands on the checkered dish towel. "I think you and I need to have another talk, young lady. You're becoming entirely too bold."

Callapher ignored the reprimand, following Mom to the door with a happy anticipation. But it was only Beauregard, standing on the porch with a wrench in his hand, the clean skin in the shape of goggles around his eyes bright and clean against his blackened cheeks.

"Sorry 'bout that, ma'am," he said. He marched a track of muddy footprints through our living room. "Went outside for a minute to check the exterior unit and got myself locked out."

"Mr. Lowett," Mom said, "this really isn't necessary. I don't want you to feel like you have to bother with this. Really."

"On the contrary, ma'am," Beauregard said, lowering himself down into the ground, "I consider it an honor. The Old Maids took me in when I hadn't a thing else in the world, and now they're jes doin' the same for you."

He disappeared again into the Bat Cave. Minutes later, a string of profanity issued up from the floor. Mom covered Callapher's ears. She muttered, " . . . don't care what they say; I will not stand for . . . *that man* in my house again . . ." In the kitchen, she dropped a cold pat of beef onto the hot skillet, slapping the pink, brain-wrinkled texture of the meat flat until it sizzled and shot out beads of hot grease.

"Take it easy, Mom," I said. "The cow's already dead."

She turned to face me. If looks could kill. I sat back down to my algebra. Callapher whispered to me in a sing-song voice, "You—got—in trou-ble."

When the doorbell rang a second time, Mom looked at Callapher. She said dryly, "I suppose you're too busy to get that."

Callapher leapt up and followed her a second time to the front door. This time, we found Dad waiting on the porch. He stood behind a large oak desk, upon which sat a shining red ribbon tied into a thick bow.

"Surprise!" Callapher shouted. She clapped her hands excitedly.

"Oh my—" Mom gasped. "Benjamin, what is this?"

"What do you think?" he asked. He stepped over the threshold and kissed her on the lips.

Mom's mouth stayed open.

"Remember that desk from your grandmother's that you absolutely loved? You never did forgive her for giving it to your sister. I looked all over for one just like it. See, it has that little slide ma-jigger that goes down so you can cover up your mess at night and pretend it's not there."

Mom stepped outside. She ran her palm over the desk. "Honey, I don't know what to say."

"Do you like it?" he asked. "I just couldn't stand to see you working on the floor all the time"—he pointed his finger at her—"and a damp floor, I should add—with all your papers getting wrinkled. It would have killed your back."

"Well, that's silly," Mom interrupted. "I don't mind working on the floor."

"Of course not," Dad said hastily. "You never mind anything."

Mom looked hurt by the remark.

The moving men from the store still stood waiting beside their yellow van on our driveway. Dad called them up and directed them to place the desk in the living room against the far wall.

"This is something you can really use, Claire," Dad was saying. "No, no, push it farther toward the hallway . . . That's fine, that's fine."

The men left. Between the movers and Beauregard, our living room carpet had turned brown with mud.

We all stood around Mom. Dad looked at Mom. Mom looked at the desk.

"What's the matter, hon?" Dad asked. "Don't you like it?"

"Ben, I love it, I do. It's very lovely . . ."

"But?"

She crossed her arms. Very quietly, she asked, "Well, dear . . . can we *afford* it?"

"Of course we can afford it." Dad spoke loudly, as if to counter her whisper. "Callapher, grab Daddy a pair of scissors so I can get this bow off."

Callapher returned empty-handed. "Daddy, Beauregard won't let me in my room because he doesn't want me to fall in the hole."

"I didn't say no!" Beauregard shouted from the hallway. "I said she had to wait . . . I'll be done right quick. Give or take a couple hours."

Mom started crying.

"Claire . . ." Dad frowned.

"I'm sorry." She walked back toward the kitchen. "I'm sorry . . . it's just a little too much today . . ."

Dad looked to us in exasperation. "What's the matter with her?"

Beauregard entered the living room. "I got pair of shears here, sir, if you need to use 'em. Well, Lord, that's a nice piece. And a big red bow. What's the occasion? Birthday? Anniversary? You forget an anniversary, mate?"

Dad considered Beauregard with impatience. "Mr. Lowett, I don't think we'll be needing your services tonight. If you'd kindly take your things—"

Beauregard threw his hands up, palms out, in a gesture of goodwill. "No offense taken. I understand. I know when a visitor ain't needed. You jes' give me a minute and I'll gather up all my things. It ain't no time to be intrudin' on a family's space; I can see that."

Dad went to Mom. We could hear their voices:

". . . can't just throw money out on a whim . . ."

". . . wasn't trying to cause a scene . . ."

". . . do something constructive for a change . . ."

Dad got fed up. He went right to the Bat Cave. Dad banging on pipes, Mom banging pots and pans. The red bow on the desk blared like a siren.

"Are they gonna get a divorce?" Callapher whispered.

I felt so terrible for her in that second, I nearly lost it with Mom and Dad.

"No," I said firmly. "They're not."

"But they hate each other."

"They don't hate each other. They're just tired. Adults get cranky when they get tired. Then they have tantrums like little babies. Come here."

I put my arm around her. We sat together on the couch. I asked her to tell me jokes, but she said she didn't feel like it.

"How did that one go? About fino?"

"I'm *not* fino!" she cried and buried her face in my arm. If she hadn't been so upset, I might have laughed.

Dad came up from his hole. He took a set of dishes from the cupboard and began silently setting the dining room table.

"Girls," Mom said to us quietly, "go wash your hands. Dinner's almost ready."

I could smell what she'd made: spaghetti with meat sauce and cheese-butter biscuits. I asked her if I could be excused to go see Mollie.

"I was hoping we could have a family dinner," Mom said. "We haven't all sat down together for so long."

"I've already eaten," I explained.

Mom's face fell. I believe she would have given in, but seeing the look of resignation on her face, Dad interceded. "What did you eat?" he demanded.

I was taken aback. He'd never taken sides on this issue. Barring from our brief conversation after my doctor's appointment, he'd never mentioned my problems again.

"A peanut butter sandwich," I answered. "And some milk and fruit."

"That's not dinner," he said. "You will stay and eat a real meal. At the table, with us."

"But I'm not hungry." This was not a lie. There was nothing in me that desired to put another piece of food in my body.

"I said you will stay," Dad said.

I looked to Mom imploringly, but she averted her eyes. "Callapher," she said, "wash your hands."

At the table, Dad took the spoons from Mom and served dinner himself. He piled a heaping portion of spaghetti on my plate, and two biscuits besides. He set the food in front of me.

"Let's eat," he announced with a grim and exaggerated enthusiasm.

I cut my spaghetti small, smaller, spooning small bites into my mouth and chewing them slowly. I might as well have been eating air or gravel for what little I could taste. Mom ate with her eyes down, but I was aware of Dad looking up from his newspaper to watch my plate. It was a cardinal sin, that newspaper. Reading at the table was expressly forbidden, right after elbows on the table and singing. The room was entirely silent but for the clinking of metal on glass as Callapher stirred her milk and sipped it from her spoon. Dad told her to stop.

"Drink from the cup or you'll spill," he said.

"Did Olivia tell you about her portfolio?" Mom asked him gently. "Her teacher thinks she has real promise. She called just to talk to me in person."

I looked at Mom in surprise; she'd never told me that Lori called. I tried to communicate with my eyes the gratitude I felt, but Mom was looking at Dad, who said, "I didn't know that. That's wonderful, Olivia. Very well done."

I ate a bite of biscuit and washed it down with the rest of my water. The meal seemed to go on forever. I didn't think I could fit any more food inside my stomach. When I'd eaten all I could, I asked if I could be excused.

"You haven't finished what's on your plate," Dad said. "Don't push it around so it looks like you've eaten it."

He might as well have slapped me in the face. So he was on their side. Anger rose hot from my belly, but I blinked hard and swallowed. I refused to give him the satisfaction of my tears. I clenched my teeth over my fork, ate every bite, forcing the muscles in my throat to open up, to swallow. Layers piled up inside me, gray hard mass growing to thickness. Chew and chew and swallow. This was too much food—more than I usually ate for lunch and dinner combined.

"I'm full, Dad," I said. The heaviness of my belly came out in my voice, with the thickness of bile and vomit. "Can I go?"

"Let her go, Benjamin," Mom said. "She's eaten enough."

Callapher got on her knees to reach across the table for another biscuit. She accidentally knocked her glass over. Milk spilled everywhere.

Dad stood to reach across the table. In quick succession, he tipped the remaining three glasses with a snap of his wrist. Milk and water pooled at the center of the table, seeping through the seam of the center leaf to drip in a thin line to the carpet. He pushed his chair away and stormed outside. The screen door slapped behind him twice against its wood frame.

We stared at each other, then looked down. Mom pursed her lips, stood, and carried the glasses to the kitchen sink. Without a word, she handed me a roll of paper towels. Together we knelt under the table to press the carpet dry. With my face only feet from the ground, the lingering odor of the busted water pipe, sharp and musty and sour, made my breath catch. The button of my pants pinched the fat of my stomach. I gagged and nearly vomited. I grabbed at the rough hairs of the carpet with trembling fingers, closing my eyes tight and pressing my mouth shut until the nausea passed.

When we'd sopped up all the milk and water, Mom told me to finish cleaning the dinner table; she was going out. I washed the dishes and put them away in the cupboard. Callapher sat at the table with her head resting against her left arm, tracing her right fingers backwards and forwards over the braid of the basket Mom filled with plastic fruit, the basket she used to make our dining room look like a little more like something she'd seen in *Home and Gardens.*

Food is made of calories, calories are made of energy, energy rolling over on itself, compounding inside me. I could have run for miles, propelled by the guilt that turned to stone in my stomach.

I pressed my balled fists into the flesh of my belly the way a baker punches through a growing bubble of rising dough. I pinched myself until red splotches appeared on my skin, chicken-scratch hieroglyphics. I didn't look at my stomach, but I could feel it: round, obtuse, and white as though I'd swallowed the moon itself. Even when I lay on my bed there was a curve to my abdomen where usually, to my relief, it sank flat between the protruding edges of my hip bones.

Locked alone in the bathroom, I knelt at the toilet, my arm braced around the seat, my head bent forward, the way Dad used to kneel at the altar when he prayed. I pushed my finger to the back of my throat. I only gagged once—but I couldn't force myself to do it. I fell back against the door in defeat.

Someone walked by in the hallway. The cadence of my father's step. I stared through the closed door in the direction of his footfalls. I wanted to hate him, but I didn't. I didn't hate him at all. I loved him so much, I felt it as a dizziness in my head. I hated myself and what I had done to everyone. Belly-down on the bathroom floor, hot cheek pressed against the cool tiles, I began the long wait for morning, when I could wake hungry and empty again.

CHAPTER 9

the most Mollie ever said about my body is that I wore such big shirts she sometimes thought I'd disappear. She addressed the notes she passed to me in school: "My dearest little bird."

I ate the most when I was around Mollie and Matthew, because I wanted them to think I was normal. I would pretend I'd eaten a pop tart for breakfast too. Or that I could have a bowl of macaroni and cheese for lunch and it would be fine, just that, just a bowl of macaroni and cheese, so what.

On her birthday, Mollie invited me to spend the night at her house. We wore paper party hats, and she blew out candles we'd stuck in store-bought cupcakes. Kari was out for Committee Night, so we slept in her gigantic king-size bed. In the middle of the night, I woke with a start. The bed was empty beside me. Blue-white moonlight lay liquid bright upon the wrinkled white bedsheets.

I went to the bathroom and sat on the toilet for a good three minutes before realizing that I didn't really have to go. I washed my hands anyway, out of habit. The cold water woke me up. As my thoughts cleared, the strangeness of Mollie's absence sank in. I felt a sudden terror at the thought of being alone in the giant old house.

In the hallway, I heard voices—two of them, low and deep and unfamiliar. They came from outside the open window. Hiding behind the curtain, I peered down to see the heads of two young men who stood on the lawn just outside the back door. One wore a baseball cap and the other a ski cap, even though the air was warm with coming summer.

The first said something to the other, who craned his neck back to look up directly at the window. I ducked away. A rock slammed against the glass pane, which shivered at the impact. A second rock—or pinecone (it sounded lighter)—struck the window. I felt my breathing thick in my throat, like it was lined with felt or dust. Like someone was sitting on my chest. But they didn't throw anything else. Instead, they knocked twice on the back door. The sound came to me from the back of a grayness in my mind. I recognized it now as the noise that had woken me.

They spoke to one another again. Their laughter pierced the still night air. When they turned to leave, the tall one stumbled down the porch steps and collided into the veranda banister with his shoulder. The men leaned against one another to balance themselves and, in this way, managed a meandering path back to the road.

The night was quiet again. The breeze blew the curtains; they lifted with the gentle twirl of a girl's skirt ruffling in a dance. I waited until I could breathe right again, then gathered my courage and tiptoed gently downstairs to look for Mollie. She sat in the library beside the window, her arm perched on the back of the couch so she could pinch two slats of the blind open with her fingers.

"Who were they?" I asked.

Mollie let the blinds fall shut and shrugged. "Old friends." She rolled her eyes up to the ceiling. "Obnoxious. I didn't want to deal with them this late."

"From school?"

"Sort of. They dropped out." She looked back out the window. The moonlight lit a white crescent upon her cheek. She acted as if their visit wasn't a big deal. I didn't believe it.

As if sensing my suspicion, she added, "One was my ex-boyfriend. Simon."

She'd never mentioned a boyfriend before.

"What was he here for?" I asked.

She shrugged. "Just fooling around, I guess."

In bed, she asked me if I'd ever had a serious boyfriend.

"No," I admitted. I didn't tell her I'd never even been kissed.

"I didn't think so," she murmured.

I felt a little insulted by her response. I tried to change the subject. "What happened with Simon?"

She turned her back to me and lay on her side. "Things."

"Do you miss him?" I ventured.

Softly, she said, "At first I did," before adding resolutely, "Not anymore."

I didn't hear the story until the next morning. We were on the road twenty miles outside Bethsaida, headed for the nearest shopping outlet. We'd been silent for half an hour, the radio playing between us, when Mollie asked abruptly, "Did you see him?"

"Who?" I turned to look in the driver's seat of a passing car, thinking she meant someone on the road.

"Last night; did you see Simon?"

"Oh. Sort of. I mean, I saw the top of their heads. I was looking down from the window outside the bathroom. But I didn't see their faces. They looked up once, but I hid behind the curtains."

"They were drunk," Mollie said matter-of-factly. "Luckily, they were too wasted to think of trying the other doors."

"What do you mean?"

"I never lock the front door—for Mom. You know that."

A sharp shudder coursed down my spine. "Do they come over a lot?" I asked.

She shook her head. "I haven't seen Simon in months. It didn't go well, the last time we talked. And I don't know who the other guy was. I didn't recognize him."

I waited for the rest in patient silence. She took her time about it: fiddled with the radio dial, ran her fingers through her hair, adjusted the rearview mirror. I think she even cleared her throat. She was like Dad at a bonfire, stirring the logs, biding time to bring a waiting story about.

"For our first date, Simon took me out to dinner. It was a real dinner too: tablecloths and real napkins. I'd never had a guy treat me like that. The most I'd ever gotten before was a $2.99 buffet ticket from Robby Happy Hands Henry for Valentine's Day."

"Robby Happy Hands?" I interrupted.

She rolled her eyes. "Worst date of my life. Not worth telling—ego bigger than brain. I've never really had any luck with dating, other than Simon. If you want to call that a good relationship . . . I mean, it was good in the beginning. He was a romantic. Bought me flowers and cards. Of course, *everyone* was in love with Simon. He was on the football team. He had these broad shoulders and this big smile—the kind with dimples in the cheeks.

"My freshman year—he was a sophomore—he got caught driving under the influence. It wasn't the first offense; they kicked him off the football team. His dad got so mad, he threw him out of the house, so Mom let him stay with us and sleep downstairs on the trundle couch. Whenever she was gone, Simon wanted to have sex, but I told him I wasn't ready. I wasn't on the pill, and I *could not* get pregnant. He said it was all right and that he understood, but he started acting shifty.

"One of my old girlfriends caught him with another girl at a game—kissing, she said. I confronted him, but he only got angry and blamed me for leading him on. He said, 'What's the use? It doesn't go anywhere.' I got so mad, I gathered up all his things and threw them on the lawn. He moved out that week.

"Gordon could tell I was taking it bad. He started walking me home from work, and I made him come over late at night just to sit there with me while I watched TV. I was so lonely. That's when Mom was getting bad for the first time too . . . you know, the Committee. One night I kissed Gordon while we were watching a movie. I guess I just forgot myself. I felt so bad afterwards and tried to explain that I didn't want to be in another relationship already. He said it was all right; he knew it didn't mean anything—that I was trying to figure things out. I wanted to make it up to him, so I agreed to visit his church. He'd been inviting me for years.

"Talk about a freak show. All these people singing really weird songs, and the building smelled like mold. Half the time I didn't know what the minister was talking about. But Gordon had a way of explaining it to me afterwards in a way that almost made sense. He talked about God as if they had this private understanding. When I started asking questions, he gave me a free Bible from the church. I started reading it at night when I was the most lonely. There were a lot of massacres and craziness in the first half—but Gordon told me to read Matthew and Mark and Luke. It was different from what I'd expected. Everything about Christ and His love started to make sense of this screwed-up world in a way that nothing else did. I tried to explain this to Gordon. He said I was beginning to believe, and I said, all right, maybe. I mean, Mollie Bauer, a Christian . . .

"What I wanted was to be like Gordon. I was so afraid for him when his mom died; his dad had left them years ago—they only had each other. But even in his grief, Gordon was calm. I cried at the funeral more than he did. He patted my back the whole time and said in that southern drawl of his, 'It's all right, Mollie. It's going to be all right.'

"I needed that, Olivia, to know it the way Gordon did, that we aren't here for a lot of nothing. He knew it like the ground he walked on. I told him that's what I wanted. He said to pray. So I prayed. Like crazy. I prayed in the shower and before bed and before I ate and everything. Then I woke up one day and realized it was about my choice. Just like waking up and saying, 'Today I will wear pants and not a skirt.' I could wake up and say I believed."

Though her talk about God was beginning to make me uncomfortable, I smiled in spite of myself. I'd never heard conversion compared to putting pants on in the morning. I held my hand out the open window, trying to cup the shape of the air. If I pushed my hand against the current it fit into my palm, rounded and resistant. But if I let my hand go limp it snapped back at the wrist beneath the force of the wind, my fingers trailing like streamers. I remembered the

Scripture *The wind blows wherever it pleases. You hear its sound, but you cannot tell where it comes from or where it is going. So it is with everyone born of the Spirit.*

"Simon said I was getting religious and weird. He was living with me and Mom again—came back shortly after Gordon's mom died. Said he was sorry, he wanted a second chance, and like an idiot, I let him. First thing he did when he got back was complain about Gordon. He was insanely jealous whenever we were together. So I stopped talking to Gordon and stopped going to church. That first weekend Simon came, we had sex . . ."

She seemed to stumble a little over the word, as if afraid of putting it in the air between us. Purposefully, I kept my gaze fixed out the window. I was ashamed to feel such an automatic puritanical surprise at her confession. I wanted to think I was open-minded, different than the prudish cohorts of my old church youth group whose judgmental airs had always riled my anger.

It wasn't that I thought less of Mollie for the act. On the contrary, she became all the more glamorous. My knowledge of sex and my previous conversations about it with less intimate friends had been limited. We whispered about it, intrigued and ashamed of our fascination, full of misinformed fantasies born of cinema romances and the genteel euphemisms of our conservative Christian mothers. Your body is a temple, and love is never having to say you're sorry.

"I didn't want to lose him again," Mollie said. "I cried some with my face away from him afterwards. I cried for a lot of things—not all bad I loved him, but for the first time I realized that it wasn't enough.

"I'd never felt convicted of anything before. I felt it like a weight on my chest—not a vague guilt but a specific thing, a specific feeling that I had to change. This switch went off in my head, and I saw everything about Simon, the way he really was: his temper, his childishness—how obviously selfish he was. I guess it was natural to compare him to Gordon—Gordon with his heart of absolute gold. But the real thing was the drinking. I don't know how I'd ignored it. The second time we broke up, I was the one who ended things. I've always wished I'd been more resolved about that decision."

"Where is he now?" I asked.

"Last I heard he was working in some tire factory a few hours from here." Glancing up, she needlessly readjusted her rearview mirror. "The last time I saw him, I . . ." She hesitated.

"You what?" I asked.

She was crying.

"Are you all right?" I asked.

She nodded, then tried to smile. "I didn't think I'd cry. I don't even know why I'm telling you this."

She wiped her cheeks dry with the back of her hand. The stuffed fuzzy dice hanging from the rearview mirror swayed heavily. I waited for her to tell me more, but the story had ended as abruptly as it had begun. It felt good, though, to be trusted with what she'd told. I was the pastor's kid. People at my old town had always talked to me in PG-13, like I was both righteous and naive by blood—and that righteousness and naiveté were somehow invariably linked.

We spent the entire afternoon window-shopping. Mollie wanted to buy some new summer outfits. As we marched from one store to the next, I began to feel tired and listless. I sat on a metal chair, hugging myself in the refrigerated air, while Mollie threw outfit after outfit over her dressing room partition. Beneath the cubicle door, I watched her bare feet tiptoe in slow circles before the mirror, the feet in the reflection keeping time like those of a dance partner. Her toenails were painted red.

"What do you think of this one?" She stepped out of the dressing room in a black strapless gown covered in tiny sparkling sequins.

"It's very elegant," I replied.

Standing before the hallway mirror, she traced the shape of her waist and thigh with the flat of her palms, looking up and down the reflection of her figure with a critical but satisfied expression. "I don't know," she said. "Might be too flashy."

"I don't think it's flashy."

She ran back behind the door. "Let me try the other one."

She reappeared moments later in a red gown suctioned tight to her figure. She wore the matching sash draped loosely in the crook of her arms. She spun once, then put her hands out, palms up. "Yes? No?"

I shrugged. "I don't know."

"Oh, come on," she batted at me with the sash. "You're not being any help!"

"Sorry," I muttered angrily.

She looked at me in surprise. "What's the matter?"

"Nothing."

She regarded me with a quizzical eye before returning to the dressing room. Her voice echoed over the stall door: "Why don't you try something on?"

I said no thanks.

"But really, you should try on this red one. It would fit you better than me . . . I'm too tall for it."

I said I didn't feel like trying anything on, thank you. She popped her head out, her face suddenly bright, and said, "Olivia, it's all right. Mom said to buy whatever. It's my money, and I can spend it all how I want."

I hadn't even been thinking of money. But now that she'd made an issue of it, I couldn't refuse the offer without seeming too proud for charity.

"Fine," I said.

I stepped quickly into the neighboring dressing room before she could suggest that we share one. She threw the dress over. It slapped against the wall like a wet swimsuit, hitting with a slick slap. With my back to the mirror, I discarded my pants and T-shirt, pulling the dress over my head. Struggling my way through the narrow gown, I got my hair tangled so bad it pulled my ponytail lose.

Mollie asked if I needed help.

"I've got it," I said.

When I stepped out into the hallway, Mollie gasped. "Olivia—you look *hot*."

I rolled my eyes.

"You think I'm lying . . . look! Look at yourself."

She took my shoulders and turned me to face my own reflection. I saw my knees protruding from under the dress, round and wide. My skin spackled purple from the cold and from the harsh light above the mirror. At my hips, the dress revealed the line of my underwear tight as a rubber band, pockets of flesh bulging over and beneath it.

"It looks beautiful on you," she said. Standing behind me, she wrapped her arms around my shoulders, hugging me to herself. "You're so *tiny*. So little." She rubbed my arms up and down briskly. "And you're freezing. Look at all your goose bumps."

I laid my hands flat against the side of my hips. "You can see my underwear."

"That's why you don't wear any. Not with a dress like that."

I looked at her in surprise. "I'd feel naked."

She nodded. "It feels good," she assured me. "I think you should get it."

"I can't, it's too much."

"Let me get it for you."

"I don't like it," I said and walked quickly back into the dressing room.

"I thought you'd look good in red," she said to me through the door. "You have such dark hair and pretty eyes. It really is your color. They do those color tests, you know, to tell you what color looks good on you. It's weird how much the right color can make you look better. Take my mom. Whenever she wears white, everybody think she looks sick because her complexion's so pale."

I dressed in my jeans and T-shirt again, pulled on my tennis shoes. I felt warmer with my pants back on. I felt safe.

"I'll bet you're all dark colors," Mollie kept saying. "You should wear things that fit you better, Olivia. You have such a cute little figure."

I leaned my head against the wall and balled my fists until the tips of my nails cut red crescents into my palms. This hate came up from my feet and into my mouth, burned in my ears so that Mollie's voice came from far away. I hated her, I hated her. I blinked my eyes hard. I wiped them dry with a corner of my sleeve, dabbing gently to keep from rubbing them red.

I stepped back into the hallway where Mollie stood waiting, holding her shopping bag in front with both hands clasped on its plastic handles. She smiled and linked her arm in mine. Swinging her shopping bag up into the air, she announced, "Well, my little bird, shall we move on?"

As quickly as that I forgave her. I wanted to kiss her cheek, a cheek blush pink that sparkled as if sprinkled with glitter. Up close, her beauty surprised me every time. But I was beginning to find it difficult to separate the color and shape of her jewel-blue eyes from their lively and intelligent playfulness. I couldn't distinguish between the stunning brightness of her white smile and the easy joy in her laughter. She was so herself, she soaked up her body. Or this: her joy became the whiteness in her smile, and her liveliness the color in her eyes. I can't explain it. I only knew this inexplicable manner with which she lived made her the most sincere person I had ever known. I thought that if I stood close enough, the essence of this beauty would somehow rub off on me. I began to believe you could be contaminated by joy or infected with beauty, the way a germ travels from one hand to another or a condition passes in a moment of shared breath.

CHAPTER 10

summer arrived. The school hallways felt moist and stank of mildew as it grew warmer outside. Through the windows came the hot sun air, carried on bluebird whistles and smelling of wet mowed lawns. I stayed after school the last week of class to help Lori clean out the art closet. She gave me a quiver of old brushes and a handful of half-full paint tubes, then told me to take anything from the storage space. There were more than a dozen old canvases left over from previous students. Some of them had hardly been touched.

"Put a clean coat of gesso on that and it will be good as new," Lori said of the largest of the discarded canvases. "You ought to take it and prep it for something. Shame to let it go to waste."

The next day, Mom picked me up from school. Together we loaded the canvas into the back of the Cheese Wagon.

"What on earth are you going to do with it?" Mom asked.

I had absolutely no idea. "Paint on it," I said with irritation.

I didn't mean to snap at her, but I'd been anxious all week. The thought of three months without painting class made me sick with dread.

Each day had become a battle for normality. Every day, by noon, I lost. It was like being unable to sleep as a child and having my parents tell me, "Don't think about it." Or someone saying, "Don't think of a purple elephant," and immediately in your obstinate brain you see the stupid elephant you were told to ignore.

Every day I woke up and told myself, "Don't eat too much." But then, I had to close my eyes and revise the statement: "Eat normal." *Normal* meant not thinking about food all the time. But as soon as I told myself not to obsess about food, it was all I could think of.

I knew what hunger felt like, but I couldn't understand or gauge the feelings of satisfaction. I'd listened to my mind for so long, I'd forgotten how to listen to my body. When I tried to eat normal, all the rules were gone, and the need to fill myself overcame me. Sometimes I ate until I lost all control, ate myself bloated and fat. Nothing was enough. I ate without tasting, even, crowding my belly . . . and still feeling, in a different place, a deep and hollow emptiness.

The summer job saved me. By some unfathomable leap of logic, Mollie convinced her mother to hire me as part-time help at the car lot office.

"You're here all the time," Mollie said. "Why not get paid for it?"

"Yeah, but what will I do?" I asked her.

"I don't know." She shrugged. "We'll think of something."

What I did was file invoices, answer phones, change Mani's clothes, and sit with Mollie while she bugged the living crap out of Gordon, who took it all with a gentle shrug of his soft, round shoulders, grateful for the attention. Every afternoon, I walked up the hill to the lot and stayed at the office from one to six. We drank tall glasses of Diet Coke, watching bad TV on the small set sitting on the kitchen counter. We turned the fan on helicopter until the entire ceiling shuddered; until, from the corner of my eye, I thought I saw a little plaster raining down.

It was Matthew who came up with our summer plan. He stopped by the car lot one afternoon, still wearing the white paper hat Mr. Burns required of all his shelf-stocking boys.

"We're making a movie," he announced, setting his camera on the countertop as proof and emphasis. The hat, light as an origami swan, blew crooked on his head in the wind of the fan.

"We are?" Mollie asked him. She sat with her bare feet propped on the desk, freshly painted toenails drying in the breeze.

"I am, anyway," he replied. "And you can be in it, if you'd like to do something better with yourselves than sit here and waste away all summer."

Mollie considered her fingernails. "What's it about?"

It was about an alien life form falling in love with a local town girl, a Cinderella meets Star Wars, fairy tale sci-fi film noir. It was to be black-and-white, with a piano score he'd already chosen.

"We'll call it *Polymorphic Dudes from Space*," he finished. "It's a working title," he added when Mollie raised her eyebrows.

We spent the afternoon planning. I was to be the town girl, and Mollie would play the alien and all the boy parts respectively (due to her tall stature and short hair). When we approached Gordon he said no way, no sirreee, he wasn't about to make a fool of himself in front of no camera. So we cast him as head of special effects. Mani was stunt double.

Matthew came to the car lot every day when his shift at the grocery store ended. We spent the remainder of each evening filming, usurping Kari's office as Intergalactic Headquarters. She threatened to fire us all once a week.

"You scared that lady half to death!" she cried after a customer came into the office screaming about a naked lady flying off the roof.

"We had a mattress on the pavement," Mollie argued in our defense. "We wouldn't have thrown her otherwise. No one wants to hurt Mani."

Her mother said, "I'm not *worried* about *Mani*."

It was funny to see Matthew so excited. He had no dignity when it came to cameras. He'd lie on his back, crawl across the ground belly to the earth, sacrifice life and limb for that one perfect shot.

"We should just hire *him*," Mollie said. "Then he'd never have to leave."

I laughed. "He's so obsessed with this stupid movie of his."

Mollie raised her eyebrows. "That's not all he's obsessed with."

"What's that supposed to mean?"

"Matthew never used to come by until you started working here."

I didn't reply.

"All that bull about the town girl for a heroine," she said. "He did that on purpose so he could look at you through that camera lens as much as physically possible."

"We're only friends," I countered.

Again, the knowing lift of her eyebrows. "S'not what he wants."

"He doesn't think of me that way," I insisted.

She propped her hand on her hip in annoyance. "Look, it doesn't matter how much you hide under those big shirts of yours, you can't hide that you're cute. Olivia, you can't make him *not* notice you."

The look in her eyes made me uncomfortable. It was the first acknowledgement between us of my silent something, of my ugliness. I felt it distinctly: she has discovered me. But discovered me at what?

As if on cue, Matthew approached me the very next day. I was walking home from the car lot when I heard the echo of footfalls behind. I turned to meet him. He approached with a determined expression and purposeful step. Standing squarely before me, he announced, "Mr. Burns hosts Bingo Night."

"Oh," I replied. "That's nice."

He nearly interrupted me, as if my response was entirely insignificant. "He's having a swing dance party afterwards. He makes me come, to help clean up. Would you want to come with me? It's tomorrow, Friday."

I was too surprised by both the question and his abrupt manner of asking to think up a good excuse. "All right," I said.

"I can pick you up at seven." He walked away as suddenly and strangely as he'd come.

I didn't tell Mollie. At the car lot the next day, Matthew was as quiet and aloof as usual. I wasn't sure if he'd asked me on a date or on janitor duty.

I remembered too late that I'd promised Callapher that Friday would be our Special Time. She was in a mood already because her newest playmates had ignored her all week. Barred from following Beauregard around, she'd taken up with a rag-taggle bunch from the trailer park beyond the Old Maids' property, four rambunctious, redheaded boys all belonging to one large and lazy Albert Speldman. The boys were busy with a new fort along the creek bed, which they constructed as cowboys, then attacked as aborigines. Since this consisted of running around the woods naked from the waist up, they argued it wasn't right for a girl: she would have to avoid the territory if she valued her scalp.

As I dressed, Callapher deposited herself forcefully on the bed. She crossed her arms. "You said you were going to spend the night with me," she said.

"That was before I made plans," I replied. "Have you seen my sandals anywhere?"

"You never play with me anymore."

"That's not true."

"Is too."

"What about the other night when we played the Barbies were on *Jeopardy*? I played that."

"You made Ken fall off the bed and get paralyzed."

"But I played, didn't I?"

She followed me into the bathroom.

"Get out." I straight-armed her out the door.

She forced her way in anyway. She sat on the tub with her hands covering her eyes so I could go.

"Why are you getting all dressed up?" she asked. "Is he your boyfriend?"

"No."

"Do you like him?"

"No. Yes. I do, but not like that." I don't know why I was trying to explain this to a six-year-old. "Kissing him would be like kissing my brother."

"You don't have a brother."

"You know what I mean."

I washed my hands. Callapher slid to the floor with a heavy sigh, throwing her arm over her eyes. "I hate him."

"Who?"

"That *boy*."

"His name's Matthew. What about your little boyfriends? Those kids you're always with . . . go find them and do something."

"They don't want me because I'm a girl."

"Well." I stepped over her and into the hallway. "You're just going to have to entertain yourself tonight. I'll be back later."

She grabbed at my ankle.

"Get off!" When I shook my foot, I accidentally hit the soft of her right cheek with my heel. She screamed bloody murder. From his bedroom, Dad shouted for us to stop it for God's sake. Dad never used to say "God" like that.

Callapher started to cry.

"Stop it!" I hissed. "You'll get him mad at us both."

The doorbell rang.

"Look, I'm sorry," I said. "I have to go."

I thought about telling Matthew I needed a second. I thought of going back to Callapher to try and cheer her up before I left. But she was being a baby, lying facedown on the floor like that, as if I'd deprived her of all reason for living. She shouldn't get away with it. I closed the front door and shut out the sound of her crying.

We drove to the dance in a joke of a car that made me feel a little better about the Cheese Wagon.

"Sorry about the smell," Matthew said.

I wondered if he referred to the greasy pizza box on the floor or the cologne that soaked the air between us.

"I don't smell anything," I lied, kicking the pizza box aside.

Mr. Burns hosted Bingo Swing Dance Night in the basement of his store. For the evening, pink and blue crepe paper had been hung in parallel loops. Beneath, bright balloons bounced across the dusty floor. There was a long table with triangle-cut finger sandwiches and Dixie cups filled with snack mix and red punch. Aside from Matthew and me, everyone was either gray or balding. Except for the librarian, whose perm looked suspiciously purple when she stood directly beneath the fluorescent ceiling lights.

"Where are the bingo tables?" I asked.

"Oh, that was over an hour ago," Matthew answered. "We'd have had to come at four for that. But I didn't think you'd miss it."

"Not really," I agreed.

Someone called my name. Ruby waved at me from across the room. She clunked to our side of the room in a pair of cumbersome white heels. She held a cup of punch in one hand, the arm of a gentleman in the other.

"Olivia, meet Harold. My dancing partner."

Harold worked his dentures to manage a somewhat wet but equally congenial, "Nice to meet you."

"It's a surprise to see you here," Ruby said to me.

I tried to shrug it off. "Oh, Matthew has to be here to clean up—so I came with him . . . to help," I finished lamely.

I glanced at Matthew, but he'd looked away as if sensing my embarrassment.

"Well, glad to have you, whatever the case," Ruby said. "Go get yourselves some punch and sandwiches. Music's gonna start soon."

Matthew walked away mumbling something about drinks. I stood along the back wall. The ladies in their pastel skirts and white blouses sat in a row on metal folding chairs, trying to look interested and interesting. The men stood on the opposite wall, thick in talk about the new road behind the hardware store and the details of their latest operations. They eyed the women and moved their sweaty hands in and out of their pockets. It was like junior high all over again.

Matthew returned and handed me a cup of punch. "I saw your last drawings hanging up in the hallway at school," he said. "I don't remember seeing them in class."

"That's because I did them at home."

"Well. They're real good."

"Thanks."

There was a slight pause.

"I think"—he cleared his throat—"you did a good job getting the texture of the flowers in that one still life. Real subtle."

"Yeah, I spent a lot of time on it."

Matthew shuffled his feet. I sipped my punch. We managed to produce, prod, and efficiently butcher three other subjects of conversation. I almost wished I were home playing Barbie Jeopardy with Callapher.

The music began. Couples took to the floor. To my surprise, they danced with a quick, easy rhythm that seemed to come to them as natural as breathing.

Matthew caught me smiling. "What is it?" he asked.

"Look at Ruby," I said and laughed. She could *dance*.

"Come on," Matthew said.

I looked at his extended hand in bewilderment. "Come on what?"

He jerked his head toward the center of the room. "Let's dance."

"I don't know how."

"I'll show you."

"Matthew, I can't."

"Come on, it's easy. Just follow me."

Without hesitation or apology, he placed his hand on the small of my back, guiding me with the slightest pressure so that his movements directed mine. There was a rhythm in his body, quickness in his darting feet. It didn't matter that I didn't know the dance. All I had to do was move as he led—right, left, forward, back, under, over, back again.

Over the music I shouted, "I didn't know you could dance!"

"My grandma taught me. She used to own the dance studio—across from the library."

"Is she here?" I asked as our faces brushed close.

He shook his head. "She died two years ago."

"I'm sorry," I said automatically. I felt flushed and silly. It was the music, doing things to me, setting hot coals under my feet, pumping my heart to the pattern of the drums. I felt the music in the laugh that came up from my belly.

Between songs, Matthew wiped his hands against his pants. His palms felt sweaty in mine, but it didn't bother me. With the music in our ears and blood, we talked easily. I liked him this way: flushed and smiling and eager. We danced five songs, swirling, spinning, flying off the floor. When the last of the set ended, I dropped onto a chair to sit and catch my breath. The metal felt cool through my pants. Matthew had a raspberry spot of red on each cheek.

With a single shake of his head, he threw his hair out of his eyes. "More punch?" he asked.

I nodded quickly.

They played a slow song now. Only one couple danced, an older gentleman and his wife. They stepped in slow circles beneath the spotted blurb lights of the spinning disco ball.

"*Mrs.* Burns's idea," Matthew said of the disco ball. He handed me a cup of punch, nodding toward the couple on the dance floor. "That's Mr. and Mrs. Brown. They had their wedding reception down here. Tomorrow's their fiftieth anniversary." Matthew stretched his long legs in front of him. He spoke quietly, to keep our conversation private. Or to bend near to me—I couldn't be sure. "As soon as they leave she'll be scolding him about leaving his pills in the glove compartment, and he'll say she doesn't know what she's talking about."

I raised my eyebrows.

"They're regulars at the store," he explained. "I see them twice a week at least. Fight like cats and dogs."

I traced the rim of my cup with my forefinger. "It's kind of depressing, isn't it?"

"I think it's hilarious."

"But fighting like that all the time."

"Fifty years," he said with a shrug. "You'd get tired of someone."

I sighed. "Yeah, well, that's depressing." I thought of how Mom rolled her eyes at Dad when he wasn't looking.

Matthew crossed his arms against his chest. "Why's it depressing?"

"Well, wouldn't you hope for something better? I mean, it's possible. For people to still love each other."

"Sure, it's possible." He was smiling.

"What's so funny?"

"Nothing."

"You're laughing at me."

"Olivia." He looked at me with a solemn expression. "Is this the face of laughter?"

I ignored him.

"You want to hear what I think?" he asked.

"Yes. Please."

"People should just stop expecting so much—if they just got used to the reality of each other and let go of their fantasies, they wouldn't be so set up for failure. Fantasy is always better than reality. It's not worth it, all that expectation."

I frowned. "I don't think so."

"It's true," he said. "Take Mollie for instance. All her ideas about fidelity and chastity."

"So?"

He extended his open palms. "Is she with anyone?"

"She doesn't seem very interested in guys," I mused aloud.

"Like I said: too high of expectations. Mollie wants someone who thinks just like she does, who has the same beliefs. She's never going to find that." He tossed his cup into the nearby garbage can. It hit the rim and bounced in. "She's just a virgin with ideas."

He looked very pompous and ridiculous saying such a thing. But the easy assurance of his assumption struck me as funny rather than sad.

"How do you know she's a virgin?" I asked.

"She's so idealistic about sex." He looked at me unblinkingly. "Are you hot?" he asked. "We can go outside awhile."

I must have been blushing. "All right," I said.

The night air had turned cool. Streetlamp light from neighboring roads lay in a foggy orange haze just above the building tops. We headed down the sidewalk along the narrow strip of town. There was nowhere to go, but it felt natural to walk.

I considered the library, the post office, the candy-cane-striped sign outside the barbershop. "When we first came here I thought I'd hate it," I confessed. "But it's not so terrible anymore."

Matthew shrugged. "I suppose you get used to it."

"You don't sound so sure."

He smiled halfheartedly. "I'm good at faking it."

"But you don't hate it."

"I guess not."

"Have you always lived here?"

"Born and raised," he quipped, raising his long arm up to snap a twig of leaves off an overhanging maple. "Same thing every day." He plucked a leaf from the stem, rubbed it into a wad between forefinger and thumb before tossing the little green bullet to the sidewalk. "Hasn't changed once. I've had the same stupid job every summer since I was twelve. But I guess I don't *hate* it." He tossed the remains of the branch over his shoulder. "If I had a choice, though, it'd be the city. Where things are happening."

I said excitedly, "That's it exactly. I went to Chicago once, with my parents. Dad had a conference to go to and took us all with him for vacation. We went downtown every night. I loved the excitement of it. Like anything could happen. Or was happening. And it was all right to plan big things."

"Things like what?"

"Things like . . . I don't know. Things."

"Vague, but all right. You've always come across to me as someone who would accomplish 'things.' " He waved his fingers in the air, as if the word could conjure magic.

"I have?"

He looked me directly in the eye when he nodded. I thought I saw something else in his gaze: something different from affirmation.

"So what exactly is it you're going to do in this city?" I asked quickly.

"Things." He flickered his fingers again. We both laughed.

"I want to study photography, actually," he said, ducking his head with an abashed glance at me.

"Obviously," I said. "You've always got that camera with you at school."

"I've got my New Year's resolution already. I'm going to carry a little camera with me every day every single place I go, so I can capture all those moments—you know, all those times you see something, random, at school, in your car—and you know *that's it*, you have to have it. You don't want to forget it. It's my resolution to catch all those. Probably sounds stupid."

I could tell that he didn't believe I would think that.

"It doesn't," I said anyway. "I hate it when people don't take me seriously. I feel like they're laughing at me. Not that they really laugh, but I can tell that in their heads they are looking at me like I'm some cute kid who hasn't grown up yet."

"The perfect picture of my dad, in fact."

"How's that?"

He kicked a stone. It skittered across the sidewalk. "He doesn't like the idea of film school. I want to go to California. He says there's no way we can afford it."

"So you're just giving up?"

"No, I'll not just give up," he said. "Mom's got relatives there. They said I could work at their restaurant. I'll go, work a year or two, save up some money. Hopefully, I can get a good portfolio together, catch someone's eye at a film festival." He shoved his hands into his pockets and watched the ground. "I don't know what kind of chance I have. But . . ." He shrugged his shoulders up to his ears. "You gotta try, right?"

"It'd be a failure of the imagination not to," I stated.

He laughed out loud.

"What?"

"Are you always this fired up?"

I pushed him in the arm. I didn't push him hard, but he fell back as if I had. He scrunched his face in a pout, rubbing his arms. "Totally uncalled for," he said.

As soon as I turned away, he pushed me on the back with both hands. He'd only done it playfully, but I was caught off guard and nearly lost my balance. He caught me with a hand on either of my arms to keep me from falling to the sidewalk. I socked him in the shoulder with my fist. Then for some reason I ran away from him, and for some reason I was laughing. It felt funny to touch him outside like that, alone. On the dance floor he was just a boy. Out here he wasn't just. He wasn't "just" anything.

I stopped running. He'd reached me. For a moment we stood looking at each other. His eyes were all bright. Above us, the town hall clock began its deep-bellied bong for the hour.

"We ought to go back," I said.

We didn't say much on the ride home. I looked out the window, frowning at myself. I hadn't expected to feel funny about Matthew, of all people. Suddenly, I wanted to be away from him and his smiles, away from his sweaty palms and flushed cheeks.

"Here's good," I said when we reached the Old Maids' place.

"I can take you all the way," he said.

"It's not far. I'll walk."

"It's dark," he retorted. "I've got it."

He drove down the gravel drive. When we turned round the bend to find ourselves in a strange light that illuminated the entire cove. Mom's living room lamp stood on the porch, shining a yellow V upward onto the house. In the grass lay two brighter bulbs encased in cages of wire mesh like hockey masks: the lights Dad used to hang in the garage when he worked on the car. And there, to my mortification, was Dad, standing on a ladder, goggles on his face, making pulp of the bushes with a saw-toothed weed whacker.

Matthew laughed. "What in heck is he doing?" he asked.

"I gotta go." I stepped out of the car hurriedly.

"Hang on!" Matthew leaned across the passenger seat to look up at me. "You all right?" He glanced at my father, then at me. "You want to get out of here for a while?"

I shook my head. "I'm fine, seriously. Good night."

I slammed the door before he could protest.

Inside, Callapher stood at the center of the living room in her pajamas and her black dress-up cape. Her hair stood on end with static; I could almost hear it snapping. She was staring out the window, seeming to have forgotten herself, holding her sparkle baton so that its tip bowed down to touch the ground.

Mom came in. She didn't even look at me, just said, "We're going to Margaret's. Callapher can't sleep with this noise."

Callapher said, "I can sleep."

Mom said, "Put your arms up."

She made her arms obediently limp as Mom shoved them through the sleeves of her jacket. She gave me a pleading look before following

Mom outside in silence. I heard the car rev to life. The twin beams of the headlights chased around the dark living room and winked out.

CHAPTER 11

i sat on the corner of my bed trying to empty my mind. Moist summer air came in from the open window. The weed whacker revved, roared, stopped. Whenever it paused, the vibrant hum of cicadas buzzed and shimmered in the air.

Moments ago I'd been walking outside with the night air fresh on my face and cool in my lungs, a pleasurable giddiness in my stomach, and talk of the city granting me the brief illusion that in other places —and perhaps in my own distant future—life could be beautiful. I lay on the bed with my hands to my face and cried. I felt Matthew's hand on my back. If he knew what I really was he wouldn't want me. If he saw me as I looked beneath the layers of clothes piled on clothes, he'd only turn his eyes away.

My eyes ached, and my head grew thick with pounding. The wet spot on the pillow began to chafe the skin of my cheek. I lay on my back, hands upon my sinking belly, studying the faces on the wall. They looked past me, their eyes alive with visions of the wonderful.

The women held their mouths just parted—to whisper a secret, to take in the air, to accept the coming kiss.

The commotion outside had stopped. I wiped my face with the back of my hand and sat up. In the dense silence, I heard myself say to the dark room, "No. No, not tonight."

The words sprang from my mouth so unexpectedly and with such authority, I felt a strange sense of victory in them. I jumped from the bed and reached beneath it for the canvas Lori had given me, dragging it to the center of the room. It took up all the empty space between my bed and the opposite wall. I gathered all of Dad's discarded newspapers from the living room, laying them pinched beneath the corners of the canvas to protect the hardwood floor. I didn't have a pallet, so I used one of Mom's old baking sheets. Cookie-size stains covered the old pan. I lined its perimeter with thick globs of paint squirted in a neat row, then sat back on my haunches, brush in one hand and cookie sheet in the other, staring at the blank white of the waiting canvas.

I closed my eyes to search the shifting neon shapes that played on the black of my eyelids. I waited for a vision to surface but saw only blue. I dry-brushed blue over the entire canvas. The stiff bristles scratched across the rough surface. I pumped my arm vigorously, making broad circles that overlapped one with the other until the color bled through the canvas, searching threads joining together.

I planted both feet firmly on the ground and balanced myself precariously over the canvas, one hand anchored to the floor, the other free with the brush. Positioned like I was in a game of Twister. My hair fell loose from its ponytail and stuck to the sweat on my forehead.

I thought of my father. When I saw him in my mind, he was always just looking up from a book, an expression of bewilderment in his eyes as they searched the room or a face before focusing and surfacing to reality. The truth of something my mother once said struck me with clarity: "You're like your father. You were born an idealist."

As I have come to understand it, Dad joined the ministry more out of obligation to his mother's expectation than in obedience to the divine leading of the Holy Spirit. Grandma Monahan had a gift for discerning God's will and a tenacity in making that will known to those who hadn't gotten the divine memo just yet. She had three sons. The first died at the age of two, the second grew up to study law. He became a divorce attorney: a career that personally offended Grandmother by gaining profit in the slow dismantling of the most holy estate. It fell to my father, the youngest, to fulfill the vow she had made to God: that if he granted her one more son after the premature death of her first, she would dedicate one of her children to the service of the Kingdom.

If you ask Dad, he'll only say that she encouraged him. He'll say that while he rebelled against the idea at first, his heart led him rightly to the church in the end. The Calling and Grandmother Monahan's injunction coexisted in his mind, distinct but in agreement.

In Bethsaida, Dad slept in on Sunday mornings. While dressing for church, Mom walked in and out of their bedroom with exaggerated care, as if afraid to wake the dead. One morning, I peered past the bedroom door. Through the darkness that filled the room, I saw the brilliance of the obstinate Sunday sunshine crisp in a golden line at the base of the closed window shade. Looking into the shadows of the bedroom, I felt I had physically come face-to-face with the very substance of my own despair. The despair of waking, lost, with no sense of direction.

In the abstract association of these thoughts I found the painting as it should be: black vacuum beneath, the transcendent blue above, and in between, the thin gold thread of sunlight that lay beneath my father's window shade. This gold would be the thin halo of angels, the gold of heaven, the promise of the other that is always just outside the closed window shade, between the fuzzy grayness of lashes clasping shut over the eye.

My thoughts compressed so tight in concentration as to become nothing. Images of my father, of school, of Matthew played forever on in the distance, but before me there existed only color and concentration. Even my own body flattened. It was a necessary tool but remained translucent between my thought and its manifestation, as impossible to see as the lightning command by which your brain tells your finger to bend.

But as soon as you notice you weren't noticing and you remember you'd forgotten, the world comes back as clear sound to popping ears. It's like being very tired and wanting to be awake while you sleep so you can enjoy it: the bliss of forgetting is only realized by remembering. I had painted for five minutes or five hours—I didn't know. But it was too late: I was aware of myself again. The paint was just paint. I was alone in my bedroom. I fell back against my bed. Blue smears stained my hands nearly to the elbows. I rubbed my forefinger into the black paint on the cookie sheet, ran it along the surface of the canvas so that a black tail smeared behind. I was weeping. There was no name for my blackness.

Curled like a fetus, my fists tight and stained, I fell asleep, a spot of drool dampening the carpet beneath my open lips.

I woke to the sound of a knock on my door. Someone's arm was pinned under my stomach. A second knock sounded and I started, fully awake. I was lying on my own arm, its fingers numb with sleep.

"What?" I called.

Mom said, "Mollie's here. Are you up? You've been sleeping the day away."

When had Mom gotten home? I peeled myself from the floor. Dimples patterned my skin, the spackled imprint of the rough carpet.

There was a third knock at the door.

"What?" I demanded.

"Don't yell," Mollie replied. "I can wait."

I looked down at my arms, at my shirt. Blue paint everywhere. "Hold on a sec. I'm coming."

I considered the mess I'd made of my room. In the harsh light of the late morning sun, I felt embarrassed for my abandon. I rushed to clear the floor, collecting the brushes and crumbling up the newspapers now spotted with dried paint. Outside the door, the floorboards creaked as Mollie adjusted her weight.

She called, "What are you doing in there?"

"Nothing." I peered around the door without opening it up all the way. "Can you give me a second? I need to change."

Mollie looked me up and down with an amused smile. The blow pop in her mouth had stained her lips and tongue green.

"What the heck are you doing, goofy?" she asked.

"I have to clean up some stuff. What are you doing here?"

She pulled the sucker through her lips with a wet sort of pop. "I've got to go out of town to pick up some things for the garage. I thought you'd want to come. Mom said she'd pay us overtime for the hours." She stared at my hands. "Were you painting?"

I shrugged. "Just working on a little project."

"Can I see?" She craned her neck to see around my shoulder. When I hesitated, she protested, "Why not? Come on, don't be embarrassed."

"I'm not," I muttered.

"Then let's see it." She put the sucker back in her mouth, the white stick bouncing in the air as she positioned the candy between her teeth and cheek. She raised her eyebrows. "Well?"

I sighed and opened the door.

She came in, walking to the other end of the bedroom to better survey the painting. "It's big," she stated.

I crouched around her legs to pick up more newspapers from the floor.

"What is it?" she asked.

"What is it?" I repeated. I stood beside her and looked down at the blue. I saw again the vision of what it could become: the bands of navy and black, the single golden thread stretched between worlds. "I don't know. It wasn't meant to be anything."

"It's big," Mollie repeated.

"I'd better clean up so we can go," I said.

Mollie seemed reluctant to leave. She wanted to look at the painting, and it made me uncomfortable: I found nothing in it deserving of admiration.

Finally she said, "I'll be in the car. Be out in ten minutes or I'll leave you."

In the bathroom, I stood at the sink in my bra to clean up. No matter how hard I scoured my arms and hands, I couldn't rub away the paint embedded beneath my skin, spots the color and depth of fading bruises. I looked up and saw a stranger looking back in the mirror. I stared a moment longer until I recognized my nose and eyes and mouth, until they became the parts of my soul, until they became me, and I had to look away.

I toweled dry and dressed quickly. As I was walking out the front door, Mom motioned to me from the kitchen to stop.

She stood with a dishrag in one hand, wiping down the counter, the phone propped between her shoulder and chin. She was saying, ". . . so you're sure you haven't seen her? Yes, well, all right. Thank you. And you'll let us know if you hear anything? . . . Uh, uh. All right. Good-bye." She hung up and looked at me. "Have you seen Callapher today?"

I shook my head. "Last I saw her she was leaving with you."

"What? Oh, yes, we spent the night at Margaret's. I came home early this morning to get some things done around the house; she was sleeping so hard I didn't want to wake her. Ruby said she got up around nine wanting breakfast, but no one can recall seeing her after that. But Margaret's at the store . . . She must be with Margaret. Still, it's strange. I'm sure Margaret would have called to tell me Callapher was going along."

"She's probably off with those Speldman boys or something and forgot to tell you."

"Probably," Mom murmured.

Outside, Mollie honked the horn.

"Gotta go," I said. "We're running errands for Kari."

"Drive carefully," Mom said absentmindedly.

Mollie and I returned around three. I saw the lights first—bright beads of red chasing the blue. The police cruiser was parked at the Old Maids'. Its many antennas strained backward in the wind of the impending storm.

"What's going on?" Mollie asked.

"Park here," I commanded.

Mollie stopped the car on the road.

I jumped out and ran up the length of the lawn. Inside the kitchen, I called for Margaret, but no one answered. "Margaret? Ruby?"

The house seemed abandoned. Its uncharacteristic silence sent a sharp shudder down my spine.

"What is it?" Mollie asked, running into the room behind me.

"I don't know. I don't think anyone's home."

For the first time, I remembered the look of concern on Mom's face as she'd spoken on the phone that morning. At the time it hadn't meant anything; finding my mother in a state of general anxiety wasn't a novelty. Now my stomach turned. Callapher.

I bolted to the back door just as Margaret entered. We nearly collided.

"Margaret, what's—"

"She's gone!" Margaret cried, running to the hall closet for her shawl.

"Who, Margaret?"

"Callapher—she's gone. They can't find her anywhere. Your mother called us hours ago, asking if we'd seen her, and I told her I thought Ruby'd sent her home." She wrapped a rainbow print handkerchief over her hair, raising her chin to knot the ends together. "At first I assumed it was nothing—she'd gotten sidetracked on the way, run into those boys and gone to play without telling anyone."

"Maybe she went home with them."

"No, no." Margaret shook her head sharply. "They haven't seen her. The boys weren't even out today. They're home sick, the flu." She ran back to the kitchen and out the door, lifting her skirt to her knees and taking long strides toward her car. Mollie and I ran behind to keep up.

Margaret looked over her shoulder to say breathlessly, "Ruby's in a frightful fit of nerves. She was the last to see the child, when she gave her breakfast. I went to the store, Ruby was napping, and Callapher wasn't here. I thought she'd gone home and told your mother so. Then Ruby woke to tell me this was not the case—she had never sent the child home. What terrible negligence on our part! And Ruby, the poor thing, she's in such torment . . . She's been tramping through the woods all afternoon, in her heels, no doubt."

I had trouble breathing. It felt like the time I'd slipped on the basement steps as a child and received a blow to the back that knocked the wind from my lungs. The same feeling of panic, of having the ground pulled from under my feet.

Margaret got into her car, looking up at us with her hand on the handle of the still open door. "The Reverend went to the Speldman place—no one had been picking up the phone—and when he discovered no one had seen her, we immediately called the police. Your mother, of course, has been in a terrible way all afternoon. We had assured her there was nothing to worry about—you know how your mother is, always fussing. But if it hadn't been for our insistence, she might have called for help earlier, and we might have saved ourselves this terrible suspense! Callapher could be anywhere by now!" She clasped at her chest. "Good Lord," she prayed aloud, "bring her home safe."

"Where are Mom and Dad now?" I asked.

"The Reverend took your van to drive through the town, and Ruby's gone door-to-door," Margaret said, getting into her car and putting the key in the ignition. "Your mother took the truck, but I do believe she is on her way home to wait for the police: they want to speak with her. Someone has to hold down the fort, in case Callapher should come home, Lord willing."

"You should stay, Margaret," I said. "Mollie and I will look."

"We can take my car," Mollie volunteered.

"Bless you, I *am* tired. But I don't know that I can stand to sit and do nothing." Her eyes darted back and forth as if reading words printed on the steering wheel. "I'll call. I'll stay home and call." She looked up at us. "Everyone in town if I have to."

Mollie and I each took one of her extended arms to help her up out of the car. We hurried toward the front of the house where Mollie had parked.

Margaret said, "A week ago she told me—and I'm ashamed now that I didn't tell anyone, but it just seemed like a natural thing for a sensitive child to say after a bad day—she confided in me her intention of running away if her family kept ignoring her. I told her that I was family and would spend all the time in the world with her if she liked, but she turned to me and—in the most sorrowful little tone you could imagine—said, 'But, Margaret, you don't even have the same last name!' "

"The bus stop," I announced. "She's always talking about taking the bus back out of town."

"I don't believe anyone's looked there," Margaret replied. "Though Sam—that's the officer—said he'd sent another cruiser through town to look. But do try!"

Mollie and I jumped into her car, speeding down the road with Margaret waving us off from behind. I rolled the window down and trained my eye on every passing tree and street sign. I told Mollie to slow down so we wouldn't miss anything. I don't know what I expected to see: a flash of blonde hair in the shadow of the woods? Footprints?

The first drops of rain hit my face, shot down upon the wind to slap my cheeks in cold pinpricks. The metallic smell of a coming storm filled my nose. The sky had turned yellow-green, full with purpling clouds.

At the bus stop, the side panels of the yellow kiosk glowed against the darkening sky like the glass plates of a lantern. The bench inside was empty. A discarded newspaper page caught up in the wind, lifted with the seeming slow motion of weightlessness, then chased across the sidewalk.

"Drive back," I told Mollie. "I want to check the library."

In town, Mollie parked the car at Mr. Burns's shop. "I'll check with Matthew," she said. "Meet me back here."

I nodded and ran across the street.

The librarian peered up at me without lifting her head. The fluorescent lights created a white glare so bright on the lenses of her cat-frame glasses I couldn't see her eyes.

"Noooo..." she said softly. "I'm afraid I have not seen a child in the library *unaccompanied*." She curled her lips with distaste over the word.

"You're sure?" I pressed. "She's about this tall, white-blonde hair."

"No." She stamped a book. "I have seen no one of that description."

I searched both floors of the library anyway. Callapher liked to hide in the corners with her books. I checked every stall in the bathroom. "Callapher?" I called. My voice echoed off the tiled floor.

Mollie met me halfway back to her car. She shook her head. "No one's seen her," she said.

We got back into the car, and she started the engine.

"Matthew wasn't there, but I talked to Mr. Burns. He said it's been quiet in town all day, and he'd have seen someone go by—he's at that counter facing the window. Said he'd seen the cruiser pass a couple times, though, and wondered what was going on."

"Where do we go next?" I asked.

"I don't know. Where else would Callapher go? The school?"

"Maybe the playground," I said. "That's not far. She'd remember the way there."

I tried to remind myself that Bethsaida was a sleepy and unassuming place. People were used to children rambling around like they owned the streets; the Speldman boys ran around town half naked all the time without supervision. The worst anyone would do was ignore her. Still, my breath came short. I saw Callapher alone in the forest, lost in the trees. I saw her run and trip over a root, sprain her ankle, break her leg. And I saw all the times in the past week she'd wanted my attention: how each time, I'd pushed her away.

"Mollie, I'm scared," I said. "What if she's in the woods?"

Mollie didn't answer. We'd reached the elementary building. The playground extended away from the school toward the dark line of silent trees, the square of land demarcated from the parking lot by a ten-foot-high chain-link fence. We looked through the wire mesh, calling Callapher's name. One of the swings on the swing set swayed backward, forward, the chains creaking as if bearing the weight of an invisible child.

"It's locked." I pointed toward the chains looped three times through the gate latch.

"She couldn't have gotten in either," Mollie said.

I started crying.

"It's all right," Mollie reassured me. She wrapped her arm around my shoulder. In my sneakers, I was nearly four inches shorter than she was. "Don't be worried yet. It's only been a few hours . . . You know she's around here somewhere."

"She wanted to spend time with me last night," I said. "I went out with Matthew instead."

"It's not your fault, Olivia."

I hugged my waist. I wanted to press out the queasy sickness rising up in my belly. "I keep thinking she must have gone off in the woods, to the creek or something. But it's getting dark. She's got to be terrified."

"Margaret said Ruby's been looking in the woods."

"Yeah, but Ruby's probably lost herself. And she's not that fast."

"We should go back to your house," Mollie suggested. "Maybe someone's heard something."

I nodded my agreement.

We didn't drive as fast on the way home. There was something resigned about the slow pace of the car, as though we'd given up. I repeated to myself what Mollie had said and tried to believe it. It had only been a few hours; Callapher couldn't have gone far. The strange thing was, I couldn't accept the alternative. I feared the worse while simultaneously believing it impossible. My life could not go that way. I saw my future existing beneath an invisible screen through which the world—the world I saw on television and in history books and in war movies—could not penetrate.

At recess in elementary school, we'd steal the identities of the children whose faces had been printed in gray grainy pixels on the back of our milk cartons. At recess, we'd pretend one of us was the kidnapper, another the lost child. Everyone else played detective. Once I was Amanda Barker, nine years old, last seen in her backyard wearing OshKosh B'Gosh pink jumpers and a pair of white tennis shoes. The kidnapper hid me under the slide and left me there, where I sat for a half hour, the gravel making rippled indents on the back of my legs.

At the house a small crowd had gathered. Kari and Gordon stood in the driveway, talking to a police officer and two of the mechanics from the car lot.

Gordon broke from the circle to speak with us. "No word yet," he said. "Your mom came over an hour ago to tell us. Some of the guys are out looking. James thinks he saw her on her bicycle this morning."

"Where?"

"Going by the lot, headed north." He pointed in the direction we'd come from. "Said it looked like she was headed for the main part of town, though I think a kid on a bike would have a time of it. That incline is nothing when you're in your car, but it's something else on a bike. Specially with such little legs as she's got."

Margaret appeared at my side. "Your mother's inside," she said. "Your father as well—he just pulled in."

I went into the house. Mom stood abruptly at the sight of me. She seemed to cross the length of the living room in a single stride to wrap her arms around me.

"Are you all right?" she asked.

"Yeah," I mumbled.

Her long fingernails poked into the skin of my back. She held me tenaciously as though, if she let go, she'd drown in our living room floor. I was aware of the hard lines of bones beneath skin. My mother was not as soft as she used to be. Or was it the feeling of my bones evident through my own skin? I could not place the bare strength as mine or hers: it was like trying to catch a person's pulse but confusing it with the heartbeat in your own finger.

"I'm all right, Mom," I said. But I held her a little longer.

God, get her home, I prayed. *God, please, please don't let anything happen to Callapher.*

CHAPTER 12

rain hit the metal awning of the window overhangs hard as beads popping off tin. I tapped the plastic cap of the blind cord against the living room window, counting in my head: Callapher had last been seen around nine. It was five o'clock now. That made eight hours, at least, that she'd been missing.

"No, no, I told you," Mom said into the phone. "Ruby—Mrs. Alcott—was the last to see her. . . . Yes, I realize that, sir. . . . I just thought in case . . . Yes, of course, we'd appreciate that. All right. Good-bye."

She hung up and put her forehead in her hands. Margaret poured her a cup of coffee. The Old Maids had brought a basket of food. The soup was heating on the stove, the aroma mixing with the pungent smell of the coffee.

"Did the police call?" Margaret asked.

Mom shook her head. "Thank you," she said, taking the coffee and setting it down on the table untouched.

Dad appeared in the front door. We all stopped what we were doing to look to him.

"There's a second storm front moving in," was all he said. He wiped his feet twice against the floor mat.

Ruby met him with a mug. "Regular or decaf?" she asked.

Dad stared at the mug and then at Ruby in bewilderment. He looked at Mom. "You're having *dinner*?" It was more an indictment than a question. "My daughter is out in the rain, who knows where—and you're all sitting here having dinner?"

"Ben, please," Mom started.

"This is ridiculous," he muttered. "I'm going back out." He reached for his keys.

Mom put her hand on his. "Take some coffee," she said.

"I don't want coffee," he muttered. "I'll be back in an hour."

I waited until he was out the door to say, "I'm going with him." I didn't want to give him the chance to disagree. When I jumped into the van, he didn't acknowledge my presence or argue against it. He didn't say anything at all until we reached town.

"You're worried," he stated.

I nodded and looked to the window but, realizing I had nothing to be ashamed of, turned back so that he could see me crying. I thought he would say, "She's all right" or, "It's going to turn out fine."

Instead he said, "This is all wrong. We shouldn't be in this place; we should never have come." He grimaced. "I think of you girls. Of everything you had to go through. It wasn't fair to either of you. I wish . . . I've always wished it could have been different."

"It's okay, Dad," I said.

He shook his head. "No, it's not okay. You deserve better, all of you." His fingers relaxed on the steering wheel, then tightened again.

The skin of his knuckles peaked white. "It's not all right," he repeated quietly.

We drove down Main Street and turned onto High. As we circled downtown, Dad watched out his window with a steady gaze, but he seemed to be looking past the buildings to something else.

"I ran away from my mother once," he said, resting his elbow against the window ledge, running his fingers through his thinning hair. "In a department store. I hid in the maternity section inside the clothing rack. I was pretending it was a jungle and that the women shopping were hippos I had to shoot."

In spite of the circumstances, I laughed.

"I heard her calling my name. She sounded totally panicked. I waited and waited until she was near tears, and then when she walked past the rack, I jumped out and shouted, 'Surprise!' I'll never forget the look on her face. I thought she was going to murder me right on the spot."

We stopped at a light. The wipers caught against the windshield, skidding loud on the glass.

"If your grandma had anything, she had a resentful memory. I don't think she let me out of her sight a single second for five years after that."

I said, "Dad, do you think Callapher's just lost?" I didn't want to say what else it could be. A stranger in a car. A face on a milk carton. Only Dad and Mom and I at dinner, always waiting.

Dad stopped the car. Without a word to me, he turned off the engine and stepped outside, leaving the door open. I got out and looked to him for directions.

"Why don't you . . ." He gazed to the right of my head, his eyes transfixed by something in the distance, then turned away, taking in the entire gray scene of rain on the empty street. He put the back of his hand to his mouth for a count of two, swallowed, blinked, and looked again at me. "Why don't you see if anyone's still in the hardware store? I'll go speak with Mrs. Klein at the ice cream shop; they stay open past six. She sees the Speldman boys in there all the time. Maybe Callapher . . ." His words trailed off.

I turned to go, but hesitated. "Dad," I said. "Are you all right?"

"I'm fine," he insisted, waving away my concern. We separated.

In the hardware store, I spoke with the man behind the counter who said he hadn't heard of any missing girl and said "Sorry" with a look of pity in his eyes that scared me so bad I ran back outside with my heart thumping like a flat palm clapping the inside of my chest.

Then I saw Dad. He had not left his place beside the driver's side door but stood doubled forward, one hand bracing the side mirror of the van, the other clasped against his bent knee. His brow was contorted as if he were overcome with physical pain. He was soaked through; a bead of rain hung from his nose, or maybe it was a tear. He moved his lips silently, quickly, a mute incantation to the empty air. It had been so long I almost didn't recognize it: prayer.

I slowed to a halt. It was like walking in on someone naked in his own bedroom. But the moment I stopped, Dad straightened. Over the hood of the van, his eyes caught mine. I didn't say anything.

"She's all right, Dad," I said, to convince myself.

"Of course," he returned. His voice sounded distant, his words as far removed as his thoughts. He turned his back to me, but I saw his hand go to his eye. "Of course she is."

We got back into the car and drove the downtown streets twice, then went back home. All the food had been cleared. Dad went to his bedroom to dress in something heavier, declaring he would walk along the creek with a flashlight. Mom met him in the hallway. I stayed in the bedroom while they talked. I heard a single sob from Mom, but other than the sound of her short cry, I couldn't understand what they said to each other.

I was ten when my parents told me I was going to have a new sister. At first I resented the idea of sharing my parents with a baby. In an effort to get me excited about the prospect, Dad took some construction paper and glitter glue and labeled a washed-out coffee tin the "Baby Name Jar." He made a slit in the plastic lid and cut ten scraps of paper for each of us.

I filled out my ballots after only the most strenuous deliberation. Ariel. Aurora. Del Monte. Oneida. At the end of the week, we gathered in the living room to hear Dad read the thirty names aloud. When he got to Calla Flower, Mom tried to stifle her laughter and snorted instead.

Offended, I stomped to my room declaring I hated the baby. When my sense of persecution had cooled a little, they informed me that even though they'd liked my ideas very much, they didn't think any of them fit very well with Monahan. They chose the name Carla, but for the remainder of Mom's pregnancy we referred to the baby as Little Calla Flower.

Callapher, Callapher, Callapher. I repeated her name in my head like an incantation, as if by thinking her name hard enough I could call her back. I lay back flat against the couch, staring at the patterns in the plaster peaks of the ceiling. I started to count. For breakfast . . . for lunch . . . nothing. With surprise, I realized I'd forgotten to eat all day. I'd forgotten food. I put my arm over my eyes and rested my other hand on my belly.

‡ ‡ ‡

I woke up to a commotion all around me. Margaret stood at the window, holding the curtain back with one hand, waving everyone to her side with the other.

"Hurry, hurry—someone's on the road! Claire! *Claire*!" Margaret bolted for the door.

"What is it?" Ruby cried, running to the window. She pulled back the drapery and squinted her eyes. "Gracious Lord in heaven," she whispered.

Two figures approached, their silhouettes blurred by the gray mist of rain: one tall and lanky, the other short, a teepee with legs. It was Beauregard, carrying a familiar pink bicycle in one hand, holding Callapher's with the other. She was wearing his neon orange parka, which pitched out at an angle to her sides in the shape of a funnel.

Mom was two seconds behind Margaret. When she reached Callapher, she fell on her knees so abruptly, I thought she'd stumbled.

"Thank God," she said, "Thank God, thank God." She kissed Callapher's cheek, her forehead, her ears, her lips. Then she held my sister's cheeks in her hands and searched the little face as if seeing it for the first time. "Callapher, if you ever, *ever* do such a thing again . . ."

"Get her inside!" Ruby declared. She'd pitched a newspaper over her head to hide from the rain.

"Good night," Margaret said. "Forget about your silly permanent for once, Ruby Mae."

"Wasn't thinking of any such thing," Ruby retorted, patting her curls absentmindedly.

Dad appeared on the porch. He looked around, searching for the source of the commotion. When his eyes latched on Callapher, I saw his shoulders drop, as if a great load had been taken from his back. He stepped forward and took her right from Mom's arms, holding her tight to his chest. Bewildered by all the excitement and silenced by Mom's anger, she laid her head gently against Dad's shoulder, wrapping her arms tight around his neck.

"I love you, Daddy," she said.

Dad closed his eyes. He laid his broad hand against the back of her head, his wedding band glinting in the light of the porch lamp. He whispered, "I love you too, Angel."

Inside, Mom and the Old Maids took Callapher to our bedroom to strip her of her wet clothes. She stood with arms outstretched as they toweled her dry. I watched from the doorway and noticed she was wearing her purple heart underwear, backwards.

They dressed her in pajamas, then set her at the dining room table with a peanut-butter-and-banana sandwich and a glass of milk. She finished both eagerly. The Old Maids gathered their things as soon as she was settled.

"Too much fuss and bother for one day," Margaret said. Then, "We'll call them all," she replied to Mom's concerns. "We'll call the lot, get hold of Kari and the men. You take care of Callapher."

They spoke a few moments longer at the door. I heard Mom mention Beauregard's name. He'd disappeared in all the excitement. I couldn't remember even seeing him in the house.

"Oh, he's quiet like that," Margaret said. "Wouldn't want a lot of attention for such a thing. But I'll send him over tomorrow if you like. Then you can talk to him in person."

The door shut. The Old Maids were gone. Even from the dining room I could hear Mom sigh. She joined us at the table.

"Callapher, dear, Daddy and I need to talk with you."

Callapher looked at Mom, wide-eyed. "Can Olivia stay?"

"You want her to?"

She nodded.

I stayed. Mom did most of the scolding. Dad nodded his head when he thought it pertinent, but I caught him winking once at Callapher.

"You're not helping," Mom told him.

Callapher explained to us that she had been headed back home to Moeller, intent on leaving us forever. She made it all the way past the city limit signs before running into Beauregard, who listened patiently to her plans and promptly convinced her to join him on his way home.

"We are very glad you're all right," Mom said. "But you are in very serious trouble. Do you understand that?"

Callapher asked if she was going to get spanked.

"I don't know what you're going to get. We'll decide in the morning."

She began to cry.

"Don't think about it now," Mom said.

"It's not his fault."

Mom frowned. "Not whose fault, honey?"

"Do you hate him?"

"Hate who?"

"Beauregard."

Mom appeared quite surprised by this. Unconsciously, she bit her lower lip, glancing quickly at Dad.

"Time for bed," he announced cheerfully.

That night in bed, I wrapped my arm around Callapher's chest and laid my face against her shoulder. I said, "If you ever do that again, I'll stop speaking to you forever."

"I didn't mean it," she whispered.

"Love me?" I asked.

She nodded. We played the I-love-you-more game. I love you more than all the sand on the seashore. I love you more than all the stars in the sky. I love you more than all the bread in the grocery store.

"You're bonkers," I said.

"I amn't," she insisted. She yawned a face-splitting yawn.

I didn't let her go. We fell asleep that way.

That Sunday we were at the table eating breakfast before church when Dad walked in wearing a suit jacket and tie. He poured himself a bowl of cereal and sat at the head of the table without explanation or apology, only an, "Angel, pass Daddy the milk."

The morning passed in familiar ritual: Dad brushing his teeth at the sink, Mom working around him to catch sight of her hair in the mirror, Callapher complaining she didn't want to wear a stupid dress. Dad drove us to church. Just like it used to be.

During the service, I watched him. He sang all the hymns. He listened patiently to the sermon. Yet somehow these gestures appeared rehearsed, and though he did his part, the father in the pew with his family, he did so with a placid silence, his hands clasped before his waist and his eyes dull.

I didn't want him to join the little circle of hypocrisy: me and Mom, singing with just our mouths like brainless puppets. I didn't want my father to sink to that. I admired his silent tantrums and even his depression more than this performance. At least a tantrum required some passion—some emotion.

After service, he followed Mom around the sanctuary, shaking hands as she introduced him to everybody. I watched him for signs of fraud, for fake smiles and tired glances toward the door. But he gave neither. He greeted all Mom's friends with genuine and almost timid eagerness. When the old usher said something in his ear, Dad threw his head back and laughed. For that single moment it was back: the light in his eyes.

As a result of his heroism, Beauregard was released from probation. Callapher was free to follow him to her heart's content and joined him each Saturday on his fishing trips to the creek. Mom's brow still wrinkled a little whenever she saw my sister scramble down the street to greet him, but once my mother makes up her mind, she has a resolve of steel. Even after discovering a brainy-looking ball of frozen worms in the freezer, she only told Callapher, "Please tell Mr. Lowett to keep the bait in *his* refrigerator," and made no further complaint.

Beauregard taught Callapher how to bait a hook and gut a fish. He taught her the scientific names for the trees that lined the creek. Together they caught a batch of tadpoles and kept them in a fish tank to watch their legs grow.

When Beauregard was at work, Callapher sat at the Old Maids' player piano. She liked to lay her hands over the keys, trying to predict when and where they would fall, trying to catch the rhythm of the invisible ghost fingers. She memorized all the words to "Love Is Blue" and "The Sound of Silence." She had a dance routine for "When the Saints Go Marching In," which she practiced in our bedroom nightly.

"What were you doing in there?" Mom asked when Callapher emerged from behind the closed bedroom door, breathless and sweating.

"Dancing," Callapher answered.

"Sounded like you were throwing yourself against the wall," Dad said from behind his book.

"Want to see it?" she asked.

"Of course we do," he replied without looking up.

Since we didn't have the player piano, Callapher hummed the tune herself. The more she danced, twirled, and flopped herself around the room, the more breathless came the accompaniment, until she danced to just a few puffing bits of song. Mom tried to censor my laughter with her eyes, but I didn't care. It felt good that we were all out in the living room together, no one hiding behind shut doors and closed window shades.

CHAPTER 13

i was dreaming. I sat on a leather chair at the mall trying on shoes.

"How about this size?" asked the attendant. He knelt before me like Prince Charming slipping on Cinderella's glass slipper. He produced a white shoe from the tissue stuffed in a shoe box. It didn't fit.

"Another," Mom demanded. She sat beside me stirring pancake batter in a big yellow Pyrex bowl decorated along its lip with little white blossoms in the shape of snowflakes.

The young man produced another box. A bit of flaming red fabric lay inside, crumpled like discarded underwear. I picked it up. It was a bikini.

"This one?" asked the attendant, whose face had become a gray mass. I looked at him hard but could not make out his features. A blurry spot existed where his head should have been, the way the heads of criminals are reduced to digitized blocks on cop shows.

I said I didn't think it would fit. He persuaded me to try it on anyway. I could change here. No one was looking. There were a lot of people in the shop. The lights were very hot and bright, and there were mirrors everywhere.

"No, the shoe," I said. "I want to try the shoe."

Mom stood. "It's wrong—it's wrong, it's wrong!" she shrieked.

"Mom, stop it!" I shouted. "Would you just, for once, would you just stop!" I was screaming at her, screaming from some hot anger deep inside.

I sat back down and propped my left foot on my right knee. Taking my ankle in hand, I turned it slightly until a seam appeared in my skin. With a quick twist of my wrist, I took the whole foot off. It didn't hurt, but there was a momentary discomfort, the air bubble tension that exists before and just as you pop a bone. I had a screw in the stub of my leg that matched the hole in the foot, which was made of plastic. The attendant lifted up a small black box. Inside lay another foot, tan, with toenails painted red. I picked it up and clicked it on.

The attendant smiled—I could see his teeth now, the floating white smile of the Cheshire cat. "There." He opened his palms to the air. "You see?"

I woke up when Callapher kicked me in the side in her sleep. I lay in bed staring at the frothy tips of the broom-brushed plaster ceiling; the pointed crescents reminded me of peaked whipped cream on lemon pie.

The irony is that I first discovered the truth from a fashion magazine.

Kari bought Mollie and me issues of the latest teen magazine whenever we did an especially good job at keeping out of her hair in the office. For kicks, we read the Dear Ms. Suzie Q advice column aloud to each other.

Dear Ms. Suzie Q, I saw my ex kissing another girl in the hallway. Do you think he's over me? Dear Ms. Suzie Q, a girl at camp told me I'd get spider veins if I crossed my ankles. Is this true?

"Here's one," I said. We were sitting in the office facing each other, feet propped on each other's chairs. We'd just come in from filming the last scene of *Polymorphic Dudes from Space.* The scene involved a car chase that culminated in a very nasty crash, for which we'd pulled a matchbox car into the curb by a bit of string taped to its metallic underside. Mollie poured a little lighter fluid over it, and I tapped it with a lit match. You could see our hands in the video.

I glanced up at Mollie. "Listen to this: 'Sometimes I go to bed crying all night. It's embarrassing to spend the whole next day at school with puffy eyes. Is there a way to make the swelling go away?'"

Mollie made a face. "Because looking good's all that matters, of course."

The last Suzie Q was printed on the bottom of the page beside the photograph of a thin woman standing before a full-length mirror in her underwear, one hand flat on her flat belly. Beside it, the question ran:

Dear Suzie Q,

My best friend hardly eats. She's really skinny but still says she's fat, and anytime I try to bring it up, she gets angry and defensive. I think she might have an eating disorder. I feel like I need to do something, but I'm afraid telling her mother would ruin our friendship. What should I do?

Sincerely,
Worried in Wyoming

Suzie Q answered:

Dear Worried in Wyoming,

First, your concern is a testament to your friendship. It's good to know there are girls in the world who care for their friends so much. If your girlfriend is merely dieting a little too much and is worried about her appearance, try to boost her self-esteem. Tell her she looks nice in an outfit or compliment the changes in her figure.

Eating disorders, however, are quite different from healthy dieting. Not only are they emotionally and psychologically damaging, they can be very dangerous to a woman's body. If you think your friend is endorsing an unhealthy or even dangerous obsession with weight, you need to let someone know. A temporary breach in your friendship is a small sacrifice to make if your friend's health is in jeopardy. On the following page we've listed some symptoms and signs of eating disorders as a reference. If your friend exhibits as many as three of the symptoms, she may need professional help.

I glanced up at Mollie. She was drawing cartoon tigers on her math homework. I imagined her writing a letter to Ms. Suzie Q. It would begin: *I have this friend who doesn't eat. . . .*

I read through the listed signs of eating disorders, keeping score with pencil dots beside those symptoms that matched my own behavior. I kept the dots light and small so I could erase them. When I got to the bottom of the page, I tallied my score: anorexia.

I sat very still. In a way, it seemed I had already known. Looking at the word, I was overcome with a sense of recognition and familiarity, the feeling you get when you look at your own face in a mirror to find both a stranger and a twin looking back. Hastily, I erased the pencil marks I'd made on the page.

"What're you doing?" Mollie asked.

"A game," I lied. "I lost."

Anorexia.

When I typed the word into the computer at the library, a dozen titles appeared on the screen. I scribbled a few call numbers on a scrap of paper and shoved it quickly into my pocket.

My stomach turned queasy as I ran my fingers along the spines of the books. I remembered the pictures I'd seen in health class: women with bone-thin legs, bulging kneecaps. Breasts deflated to hang in empty flaps of skin. Gathering a small stack of books, I retreated to the most secluded corner of the library, where I sat staring at them for a few minutes, paralyzed.

I opened the first. There were photographs. Girls with arms and legs streamlined straight, their heads seeming too large, disproportionate to their bodies like the head of a fetus to its developing form: translucent skin, black bead eyes. A woman standing with her back to the photographer, arms outstretched as if she were a criminal to be searched. Her pelvis pointed sharply through her skin like the twin points of clavicle bones, the padding that should have been her thigh and buttocks having been sucked up tight into her body.

Girls stared up at me from the books with hungry, vacant eyes grown large against shrinking faces. Anxious for warmth and protection, they cradled themselves like infants, their breasts flat and their wombs dry. No longer women but children, they wrapped their arms around their figures to guard the hard-won pocket of air inside. My hands trembled as I turned the pages. I was a little kid watching a horror movie with my hands over my eyes, looking through my fingers—almost against my will. The way you look at car accidents on the highway. I was not like these women. I was *not*.

Then I heard my mother telling me to eat. I heard the doctor. How strange it had been at the time, his ability to anticipate my habits. For an entire week after that appointment, I'd racked my brain to figure out how he knew I made my bed every day. I felt ridiculous and embarrassed now for having thought him brilliant. His understanding was the product of education, not empathy, and certainly not telepathy. To him, I was just another condition from a page, another case study observed, analyzed, and categorized. Before my mind had come into its own, it had been dissected to fit into a textbook.

My conception of eating disorders had one shape, and my counting and anxieties and self-loathing another. Suddenly they began to merge, like a double image coming into focus. The torments of my mind and the source of my hell now fit into a prescribed form. They had always had a name.

With my head in my hands, I grasped at my hair, as if by pulling it out I could pluck the diseased thoughts, seeds festering in the roots of each strand. Then I'd be left with a scalp of pinholes, the head of a bald Barbie doll, with breathing holes for my brain.

"Excuse me, miss?" The librarian stood at the end of my table. "We'll be closing in ten minutes if you have anything you'd like to check out."

She glanced at my stack of books. I covered the titles quickly with my jacket.

"Thanks," I said.

When she was gone, I went back to the stacks and shelved each of the books in its proper place. I walked out the front door, averting my eyes from any that might be watching from behind the desk.

That night the Shoe Box was unbearably quiet. Mom and Callapher were with the Old Maids. At the dining room table, Dad worried a crossword puzzle. I paced in my bedroom anxiously, conscious of every printed eye staring at me from my wall. I needed to get out.

I told Dad I was going to the car lot to do some work for Kari. As I walked, I repeated the black word to myself to the rhythm of my footfalls. The skinny pointed A, the incising spit-wet X. *An-or-EX-i-a, an-or-EX-i-a, an-or-EX-i-a.* I tried to make it stick. I tried to hang it about my neck, a name tag or a label. But a part of me refused. I was overcome with a perverse desire to own this thing I'd created. It had to have its own name. It had to be mine, not some disorder shared by girls everywhere. I'd begotten a separate identity, the way ancient gods gave birth to offspring straight from their heads, in agony. I'd created this willpower that lived its own distinct existence, ruling over me.

And they'd already tamed it. In their white coats, scribbling notes in a lab, they'd named the parasite feeding off my body. I'd been betrayed. The one thing in my life that provided safety and promised glamour had made me the cloned replica of a thousand women, the poster face for a mental case.

The bell chimed over the door as I entered the office. I tapped on the small one-way mirror planted in the wall adjoining the garage.

"It's just me," I called to Gordon.

If I looked hard, I could discern shadows moving beneath the reflections, the intimation of the world behind the looking glass. I thought I saw the ghost of a hand wave back, but maybe it was my imagination.

"Hey," his voice called back. "I'll be there in a minute."

We hadn't done a thing in the office that week but film Matthew's movie. A foot-high stack of invoices sat piled on the front desk. I carried them to the kitchen table in the back and began organizing them into neat alphabetical stacks. The papers were soft at their corners. They stained my fingertips with the silvery residue of penciled words.

I'd been working for nearly an hour when the phone rang.

"Gordon, you want me to get that?" I called.

He didn't answer. The phone rang again.

"Gordon?"

After three more rings, the caller gave up. It was well after office hours, anyway. But no more than a minute later, the phone rang again. I sighed, got up, and went to the front desk.

"Bauer Auto Sales," I said. "How may I help you?"

"Olivia, it's me—"

Gordon entered the office. "Were you calling me?"

I held my hand up to him, alarmed by the urgency in the voice on the other end. "Mollie?" I asked. "What's wrong, you sound—"

She interrupted me: "He's here—he's been drinking."

Gordon started when I said Mollie's name. He reached for the phone, but I pulled away. "What is it?" he mouthed silently.

"Who?" I asked Mollie. "Who's at your house?"

"It's Simon. I was upstairs getting ready for bed when I heard his car on the lawn. He got out and started yelling. He's completely wasted. . . . Olivia, I'm scared, he's . . ."

"It's Simon," I told Gordon.

His expression hardened. "I'm going over," he said.

I said, "Gordon's coming. Hold on—we'll be there in a second."

"No," Mollie said, panicking. "Don't let him come by himself. Tell him not to—not by himself."

"I'm calling the police," I told her.

"Olivia, wait."

I heard a noise muffled through the receiver, the barely discernable sound of shattering glass.

"What was that?"

"I can't believe this is happening—"

"Mollie—what?"

"He broke the window downstairs—he threw something."

"Get upstairs." I looked around, but Gordon was already gone.

"I am upstairs. I'm locked in Mom's room. I can see him outside—he's pacing on the lawn."

"Mollie, Gordon's coming. I have to go—I have to call the police."

She tried to protest, but I hung up and dialed 911.

"Nine-one-one, please state the nature of your emergency."

"Someone's trying to break into my friend's house—it's a young guy, and he's drunk."

"Is he in the house?"

"I don't think so. He broke a window."

"Are you at the house, ma'am?"

"No, I'm in the neighborhood . . . it's . . ." I floundered for the address. "It's 1136 Ellis Lane—I think, but I'm not sure. It's on the end of town, behind the Bauer Used Car Lot, a big old farmhouse—green, with a wraparound veranda."

"Ellis Lane, 1136 . . . One moment, ma'am. Please stay on the line."

She gave directions to a policeman through a thick static, her voice small and far away. As soon as I heard her get out the name of the street, I dropped the phone and ran out the front door. At the clearing, I hid in the shadows of the last line of trees.

A young man stood on the lawn, and though I'd only seen him from above that one night weeks ago, I recognized him. The yellow of the porch light glared bright on his face and figure, casting an elongated shadow with arms stretched so they swept the length of the lawn when he spread out his hands. He climbed the porch steps and began pounding against the door.

"I know you're home!" Simon yelled. His words were thick and slurred. "And I just wanna talk . . . Just come out and talk. You've been ignoring me, and I don't like it. *Get out here!*"

He flung his arm wide through the air. The extravagant gesture was too much, and he tottered on his feet, nearly falling forward to the lawn.

"Come out and talk to me . . ."

I didn't see Gordon until he leapt on Simon. It was as if he appeared from thin air. At a breakneck run, he threw his broad arms around the younger man. Both fell to the porch in the impact of the collision. Simon floundered beneath Gordon's heavy weight, letting out a piercing shriek of surprise and anger. Gordon pinned his shoulders to the porch and punched him in the face—once, twice, again and again.

I ran to the house. Just as I reached the porch, Mollie burst through the front door.

"Stop it, Gordon!" she shouted. She grabbed his shoulders and pulled him back. "Stop it—you're hurting him!"

Blood covered Simon's face, but Gordon hit him again.

"Stop it!" Mollie screamed.

He looked up at her and blinked, as if waking from a dream. He dropped Simon against the porch and stood, his eyes trained on Mollie's, unflinching. "You all right?" he asked.

She nodded. "Yeah." She bit her lower lip, hugging herself tight. An involuntary intake of breath rattled her shoulders. "Yeah, I think so."

Gordon stepped over Simon. He put his arm around Mollie. "Let's go inside," he said, leading her back into the house.

Simon's lip was split, and his nose had already begun to swell. I was convinced it was broken. He rolled to the left, then right, as if gaining momentum. He tried to raise himself on his elbow but wobbled and fell back against the floor. Moaning, he turned his face away, opened his mouth, and threw up on himself and the porch.

Inside, I found Mollie and Gordon together on the couch. Mollie rocked back and forth, perched on the very edge of her seat. Gordon watched her anxiously but sat apart, his broad hands still at his sides. Simon's blood stained his knuckles.

They found Simon's car a mile down the road, nose-dived into a ditch. He'd been at a party out of town. It was a wonder, they said, that he'd managed to drive so far in his state.

"Especially on roads like these," Margaret said when she heard the news. "It's positively treacherous around here as soon as you pass the city limits."

That week I practically moved into the old farmhouse. Kari stayed out late almost every other night, and Mollie was too shaken to sleep alone. Mom said she could stay with us, but Mollie didn't want to be an imposition. She pulled a mattress out of the basement sofa bed, and together we carried it upstairs so I could sleep on the floor beside her bed.

Gordon duct-taped a black garbage bag across the broken window.

At night it bulged out and sucked in with the direction of the wind, like a lung filling and collapsing. He stopped by every night to check all the locks and make sure we were all right. Frankly, I didn't see the point of locking the front door with a hole in the window two feet away, but I didn't say anything. Gordon did it as much for himself as for us. I suppose it gave him some peace of mind. I was strangely in awe of Gordon that week. I couldn't forget what he'd done to Simon's face.

I had always thought Gordon liked Mollie. I hadn't realized that he loved her.

I mentioned this discovery to Matthew. We were sitting on my porch together, leaning against the house. He'd brought over his sketchbook and talked with his eyes fast on the horizon, scarcely looking down at the paper over which he scribbled briskly. When I told him about Gordon and Mollie, he was only surprised that it had taken me so long to notice.

"Gordon's had his eyes on her forever," he said.

"But he's so . . . *old*."

Matthew raised his eyebrows. "He's only twenty." He extended his right arm stiffly ahead, holding his pencil upright and squinting at it to measure the scale of a distant object. "Mollie's sixteen. Four years' difference. A lot of women end up with older men."

"But *women*," I retorted. "Not girls. Mollie's just a sophomore."

"I wouldn't worry about it," Matthew said. "The only other person besides you that doesn't know what's going on is Mollie herself. And if Gordon spends as much energy ignoring her this year as he did last, she'll never know."

Matthew seemed to think less of Gordon for his avoidance of the situation. I said good riddance; Mollie deserved better. Gordon was so . . . so dull and nice and kind. Not at all exciting and not necessarily attractive.

As if reading my thoughts, Matthew took up the subject again: "You know, Mollie might give him a chance if she knew."

"I don't think so."

"How do you know?"

"Because they've been friends forever."

"Friends become lovers all the time," he retorted, rather archly.

I felt his eyes on me but avoided his gaze. "Well, I don't think she'd go for him."

"Mollie Bauer, Mollie Baker," Matthew singsonged, returning attention to his drawing. "Wouldn't make much difference. Drop the U, add the K."

Seeing I was annoyed, he stopped. "Oh, well, it's for the better. Gordon will stay in Bethsaida forever. He'll be a fat old townie by his thirties."

I didn't answer. Hoping he would consider my question somehow unrelated, I waited a long while before musing aloud, "How is it that you always see the most gorgeous women with the most plain, unattractive men?"

He shrugged. "I guess girls are more forgiving. Pretty girls pick ugly guys all the time." He straightened up and began with a new breath as if opening an entirely new subject. "So you've got two types of people in this world: the attractive and the unattractive. Some unattractive people want to be attractive. If they're pathetic about it, they spend their lives hating the people that are; if they're ambitious, they try to make themselves beautiful—diet, exercise, plastic surgery, makeup." He said the word *makeup* as if it tasted bad.

"What is that thick crud girls put on their faces, anyway? Foundation? Is that what you call it? It's like they don't get the concept of airbrush. Nobody looks like the magazines. Cinematography, photography . . . a lot of mean tricks. People change on film."

He studied his drawing, cocking his head to the right and squinting his left eye. Then he selected a new pencil from the row he'd laid neatly beside him on the concrete slab, concluding, "A lot of makeup makes me nervous. Plain girls are more kissable."

"Liar," I shot back. "You're telling me that someday when you're a famous photographer shooting an ad in Europe with some drop-dead gorgeous Parisian, you wouldn't be attracted to her?"

"I didn't say that," he replied calmly. "I said plain girls are more kissable. A guy will have a fantasy about the Parisian model, but he doesn't imagine waking up next to her in the morning."

I watched his face, the way he pinched his lips tight when he was concentrating. So that's why he liked me: I was plain. Great.

That night I stayed at Mollie's again. Sleeping on the pull-out bed mattress made me think of cottage cheese. I rolled on my side, punched the pillow in, and resituated myself on the lumpy makeshift bed.

"Are you still awake?" Mollie whispered.

"Yeah."

"I can't sleep."

"Me either."

There was a silent pause. I heard the shifting of bedclothes, then looked up to see the outline of Mollie's face forming to visibility over my own. I was so surprised, I started, nearly hitting my forehead against hers.

"Sorry," she whispered. She got out of her bed and lay down on the mattress with me. I pitched the covers up to let her in. We lay with our heads on the single pillow. Her hair brushed my cheek. It was stiff with gel, rough at its spiky tips like broom bristles.

"Your feet are cold," she said.

"They're always that way."

"You always look cold," she said.

"What do you mean?"

"I don't know . . . you always look . . . bundled up. You hug yourself when you walk around."

For some reason my heart began to pound. There was the word: *anorexia*. I wondered if Mollie knew. I opened my mouth, but something different from what I'd expected came out: "What really happened between you two?"

"Me and . . . ?"

"Simon," I supplied.

"We broke up." She shrugged.

"But why does Gordon hate him so much?"

Mollie laughed. "Gordon doesn't *hate* anybody. I don't think he's capable of it."

"Well, you didn't see his face when he was beating Simon up. I'm telling you, he was enjoying himself."

"That's stupid."

"I'm serious. What's he got against Simon?"

Mollie shrugged evasively. "He just never liked him. He thinks he's a bad influence. He always thought I could do better."

She was silent so long, I resigned myself to this inadequate answer. Outside, the wind chimes hanging from the veranda caught in the breeze. They played a brief string of discordant notes. I could almost hear the trash bag on the broken window breathing in, out, sucked through the broken glass with a wet *sfwap*.

I was nearly asleep when Mollie said, "Olivia—do you ever . . . Have you ever had something you wish for all the world you could take back? Just one thing."

I blinked in confusion. For a moment I wasn't sure if she'd really spoken or if I had been dreaming. "Say what?" I asked.

She propped herself on her elbow and leaned in close, whispering: "Do you have things you regret . . . ? You know: secrets."

Slowly, my thoughts sifted from dreams to coherence. There was a strange and trembling urgency in her voice.

"What do you mean?"

"I don't know." She lay back down. "It's nothing."

I wanted to stop there. I wanted to pretend it really was nothing and go to sleep. I played the word in my head again, my word, the word that made me, the sharp A and X. Anorexia.

I said, "Tell me."

Mollie sighed. It was a sigh of resignation, the realization that she could not retract. She said, "I've never told anybody this. I don't even know if it's true. I mean, I know it happened, but sometimes . . . but I can't remember it well. I was drunk."

"Remember what?"

We were whispering.

"I was at a party with my girlfriend Chelsea. It was just after Simon and I had broken up, maybe a month or two. He was at the party, him and two of his friends. It was the first time we'd seen each other since the breakup, and when I went to say hi, he just turned and walked away from me—looked through me like I wasn't even there. It killed me, Olivia. So I drank myself stupid. He left at some point, but his two friends were there. Big guys."

I felt her shiver next to me.

"James and Eric, I think. They were drunk, but not as far gone as I was. They told me they'd take me to him. It's like black patches in my memory: I see some things and not others. As if the memories have been erased, or like they aren't there at all . . . Don't you think that's weird? How our brains work? How you can hold on to some things forever, and other things that were right there before your eyes are gone?"

She was starting to scare me a little. I reached my hand across the bed, just to touch her, but she clasped her palm to mine and squeezed painfully tight.

"What happened?" I asked.

"I went with them in their car—then I don't remember things exactly. But we couldn't have gone anywhere, because when I woke up the next morning I was still at the Barkers' house, where we had the party, on their living room floor. I wouldn't have thought anything of it, except that Chelsea was all worried. She said she hadn't seen me after one and was freaking out all night because no one knew where I'd gone. I told her nothing had happened, that I'd been at the party all night. Then I remembered—like a part of a dream—I remembered getting in their car, and a face over mine . . . I remembered waking up what must have been a long time later . . ."

She stopped. I couldn't see her face; I only realized she was crying when I heard the tears in her gasp for breath.

"I was lying in the backseat. But my pants . . ."

This time I think my heart did stop. I realized what she was trying to tell me.

"Mollie—are you sure?"

She shook her head. "I don't know."

I didn't know what to do. She clenched my hand so tight, I felt it would break beneath the pressure. Freeing my hand, I put my arm around her. She held me tight, burying her face under my chin. Her tears soaked through my shirt until it clung wet to my skin.

"Maybe it was just a dream," I said. "Maybe nothing happened."

She shook her head. "No . . . no. I say maybe it's not real. I say maybe it's just a dream." She sobbed. "But I remember, Olivia. Just that one minute. But I saw him over me. I *remember*."

I had nothing to say. It felt wrong to even hold her. Clearly, as if it had physical shape, I saw my envy of her beauty rising up to condemn me. I despised myself for all the times I'd hated her on account of the body she had, a body that she'd never asked for, an object that on the nearly forgotten night had been as separate from herself as the mannequin on display beneath the car lot lights.

Eventually she calmed down. "I can feel your ribs," she said, clasping me tighter. She said it without surprise and without judgment. Stated it merely as fact.

I never felt more close to her and never so far away. She had told me everything.

In return, I told her nothing.

part three

CHAPTER 14

collage

(kol LAJ)

1. An artistic composition of materials and objects pasted over a surface, often with unifying lines and color. From *coller* (French) = to paste

a woman dressed as a mermaid glides beneath the surface of the water, her bare belly flat as she stretches to look over her shoulder. Her hair billows behind as she gazes upward to the light with thick lips pursed, the scales of her tail translucent.

A woman wearing a black coat with a high collar crawls along a marble floor, her right leg extended back, her body resting on the knee of the left. On both feet she wears stiletto heels. Because of her position and because she is wearing nothing but black lingerie beneath the coat, her legs are exposed. She stares with the alert hunger of an animal, with eyes rimmed in black.

A woman in a top hat stands facing forward like a criminal for a mug shot. Her mouth is parted slightly to breathe out, to take in.

These were the pictures glued to my wall.

Pictures of beautiful women surface even in my earliest memories. When I was small enough to fit in my father's lap, he read to me from a book of collected fairy tales. It was thick as the E section of his encyclopedia collection, with a white cover and gold calligraphy. Inside were pretty princesses in pink dresses, followed by their ladies-in-waiting. Ladies-in-waiting meaning, of course, women in suspense. Women waiting: women hoping. Who's the fairest of them all? Someday my prince will come.

I would lay my cheek against Dad's button-up shirts, feel his voice reverberating in his chest and then vibrating in my ear. I heard him twice: the voice from his lips and the echo inside. He read to me until the black blurbs on the page became words, and I could read the stories myself. Though there was no need; I had long since memorized each.

Sometimes Dad made up his own fairy tales. He'd start with something like, "Once upon a time, in a land far, far away near here, lived a queen who wanted a child. One day she gave birth to a little girl who had hair as black as a raven and skin as white as snow. 'I'll call her Snow White,' she said. When Snow White was big enough, the queen sent her through the woods to visit her grandma and take her some Metamucil muffins. But on the way she ran into a big bad wolf, who said, 'I'll huff and I'll puff and I'll blow your house down.' "

I would get mad and tell him he was saying it wrong. He'd reply, "Are you telling this story, or am I?"

If I was good at the grocery store, Mom let me pick something out from the candy rack at the cash register. But what I really liked were the bridal magazines. If Mom was feeling generous, and if I'd been especially obedient, she'd purchase one of the inch-thick magazines. I'd lug it home, take it to my bedroom, and spend hours poring over the pictures. I liked to pretend that all the models inside were princesses. They were all sisters. I had to pick the prettiest one, because it was always the prettiest one who got the prince.

In the bathroom, I would scrub my face until it turned red, trying to rub away the faint mole beside my nose, trying to wash out the imperfect blush in my cheeks—trying to make my skin as flawless as the women's in the magazines, as cream-clear as the watercolor skin of Snow White, crisp between the outlines of her face as it lay printed upon the page.

Now, so many years later, I can see the fear beginning to take shape in little girls' eyes. I see their furtive glances at the magazines, the gleam of something like lust that shines in their eyes as they feed on the glossy pages. I see them stand behind a beautiful woman and trace the lines of her figure with their eyes, holding their crossed arms tight over their own bodies. I see them searching through advertisements for cologne, shampoo, dental bleach, lipstick, dish detergent, tennis shoes, tight abs, and lingerie—hoping to find their own faces.

Looking at pictures of yourself is like hearing your own voice play back from an answering machine. You know your voice as it exists warm and in your head—but that sound coming out of that machine is loud and full, low and stupid. Is it really the voice everyone else hears? Pictures are like that. I looked at photographs of myself in surprise, because the shapes looking back did not reflect the shape of my soul as I knew it: all the warmth, the desire, the brilliance, the despair burning inside me.

Mom kept our family photo albums in chronological order atop Dad's oak bookshelf. We had to wash our hands before looking at the pictures. I always liked looking at the ones taken of my parents shortly after they first met. The world was different then, smaller, tinted with a golden ambience, as if each photograph had been stained in tea. In the photos, my mother's hair is long—black wavy locks that nearly reach her waist. Dad's shirts are unbuttoned at the top. He wears jeans with gold medallion buckles the size of ashtrays. From the albums he has been solidified in my memory as a man happy to be outside, energetic and always laughing. There is Dad holding up a walleye he caught while fishing with his brother. Dad shaving his head to play Lex Luther for Halloween. Dad lighting a birthday cake for his mother with a blowtorch.

During his years in seminary and after his graduation, my father's pictures change. He begins to wear white collared shirts, red ties tight around his Adam's apple, black suits with box shoulder pads. He looks up from his office chair, his complexion pale, an expression of surprise on his face, as if caught off guard that anyone has found him there . . . as if bewildered by the fact that the large oak desk in the room with the maroon carpet is the end of the line, the culmination and extermination of dreams.

Dad was to begin teaching at the end of August. The first of the month, he woke up at nine and drove to Bethsaida Christian Academy, where he remained until dinnertime. He repeated this schedule the next day and the next. It was good to see him leave in the morning and come home in the evening looking tired and relieved. The Working Father.

But my happiness with the new arrangement was purely selfish. I'd seen his place of employment, and I felt for him. The school boasted classes K–12, the combined attendance of which had never exceeded 175. All classes were held in the two-story brick building adjoining the Old Maids' church. From its pipes came the rank odor of neglected plumbing. I couldn't pass the building without a sense of malaise following me like the trail of that singular, dank smell.

Due to limited space, Dad shared a classroom with another teacher, who came to visit that first sweltering week of August. When the doorbell rang, I found him standing on the porch behind a cumbersome fruit basket packed in plastic wrap gathered at the top in a red bow nearly as large as his head. He was short and balding, freckled on the hands and cheeks; but his age seemed most evident, somehow, in the tweed jacket he wore, beige and rough and heavily patched at the elbows.

"Is this the Monahans'?" he asked.

"Yeah," I said. "Can I help you?"

"I'm Mr. Oreck," he said. "I come bearing gifts. Compliments of Mrs. Oreck."

"Tell him to come in," Dad said, joining me at the door. "Claire—company!"

Mom entered the living room, wiping her hands dry on her jeans. She looked at Dad questioningly.

"Pat Oreck," the little man said, extending his hand.

Mom exclaimed at the sight of the fruit, hurrying to relieve him of the burden. "Mr. Oreck, you shouldn't have."

"Not my idea," he said. "All the wife's doing. And please, it's Pat."

"Would you like some coffee?" Mom asked. "Something to eat?"

He accepted the offer of coffee but politely refused any food. So Mom went directly to the kitchen and began cutting banana bread into squares, then fanning them in rows on her prettiest pink crystal plate.

"I don't want to intrude," said Mr. Oreck. "I only wanted to stop by and say hello, welcome you to the school." He sat delicately upon the edge of the couch as if to demonstrate his intention of departing quickly. Despite his protestations, he gladly accepted his cup of coffee and even helped himself to a slice of buttered bread. Mom smilingly placed the platter well within her guest's reach upon the coffee table and joined Dad on the love seat, crossing her legs to put them at best advantage.

Dad and Pat talked awhile about the classroom, about the curriculum, about the principal—a balding man who donned a red baseball cap every morning and afternoon to drive the school bus. They spoke of the colors of the walls.

"Nobody likes a blank wall. I don't," Mr. Oreck asserted. "White walls—so uninspiring. If it weren't for the school board, I'd have painted every inch a good bright yellow by now. Or blue, I hear, has a calming effect. I once knew a lady who painted her office bright yellow. Every time you walked into the room you had the distinct impression of having stepped into the great outdoors—back to sunshine, to brightness. That was Mrs. Polaski. She was the secretary of the school nearly fifteen years, then left without so much as a notice." Unexpectedly, he turned to me and winked. "A complaint against the basic immodesty of the new uniforms, I believe."

I had just been getting ready to leave the room, but this inexplicable gesture seemed an invitation to stay. Strangely, I found it welcoming.

"Well, hello," said Mr. Oreck, setting his cup down on the coffee table. "Who have we here?"

He spoke to Callapher, who had entered the living room wearing two star stick-on earrings, a plastic pearl necklace, red lipstick, and mother's white lingerie nightgown, the V-cut of the neck exposing a triangle of skin that ended at her belly button.

"And what is your name, mademoiselle?" Mr. Oreck asked.

"Cecilia Valentine," she replied. "I'm going to the ball."

"A ball? Oh, but you can't go to the ball," he said solemnly. "You haven't any glass slippers."

Callapher lifted the nightgown to consider her bare feet. "It's a barefoot ball," she explained. "What's wrong, Mommy?"

"Nothing, dear," Mom said, standing abruptly to take Callapher by the hand. "Why don't you show Mommy where you put your own clothes." They disappeared quickly down the hallway.

Despite the brief embarrassment, Mom seemed to brighten significantly after Mr. Oreck's visit. Her cheeks looked flushed and bright in the sunlight as she stood at the front window watching his car drive off. "I like him," she pronounced.

"Looks like it's going to be a more pleasant arrangement than I'd anticipated," Dad agreed.

Mom thought a moment before saying decidedly, "We should have company over more often."

"We have the Old Maids every other day," Dad replied.

"They're family. I mean real company. Do you remember the Christmas parties we used to give?"

"I couldn't possibly forget: you turning the house upside down for a month and baking until there wasn't an open spot left on the kitchen counter. And every time afterwards swearing never to do it again."

Mom sighed wistfully, letting the curtain fall. "Seems like a very long time ago."

She and Dad spent what remained of summer arguing the matter of Callapher's education. As the daughter of faculty, she was eligible for a scholarship to the private school. Dad said it was silly to send her to another new place just after she'd grown accustomed to one, but Mom argued that the Christian school would be a better environment.

"Better, how?" Dad asked. "She'll be in a roomful of strangers again. One move is enough. Besides, the classes are small. There're only fifteen first-graders this year."

"Exactly," Mom replied. "She'll get that much more attention from the teacher. She won't have to compete with thirty other kids." Mom was also a die-hard fanatic on the subject of Bible literacy. She was all about cramming young heads full of Scripture. *Instruct a child in the way he should go, and when he is old he will not turn from it.*

"I don't see why you insist on keeping her in the public school system," she said, "when you know she'd get a better education in a private institution."

Dad pointed his forefinger. "That is entirely speculation."

"I think you should just admit this isn't about Callapher," Mom retorted.

"I don't know what you mean."

"You know exactly what I mean, Benjamin, and don't pretend otherwise. I won't let your cynicism jeopardize her education."

Dad insisted that Callapher didn't need any more Bible instruction. "She's been soaked to her saturation point."

His case in point: we were in the living room one night when we heard Callapher singing from behind the closed bathroom door. She'd disappeared a half hour before, book in hand.

Mom looked up from her desk. "What do you think she's doing in there?" she asked.

"I haven't the foggiest," Dad murmured. His reading glasses slid down his nose. He pushed them back up again.

The song got louder. Dad looked up and listened. Callapher was singing the words of *Horton Hears a Who* to the tune of "A Mighty Fortress Is Our God."

"Oh, for heaven's sake," Dad said.

She reached the last punch of the chorus: "Because a person's a person no matter how small!" The toilet flushed.

"My dear," Dad said to Mom. "I think we may satisfy ourselves:

we have successfully brainwashed our children."

Two weeks later, Callapher returned to the public elementary across from the high school.

I was grateful for the beginning of the semester and the return to the busyness of school. Routine saved me from depression, compartmentalizing the days into manageability. I was treading water: moving a lot, keeping my head above the surface, but not going anywhere.

Each morning, Mollie picked me up for school. She drove a different car every other week. By mid-September, I'd served two detentions for tardies. Matthew and I had painting and drawing class the last three hours of school, after which I went right to the car lot to work from then till anywhere from five to close.

On weekends the three of us went to town to see dollar student movie specials at what Mollie dubbed the Sticky Floor Theatre. She also named the employees. The candy counter clerk with ghostly pale skin and black, greasy hair was Gravy Girl. The late-night manager with the beer belly and dirty blond rattail was The Hedgehog King.

Matthew pointed out that he didn't think it very Christian of Mollie to call people names. She replied that she only called them names behind their backs, and if they wanted they could call her Pumpkin Head if they liked.

"Pumpkin Head?" I asked.

"Yeah, Pumpkin Head. Don't you think my head is huge?"

I'd never heard Mollie say anything remotely self-conscious before. "No, I don't think your head's huge. What are you talking about?"

"I've got this stick figure and then this big, round face. Like a pumpkin on a pole."

She drew me a picture on a napkin: a stick figure topped by an exaggerated bubble with eyes and a crooked smile. "See." She held the napkin up beside her face and smiled. Through her teeth she added, "Just like me."

Despite her brief show of self-deprecation, Mollie didn't seem to think it such a big deal to have a pumpkin head. There wasn't a moment in her presence that I forgot her beauty, but sometimes she'd make me laugh hard enough to forget my own lack thereof. It was good to laugh, and it was good to see her every day. Until Mollie, I'd never had a girlfriend I considered an essential part of my life. The only time I didn't welcome her company was on Sunday mornings.

I suppose it was nice to have someone else to sit with besides my mother, but Mollie's enthusiasm for church made me uncomfortable. She listened intently to Pastor Evans's sermons. She sang all the hymns. She even went down to the altar to pray with people. Occasionally she missed service to volunteer in children's church downstairs. I was always glad for those mornings. Her absence absolved my responsibility for what was said from the pulpit; if she wasn't there to hear it, she couldn't talk about it afterwards. I'd had enough from the pulpit all my life. *I* could give the sermon, if it came to it.

Matthew was weird about me going to church. "I didn't think you were into that sort of thing," he said skeptically.

I laughed at the peculiar expression on his face. "What do you mean, 'that sort of thing'?"

He grinned at my response, but it seemed forced. I saw the bewilderment in his eyes.

"You know, going to church, praying, all that. Jesus Christ and save my soul." He clasped his hands to his chest, rolling his eyes upward. "Bleeding hearts of the world."

"No." I rolled my eyes. "I'm not into 'bleeding hearts' and 'save my soul.' Seriously."

Later, it occurred to me that I'd omitted the name Jesus Christ, and that perhaps doing so had not been entirely unconscious. I could hate Pastor Evans's sermons and grimace at the hymns and roll my eyes at the Styrofoam-bread-square-grape-juice Communion. But somehow I couldn't defame Christ. Call it brainwashing, call it superstition, but to mock His name for approval would have been like cheating an honest man of his reputation with malicious slander. I didn't like church, but I didn't have to spit on Jesus.

"If you don't believe all that, why do you go?" Matthew persisted. "Isn't that hypocrisy?"

"No," I retorted. "I don't say that I believe those things."

He shrugged. "So quit church."

"Why are you picking on me about this?" I demanded. "Mollie gets all excited about church, and you never bug her."

"Because she's into it," he shot back. "I may not get *why* Mollie likes it, but at least she's honest about what she believes. You hate church, but you go anyway."

"Mom wouldn't understand if I didn't," I said.

"Tell her to get over it."

I frowned at him. "Look, she's had a hard enough time. If I quit church, she'll think I've gone to the dark side. She'll freak out."

"Suit yourself. But it sounds like hypocrisy to me."

What Matthew said really bothered me. I'd long felt justified in my spite for hypocrites; I'd never considered myself a member of the club.

But I couldn't bother with my eternal soul just then. It was hard enough to get up every morning and deal with the mortal body.

CHAPTER 15

halloween marked my first acquaintance with Beauregard's mother. By a freakish stroke of misfortune, she once again found herself homeless at Margaret's doorstep.

Callapher had spent that week begging Mom to let her join the Speldman boys trick-or-treating.

"Where on earth will you go?" Mom asked. "To the trailer park and the Old Maids'? We live in the most secluded neighborhood in town. You'd get more candy if you just took your pillowcase up to the Dairy Mart and spent five dollars."

Remembering something Dad used to say in his sermons, Callapher promptly replied, "Yes, but Mother, it's the principle of the thing."

Dad was so amused by this, he promised to take Callapher out trick-or-treating all night, just the two of them. When it came to costumes, he suggested she dress as Princess Leia. "We can pin two cinnamon buns to your head and wrap you in white bedsheets."

Callapher said she'd rather be a kitten or a ghost but couldn't make up her mind between them. She deliberated all week and finally decided to dress as both, creating an elaborate story of how she'd been a happy little house cat crossing the street when she got "ranned over" by a semitruck and died instantly.

Mollie and I dressed as fat old men. We dusted our hair and eyebrows with baby powder and wore extra large plaid button-ups stuffed with pillows. Using one of Mom's old eyeliners, I drew wrinkle lines in our foreheads and down the corners of our mouths. We were still dressing when the doorbell announced Matthew's arrival.

Mollie opened the door and looked him up and down. "Where's your costume?" she demanded.

He looked over her shoulder to meet my eyes, saying with feigned blankness, "We're dressing up?"

Mollie said we weren't leaving until he put on something. "I know," she exclaimed. "We could do you as a woman!"

He said an emphatic no.

She scrounged up a white bedsheet. "Cut some holes in it and be a ghost."

"This will do fine," he replied, tying the corners of the sheet about his neck.

Mollie looked at him with her hand on her jutted hip. "What's that supposed to be?"

He flicked the knot with his forefinger. "A cape."

"Cape of what?"

He frowned. "What do you mean, cape of what? It's not a cape *of* something. It's a cape."

"Of good? Of evil? Are you supposed to be some new super hero?"

Matthew said he didn't see why it really mattered.

"Well, fine, we'll call you Poop. Mr. Party Poop."

Mollie drove us to town so we could walk the more crowded neighborhood behind the main strip of downtown shops. We covered every street, Mollie and Mr. Poop arguing half the time about the importance of childhood rituals like wearing costumes. When he said he was tired, she began to protest and looked to me for support, but I sided with the Poop. I was exhausted from all the walking under the weight of my three-pillowed belly and butt, and I was more than a little annoyed with their absurd argument. Mollie finally said we could stop if we got food, so we went to Waffle House for pancakes.

Halfway through dinner, we heard the sound of sirens approaching from a distance. The noise grew nearer until they passed with the flashing of blue and red on the street just outside our window. Moments later, a fire engine followed the cruiser, its great horn bleating.

"Probably a child dying somewhere," Matthew mused. He raised his eyebrows, lifting a candied apple from his bag as case in point. "Poisoned."

"Look at that," Mollie said, her face pressed against the window. She pointed.

We ran outside. An orange-pink haze lay thick on the horizon, glowing from beneath with light that pulsed in the steady rhythm of a drumbeat.

"Do you think it's a bonfire?" she asked.

Matthew said, "More like a fire, fire. We ought to go check it out."

I argued against this idea. "How will you know where it's at?"

Mollie frowned. "It's over the car lot."

"Is not," Matthew retorted.

"Let's get out of here," I interrupted, sick to death with both of them.

We drove to my house. Dad stood on the lawn, looking over the roof at the brightening light. He was talking on the phone, in and of itself an aberration of nature.

"No, I just got off the phone with her. She says she'll stay with Ruby until you get back. Do you need anything?" he asked. "Of course . . . certainly."

Mollie and I ran to his side.

"There was a fire at the motel," he explained, his hand over the receiver. "Spread through the whole complex."

"Who are you talking to?" I asked.

"It's Margaret. She's at the motel. Beauregard's mother is going to stay with her for the night."

"I better go make sure Mom's up," Mollie said.

"It's a good three miles from the car lot," Dad assured her.

Mollie knew this but hurried off anyway. Matthew followed, saying something about borrowing a car to get some pictures.

Callapher came out to stand with us, her nose and cheeks a raw pink where she'd rubbed her skin clean of makeup. We watched the sky colors blend and morph with the liquid pastel of a watercolor. Mom found us on the lawn when she returned home. She was on foot, carrying a plastic bowl half full of caramels and bubblegum.

"Did she get in okay?" Dad asked. "She" being Mrs. Lowett.

Mom nodded wearily. "They were trying to find her a good change of clothes for the night when I left." She joined us; together we silently watched the night sky as if it were the evening television feature.

"Can you believe it?" she asked, propping one hand on her hip, crossing the other over her waist. The gesture seemed somehow protective. "Some people never get a break."

The next day was bright. The beautiful sunshine and crisp, sweet air made the strangeness of the previous night all the more foreign. The fire itself seemed far away and impossible. But there was Mrs. Lowett as proof of the ordeal.

She was seated at the Old Maids' kitchen table when I stopped by in the afternoon to take Callapher home for dinner. She looked older than I'd expected, a short, stout woman with mushroom-colored patches beneath her eyes. Her wiry gray hair lay in unteased curls molded exactly to the shape of a large curling iron. She wore a green-striped T-shirt beneath a heavy sweater, the thick knit collar fanned flat on her shoulders. I could smell the acrid stink of smoke heavy on her clothes.

"Olivia, Mrs. Barbara Lowett," Margaret introduced us.

"Pleased to meet you, ma'am," I said.

Mrs. Lowett extended her hand, but she didn't look at me. I accepted the greeting; her hand felt moist and shapeless in mine.

"Pleased to meet you," she said.

I was anxious to get Callapher and leave, afraid that our presence made the woman more self-conscious, but the moment I sat down she began a detailed account of the fire, glorying in the shock of her own misfortune and demanding due sympathy.

"All I got," she said, gesturing toward the things now carefully organized in a cardboard box from Margaret's basement. "Couldn't grab nothing more. I was sleeping in my chair, watching my show, and the alarm goes off loud enough to split your head. I run outside and see my neighbor's roof—that would be Patty—smoking black, with big flames all over. So I run back inside and just pick up everything I can carry in two hands, and that's all I got. I got a picture—"

She rummaged through the box to produce a silver-framed photograph of herself and a young man I assumed was her husband. I'd never heard of Beauregard's father.

"That's Jeremiah," she said, tapping the man's face with the flat of her forefinger. "S'all I got now, just a picture of him." She dabbed at either eye with the corner of a Kleenex.

Margaret came up from behind. "Now, don't you worry," she said, laying a hand on Mrs. Lowett's round shoulder. "It'll be all right in the end. Beauregard's got more of your things—remember? A whole row of pictures we set him up with when he first moved in."

Mrs. Lowett's lips straightened at the mention of her son's name. "Don't even know who the pictures are of. I can take them back, and I *will* take them back," she asserted indignantly. "No point in him having them if he can't bother to acknowledge them as his own flesh and blood."

Margaret gave me a look of warning: don't say anything. The gesture was unnecessary. As soon as Callapher appeared, I took her hand and we left the house.

Mrs. Lowett remained at the Old Maids' for two weeks. Each day, Margaret drove her to and from work. She slept in the spare bedroom upstairs and sat in the living room evenings watching *Jeopardy* and *Wheel of Fortune* with Ruby.

She never spoke to her son, but the disregard was mutual. Beauregard went about his typically mysterious daily affairs without once acknowledging her presence. Though his manner lacked spite, this casual dismissal of his own mother was far more disturbing to me than any blatant exhibition of hatred. She might as well have been a new piece of furniture unworthy of comment, a fly on the wall not worth swatting.

Of course, I was beyond surprise when it came to Beauregard's behavior. It was Mom's reaction I hadn't anticipated. She made a pot of soup and a pan of cornbread and carried both to the Old Maids in a picnic basket. On the table she left a note saying she'd do anything she could to be of help. The small contribution was her only comment on Margaret's newest resident.

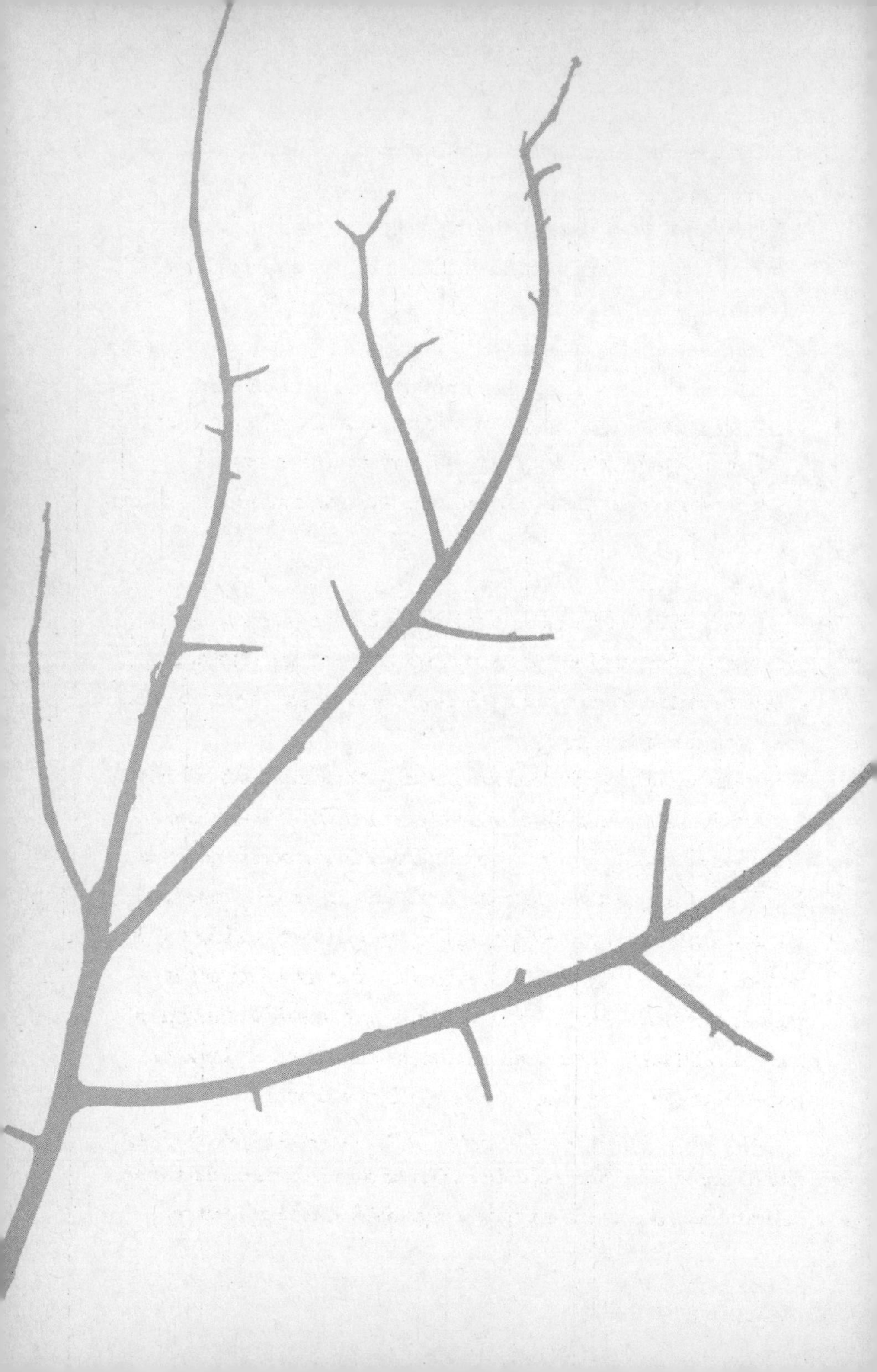

CHAPTER 16

scale

(skayl)

1. A system of ordered marks at fixed intervals used as a reference
2. An instrument or device used in such measurement
3. A progressive classification of size, amount, importance, or rank

i measured the changes in my body by the increasing tightness of my pants, by the disappearing shadows that once outlined the contour of my breastbone. I fought the temptation to step on the scale.

Scales are like the cardinal sin of eating disorders. With effort, I ignored the existence of the one-by-two-foot plank of plastic and metal stored under the sink, with a little face of numbers and a red needle bouncing in its vacuum like the bubble in a level. I imagined standing on it and the needle flying up. One hundred and fifteen? One hundred and twenty? More? Standing in the shower, water beads bouncing off my clenched eyelids, I barred my fists tight. I imagined the scale and said, "Get behind me, Satan," then laughed. I prided myself that I was cultivating a sense of the ridiculous.

And some days it was ridiculous. I could almost see it: the absurdity of measuring your worth by inches of skin. But some days were unbearable. If I counted them on a calendar, I would say that by

November I was having two, maybe three days each week when the myriad moods of my twelve waking hours averaged out to what you could feasibly call good. Two to three days when I managed three meals and more without any crippling anxiety, when I ate without my stomach swelling and aching in revolt, when I went to bed and only had to count once before falling asleep.

Maybe an outsider wouldn't consider three days out of seven that great. But I wasn't shooting for great. I was thankful for anything above survival. And two or three out of seven was better than none. Normality, in all its robust, unthinking glory, seemed impossible.

I was most content at the drawing board or easel; in the effort of concentration my thoughts went blank as white noise. I needed the brief escape. I imagined the rest of my life progressing from one point of discovery to another, a forward momentum propelled by the energy in my chest that rose fresh as birdsong each morning. Motionless, but for the swoop of my hand and the darting of my eye, I flew forward in a steady rush of anticipation.

It was this same passion in Matthew that made his presence, and his alone, tolerable when I worked. I couldn't stand to have anyone watch me paint or draw, but it felt right to have Matthew working beside me, complicit in the act of creation. We ate lunch together every day and sat beside each other in drawing class. I could sit whole hours without speaking, just feeling safe with the reassuring rhythm of his drawing hand beside mine.

When I got to class one Tuesday, Matthew beckoned to me from Lori's office door. "She wants to talk to us," he explained.

Lori looked up at us from her desk. "The fall concert is this

Friday," she said. "All the little kiddies and high schoolers will be showcasing their choirs. Usually we hang up artwork—so people will have something to entertain them while they stand around with their punch, I suppose. Anyway, we're doing it big this year. The elementary and junior high are participating, so I'm going to need extra help hanging the work. You'd get the whole day Thursday excused from classes, then you'd stay after to finish whatever's left. The other art instructors are coming—we'll order pizza or something. And I know both of you have pieces that won't embarrass me, so I'll let you choose your own wall and decide what to hang from your own work. At least there're some things we can be proud of in this school."

She slapped Matthew twice on the arm. It was a mechanical gesture. I always imagined Lori had to practice affection the way other people practice piano or learn foreign languages.

"So. Are you available?"

"Sure," Matthew said.

"I think so," I followed.

"Good." She clapped her hands together once. "Come see me Thursday morning, first thing. I'll have a note to excuse you from classes."

Matthew and I returned to our shared table in the drawing room.

"Hey," he said.

"What?"

"They're playing that new film I was telling you about at the Sticky Floor. D'you wanna go?"

"When?" I asked, with what I hoped was an opaque expression. I didn't want him to see my reluctance.

"I was thinking tonight. There's a seven o'clock and a nine thirty. But you probably can't do the late one with your curfew."

"I don't know," I said, annoyed at his mention of my parents' rules. I knew he didn't mean to be condescending, but I hated the way *curfew* came out of his mouth.

He leaned back in his chair to consider me, crossing his arms complacently over his chest. "What else could you possibly have to do? You and Mollie have to braid each other's hair or something?"

I frowned. Fine. "I get off work at six tomorrow," I said. "You can pick me up at my house."

"Quarter to seven?" he asked, brightening immediately. I'd been forgiven.

I nodded.

Since the summer, Matthew had developed the habit of calling now and then, asking would I like to see a movie or get food. As comfortable as I felt with him while working, there was an awkwardness to anything we did alone outside of class. At school everyone else shared the table. At the car lot Mollie's laughing commentary kept our conversations animated. But when it was just the two of us, his eagerness to stand nearly touching me alarmed me every time. I liked being with him when his eyes studied his paper; I did not know what to do when his eyes studied mine.

I said nothing of these feelings to Mollie, and I tried my best not to encourage Matthew's interest. But just when I thought he'd given up, he'd call again, sometimes weeks after our last date. Each time he called, I was convicted of having once again led him along just enough.

The next night, I sat beside him in the movie theatre, conscious of our arms brushing on the slim, shared armrest between us. My shoe bottoms stuck to the tacky floor.

"Do you want some food?" he asked.

"Sure," I whispered back.

He returned fifteen minutes later with a large soda and a tub of piping hot popcorn. I ate some, chewing each of the kernels slowly. They left my fingers and lips shiny with grease. His knuckles brushed mine when I reached for more. I pulled back my hand, aware that his gesture had been purposeful.

It was difficult to pay any attention to the film. It was long and quiet, and I was acutely aware of the arrangement of my legs: crossed, feet flat, or ankles tucked. By the time we left, I was exhausted from the effort of trying to appear nonchalant.

"That was a bust," I said enthusiastically. I meant the film, but realized after the fact that he might interpret my comment as a judgment on the date as a whole. So I added, "It's been forever since I've seen a good movie."

"It was fairly abominable," he said, head bowed down.

"You finish our homework for Lori yet?"

He answered dully. He was being weird. He didn't banter eagerly or volunteer some new stupid joke to keep up conversation when I fell silent. Instead, he quick-stepped toward the car, hands shoved deep in his pockets, his brow furrowed as if in concentration.

He parked on the street just before the Shoe Box driveway. We hadn't said five words together since leaving the theatre.

"Thanks for the movie," I said, grabbing at the door handle as if it were a lifesaver.

"Sure," he said to the steering wheel.

"Well. I'll see you tomorrow."

As I opened the door, he reached across and placed his hand on mine. He said, "Olivia," then thought better, closed his mouth, and kissed mine.

I watched it coming, as if in slow motion—and I let him do it. His lips felt warm and soft and everywhere. He held my gaze a moment, then, taking my hand all the way in his and squeezing it once, tight, he leaned in and kissed me again. He tasted a little like the salt of tears and smelled faintly of aftershave. I was the one who pulled away. He looked hard into my eyes, unabashed in the asking. Then he recovered himself and sat back in his seat.

"Good night," I think I said. My voice was unsteady. My heart pounded hard. When I stepped into the cold night air, I felt that I'd been sweating under my arms. I don't even know if he said good night back.

Inside, Dad asked, "Have a nice time?"

I looked at him, blindsided by the unexpected presence of company. Pat Oreck sat across from my father, a half emptied cup of coffee in his hand. Mom was with them. She sat in her desk chair, legs crossed, back straight. They had stopped speaking the moment I entered. Six eyes stared at me.

"Yeah—it was all right," I managed.

Blushing, I turned and went straight to my bedroom, but when I opened the door there was a scream of protest.

"I'm getting naked!" Callapher exclaimed indignantly.

"I've seen you naked a thousand times," I said.

"Get out," she insisted.

I returned to the dining room and sat at the table, slightly dazed, longing for a place to disappear to so I could lie still and think, memorize, and replay the fact of Matthew's lips on mine. The first kiss.

"You all right?" Mom asked. She'd come into the kitchen to warm her coffee.

"Yeah, fine. Callapher's using the bedroom," I said, as if it were an explanation.

"I told her to take a bath," Mom stated, apparently unaffected by the fundamental change in my person.

I found this slightly annoying, but it gave me, simultaneously, a strange sensation of superiority—that I was living life and touching my first boy while they sat and had coffee, having long since pronounced their tired disappointment with such things.

My book bag lay slouched in the corner. I took out my algebra book, opened it at random, and positioned my hand over an old sheet of previously worked problems. I tried to recount the strangeness of the night, but the talk in the living room continually interrupted my thoughts.

Pat was talking about a conversation that took place in Dad's class that week. Apparently a student's mom had had her purse stolen, and the boy told her that the Bible says if someone takes from you, you are to offer more. His mother's reply was immediate and concise: "Don't be stupid." So he challenged Dad about it. Did the Bible mean what it said?

"Another naive but well-meaning zealot, I'm afraid," was Dad's opinion of the boy.

Pat said, "That's a little unfair."

"I'm not being serious," Dad replied.

"You mean the man just took her purse?" Mom asked. "In the parking lot, in front of everybody?"

"Just last week," Dad said shortly. "Would anyone like more coffee?"

"I've just gotten some," said Mom.

"No, thank you," Pat answered. Turning to Dad, he continued stubbornly, "It seems to me that you failed to answer the question asked."

"Which question would that be?"

"The boy asked what Christ's lesson meant. You said it was a metaphor; a principle."

"I believe we concluded that the principle is love," Dad replied with an arched expression.

"Certainly . . . love. Of course." Pat crossed his hands on his chest. "But you know as well as I do, Ben, that love is practical. The apostles did not differentiate between love and practical acts of kindness. 'Suppose a brother or sister is without food and clothes. If one of you says to him, "Go, I wish you well, keep warm and fed," but does nothing about his physical needs, what good is it?' "

Dad retorted, "I never said anything against the idea."

"Idea," Pat repeated. "That's the problem. You didn't say anything at all, just let the word float there in the air, an idea. Love is not an ambiguous state of mind or emotion. If we leave it at that, it becomes too lofty, an unreachable end; and when a thing becomes impossible, what incentive have we to pursue it? The perceived impossibility only justifies our complacency."

"But you have to differentiate between generosity and naiveté," Dad said. "Innocent as doves, wise as serpents."

"I fail to see the correlation."

"Surely, there are times for discretion," Dad replied. "Yes, as Christians we are to do good—but not recklessly. Take my wife's aunt, for instance. Seven years ago she opened her doors to that man in her basement, and he's still there. She had no contract with him, no plan for his future, no idea how long he would stay. And that's only a minor example."

He waved his hand, as if Beauregard's story was insignificant compared to other instances he didn't wish to name.

"Really, Pat, what did you expect me to say? That to be a Christian his mother shouldn't just forget about her stolen purse but pack up her best china as well? It's a metaphor. It would be impractical—no, presumptuous—even to suggest otherwise. To the boy or his mother."

"You know quite well that I would never advise you to do such a thing. I'm just telling you that you're a lousy teacher, that's all."

Dad laughed.

"You think I'm kidding. You let those kids lead you around like you had a rope to your neck. You can't say the word *love* and let it rest at that. You have to *teach* them. Of course, I've only known you a few months." Pat studied the contents of his coffee cup, then lowered his voice gently. "But it seems fair to assume you've resigned more than your credentials."

The pipes in the walls strained as Callapher ran her bath. For a few minutes, I lost their conversation in the noise. When the water shut off, Pat was pointing to the Bible that sat on our coffee table and saying, "This is full of truths that sound like contradictions to us. Anyone who reads the first chapters of Matthew and doesn't find the teachings of Jesus either otherworldly or insane is reading with blinders on his eyes." He frowned. "Impractical. Do you suppose Peter was being *practical* when he stepped out of the boat and walked on the water?"

"It sounds good in that context, certainly," Dad agreed. "But we're not walking on water here. We don't live in the days of Christ. His presence on earth allowed for such miracles, as validation of His identity, as promptings to faith . . ."

Pat raised his eyebrows. He looked to the right, then to the left, as if expecting someone to walk into the room. "I'm sorry—has He gone somewhere? Is His presence lacking?"

When Dad tried to reply, Pat raised a hand to stop him. "He promised that we would do as He did—that, indeed, we would do greater things by the power of His Spirit within us. Or," he added with a hint of sarcasm, "do you suppose that was simply another of His cryptic 'metaphors'?"

Dad lowered his head and pinched the bridge of his nose between his forefinger and thumb. "Pat, I have been with the church for twenty-two years, and in all that time I never once came across what goes on in that book." He gestured toward the Bible. "It's not like I haven't looked."

Callapher called my name.

"She wants you," Mom said to me, walking to the kitchen with the collected empty coffee cups.

"She can do it herself," I said.

Callapher called again. I sighed, closed my book, and went to the bathroom. She was standing in the tub, tracing her name in the fog on the wall tiles. When I entered, she sat back down, her butt rubbing loud against the bottom of the tub.

"What?" I asked.

"It's time to wash my hair," she said, annoyed at having to explain.

"You know how to do it yourself."

"But I like when you do it."

"Only babies have their hair washed by someone else."

"I can't," she whined. "I get soap in my eyes, and it burns."

I said, "Hand me the bottle."

She tilted her head back and covered her eyes with her hands while I slathered up her hair.

"Don't get it in my eyes," she said.

"I never get it in your eyes. Tilt back."

I rinsed the water from her hair with a plastic Snow White cup. She made me play baptism.

"In the name of the Father, the Son, and the Holy Spirit," I said, pouring the water over her head.

"Amen!" she declared.

"Go." I laid my hand on her head. "And sin no more."

When Callapher had gone to the room, I washed my face and brushed my teeth. I stared hard at my face in the mirror. With my elbows propped on the edge of the sink, I leaned closer toward my reflection, trying to see myself as Matthew had. Lips pursed.

"What are you doing?"

I jumped. Callapher stood in the doorway, watching.

"Get out!" I shouted, slamming the door in her face.

"But you're not even in your underwear!" she exclaimed.

I waited in the bathroom a few minutes, sitting on the toilet. I heard Callapher walk away, pronouncing to the air, "Go and sin no more."

The more I thought about kissing Matthew, the more stupid I felt about the entire thing. I was certain it had ruined our friendship, and the next morning I prepared for school with a queasiness in my stomach that I mistook for dread.

On the drive to school, Mollie said I looked funny. "Are you sick?"

I shook my head. "I just woke up."

"Well, you look terrible."

"Thanks," I muttered.

I went directly to the art room as Lori had directed, scanning the empty classroom, anxious for the sight of Matthew. He stood beside Lori's office, two pink slips in hand.

"There you are!" Lori exclaimed, emerging from the supply closet. "Matthew has your excuse form thingy."

Matthew handed me the slip. He looked directly at me, but I averted my eyes.

"Wait a minute," Lori called, when we both turned abruptly. "I want to talk to you a second. I've got to drive to the elementary to help Samantha get things from her classroom. In the meantime, there are stacks of work from the Drawing I and II classes that need hung. There's that long empty wall in the hallway just outside the gym and another facing the cafeteria. Hang the drawings the way I said, the bottom third of the paper at eye level—well, Olivia, maybe a few inches above in your case. You can either split up and do a wall each, or work together. I don't care—so long as it gets done. So?"

"I can do the wall by the cafeteria," I volunteered.

"I'll help." Matthew said.

"I think it'll go faster if we split up." I felt Matthew's eyes on me but didn't look his way.

"Whatever she wants," he agreed in a begrudging voice.

Lori propped her hands on her hips and studied Matthew, then me. She frowned. "Something going on between you two?"

"No," I replied quickly.

"Good," she said disbelievingly as Matthew crossed his arms. "You'd better check in with your first-period teachers. Then start in the main hall. Try to get through the stack before classes change so people aren't given the chance to trample everything."

Matthew followed close behind as we left the art room, but at the hallway we went our separate ways. When I saw him an hour and a half later, he was working back in the painting studio, hanging first-grade paper mobiles from the ceiling with paper clips and string. Lori kept us busy in separate parts of the building throughout the morning; I was saved, momentarily, from Matthew's unnerving presence.

Dad had given me the truck for the day. At twelve thirty I drove home to pick up the painting I'd wrapped in plastic the night before: the large canvas of blue, of gold. I carried it into the school myself with some difficulty and managed to prop it against a drawing table so I could go back and move the truck. When I returned to the room, Lori was standing before the painting, arms crossed, frowning.

"I did it at home," I said, strangely apologetic.

She stared for a count of three and pronounced the painting the most solid piece of work she'd seen from me yet.

"We'll hang it in the front hall," she decided.

Her praise left me flushed. I whirled out of the room in a half skip, nearly colliding directly with Matthew's oncoming chest. He looked down and smiled, as if expecting me. I was struck again by how tall he was, as if I'd never really noticed the fact before.

"I was looking for you," he said. "I still haven't decided what to show. I've got a whole new series of photographs in my basement, but I can't decide between them. I was thinking maybe you could come with me real quick to look at them after school? Since your mom's not expecting you back till late anyway."

Unprepared with any good excuse and flattered by the request, I agreed unthinkingly. I saw the trick in it, of course, but it was too late to get out of going.

We left the school at a quarter after five. I drove behind Matthew with both windows down. The wind roared in my ears and made chaos of my hair. Soon we'd passed all signs of civilization, climbing high and higher around the winding roads that hugged the mountains. We came to a sudden stop and silence before a log cabin situated upon a steep incline, surrounded on all sides by untamed forest.

The house was not what I'd imagined as Matthew's home. I'd never met his parents. I couldn't remember the name of his sister or whether she lived away or at home. For a moment, I couldn't even think of his last name. Momentarily, fact and vague fiction collided, until the latter gave way to the reality of the present cabin in the woods that held Matthew's life and memories. It surprised me that I could know so little about one of my closest friends. It felt like an indictment of my own vanity, as though his existence began when he stepped through the boundaries of my world, beyond which lay the invisible and unknown.

These thoughts passed through my mind in an instant. We had reached the front door.

Inside, the air lay thick with the moist air of breathing plants. They filled the living and dining rooms in a proliferation of waxy green leaves. A miniature fountain trickled and burbled on the end table. On the wall, a cat-shaped clock meowed the turn of the hour with a switch of its black pendulum tail.

Matthew dropped his things, disappearing wordlessly into the kitchen. He asked if I was hungry. I said I wasn't.

"Down here," Matthew said. I followed him down the basement steps into a humid darkness. "My territory," he explained. "Mom said if I cleaned out the basement it was mine. Dad helped me convert the old storage room into a darkroom."

He walked the length of the basement pulling hanging cords, which clicked lights to life. They shone from behind milky opaque squares in the ceiling.

"It's really too dark right now, but I'm ordering better light to suspend from the corners. And I've got this bright lamp over my desk, which helps."

His photographs—black-and-white—hung from string extending the length of the basement. Each picture was attached by wooden clips, like freshly laundered shirts hung to dry. There were three such rows, the second two feet behind the first, the third two feet from the second. I walked carefully among them, studying the pictures in turn. I recognized corner shops in town and some of the more famous and ancient neighborhoods, where the overgrown limbs of ancient trees hung to the ground. The scenes were familiar corners of Bethsaida life, but they seemed different in the photographs, impenetrable and still as worlds encased in snow globes.

My favorite was a picture of the Osage orange tree that grew alongside the library yard. Its black, craggy limbs split the white sky with their beautiful winter-dead irregularity.

"This one." I pointed. "You should show this one."

Matthew came up from behind. He stood close enough that I could feel his breath on my neck. When he saw the photograph I'd chosen, he nodded in agreement.

"That's one of my favorites. I've got a whole series."

With his hand gently resting upon the small of my back, he directed me forward. Together, we bent beneath the first row to stand before the second. "These," he said with a gesture. "Did them just two weeks ago. Recognize this one?"

I stared at the picture, but I couldn't place the pattern of the bare forest roof with anything I saw in daily life.

"That's just outside the car lot."

"Really?"

"That cropping of trees that comes just up to the pavement of the lot. I had to lie half under a parked car to get the shot."

I laughed at the thought. Matthew had no dignity when it came to his photography. I reassured him that the series was quite striking.

He took them from the string and stacked them with a sheet of clean white paper sandwiched between each pair to protect the glossy surfaces. "I'll take them to Lori tomorrow," he said. "She'll have left the school by now. And the concert's not until seven anyway."

Upstairs, he tried a second time to offer me something to eat, and a second time I refused politely. He didn't seem to expect me to leave. I sat across from him in the den. A large potted cactus sat on the floor just to the left of my feet. I scooted over on the couch to escape the potential sting of its furry yellow prickers.

Matthew nervously kneaded the knuckles of his left hand with the fingers of his right. When conversation came to a halt, he stood without provocation, and sat directly beside me. The couch cushion sank so that we sat mashed together, thigh to thigh. It was before us: the business for which we'd both agreed to this meeting.

I reminded myself that I had no intention of encouraging it. I turned my face toward his, intent upon making this clear. When he opened his mouth, I half expected an apology. What had happened between us last night would not be happening again. Instead, he lifted his hand to brush my hair back from my forehead. The gentle touch sent a quick shudder down my spine. Involuntarily, I smiled. He accepted this as an invitation and kissed me.

"I was so afraid I'd scared you off," he murmured. "When you didn't say anything to me all day I thought you'd changed your mind."

He took my hand. That felt right and natural. When he kissed me again, I lost consciousness of it, no longer watching myself, curious about the act but lost in it, unfurling beneath.

. . . It could have been a single minute, if the cat clock had not intervened to convince me of the time. I pulled away.

"What is it?" he asked, breathless.

"Nothing," I said. "It's just—it's a little fast, that's all."

"Sorry." He smiled sheepishly. He kissed me to the left of my lips. "I've wanted to do that since the first time I met you."

"Kiss me on the cheek?" I asked.

He laughed. "Kiss you at all."

That abruptly, I imagined my bare skin and fat exposed to his hand. I thought of the flatness of my bare breasts as they stared at me from my reflection in the bathroom mirror.

He leaned in toward me again, but the front door was opening in the living room. In an almost synchronized effort, we pulled away and sat upright. A woman walked in with a grocery bag in either arm.

"Matthew, please!" she said. "A little help!"

He sprang to his feet with the earnest agility and obedience of a little child. I looked down to straighten my shirt. His mother hadn't seen us, but I was embarrassed by how quickly we'd pulled apart. By how quickly the boy kissing me had become this woman's son.

"Mom, this is Olivia," he said, looking to me. In his eyes I saw the boy who was not a child, the one who was thinking of my lips and my body.

"Nice to meet you," I said.

"Heard all about you," his mother replied without any real interest. She offered a backward wave of her hand. "Sorry the place is such a mess. Haven't been home at a decent hour all week. Matthew, did you offer her something to drink, or did you just let her sit there?" She emerged from behind the refrigerator door where she'd been stacking yogurt in the crisper.

"I have to get going," I said to Matthew.

He followed me down to the truck. When I turned, he was standing so close as to press me against the car door.

"I'll see you tomorrow?" I asked, looking over his shoulder to avoid his gaze, for he looked at me with an expression in his eyes I could not genuinely return.

He planted a dry kiss on my lips. "Tomorrow," he said, smiling. "All right." Then he paused. "Something wrong?"

"I don't know—I don't know if we should do this."

Matthew looked to the right and then to the left. He seemed entertained by my statement. " 'Do' what?"

"What just happened—"

"Was just a kiss," he finished for me.

He'd stopped smiling, but the amusement that lingered in his eyes gave me the courage to confess.

"I didn't mean for it to happen. I'm not ready for this."

Now he frowned. "Olivia, I like you, all right? I just like you. And I want to spend time with you." He nudged my arm, a platonic gesture, somehow ill fitting and strange in that moment. It struck me that it was already too late for friendship. It had been too late the moment we met. "How can that be wrong?" he asked.

"It's not about being wrong," I said in frustration.

It was his turn to be angry: "Then why didn't you say something?"

"I don't know. I'm sorry."

He stepped away from me. "You want to be friends," he stated.

"I don't know what I want."

"I thought you wanted *this*." He extended his arms. "But I guess I was wrong."

When I said nothing to assure him one way or the other, he turned his back to me.

"I should go," I managed timidly.

He did nothing to acknowledge my leaving. I got into the truck and pulled out without looking back, but I sensed him becoming small and smaller behind as I drove hard and faster forward to the safe place within, my own arms wrapped around me, my knees tucked up tight, my body an impenetrable kernel of self-sustaining strength, untouching and untouched.

CHAPTER 17

mr. Oreck attended the fall concert with my parents to see Callapher sing. During intermission, he stood with my father against the high school sports trophy case, a plastic-wrapped wad of crumbling bake-sale oatmeal cookies in one hand, a paper cup of toxic hot-pink punch in the other. Dad waved me over.

"We were talking about your painting," he said, gesturing toward the canvas hanging on the wall opposite.

I looked at the painting. I didn't consider the ceiling-to-floor bulletin board backdrop very flattering.

"What's the title?" was Mr. Oreck's first question. His second was, "How much?"

I blinked. "Seriously?"

"Certainly," he replied. "I'd like to have it in my library at home."

"I'm flattered," I said, "but I don't know . . ."

"If you're too attached to it, I can understand."

"No, it's not that," I said hurriedly. "I've just never priced anything before."

Mr. Oreck slid his eyes across the painting, up then down. "You think about it," he said. "And let me know. I'm very interested."

The compliment of his offer made up for the awkwardness of the night. All evening, Matthew and I skirted back-flat to walls of hallways and classrooms in an attempt to avoid each other's sight.

"What's the matter with him?" Mollie asked.

"He's been like that most of the night," I replied.

Mom and Dad stayed late so Callapher could escort them through the hallway in which she was the proud exhibitor of a purple clay cow that resembled a fat frog and a crayon landscape featuring a blue beam of sky lining the page top, a flock of twenty black V birds, her specialty, flitting through the white beneath.

After a quick word of praise for both the clay cow and the crayon birds, I left with Mollie. She sang with the radio, flubbing every other line.

I blurted out, "I kissed Matthew."

Mollie raised her eyebrows, surprised by the suddenness of my confession. But she only said, "And . . . ?"

"And what?" I asked.

"Did you like it?"

I studied the passing trees. "I don't know."

She frowned. "Well, would you want to do it again?"

I thought a moment. "It's weird. It's *Matthew*."

Propping her elbow on the windowsill, Mollie curled a lock of hair around her finger. "I guess it would be kind of strange, considering you've been friends and all." The tone of her voice implied that she didn't understand at all what would be weird about it.

"What should I do?"

"Well, that depends. Do you want to be with him?"

"I don't know. I mean, I never did—and when he kissed me I was so surprised, I just let him . . ."

"But you kissed back."

I nodded. "Then I told him I wasn't ready."

She frowned. "What did he say today?"

"He didn't say anything!"

"You need to talk to him."

"How do you talk to someone who's ignoring you?"

"Maybe he thought *you* were ignoring *him*."

"This is so stupid," I muttered.

Mollie parked the car in our driveway. "Here," she said, turning in her seat to face me. "We'll role-play. I'll be Matthew and you be you. Now, tell him—me, I mean—what you want to tell . . . me."

I gave her a warning look. *"Mollie . . ."*

"Mollie? Where?" She looked over her shoulder. "I don't see Mollie."

"Look," I said, "kissing you was nice, but you're one of my best friends, and I don't want to ruin our friendship."

"You didn't like it?"

"It's not that I didn't like it, I just think that—"

"So you did like it?"

"Yes, I said that."

"So what's the problem?"

"I'm afraid it will change everything . . . it won't be you and me and Mollie hanging out anymore."

"I don't know why you keep talking to me as if Mollie were in the car. Why do you always make this about her? You don't want me."

"I didn't say that."

"You don't love me!" Mollie dropped her head against her

window and groaned, covering her face with her hands. "Oh, I'll die of heartbreak."

I got out of the car without saying good-bye and slammed the door angrily.

She called the house half an hour later to repent. I didn't answer but listened to her voice on the answering machine, sounding chintzy and small and far away:

> "I just called to say I love you.
> I just called to say how much I care—I do—
> I just called to sa-ay I lo-ove you
> And I mean it from the bottom of my heart.
> Of . . . my . . . he-A-ert.
> Ba dum dum. Ba dum dum dum."

I called her back.

"Sorry," she said.

"It's all right."

We sat silently on the phone together a minute.

"You really will have to talk to him," she said.

"I know."

"Are you sure about this? I mean, is there something else? He is just Matthew—I get that. But he's a sweet guy. What are you afraid of?"

We talked for another hour, but I never answered the question.

When I told Mollie about Mr. Oreck's interest in my painting, she was duly impressed. "Really?" she asked. "How much do you think he'll pay you for it?"

"I have absolutely no idea."

"It's pretty big—you should get a lot."

"Paintings aren't priced by inches," I said, but she didn't seem to hear.

"I don't think you should accept anything less than a thousand dollars," she stated emphatically.

I laughed out loud.

When Mr. Oreck approached me a second time, I said yes with little hesitation. Under Mollie's duress, I asked $300, and to my surprise, he agreed readily. So readily, in fact, I almost believed Dad's opinion of the price: "A steal," he called it. He suggested I come by their classroom that week.

"He wants to pay you in person. And call him Pat," he insisted. "He doesn't like Mr. Oreck."

I stopped by on Friday and waited outside their classroom door until the last of the students had filed out in their parade of navy blue and starched white. Dad waved me inside.

Anticipating my arrival, Pat had already collected his coat and bag. "I thought we'd talk at the café on the corner," he said, with a glance at his watch. "Four o'clock—too early for dinner. But they've got great pastries, and the coffee's the best in town."

"Sounds all right to me," Dad agreed. He glanced at me furtively. "But it's up to Olivia—I don't know if you need to be anywhere else," he said to me.

I understood his concern. "I don't have to be anywhere. Sure, we can go."

At the café, I ordered a hot tea and—for the appearance of normality—a banana nut muffin. Dad and Pat asked for cherry pie and ice cream.

"Don't tell your mother." Dad winked at me.

I felt as if I lived in shared conspiracy with Dad regarding food. Since the one incident at the dinner table, he'd never mentioned my weight or eating again. His only acknowledgment of my diet was our now traditional weekly trip to the grocery store, a chore he'd retained even though he worked full time as opposed to Mom's twenty hours a week. He let me pick out things "I liked" and treated my habits in general with an eager, if bewildered, solicitude. The fact that he didn't understand my ways bothered me more than all of Mom and Aunt Margaret's fussing that I clean my plate.

I worked carefully and slowly on the muffin, trying to concentrate on the taste and resisting the urge to pick out the nuts with my fork. Dad and Pat finished all of their pie and let the waitress warm their coffee. They spoke about the day, about school in general. My father had always been good with people, but it was a little strange to see him laughing with a friend.

They could have easily enjoyed a two-way conversation, but Pat made a point of forcing me to talk. He inquired after my classes and my work, listening in turn with his eyes intent upon mine, as if the story of my life were the most interesting he'd ever heard. The authenticity of his undivided attention began to feel like flattery.

He was particularly curious about life in a studio. "I like so much of everything in painting. Well, there was the one piece . . . can't think of its name. Saw it in the museum in New York. Confound it, what was the title?" He leaned back in the booth to study the crisp cut glass of the overhanging Tiffany lamp and frowned, pressing his two front fingers against his lips. "I can see it in my mind clear as a bell, but the name is gone. Well, my mind's not what it used to be." He looked at me, and his eyes sparkled. "Do you know that I spent an hour and a half looking for my glasses yesterday, only to find them on my face?"

I laughed.

"Laugh at me if you like," he said, rearranging his napkin in his lap. "But your father knows what I'm talking about. Losing your own mind. How the body grows old. 'But Alas, so long, so far / our bodies why do we forbear? / They are ours, though they are not we; / We are the intelligence, they the sphere.'" He pointed toward Dad. "I've still got that. That's the way it goes. Some things here, others—*fwish*!" He waved. "Gone like the wind!"

"What was that?" I asked. The words he'd recited lingered in my mind bright but without shape, like the neon afterimage burned on eyelids after a long stare into brilliant light.

"You like poetry?" Pat asked.

"I liked that."

"John Donne," Dad supplied.

"Exactly right," Pat said, pleased. "A metaphysical poet of the seventeenth century. That bit is from 'The Ecstasy.' Lines 49 or 50 or something or other."

I rolled the delicious word around in my mouth: *ecstasy*. Joy transcending, a raucous fire in the body—the soul shot out in a backward thrown cry.

Pat asked, "What literature courses are you taking now?"

"I'm not in any," I replied. "I used all my extra periods for art classes."

"Olivia, literature *is* art," Pat declared indignantly.

I apologized and meant it. I felt truly sorry that I'd never heard of this John Donne and his fabulous "Ecstasy."

Pat drilled me about my knowledge of literature, a meager education that amounted to little more than a few Shakespearean plays, some post–World War II novels, and very, very little poetry not counting the

Psalms. He took a notepad out of the pocket in his jacket lining and scribbled something, then ripped the notebook paper from the pad and handed it to me across the table.

I studied it: titles of works by Milton, Donne, Yeats.

"You read those," he said, "and we'll do this again some time so you can tell me what you think."

"All right," I said. I folded up the list and tucked it in my jeans, where it stayed the rest of the week.

Mollie insisted that you can't mess with a guy's head. "Whatever you do," she said, "don't say you're interested and then change your mind. It's not fair. Don't go to him unless you're really willing to put all your eggs in the basket. Or whatever."

So I didn't talk to Matthew. At school, we retained a semblance of friendship, but every word was forced and rehearsed where before it had been natural and easy. We still sat together in class and at lunch, but he spoke mostly with the other people at the table, and only politely to me.

Sometimes, at night, I practiced kissing him in my head. I imagined being with him. I remembered his smell. But in the daylight, struck by his scowl as if it were a direct slap to my face, I always turned away, embarrassed by my fantasies. I started working overtime at the car lot. Saturdays with nothing to do, I drew in my sketchbook with a near violent urgency, as if by filling the pages I could escape the deep, powerful sadness seeping into my bedroom in the hot sunbeams from the window.

Keeping a journal helped. I had a new black, bound notebook in which I counted my food pyramid every day, to make sure all the foods fit. It was satisfying to feel the soft pencil tip against the bare and blue pinstriped page. It was comforting to see my life reduced to a neat and orderly pattern of symbols adding up to a predetermined sum. Sometimes I added up the calories, sometimes the fat. I tried to calculate how many miles I might have walked that day. I was still banned from jogging outside, and I couldn't run in place. Mom would feel the rhythmic vibrations of my bedroom floorboards from the kitchen. But I never sat if I could stand. In the bedroom, a folded square of towel beneath my butt, I pumped sit-ups until the sweat drenched my face and back and underwear.

That week after the art show, I was given another distraction to fill the hours. Dad came home from school one day with three books in hand, compliments, he said, of Pat Oreck. They hit my desk with a dull thud.

I suppose it was a sense of obligation that inspired me to actually pick up *Paradise Lost*. Pat had been very good to my family, and in some strange way I felt I owed him something. In bed, I propped myself up on my elbows and plowed through the first pages. It was difficult reading, but surprisingly I found myself absorbed. I thought Milton a delusional egoist for claiming he could explain the ways of God to man, but I had to give it to him: there were times I stopped reading, breathless.

> *A mind not to be chang'd by place or time.*
> *The mind is its own place, and in itself*
> *Can make a heaven of hell, a hell of heaven.*

My personal hell existed within the confines of my skull. I'd gone beyond thinking my body was the trouble. The real culprit, I knew, was the mind. But I'd never considered my fear a spiritual matter. I didn't understand that the body and the spirit are connected, that the abuse and suffering of one affects the other, wind in the belly of a kite. They move together.

I'd spent every ounce of mental power counting the calories in my food and the hours between meals. I'd never given my imagination leave to flirt with the idea of God. Didn't the Bible speak of angels doing battle? Of Christ resplendent in glory? Of the church as a living body? These ideas had been lost to me beneath the felt figurines of Sunday school lectures. If God were the God Christians claimed Him to be, surely He would shoot adrenaline down the very fibers of my soul. I went to bed thinking of angels conferencing, of spirits scheming, of the Garden dripping with sensual delight. If there was a kingdom of a living God, and if it were made of such visions as this . . . I felt the danger of thinking too much about it.

But then I went to church, and the dreams of another world snapped to nothing, like smoke dispelled. I saw only a preacher with a double chin, a tone-deaf choir director, the principal of the Bethsaida Christian Academy sleeping through the sermon with chin flat to his chest. This was not the world of books. Books, I reminded myself, are constructed fantasies born of men's minds. And the Bible is only a book.

With Margaret's help, Mrs. Lowett moved into a studio apartment out of town. She said she needed to be closer to work, but I suspected she wanted to be farther away from Beauregard. Margaret fussed over the situation all week.

"She's not got enough for that rent—I know she doesn't."

"It's her business, Margaret," Ruby said. "She's a grown woman. She can take care of herself."

"Well, I don't like it," Margaret replied. "I don't like it at all."

That Sunday, Margaret stepped up to the pulpit dressed as a turkey to announce the annual food drive. She wore a brown sweat suit stuffed with pillows and a plastic beak from an old Halloween costume. Ruby accompanied her as a Pilgrim. Halfway through the announcement, her cap gun went off. There was a small puff of smoke, and the parishioners in the back row started to attention. Pastor Evans regained the pulpit to make a joke about keeping the snipers off the platform. Everyone laughed politely, and the service continued without any more excitement.

CHAPTER 18

we had our first real snow Thanksgiving week. Ruby called to warn us.

"The big green blob is moving in fast," she told me. I could hear the weather channel playing in the background. "And the blue blob is behind it, coming right for our county."

Mom sent Dad and me to the store for batteries and candles and milk. When Callapher insisted on joining us, Mom made her wear a blue snowsuit, mittens, and a hat. She looked like the bloated blueberry girl from Willy Wonka. When I laughed at her, she kicked me in the shin, lost her balance, and fell to the floor.

"S'not funny," she said when I laughed harder.

Dad suggested we sew her into the suit for the duration of adolescence, to reduce the probability of injury. "You could run into every thing and just bounce off," he said. "And it would certainly prevent unwanted contact with the boys."

But as soon as we'd left the Shoe Box, he pulled into the Old

Maids' drive to help Callapher out of her wrappings.

"I can't have you embarrassing me now, can I?" he asked.

Margaret was bent over her flower beds, struggling to spread a tarp over the little plot of ground. Dad rolled his window down and said good-naturedly, "Nice blizzard we're having."

Margaret turned, holding either end of the tarp up in her outstretched arms. The wind caught the plastic and blew it into her face. She struggled to free herself, sputtering, "Blizzard my foot. This is the good Lord's dandruff." She punched the plastic sheeting down and held it to the earth with her foot. "Feather dusting."

"Watcha doin'?" Callapher leaned out her window.

"I'm covering the flower bed, dear."

"Aren't the flowers dead?"

"You don't shoot a dog if it's not suffering yet," Margaret retorted. "I've got to protect the soil so that it'll be ready when the flowers come back in the spring." She addressed the flower bed. "Isn't that right, my darlings?"

As we drove away, Callapher asked, "What's she mean about killing a dog?"

"I suppose that's Margaret's way of saying she's close to her flowers," Dad replied.

"Maybe they're like her pets, huh?"

Dad agreed this was probably the case.

At the store, Callapher pushed the shopping cart until Dad got sick of her running into his heels and demoted her from driver to passenger, where she sat among the groceries. When we turned corners, she peered over the edge of the cart, pointing her forefinger at other shoppers, squinting her eyes, and making laser *pshew, pshew* sounds.

"Please don't shoot everybody," Dad said.

Callapher examined each item he put in the cart.

"Eww, beans." She extended her arm toward Dad, the offensive can in hand. "We don't eat this kind, Dad."

"They're not for us; they're for Margaret's food pantry."

Callapher brushed her bangs out of her eyes with the back of her hand. "Margaret puts soup in her purse and passes it out on people's houses. She takes stuff to Beauregard's mom, too, but she said I wasn't supposed to tell anybody that."

"Well, I won't tell," Dad replied.

She stood up with her hands on either side of the cart for balance. "How come Margaret can't buy this stuff herself?"

"Because generosity begets generosity. Sit down, Angel."

Callapher said she thought begetting was about babies.

"You've heard that it's better to give than to receive?" Dad asked. "Well, sometimes when people on the receiving end learn to appreciate a gift, they are grateful and want to give back. Imagine if you went to a Christmas party and they were having a gift exchange. Wouldn't it feel good to have a gift to give after you received one?"

"So, you give Margaret soup, and she gives poor people soup," Callapher said.

"Something like that."

"Then, maybe, those people will give somebody soup."

"That would be an ideal way for things to go, I'd say," Dad murmured, studying the label of an oatmeal box.

Mollie was at the house when we got back. "Hey, Callapher. Hey, Mr. Monahan," she said when we walked in the door. She turned to me, clasped her hands together and cried, "I know you're not supposed to work today, but come back with me, please. I can't stand to be alone in that office when it's like this. Nobody's going to come, and it's going to be *bo-o*-ring."

"Why aren't you closed?" Dad asked. "These roads will be impassable within a few hours."

"Nobody closes roads down here," Mollie replied. "Snow three feet deep wouldn't keep people from going to work. Mom hasn't closed the office seventeen years running."

I agreed to go back with her, but wanted to change into warmer clothes first. Mollie followed me directly into the bedroom: she was consistently unceremonious and indecent when it came to getting dressed. I turned my back to her while I pulled off my shirt.

"What are these?" she asked, looking at the books on my desk.

"Oh, Dad's friend Pat Oreck gave me those to read."

She turned her head to the side to read the titles. "Milton? You're reading Milton for *fun*? Are you crazy?"

I pulled my head through a new sweater. "It's kind of interesting."

"I don't know," she said doubtfully, picking up the book to weigh it in her palms. "I only like books with pictures."

I thought she was teasing, but later that evening she said, "If I ask you something, will you be totally honest?"

We were sitting at the front desk. Outside, snow fell in sideways sheets like a heavy rain.

"All right," I answered nonchalantly.

"I mean it," she said, kicking her feet down from the counter to wheel closer to me on her chair. "You have to swear to tell the truth."

"On the Bible?" I asked.

"No, not the Bible. Your own mortal soul will be fine."

I swore on my own mortal soul. "What?"

She looked down, suddenly bashful. With her fingernail, she picked at a piece of tape stuck flat to the desk. The hot-pink polish she wore daily had chipped to reveal the white moon crescent of each nail. "Do you ever wish I was . . . I don't know . . . an artist? Or smart—like you?"

I looked at her in surprise. "Are you serious?"

She shrugged and smiled, as if aware that she was being slightly absurd. But she continued, "You're always talking about things Lori's teaching you or about something you've read. You're reading freaking Milton, because you *want* to. And you use big words."

"I what? Words like what?"

"I don't know . . . You used one the other day. Juxto-something."

"Juxtapose?"

"See!" she exclaimed. "I don't even know what that means."

Nothing she'd said had ever surprised me so much.

"No, I don't care that you're not an artist," I insisted.

"But don't you wish you could talk with me about those things? Instead of me just saying, 'Wow, Olivia, that's so amazing' or, 'Olivia, you're a genius'?"

"Of course not," I replied. "I like talking about what we talk about."

She considered this silently, crossing her arms on her chest. Then she laughed. "What, Hedgehog King and Gravy Girl?"

And that quickly, any suggestion of insecurity on Mollie's part vanished. She never mentioned the subject again.

I never thought of our friendship quite the same way after that. Before, I had always felt a step behind Mollie. Next to her bright smile and long legs and magnetic charm, I wanted to imitate her the way Callapher sometimes tried to copy me in dress and mannerisms. But while I was coveting Mollie's body, she was envying my mind. The grass is always greener.

When I was honest with myself, though, I had to admit that I envied more than Mollie's beauty. I envied her peace of mind. Her exuberance. The effortless way she laughed. Despite what she'd been through only recently, and despite the lonely life she had at home, she seemed to get an irrepressible pleasure from nearly everything.

Sometimes I flattered myself that my friendship made her happy, but she looked even at me sometimes as if she had a secret—the way a woman might look over the shoulder of a friend to share a glance with her lover. It was maddening. She was flippant one moment, sincere the next. She never judged—she never doubted. I knew it all pointed to one thing.

It had never felt right to envy Mollie in the first place; it felt positively sinful to envy her for her faith. I wondered what this meant and concluded that I was simply destined to desire whatever she had, like a child throwing tantrums over her big sister's things. That if Mollie and her long legs had a Buddha seated on the bedroom dresser, I'd want one too.

I was not yet considering Jesus the man or Jesus the God. I thought only of Christianity: the club whose members wore suit jackets to service and promise rings to school, a fashion trend characterized by crosses on necklaces. Christ was nothing to me of flesh or spirit. He was one more poster face advertising five quick steps to forever happiness.

Every magazine promises that. After a while, you get a little pessimistic.

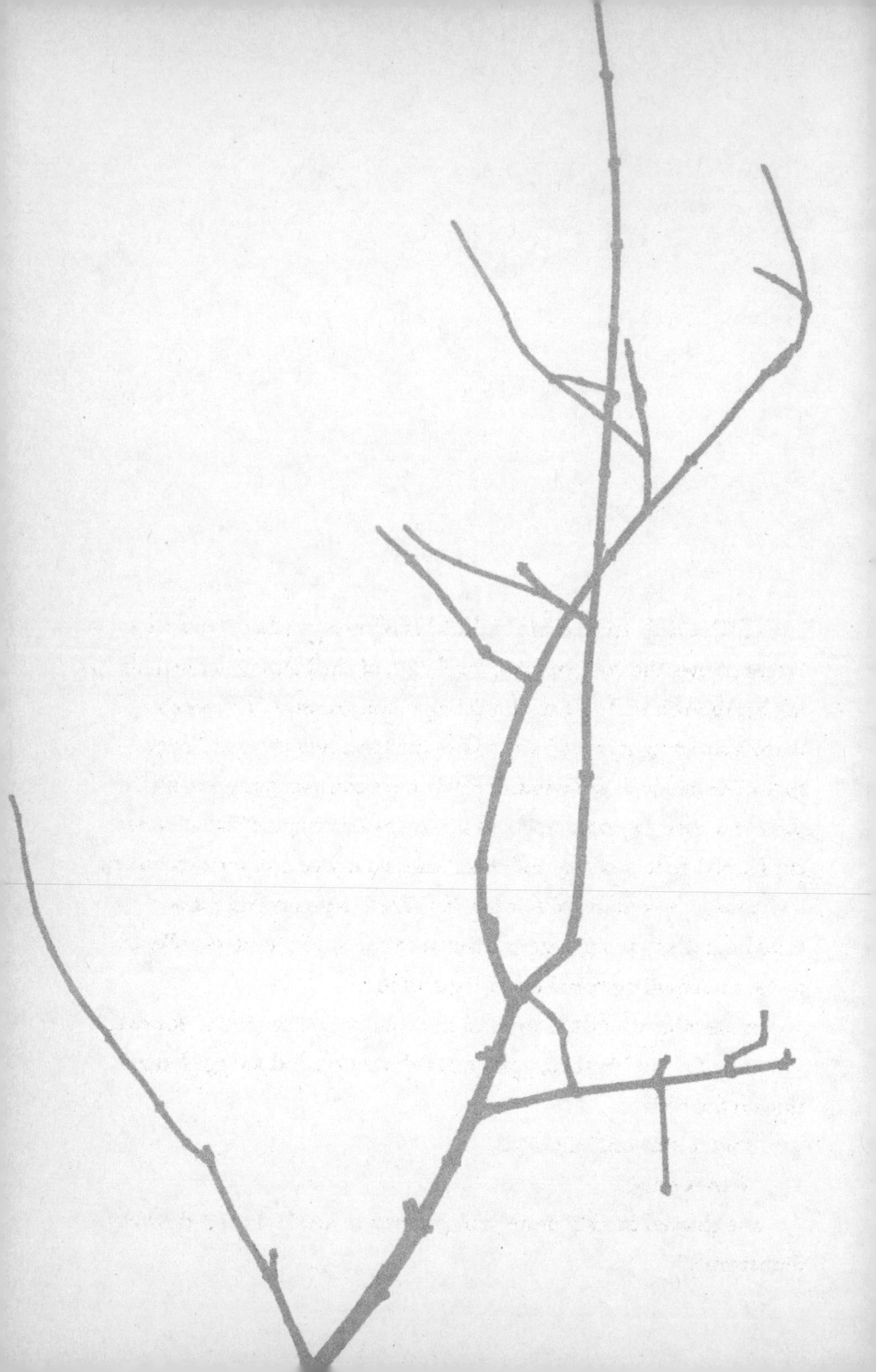

CHAPTER 19

the old vacuum roared in Mom and Dad's room. I stepped over the cord running the length of the hallway, walked into my bedroom, and threw my book bag to the ground. Callapher's Barbies sat straight legged and stiff jointed in a row upon the bookshelf. The blinds of the window shade were conspicuously clean of dust, and crisscrossing our carpet lay the patterned path of the sweeper as it had gone this way and that. I opened my desk drawer to survey the damage: a bouquet of pencils sharpened to points and rubber-band bound, my scrap paper stacked into a neat pile, erasers collected in the cardboard bottom half of a matchbox.

In the other room, the vacuum died. Mom appeared in the doorway.

"What's this?" I asked, pointing to the bucket and sponge left sitting on the floor.

"I want it down," she said.

"What down?"

She glanced quickly at my collage, then at me. "I want it down by dinnertime."

"Or what?" I asked defiantly. "I won't eat?"

She said nothing. As she left the room, I opened my drawer a second time. The magazine I'd bought the day before was missing. Kneeling on the floor, I pulled out the shirt box I kept beneath the bed. It was empty. I swung open the closet door, looked to the floor. Every magazine I'd stashed in my room was gone.

I found Mom seated at the dining room table, sipping a tall glass of water calmly, as if she were waiting for me. "I had to," she announced before I'd said anything. "Your room hasn't been cleaned once through since we got here. Callapher's things were everywhere . . ."

"Where are my magazines?"

She stood and carried her still-full glass to the sink. "I threw them out," she said.

I followed her into the kitchen, kneeling down to search the garbage can under the sink.

"They're already outside," she said. "I took them to the curb."

"You went through my things—through my desk, under my bed. Mom—you just can't do that!"

We stood face to face.

"I'll not sit by and let you do this to yourself," she said. "Do you hear me? I won't."

I crossed my arms and stared at her with burning eyes. "Do what?"

Turning her back to me, she reached up to retrieve a small leather-bound journal from above the refrigerator. "Explain this." She fanned through the journal. On the quick snapping pages I saw my food triangles, the rows of numbers, the calories counted.

"This is recent, isn't it?"

I wanted to deny it, but there was no point. I'd dated each entry.

"Olivia." She searched my face with pleading eyes. "What's gotten into you?"

I raised my chin defiantly. Mom tried to set the journal on the counter, but it tipped and fell, hitting the floor with the slap of leather against tile.

"I told Dr. Palmer I'd give you a chance, but I've waited long enough," she whispered. "I think you should see a counselor."

I shook my head empathically. "I'm not going to a counselor—"

"Yes, you are," Mom stated. She nodded to herself, her voice softening again, her eyes escaping mine to shift across the floor. "I'll make some calls. We'll find someone Dr. Palmer trusts. You need help, Olivia. I can't help you."

"I'm not going to a counselor," I repeated. "And I'm not taking down my pictures."

"Then you won't sleep here tonight."

"Fine!"

I marched to my room and slammed the door behind. I threw the first clothes I grabbed into Callapher's going-to-Grandma's suitcase, slung my book bag across my shoulder, and left the house without a glance or word to my mother. At the door, I nearly collided with Dad, who caught me by either arm and looked down in concern. I shook my way past him, but as I flew down the porch steps to the lawn, I could just hear his voice.

". . . the matter with her?"

I ran to the Old Maids'. I didn't want to see Mollie and have to explain to her the fight with my mother. But even as that excuse flitted through my head, I knew the truth: I didn't want to be with Mollie because I didn't trust myself around her. Sometimes I hated her long legs too much.

"Good gracious, Olivia. You're the last person I'd have expected to see," Margaret declared at the sight of me, straightening the elastic waistline of her dress. She wore a bit of Kleenex tucked into her anniversary watchband. She looked me up and down. "Walking out in this cold without so much as a scarf and hat! Come in, come in and get warm immediately!"

I followed her into the kitchen. She set me down at the breakfast table beside the window.

"Would you like something to drink?" she asked. "Do you like tea? Or maybe some hot chocolate? We've got some oatmeal cookies just baked yesterday, if you're hungry."

I shook my head at first but changed my mind. "Maybe some tea."

"Right, some tea," she agreed happily.

She set a kettle of water to boil. From the cupboard, she produced two teacups and saucers, each delicate at the tip with the thin thumbprint vein and shape of flower petals. She rinsed each, drying their insides out with the balled-up corner of a fresh dish towel. I didn't like tea much, but there wasn't an ounce of evil in it. And I enjoyed watching Margaret perform the familiar ritual with slow deliberation, as if each motion provided her with its own particular pleasure.

"It's funny you should come by," she said. "Ruby's in the other room sleeping, and I'd just put myself down for a nap, but for some reason I couldn't fall asleep—a rare occurrence, I assure you. You know what my husband used to say, rest his soul . . . he used to say that when he was young he took his naps, and after he turned thirty his naps took him!"

Margaret rarely spoke of her late husband. It was difficult to attach the short, skinny man in the photographs hanging in the living room with the woman before me now. For a moment, the fact of her history appeared to me with clarity, like a shadow following her figure: piano lessons maybe, childhood Christmases, her first kiss. The phone call that her husband hadn't made it through the night. The vision left me convicted for every time I'd rolled my eyes at her behind her back.

She prattled on. "I'm always glad for a bit of company. Ruby's arthritis has been bothering her something terrible today, and I'm afraid it's made her quite a bore. When her hands get bad there's no music in this house for days, and I about lose my mind with the silence."

She set the tea things on the table. "Sugar? Milk? Or I suppose I should say cream? Sounds more proper that way, don't you think? Just nice to say, 'Sugar or cream?' "

I smiled and said I would like both, thank you.

She made me sit back as she poured, so I wouldn't burn my face on the escaping steam. I stirred the water. Deep amber swirled from the steeping teabag, the color feathering out like a drop of ink diluting.

"Well, this is nice." Margaret sat opposite me. She lifted her cup to her lips with both hands. It was a strikingly elegant gesture for a woman of her size. "Now, you be sure to let me know if you want anything else—I've got things besides cookies too. Toast, some little biscotti things. I don't like them, personally, but you're supposed to dip them in tea or coffee, I suppose. And then there's some strawberries with cream—"

Without warning, she slammed her right hand hard against the windowpane. I jumped an inch off my chair in surprise.

"Scat! *Scat*, you!" she shouted.

Two squirrels jumped down from the bird feeder, which swayed sharply back and forth in the wake of their sudden leap.

"The little rats! They'll eat my birds out of house and home. I don't know how they get up there!" She set her teacup down against its saucer with a delicate *tap* of china to china. "Now, what's on your mind? You've got something on your mind. I can always tell when someone's about to have a good cry. It's a sixth sense."

I blushed.

"Don't you be embarrassed." She gave my hand two flat pats. "Look, you go and cry whenever you like. Everybody needs a good cry now and again. The Good Lord Himself wasn't above it."

"It's nothing," I said.

She watched me in silence for a moment, thinking. Then she began, "Olivia, I've seen something in you that I haven't seen in many people. You are a very talented young woman. Now, I'm old, and I know I'm silly, and I may not know much of all that philosophy and theocracy and highfalutin priddle praddle like the Reverend . . . but I know what I know, and it seems to me that God doesn't just parcel out His gifts so they'll be wasted, and I don't believe He cares for His children to live punishing themselves without reason."

Reluctantly, I met her gaze.

"You're a lovely young woman," she said, bowing her head toward mine. "And someday you'll see it."

The phone rang. I knew it was my mother before Margaret even picked up.

"Yes . . . yes, she's here," she said, glancing at me from where she stood by the window. The Old Maids had an ancient phone, with a twenty-foot rubber cord twisted like an umbilical. It tied itself around Margaret's thick waist as she turned. "I see. . . . Yes, I'll ask her." She placed the receiver against her breast and turned to me to ask, "Your mother would like to know if you're coming home for dinner this evening."

I shook my head. "Tell her I'd rather not."

Margaret turned back toward the window, put the phone to her ear, and said exactly, "She'd rather not. . . . All right. Yes, it's no bother. . . . Of course, dear. . . . Uh-uh. Good-bye." Margaret returned to her seat.

"What'd she say?" I asked.

"That you were to let her know when you'd come to your senses, and to not be a bother to us in the meantime or I have the right to kick you out."

"Can I stay here?" I asked.

Margaret waited a moment, considering. "All right," she said. "I don't want to get between your mother and you, whatever the trouble is, but if you insist on staying out of your house, I'll put you up here. You'll have to sleep on the couch, though—I'm having the bed in the spare room taken down this afternoon. In fact, George ought to be here any minute."

I said the couch was fine, and she told me to make myself at home; she had to get things cleaned up before Mr. McFanny arrived.

In the living room, the sunlight slid in silent shapes upon the carpet and across the piano, the beams spliced by the glass fronts of picture frames. The white glare of each reflection blocked the image of the face beneath. When the wind blew, the lights changed, swayed. I lay belly flat on the sofa with the intent of resting a moment. I needed to think. To count.

When I woke an hour later, Margaret was in the kitchen arguing with George McFanny about the dismantling of a king-size bed.

"Now, George, you listen to me. We're going to take that bed apart, and we're going to deliver it to Mrs. Lowett, and we're going to do it today."

"Looka here, Ms. Margaret, ma'am, I ain't fixin' to argue with you 'bout the dumb bed. What I'm saying is that them roads don't look good to me. Iris and me got a patch a' ice big as Grandma's hot water tub, jest pooling out all over the back of our driveway. If you think I'm gonna load up my Chevy and cross this town five times over to put together some bed, you got another think coming."

Margaret protested, "That woman's been sleeping on the floor for a month, and not a soul knew until this afternoon. It's twenty below out there, and she's sleeping on a bunch of blankets and towels! Now, it won't take us more than two trips to get that bed to her—"

George counted on his thick, grease-painted fingers. "Now wait a minute. That's two trips the first time—there and back—and two trips the second time—there and back. Two plus two is nearly five, which is what I said the first time. I ain't driving over this town five times."

"George!" Margaret stamped her foot.

"S'no good, I'm not doing it." He threw his hands in the air and turned his back to her.

"All right, two trips," Margaret conceded. "Two. We'll take her the mattress and bring her the frame later. Just two."

Margaret rounded up Beauregard, and the three disappeared upstairs. A thud against the second-story floor sent the ceiling shaking. The crystal teardrops hanging from the dining room chandelier rattled and clinked. Moments later there was the sound of something scraping against the wall. They were straining to squeeze the king-size mattress around the corner of the stairwell.

"If this ain't the most featherbrained idea I've ever heard of,"

George said from the top of the stairs. "How'd you git this thing up here in the first place?"

Slowly they managed to reach the bottom of the stairs, where Margaret found herself wedged between the foot of the mattress and the hallway wall. Beauregard tried to push the mattress around the bend by shoving, but only succeeded in pressing Margaret into the wall so hard she let out a gasp.

"Don't squash her to death!" George cried.

Margaret began to laugh. She laughed until she couldn't breathe—something that had been difficult to begin with, what with the better part of a master bed pressed to her belly.

"Somebody help the woman!" George cried.

I ran to the stairs. Taking the mattress in either hand, I pulled while Beauregard and George shoved. After a moment's resistance, it unplugged itself from the corner turn. Margaret sat down to catch her breath.

"Plumb foolishness," George said, taking off his cap and slapping his thigh with it. When Margaret caught a second fit of hysterics, he brushed the top of the hat, placed it back on top of his head, and looked away as if embarrassed. "Silly as a schoolgirl, I swear."

They proceeded to wrap the mattress with plastic sheeting Margaret had bought that morning. Then we all helped carry it to George's truck, where he lassoed it down with some rope thin as twine.

Standing atop the mattress, he pulled at the delicate rope now holding it in place. He stood up and tipped his hat back on his forehead with a deep frown. "Not gonna hold, I don't think."

"Haven't you got any bungee cords or the like?" Margaret asked.

"Left 'em in the garage. Warn't planning on hauling anything today."

"Well, that's ridiculous," Margaret said. "I told you we were moving the bed."

"And I told you I warn't planning on doing it." He turned to step down to the ground. "Well, it'll have to do. We're only doing this once."

"Will it stay?"

With his hands on his hips, George considered the matter. He looked the truck up and down. "Maybe. I'm a bit afraid if the wind picks up it'll catch beneath her. Blow her up."

Margaret pursed her lips. Lifting her skirts, she started to climb atop the truck bed.

"Get down from there, woman," George said, but even as he spoke, he hurried to offer her his hand, and with the other across her broad waist, gave her a helpful shove upward.

"I'll stay with it," she said.

George looked up at her, blinking. "What, sit back there? The whole way? I don't think so. Not in this cold. You'll freeze yourself to death. And if you don't get your fingers froze, we're liable to get arrested."

Margaret was situating herself on the mattress, butt flat against it, her back to the middle cabin window. She nestled down, wrapped her coat around her waist.

"No such thing," she said, looking down to button her coat up to her chin. "We'll just keep an eye out. Olivia—run inside and get me my orange scarf, the one with the polka dots. Then we'll get going. It's already getting dark, and I promised Mrs. Lowett we'd get her something soft to sleep on before bedtime."

I returned with Margaret's scarf. She took it with her white-mittened hand.

"Thank you, dear. Exactly the one. Now, I'll be back—oh, I don't know—two hours, I think. Ruby left just before you woke—she's having dinner with her Bible study tonight and ought to be out until eight. Beauregard's content in his underground hole, so for all intents and purposes, you've got the house to yourself. Eat anything you like."

I went back inside, rubbing my hands together until the numbness in my fingertips became the tingling pain of recirculating blood. The truck revved to life just as the kitchen door shut behind me to stifle the noise of its engine. Out the living room window, I saw Margaret clap her mittened hand twice upon the roof of the cab. From behind the glass, the gesture was silent and passed like slow motion before my eyes, as if Margaret moved beneath deep water. Or perhaps that is the illusion of memory.

After Margaret left, I moped around the house restlessly. I made a salad and left half of it in the bowl in the sink. I washed my face. I watched television. At seven the phone rang. Beauregard—whose presence I felt only in the occasional creaking of floorboards downstairs—did not attempt to answer it. It rang again at seven thirty and then again five minutes later. Assuming it was my mother, I stayed in the living room, refusing to pick up. When it rang a fourth time, I turned up the volume on the television.

Somebody knocked on the back door. I went to the kitchen. Peering through the white ruffled curtains, I saw my father's black-coated chest. My mother's tenacity surprised me: she'd sent an ambassador, I thought.

I opened the door, and a confetti cloud of snow rushed in.

"Hey, Dad," I said with a sheepish bow of my head.

"Hey, honey," he returned, brushing quickly past me to stand at the kitchen table. "You weren't answering the phone."

"I was in the other room."

I waited for him to open with his usual beginning to most our private conferences: *Your mother . . .*

He said, "There's been an accident."

"An accident?" I repeated. My first thought was of Callapher. But as my mind raced, I placed her at home with Mom, safe.

"A car accident," Dad stated. "A deer jumped out in front of George's truck. Margaret was thrown when the mattress flew up." He spoke with an unnatural calm, laced with sympathy, a tone developed during late-night hospital vigils with mourning parishioners. He stated, "She didn't make it."

I was too stunned to speak. My hand flew to my mouth—a gesture that seemed appropriate but felt strangely rehearsed, a reaction learned from television and cinema.

"Beauregard doesn't know, of course, but I don't think it's the right time or place to tell him. Your mother and I are picking Ruby up at church to give her a ride to the hospital. We need you to stay with Callapher."

I nodded, running to the hallway for my coat. The van was out front. It seemed silly that he'd driven. I felt ashamed of my tantrum, of not answering the phone. As we drove back to the house, Dad explained matter-of-factly, "George is still in the emergency room. He's all right but had to have a serious row of stitches . . . want to make sure he got his truck towed all right. . . ."

I listened halfheartedly. Already my mind had begun to edit memory. All evening I'd sat on the couch with the world as usual because I didn't know. How long had Margaret been dead?

It took so long just to drive to our house. A bedroom door slammed just as we entered the Shoe Box. Mom appeared from the kitchen, buttoning her coat. She carried her purse and a second, larger bag on the crook of her arm. "Callapher doesn't want us to leave," she said to Dad, laying her gloved hand upon his elbow.

Dad walked to the hallway. I tried to catch Mom's eyes, but she averted her gaze, pretending to inventory the contents of her purse.

"Olivia," she said, all business, "your father and I will be gone for a couple hours. Callapher didn't touch her dinner, so try to get her to eat something. There's lasagna and some leftover macaroni in the fridge. Don't leave the house under any circumstances—we might need to contact you."

Dad had returned. "She's locked herself in," he said.

"I'll talk to her," I said eagerly, hoping Mom would look up. But she left without a word or glance in my direction, following behind Dad with her eyes focused steadfastly forward.

At the window, I stood transfixed by the stillness of the night, by the amber fuzziness of the streetlamp on the corner. It clicked to life automatically each evening at dusk, regular as sunrise. Snow spun in loops by the light of its single bulb. A thin layer of cold air lay flat on the windowpane. It could have been Christmas Eve or a night for books and hot chocolate. The world could have come down on us yesterday; it could have come down on us later. This evening was no different than any other to the unmoving, solitary lamp. There was nothing special about it. We were simply one of the families who would not be sleeping this night.

"Callapher?" I knocked softly on our bedroom door. "Can I come in?"

The lock clicked, and I heard her feet padding across the creaky floorboards. When I opened the door, the room appeared empty and entirely still but for a disturbance in the ruffled lining that hung from our bed to the floor. I knelt down and peered underneath.

Callapher lay on her belly, her chin propped on the top of her clasped hands.

"What are you doing?" I asked.

"Nothing."

"Did they tell you?"

She looked down. "That Margaret's dead," she mumbled into her hands.

I didn't know what to do. After a pause, I ventured, "Do you want to come out and sit with me? I'll make you something to eat, and we can talk."

"I don't want anything."

"You want me to wait here with you?"

She said no.

"How come you're under the bed?" When she didn't answer, I asked, "Are you hiding?"

Abruptly, she burst into tears. "I don't want Mom to die."

"Callapher! Who said Mom was going to die?"

"She's going to get in a accident. Like Margaret."

I reached under and managed to get my fingers through her belt loops. I pulled her along the floor; she slid easily against the hardwood. As soon as I reached for her, she began to squirm eagerly out from beneath the bed. She straddled my waist, her arms so tight around my neck that I found it difficult to breathe.

"She's not going to die," I insisted. "What happened to Margaret was an accident. They weren't being careful."

"Because they weren't wearing their seat belts?" she asked solemnly.

"Probably," I said. "Margaret wasn't wearing a seat belt. But Mom's a very, very careful driver."

"Mommy always wears her seat belt."

She settled down as I rocked her, hiccupping into my shoulder.

"You want me to make you some lasagna now?"

"A milk shake," she stated.

"All right, a milk shake."

We went to the kitchen. I pulled two scoops of vanilla from the carton, lobbed them into the mixer and added milk, five ice cubes, and a silky line of chocolate. I chunked everything together until it poured smooth and set it before Callapher in a large glass, ignoring the desire to taste it, closing my lips instead to plant a kiss on her head.

"Stay here," I said. "I'll be back in a second."

In the garage, I found a windshield scraper and took it with me back to our room. Callapher followed, sitting cross-legged in the doorway frame.

I stood on the bed with either palm flat against the wall. The magazine pages felt cool, slick to the touch. Curling my fingers, I dug my nails into the pictures. I ripped through the eyes of a model that stared at me through a haze of blood-red heat. I opened the body of a woman's thin stomach as she stretched in a red bikini near the flat surface of still pool water. I peeled away what would give to the grab of my fingers and scratched what obstinately remained with the ice scraper, pulling it along the paneling in long, crossway strips. My fingers cramped from bending against the flatness of the wall. I was scrambling up a steep incline without proper hold.

Callapher observed, "You ruined it."

"It's all right," I said. "I have to clean it up now."

"Why?"

"Because I don't want to look at the pictures anymore."

"Because they make you sad?"

I looked down at her in surprise. She waited for my reply.

"Yeah," I said. "I guess so. You want to help?"

She shook her head yes. I gave her a ruler, with which she scraped the wall vigorously, her tongue sticking out of her mouth in concentration. Watching her work so energetically, my shame deepened. I'd grown accustomed to evoking my mother's anxiety and my father's bashful, silent embarrassment. But I'd forgotten that, like any adult, a six-year-old can love with a love that hurts.

In two hours, we uncovered most of the wall. Pieces of the photographs remained, but each scrap was so small it concealed the image of its whole, as a puzzle piece becomes mere color abstraction without the entirety of the picture to which it belongs. Where completely exposed, the wood was stained with the green-white residue of petrified rubber cement. I scoured the wall with a wet soapy sponge. Wrinkled papers blew about the bedspread and cluttered the floor.

Then I lay flat on my bed, letting the slick papers stick to my skin. My fingertips were puckered white and withered from long immersion in the water. Callapher lay beside me, running her finger people up and down my arm.

At eleven thirty, the front door opened. George entered first. He looked larger somehow in our little living room. Or perhaps it was the gray of his complexion in the orange warmth of the two lamps that made him seem so strange. Mom and Ruby appeared behind him.

When Dad went to Mom, she patted his arm the way a mother

pats a child's back. Resolutely, she said, "Everything's going to be fine."

She made a pot of coffee, wrists snapping with quick efficiency as she turned the coffee mugs open-end up. The adults sat at the table. I stood to the side.

"I shoulda known not to give in to her like that," George said, "but she was so darned determined to get that thing to Mrs. Lowett soon as possible." He shook his head. Without his ball cap, his black hair lay flat, sprouting starburstlike from the center of his scalp to come to gathered points.

He said, "I didn't see it 'til it was too close—jumped right in front of the truck not fifteen feet ahead of us. We'da been all right but for the surprise of that. I seen deer in these parts all the time but never on such a street as that—shopping lots on both sides, and a factory. I don't know where an animal like that woulda come from."

His chest heaved as he labored for breath between words. "But I stand on the brake—you know, gut reaction—I remember too late that I shouldna done it, and as I think it, I hear this sound behind me like a great big gust a' wind, and quick as lightning, just then, I feel the truck bed get lighter—or maybe I'm imagining it. That mattress flew right up—the rope swiveled right out—I heard this sound . . ."

He stopped at this. Ruby looked to the right, then down, and quickly left the room.

"Give her a minute," Mom said, even though no one had moved to follow her.

She slept at our house that night. Dad offered her the bed that Callapher and I shared, but she shook her head. While Mom stretched bedsheets across the couch, I found myself standing in the hallway with Ruby and Ruby alone.

She clasped my upper arm. "Isn't this a terrible thing that's happened?" she asked in a near whisper. I looked into her asking eyes.

Broke her neck, the coroner would pronounce over Margaret's body. Died on impact: we shouldn't worry; she'd felt nothing. A quick blow to the proper juncture, and her soul escaped with the snap of vertebrae, the snap of a rubber band pulled tight, released. Of course I wasn't there, but in my mind I can still see the mattress catching the wind like a sail, bellying up. I can see Margaret's red hat spin against the darkening sky.

Mom appeared in the bathroom doorway. I was washing my face.

"Thank you," she whispered. I looked down. In her hands, she'd gathered a pile of crumpled papers from my floor. White and curled, they blew about in her palms like bits of ash. My little paper kingdoms.

CHAPTER 20

figure

(FIG yer)

1. The outline, form, or silhouette of a thing

ground

(ground)

1. A surrounding area; background

mom handled the mysteriously mundane business of burying the dead, the details of which remained as invisible to me as the preparations of every wedding I'd ever attended. Bury a body, figure in the ground.

There's a verse in the Bible that goes: "What right does the pot have to say to the potter, 'Why have you made me this way?' " Dad frequently quoted it from the pulpit when he addressed the trials and temptations of life. We are just bodies of clay, piles of earth, spinning wild upon this globe, pressed in on all sides and molded by the Artist's hands into vessels with purpose.

If I were made of clay, I would hack off a bulge from my hips and remold it to my breasts. Adam was molded from dust, brought to life by breath shot through his nostrils from the kiss of the living God. Ashes to ashes, dust to dust.

Why have You made me this way?

Mom moved with authoritative purpose, her brow furrowed in concentration. She'd been the same way when Dad lost his ministry, busily moving from one task to the next with sustained, inexhaustible energy, as if by forward movement she could keep a step ahead of what loomed behind. She helped Ruby clean the farmhouse for the funeral reception. They pushed the dining room table and living room chairs against the walls. They vacuumed the carpets, dusted the furniture, and wiped the windows spotless.

Beauregard did not deal kindly with all the upset of routine and the constant barrage of company. Twice Mom tried to set him down and speak with him face to face. On both occasions he ran from the room, urgently waving his hands at his ears as if to ward off a buzzing cloud of insects. From the basement we heard him groan, teeth grinding, guttural moans of frustration, two at a time, followed by complete silence. When people knocked on the door, he repeated the sound, banging a broom handle against the basement ceiling. The teacups and saucers rattled in their cupboards.

People came all day. We received condolences, flowers, and more variations of the Crock-pot casserole than I would have thought creatively possible. That evening, Dad tried to cheer Callapher by draping a dish towel over his arm like a maître d', flourishing a plastic spoon over the proffered dishes, and saying, "Madame, which shall it be: the tuna casserole, the beef casserole, or the Casserole Surprise?"

Callapher said she wasn't hungry. I said the same. For once, no one tried to argue.

We arrived at the funeral parlor at three. The room was laid with patterned carpet and decorated with cheap watercolor prints that hung against dizzying wallpaper. In its emptiness and décor, the room had all the lonely air of a hotel lounge at midmorning. The casket stood at the front, framed on either side by wreaths of flowers propped on brass easels. Strangely, in arrangement and combination, the candle flames and the reflection of fresh flower petals in the casket's polished wood grain reminded me of the Communion table in our old church's sanctuary. I blinked away the comparison. The pungent smell of lilies sickened me.

The top of the casket had been propped back. This lid seemed monumental in weight, waiting to fall with a sound, I imagined, like the banging of discordant keys on a piano. The interior was lined in white fabric that gathered along the edges like the ruffles of a baby bassinet. From the foyer, I could just see the tip of Margaret's white forehead, the blur of her gray bangs.

Callapher kicked her way out of Dad's arms and ran back into the hallway. Dad followed and knelt beside her. I could hear him murmuring gently. My breath caught for my sister: I didn't want to see this any more than she did.

But Mom was walking toward the body. I had no choice but to join her. Together we stood before the casket. Margaret's body lay pressed tightly inside, folded like clothes in a suitcase waiting to be closed. She appeared shrunken in height and stature, her complexion very pink, the colors painted in a powder-soft film over her skin. Her hands lay clasped on her collapsed waist, the skin of each fingertip flat and nearly translucent against the skin of her hand. I looked very hard at her face without recognizing anything of Margaret at all.

A framed photograph of her last church directory picture lay propped inside the casket lid. I studied the photograph: Margaret smiling as if she was sharing an inside joke with the photographer. She was keeping a secret from us, her cheeks flushed and shining, her eyes sparkling. The picture was nothing but ink transferred onto a flat piece of paper. But those colors on that flat piece of paper held more of Margaret than the three-dimensional painted form now lying before me in a bed of white satin and flower petals. The life that once lived in the body now lived in the picture. The spirit had escaped the first and now flitted behind the printed page inside the silver frame, teasing me from the corner of the eye only to vanish when stared at directly.

I stood with Mom and Dad and Ruby in a line beside the casket as people began to arrive. From an invisible source came the tentative play of piano music. I recognized everyone from the church but knew most by face and not name. They hugged me anyway, leaving my clothes with the funk of their accumulating perfumes.

Callapher sat in the front row of chairs lined to face the casket as pews face a pulpit. She swayed her feet back and forth above the floor, twisting the buttons on her winter coat, which she'd refused to take off. The hood hung limp on her back, puffing her hair up all around her. It stuck to her cheeks with static. I gestured for her to stand beside me. She shook her head resolutely.

No other relatives had come. Mom's father died of cancer when I was five. Margaret had one living brother, much older, who lived in Florida belted to a wheelchair, his legs long lost to diabetes. His own children were grown and divided amongst the states.

It was wrong, somehow, this scarcity of family. I saw Margaret as a woman surrounded by generations, the matriarch over her brood. I realized this had been a trick of the imagination, an illusion created by the far reach of her generosity. She did not belong so much as she gathered; she was surrounded by love because she opened her arms in hospitality.

Unwittingly, I'd been standing with my knees locked tight. A faint wave of nausea crept up from the bottom of my stomach. Excusing myself, I went to the bathroom to splash cool water on my face. When I returned to the foyer I found Matthew standing with his hands in his pockets, pretending to study the framed print of a watercolor lily pond. He turned abruptly when I said his name.

"Hey." He stepped forward, taking his hand from his pocket to extend it as if for a handshake. He stopped and reconsidered, running it through his hair instead.

"How long have you been out here?" I asked.

"Not long." He paused, thinking. "How is everybody?"

By everybody I assumed he meant my family—my mother, whom he considered a Puritan, and my father, whom he considered an eccentric. I wanted to appreciate his attempt at kindness, but I answered automatically. He returned with hasty, rehearsed sympathies, his eyes darting briefly to the casket at the front of the adjoining room. I realized that he had no intention of viewing the body.

His proper condolences dispensed, he talked about everything besides the funeral, telling me about his last batch of photographs, about how I'd missed a cafeteria catfight between two freshman girls that had the whole school talking. We both laughed at the story more than we should have. We both laughed as if it were funny.

"Oh, before I forget," he said, reaching into his pocket to retrieve a crumpled envelope. He pressed it against the wall, ironing it over twice with the flat of his palm before handing it to me. "I was going to buy flowers, but Mollie said the Old Maids—I mean Ruby—wanted donations for the church."

I took the envelope from him, noticing that his knuckles were chapped from the dark room chemicals and winter air. When my fingers brushed his hand, he unconsciously jerked it back ever so slightly.

"You didn't have to," I said. I studied the heavily scrawled *for Old Maids* written on the envelope. I looked at his freshly washed and still-wet hair. I looked at the red plastic stem, remnant of a Goodwill price tag, sticking out of his suit jacket collar. An overwhelming feeling of gratitude came over me. Impulsively, I stepped forward and put my arms around his neck.

"Thank you for coming," I said.

I could feel his back tense. Very lightly, he placed his hands on my arms, not exactly holding me but acknowledging the embrace nonetheless.

"Yeah. Sure," he said. Then, more emphatically, he added, "I wanted to come."

For the next hour we sat together on the wooden bench in the foyer watching the people as they filtered through the front doors. I was acutely aware of our silence, but it was not uncomfortable. I wanted him to stay and sit beside me all night. I think he would have had Mollie not interrupted.

She came wearing a black dress and black pantyhose that accentuated the shape of her legs. After hugging my mom and giving Ruby a kiss on the cheek, she returned to the foyer and stood before Matthew and me. She considered our silent surveillance of the visitation until Matthew begrudgingly stood and said, "I'll let you guys talk."

As soon as he left, Mollie linked her arm through mine and led me on a circuit around the hallways of the funeral parlor. It was the first time we'd spoken since the accident.

"How are you?" she asked.

"I'm fine," I said.

"How are you *really*?"

I shrugged. "It's weird. I don't quite believe it happened."

She nodded.

"It really scared Callapher to see the body," I said.

"When I went to Gordon's mom's funeral I couldn't stand to look at the body. I thought it was so dreadful that people kissed it goodbye. That they stood there staring at it."

Mollie thought I'd spoken of Callapher only to disguise my own confusion. I began to interrupt her but realized she was right. I might as well have been speaking of myself.

She was saying, ". . . but I think it's necessary. It forces us to accept the fact that there is such a thing as a body and such a thing as a spirit—that one day they'll separate."

"But I can't think of Margaret's spirit without thinking of her face," I countered. "They're the same thing to me. Mollie, what if we just made up the idea of heaven to save ourselves? What if it's just an illusion?"

"Faith," she replied simply. She quoted: "'Faith is being sure of what we hope for, certain of what we do not see.' It doesn't matter what you see. It matters what you know. I know."

I was exasperated. I hated answers like that. "It's not that I don't want to believe," I retorted. "But I can't just assume things are the way I want them to be. I can't base my whole life on wishful thinking—on Christian storybooks."

"But we didn't just make it up, Olivia. We're basing it on a Bible that's been preserved through centuries—"

"A book," I clarified, interrupting.

But she continued without stopping: "—on thousands of believers who've gone before us. There's an entire history behind us, reaching all the way back to Christ. It's bigger than you or me or our own ideas of what's true and real."

I withdrew my arm from hers. "I believe in a God," I said defiantly. "But sometimes I fear His nature."

Mollie's eyes slid down over my body. I realized that unconsciously I'd wrapped my arms tight around my waist.

Mollie bit her lip. She took a breath and said, "Sometimes I don't understand you, Olivia. You're so talented and so pretty." She looked over my shoulder, glancing to where my parents stood beside the casket. "You have this family that adores you. I know Margaret's death is a surprise, but somehow I don't think that's what we're talking about."

I looked at the floor. She *did* know. She'd always known.

"You have everything," she continued softly. "This whole life ahead of you. I hate to see you this way, depressed. What is it?"

What was it? I fought to keep my gaze steady. I studied her eyes, the clear jewel-blue eyes of a mannequin, of a magazine. How could I explain it to Mollie, Mollie who was born with the fortunate disposition to be content with everything and amiable with everyone?

"I don't know what I want," I told her. "Nothing." I shrugged. "Everything."

My cryptic answer annoyed her, I could tell, but she said nothing. She stayed at the funeral parlor for an hour before leaving, sitting with Callapher on her lap and braiding her hair into two pigtails.

"I can't come to the funeral tomorrow," she said to me as she put her coat on. "Gordon needs someone at the front desk, or he'll be there alone."

"That's all right," I said. I looked at her hard. I was seeking forgiveness—a gesture, a glance to say it was all right between us. She turned away before I could find what I was looking for.

At home, Callapher fell asleep almost immediately. I lay fully awake beside her in our bed, staring through the blank wall.

I woke in the middle of the night with a start. I lay awake for nearly an hour, trying to sleep. My belly sank flat: the hard-won prize for the meager dinner I'd allowed myself. I went to the kitchen to pour a glass of water. At the dining room table, I debated between a slice of bread or a piece of fruit. I wanted the slice of bread, but it was wrong to eat such a thing at such a time. No, I had to retract, recalculate. I can eat when I'm hungry; that's the new rule. But it should be something normal. Normal people ate ice cream and cookies for late-night snacks, not plain slices of wheat bread or sixty-calorie apples.

I cradled my head in my hands. The drinking glass was sweating a little puddle of water on the table. It spread to wet the corner of Mom's Bible. The book was black-leather-bound, its rice paper divided by the frayed red ribbon of a sewn-in bookmark. I scanned the concordance for the word *heaven*. In Revelation I found a lot of weirdness fit for Milton. Wheels with eyes, scrolls to be opened, judgment poured like tar from cauldrons. I went back to the beginning of the New Testament, but Jesus gave very little physical description of the eternal-happy-ever-after. It seemed heaven was not so much about a place of glory as it was about proximity to the source of glory: "I go to prepare a place for you," He'd said, "and where I am, there you will be."

When I tried to pin down an exact image of heaven I saw only a profuse cloud of white, brilliant with light. I never saw wings or golden gates. Though in the back of my mind there existed the vague idea of a city, it had never been clarified or perfected by effort or real imagination and floated like a strangely illustrated facsimile embarrassingly reminiscent of the Little Mermaid's undersea palace.

As a painter, I'd learned that the laziness of my imagination was rivaled only by its caprice. Memories changed with time, replacing the past. Facts I'd memorized vanished like etching in sand washed daily smooth by the tide. Nothing I created ever matched its original inception, for the idea first conceived was always too vague to bear translation to a page or to canvas. I read whole novels with just the words before me, never solidifying the faces of its characters.

In this shifting memory, among this host of ill-defined figures, was Jesus, an obscure collage of ideas and art and fantasy. Whenever I'd prayed in my life, it had been to the floating and benevolent face of the painting that hung in our old church: kind eyes, Jewish curls, a plain robe glowing through a haze of desert dust. All these years, I'd been praying to the memory of a painting. My prayers had never gone beyond the canvas of another artist's dream world. I'd prayed to an idol carved from stone, a god given name and shape by its creator.

You don't exist, I thought. *Or You don't care.*

The clock on the kitchen wall above the sink tick, tick, ticked. The tree outside the window leaned in the winter wind. The sharp shadows of its branches swayed across the table with the slow forward and inevitable backward of a swing on a swing set—rising up only to sink back.

And then a voice said, *Do you want to be healed?*

I sat up, surprised but not frightened. The voice had not been audible, but each word surfaced in my mind with clarity. I waited, daring the air before me.

"God—help me," I said aloud. My own voice sounded strange in the silent room. The house seemed empty, as though my parents and my sister had been sent away, and all the world outside the windows had been suspended.

I waited without believing in a reply. My words were insincere. I'd spoken them in earnest but with the obstinacy and childishness of a dare. I wanted a god to crack the ceiling like eggshell and strike the darkness with widening seams of brilliant light. That would never happen. And I didn't expect it to.

I envied the hope of the parishioners planning to attend Margaret's funeral. In turn, I resented their obtuse, blind optimism. After hearing of the accident, I couldn't avoid the idea of Margaret in white flitting about some glorious ever-after. I'd never have admitted to believing in these silly pictures, but at the funeral, seeing her body dispelled them permanently.

I poked the soft of my stomach with my forefinger, remembering the fallopian tubes on the poster in the doctor's office. In textbooks, organs are clean. They situate prettily within the lines, distinguishable one from the other by the diluted watercolor pastels of storybook illustrations. If I were to open my belly with a knife, I would find blood, sinew, and pulsing pressed meat.

I'd seen surgery performed on cable television. I'd seen the living tissue of an exposed brain visible between skin pulled back from a scalp like tent flaps opened. The surgeon prodded the pink, sweating membrane with a slight metal rod. Each time he touched the patient's brain, lights flashed in tandem rhythm on the machine stationed beside the anesthetized man's head. They were trying to pinpoint which sections of the brain were responsible for what: coordination, concentration, decision, emotion.

I found the operation sordid, not for its premise, or execution, but for the reality of the brain. The head was not a vast cavity of glitter and cinematic pictures. It was gray tissue squeezed in too tight.

In the bathroom, I stripped down to my underwear and stood on the toilet so I could see the reflection of my entire body in the mirror over the counter. I pretended it was the chair in Lori's drawing exercise. I stared hard until it was my body that gave the air shape. Then a strange thing happened. When I saw this body as an object in the room—when it became merely one thing that gave other things shape and not the only shape that I saw—it appeared slight. Small. Almost frail.

I stepped down from the toilet and dressed slowly. My hands were trembling. In the bedroom, I lay in bed with them flat at my sides. I felt very funny. Sort of excited and liberated and scared. It was like waking up. Or putting on glasses. It was like learning that perspective was an invention. I was giddy with the shock and wonder and pleasure of discovery.

I pressed my cheek against Callapher's little shoulder. She lay belly down, her face pressed flat against the pillow, her cheek squashed up against her nose. I put my arm across her back, feeling for the movement of breath. When I couldn't feel anything, I sat up in a sudden panic, rolling her over to lay my ear against her chest. I held my own breath to listen for hers. With my fingers pressed to her lips, I finally felt it: the gentle hot whisper of life, exhaling.

I curled up against her. Her lips puckered a little, mumbling mutely in the language of dreams. I placed my hand on her chest, hoping to hold her soul to earth by the press of my palm.

CHAPTER 21

"don't put it in there; it won't last," Ruby said of the flower Callapher had stuck in a warm can of Pepsi. We sat in the van waiting for Mom and Dad. The black hearse idled directly ahead of us, the driver waiting at attention beside its open front door.

"I don't have water," Callapher protested. "It will die."

"It's already died, dear. Flowers can't live without roots. See, the tip's been nipped."

The back door opened with a sudden violent onslaught of cold air; Mom placed another flower arrangement behind the seat. "They said they'd deliver the rest," she said to no one in particular. Then, "Dad's coming."

At the cemetery, we stood around Margaret's future grave as Pastor Evans said the final prayers. My temples ached with a pulsing, steady rhythm. I concentrated on the ground, wishing I could cry or look more disturbed. When everything had been done and an amen said, I marched behind Dad down the hill toward the van. While we were waiting for Ruby to conclude her good-byes, I caught him staring up at a fixed point on the hill. I turned to follow his gaze and saw a figure in a brown coat standing in the distance, nearly hidden by the line of trees that delineated the cemetery from the neighboring undeveloped land.

"Who is it?" I asked Dad.

He studied my face, as if considering his answer. "Mrs. Lowett, I believe," he answered finally.

I turned back, but—as if sensing my intrigue—Mrs. Lowett had disappeared.

"Does she know?" I asked.

"What happened? About the accident only, not the circumstance. Ruby told her as little as was necessary. She doesn't need to know more."

As we left the cemetery, we drove beneath a tall arch at which the ends of the circling stone walls met. A metal placard hung on the left stone buttress of the archway. On the placard, beneath the name of the cemetery, was the raised silhouette of a carriage driven by a man in a top hat. I stared at the molded figure, struck by its strange familiarity. A mere moment of déjà vu, perhaps. For I couldn't place the recognition it aroused.

On a folding table set up in Margaret's cleared living room, Mom set out plates of wet and crisp vegetables, triangles of salami with cubes of cheese, and a Crock-pot of chunked soup. The walls of the house shrank in with each new guest. There was no music but a great deal of buzzing talk, pierced by the occasional and seemingly impertinent sound of laughter.

I paced amongst the thick of black suits and dresses, unaware of the indistinct faces crowding near my own, breathing through my mouth to escape the dense competition of purple perfumes. The image of the man on the placard would not leave my mind. I avoided eyes and talk, like an uninvited stranger at a party. I found an empty seat and anchored myself to it.

"Don't know what she'll do with it all," said one woman.

"You think she'll keep it on?" her companion asked.

"'Course she will; what else would she do with herself?"

"Well, what about Lowett's boy? What about him, is what I say."

They were discussing the matter of Margaret's will. She'd left the house and land to Ruby. The women behaved as if this were an unexpected turn of events.

"Well, I don't know who else she'd give it to," said the one. "It's not as if she had family lined up for the taking."

My particular metal folding chair sat flush with the back of the couch so that the women spoke behind me. The hat of the ringleader brushed my neck when she turned her head. I listened accidentally. I was still trying to figure out the image of the footman.

"Remember the time she dressed as Moses?" one woman cried.

They all laughed, and in a flash I remembered. I had dreamed his figure when we first came to Bethsaida. A man in a suit opening a door.

I stood. "Excuse me," I said to absolutely no one in particular. Taking my coat from the pile on Margaret's bed, I escaped the farmhouse and ran for the Shoe Box. I took the keys for the truck from the counter and left a note in their place:

Gone to the cemetery. Back soon. ~Olivia

‡ ‡ ‡

I stood beneath the archway, craning my neck to gaze up at the placard. The little sculpture was dirtied black but rubbed to a bronze sheen at its upraised parts. It would smell, I decided, like an old penny that has warmed an hour in your palm or pocket. I tried to envision the peculiar dream. What I remembered most was the anticipation it left me with. A sense of destiny or of destination. A sense of joy. That there was a journey to take and a driver to take me.

That's all it had been—a silly dream. The carved image was merely a coincidence. Any semblance of circumstantial design was the result of my imagination connecting this moment to another in the past, a comforting but contrived symmetry. A bit of burning sun glinted sharply over the corner of the stone arch above, blinding me temporarily.

I walked away. The road was just wide enough for a single parade of cars. The one-way street implied permanence: a coming in, without an exit. With alarm, I realized I had no idea where to find Margaret's gravesite; I'd paid little attention when Dad drove us to the plot earlier that day. But then it occurred to me that I'd come without any real intention of visiting her grave. So I left the cleanly laid way of the paved road.

The surface of the snow broke underfoot like a sheet of burnt sugar. My boots left clean footprints to trace my route. The shape of the air was grand around me. I was alone and insignificant. The sky was too large. I might fall into it. Somehow, I remained fixed to the ground. I parted the thick resistance, the bow of a boat displacing still, heavy water.

The forest rose to meet me, the ancient trees watching with silent equanimity the fast-breathing speed of my life. I entered the woods. Back to the living, I thought. In the field lay the dead, kept at bay by layers of earth. Here, life soared underground in the pumping strength of fist-tight roots punching through the earth.

I'd not come for the placard; I'd not come to see Margaret; I'd come for the loneliness. I needed to escape the walls of people closing in—the church, the well wishers, then my mother and the doctor. Soon there would be a psychologist or a psychiatrist. I didn't know the difference. What did it matter? He would be an educated somebody with a paper and pen, ready to translate my confusion into clean little words and tidy prescriptions.

It felt quite necessary to be rid of this body entirely. Shed it like wet clothes, like snakeskin, and be done with it. The trees waved their consent.

I took off my hat and unwound my scarf from my neck. Pulling the middle finger of my glove to a tip, I slipped my hand out from inside. I laid each article neatly upon a rock jutting up from the ground, its surface dry and clean of snow. I unbuttoned my coat, folding it beside the gloves. I took off my shirt. My stomach heaved at the shock of cold: my diaphragm snapping an involuntary intake of breath. With slow and methodical gestures—feeling as though I'd performed the ritual before, in a dressing room or a doctor's office—I discarded everything until I stood motionless and nearly naked, the thin fabric of my underwear clinging to my body like a second layer of skin.

The body resisted. The skin rose up, each pointed hair sharp as the prick of a needle. The blood soared to crowd and cushion the brain. I demanded the pain. This was it: the will against the body. I had come to the place between instinct and choice where the spirit must reside. That priests might torch their own heads in protest, that an injured man might hew his own beloved but diseased limb to save those parts yet living. That women, voluntarily, might starve themselves.

I lay down, back flat to the frozen ground, arms outstretched in a jumping jack, in a snow angel. I burned my eyes on the patch of white sky above. The overarching branches bent at their elbows, dividing into the intricate network of neurons or of veins. The snow became visible only when it drifted in front of the dark trees. It seemed the sky itself was breaking down, bits of the heavens drifting lazily, spinning, left, right, down, down.

The hard, throbbing pain of cold pulsed in my hands and feet and face to the rhythm of my heartbeat. Arms and legs shaking violently. Teeth bashing together hard as rock. I braced myself. Quick as that, the body obeyed. It couldn't run away without my permission. It couldn't cover itself if I demanded nakedness. I'd been its prisoner long enough. By the power of will, I held it down as it trembled in protest. I concentrated on the trees above. I traced the tip of a finger stem to the bough, to the trunk, then beneath the earth to the web of roots spreading outward again. In textbooks they show the earth sliced from the side, so you can see the roots fanning in the ground just as the boughs break the sky: the bottom half a reflection of its top. The single trunk between connects the visible to the hidden.

I am the Vine, and you are the branches, Jesus said. I am the touchstone between all that is visible and that which is not. I reminded myself: that Jesus had a body like mine made of dust, of flesh and blood and bone with a little brain of gray tissue.

This is why I'd come. To be alone with *Him*. To have it out with Him. Why, why, why did You make me this way?

The trees didn't answer. I was invisible to them, a camouflaged animal, joining its environment. My body was disintegrating fine as glitter, becoming, like Margaret, a part of the earth. My legs and arms had disappeared. My nose and ears were vanishing. Soon I would be without head or face—only vision, given shape by the tingling gold pain that framed the contour of my temples and formed to the back of my still-present eyeballs. I laid my palm against my chest. Only where my own skin touched skin could I feel. My heart pounded angrily against its cage of ribs. A different heart from the one of my childhood—I'd lost the pink-lined box in which I'd kept my felt-board Jesus.

A great gust soared through the trees, a wind that split the forest ceiling and shot back up from the ground like a diver cutting the depths of a pool to arch back to the surface. Black strings—no, my hair—flew up in chaos. My breath caught. The trees groaned with a creaking like the shifting of beams in the bowels of a great ship at sea. It was the wind of Pentecost coming, exultant with fingers of fire for waiting disciples, the deposit of the Holy Spirit. I knew spirit to be a wind invisible and liquid, something you could grasp at without catching. It was spirit I saw in Margaret's eyes. Now her body would decay, her eyes fold into shadow. How was I to understand a spirit without the body?

Do you not know that your body is the temple of the Holy Spirit?

The snow fell from the opaque sky. The ground kneaded my back. Was it possible? That the Spirit of God is known as all spirits are known: in the face of its host.

In her robe of tablecloths, Margaret had once pronounced for Christ: *Whatever you do unto the least of these you do unto Me.* Each time she touched another or fed the poor or opened her arms to the weary, she was showing compassion to Christ. In loving her fellow man, she had loved Him. In loving Him, she accepted His love for her. It was a web of human touch, of the Spirit of Him who loved passing from body to body like nutrients through veins or through tree limbs.

Then I saw it: the church a divine network shooting outward, each branch alive by the power of life surging upward from the root. I saw the body of Christ dead, embalmed, then risen. The spirit of Christ no more tangible an abstraction than my own but—as air or wind or warmth or love—no less real for its invisibility. Those who love in His name are the visible manifestation of the Kingdom unseen.

Clear and bright, here, oh, God, oh God, it was true, it was real and I saw it, there, *here*, in the past and unfolding in the future: the beauty of Christ . . . a love never ending that defies the dying of the world.

The vision overwhelmed me in a moment, the web of love and life bursting outward like a firework exploding.

Reeling in the after-glory, the pattern of the tree limbs imprinted on my eyelids, I tried to stand. I tried to raise my head. But I'd snapped the circuit between spirit and body, and the body had escaped me. I lay paralyzed until, of an effort not my own, I was lifted up.

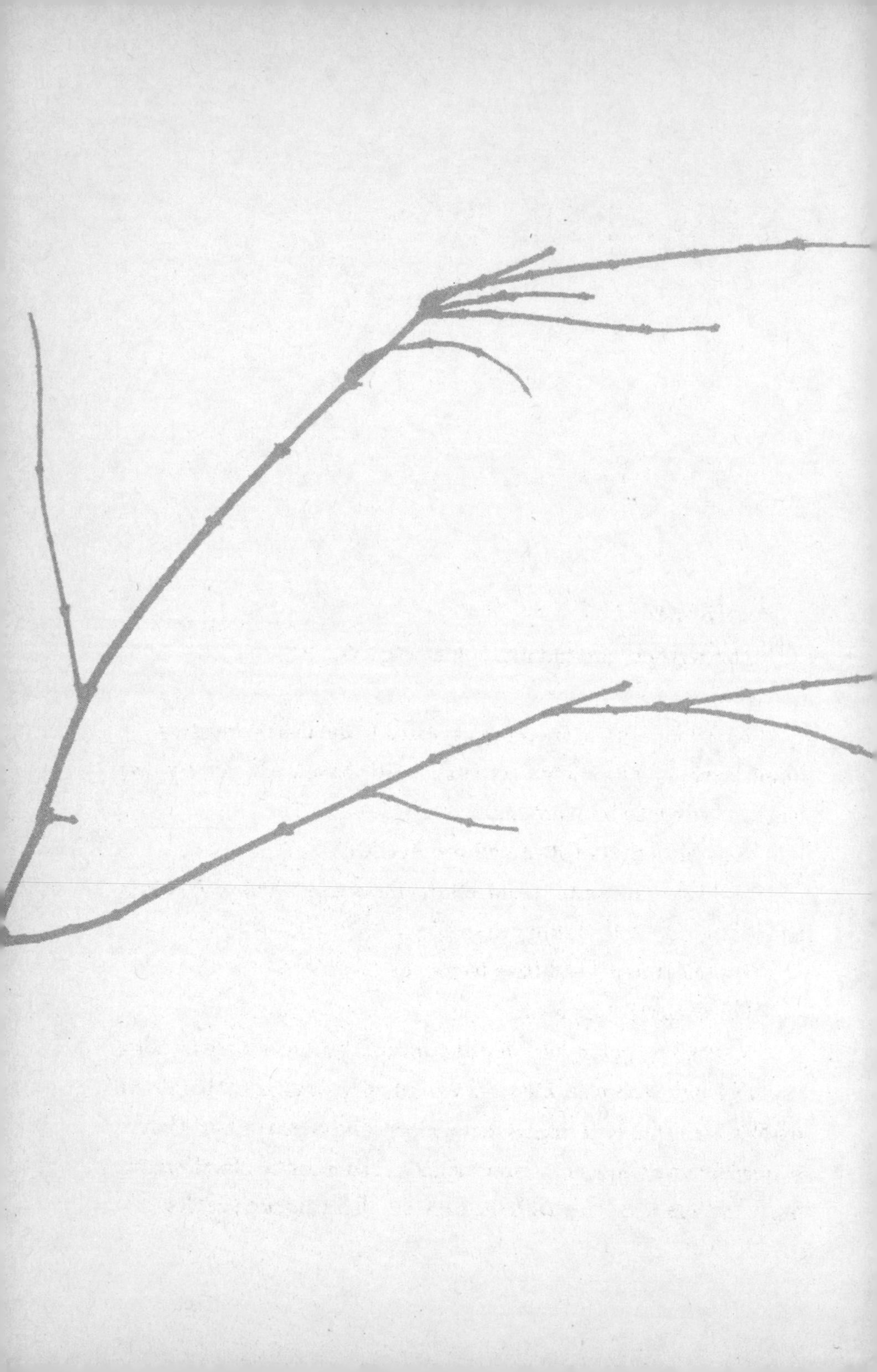

CHAPTER 22

"olivia!"

Arms wrapped around me. Something soft.

"Olivia!"

I forced my eyes open. Mom appeared in the dissipating gray. Immediately, I looked down in shame for my nakedness, but my coat had been wrapped back around my shoulders.

"Are you all right? Olivia, can you feel this?"

I nodded. "I'm sorry," I said, tasting the warm saltiness of blood: I'd split my lip in the attempt to speak.

"We've got to get you back to the car."

"I'm all right," I insisted.

"You have to get inside," she demanded. "Your hands are freezing."

My hands were pale, the surface of my skin strangely shiny. I stared dumbly at the ten bent fingers that no longer belonged to me. They seemed far away. Suddenly I was standing. The shock of blood returning to my legs struck me with the pain of a thousand hot needles.

"It's all right, it's all right," Mom said. "You're going to be fine. We've got to get you dressed."

She'd spread her coat on the ground so that I could stand with my feet protected from the snow.

"Hold on to me," she commanded, placing my hands on her shoulders. I slipped once, unable to grasp them with my unfeeling fingers. I managed to balance with an elbow on either of her shoulders as she helped me into my pants. She lifted my feet and pulled on my socks. My sweater had fallen in the snow. Mom took off her own and pulled it down over my head. I stood dumb and still as she dressed me, not so willingly obedient as simply incapable of protest, like the mannequin with glazed eyes and glossy skin.

I wouldn't have thought it possible, but Mom lifted me up as if I were a child, with one arm beneath my back and the other beneath my loose hanging legs. Her bare arms lay exposed to the winter sky. She left her coat behind. It lay flat on the ground, its arms open so that its black silhouette against the white seemed a tangible haunting of my own figure there on the snow.

The van was ahead of us, parked where my footprints began. Mom set me down to open the passenger door. I leaned into her body to balance. We didn't speak as she drove; talk was impossible. The world behind the window spun, a disorienting kaleidoscope of white, black, and yellow. The gabled attic windows of the Old Maids' farmhouse rose up from the confusion. I heard the ignition of a car in their drive. People standing on the lawn, dressed in black.

We reached our driveway, and Mom jumped from her seat. She flung open my door, pulling me out like the car was on fire. I wanted to laugh and tell her it was all right, that she didn't have to worry. I wanted to tell her that I understood, now, and things were going to be all right. She looked so worried. She needed to sleep. To rest and smile.

Water thundered against the bottom of the bathtub. Mom knelt over the side, testing the water temperature with the flat of her wrist as if preparing a baby's bottle. She worked again at my legs—rolling up my jeans. I sat upon the tub edge, my feet in the bath. Still kneeling, Mom wrapped her arms around mine from behind. Together we leaned forward, until I saw our hands shimmer beneath the surface of the water. I did not know my hands from hers. The pouring water roared. I turned my head to better smell her smell: musk and the faint hint of sweat staining the underarms of her blouse. Her voice gained clarity in my ears. "Keep them under . . . that's right. Just keep them under."

I didn't know what she was so worried about. Then the pain began. It gathered slowly at my wrist, a viscous slow line of heat that began to throb and pulse. The stump ends of my wrists burned like torches, my hands growing back. The wrist unfolded the palm, the palm pushed forward fingers. Each tip roared in silent flame. I must have moaned. Mom's grasp tightened.

"It's all right," she said. "It's all right."

I bit my lip to keep silent. It still tasted of blood. I slipped on the edge of the tub, nearly falling in. Mom let go of my wrists to catch my waist. The pain filled my mind, blinding me to everything else. In coming back, my fingers and toes made the rest of my body vanish. I was only aware of their burning shape and of Mom's arms around me.

When I surfaced again, the confusion had gone. Mom examined my raw fingers, bending each back gently. I heard someone crying. My confusion was still so great that for five whole seconds I mistakenly assumed the sounds came from me. Then I felt hot tears on my neck. Mom was shaking.

She sat on the toilet, cradling her forehead in her hands. When I forced my way onto her lap, she didn't protest. I wrapped my still dripping hands about her, burying my face in her neck. After a while, it was difficult to tell if she held me or I held her. I suppose we balanced each other.

That evening I lay in bed with my hands snug beneath the warm pile of covers. I was conscious of them curling like two pets—strange little things with their own personalities, sleeping with me under the covers.

I gazed up at the now blank wall beside my bed. Bits of paper still glued to the paneling flickered like candle flames in the breeze of the spinning ceiling fan above. I closed my eyes. The wall was naked. I was naked. I'd lost something, but there were no eyes looking down on me anymore.

Voices murmured through the walls. Dad was warning Callapher about the skillet. I smelled pancakes and bacon. Breakfast for dinner: Callapher's favorite. Metal clanged against the stove. My mother's laughter rang out, unexpected and lovely.

A car pulled into our drive. Its doors opened, slammed shut. Dad answered the doorbell with a sound of surprise. Callapher ran down the hall and back to the living room again. Curious about the commotion, I followed her into the living room to find George McFanny in the doorway, his large boots chunked with mud.

"I brought a couple bags a' things," he was saying. "Took 'em to Ruby, but she said she wanted all donations to come here. Says you'd take 'em, Mr. Monahan."

At Mr. McFanny's feet lay three shopping bags filled to bursting with groceries.

Dad considered the pile. "Of course, George. I'll take them to Mrs. Lowett tomorrow."

"I'd take 'em myself, but seems Mrs. Lowett's being relocated to a new abode, and it might make it easier if'n she gets the stuff after she's done shuffling things about."

"Yes," Dad said, nodding. "I have the address—I'll be sure she gets them." He set the bags on the table, propping his glasses on his head to peer into each.

"Double-padded," he said of the toilet paper situated at the top of one pile. "They've certainly bought the best." He noticed me standing in the hallway. "There she is! I was beginning to think you weren't going to come out of there."

I looked at Mom, surprised. She hadn't told him.

There were times I'd hated her for the way she watched my plate and body. My prison guard, my drill sergeant, my mother.

That evening, I ate the meal she'd prepared. Under the table, I clasped her hand. I was sending her signals, tappings like Morse code. *Yes,* I wanted to tell her. *I promise.*

Late that night our doorbell rang a second time.

"Sorry to bother you so late." It was the choir director. Mrs. Something-or-Other. She elbowed past Dad carrying a pan of sheet cake, a plastic Kroger bag slung from her elbow.

"That's very kind of you," Mom said. "But we've plenty of food from the reception."

"It's not for you," the woman replied curtly. "'S for that woman Miss Margaret was helping out. We've all got wind of it, what she was doing. Just like Margaret. Went out in a blaze of glory, she did, and nothing else woulda been fittin'. I was gonna buy her a big bouquet of all the best, but I got to thinking, and it seemed she might have wanted something more practical left in her wake. So here's a cake and some goods—flour and sugar and a few eggs—and you make sure that lady gets it all. And I've got a check here for the rest of what it woulda cost me for them flowers. You all have a good night, you hear."

She left as abruptly as she'd come.

Dad looked up slowly from the check he was holding. "Claire, this check is for $300."

Mom examined the check over his shoulder. "No flowers would have cost her $300."

Dad shook his head slowly. "I'll tell you what," he said, then proceeded to tell us nothing.

By week's end we'd run out of room. Boxes of rice and cereal and corn bread mix lined the countertops. There were bags filled to bursting with flour, sugar, potatoes, and fruit, stacked cans of beans, corn, and soup. Dad filled our picnic cooler with ice for the overflow.

"I just hope Mrs. Lowett has a good-sized pantry," he said, "or she's going to find herself dangerously swamped."

Callapher jumped up in his lap with a flying leap that nearly knocked his wind out.

"Is it like begetting?" she asked.

He brightened. "Yes, Angel," he said when he'd caught his breath. "It's exactly like that."

EPILOGUE

Resolution

(REZ e loo shun)

1. An explanation, as of a problem or puzzle; a solution
2. In photography or magnification, acuity or sharpness; focus

my afternoon in the forest has taken on an unfamiliarity and abstractness, as carefully preserved memories sometimes do. But I consider it the beginning and the end: the day I met the Servant in white, with His hands outstretched in welcome and the door open beside Him. This is the God-as-man who once hung stripped and flayed and knew to the fullest the grief of the physical body. I'd grown up thinking that it was my responsibility to invite Him into my life if I so cared. Now I see the absurdity of this. All my life, the very deep ache of hunger was His call to me.

When Jesus healed people, He frequently warned them not to tell anyone. I don't tell many people. Anyone can explain away my vision as the calculable effect of desperation and hypothermia. Miracles and revelations don't translate well in English. Some things are more beautiful kept hidden, like romance and kisses and prayers. I once feared I would live life without such things. Men, I knew, would turn away from the grotesque size of my body. At the same time, however, I believed that God would turn away from its inconsequence. I was too large and too small to warrant love.

The first time I flew in a plane, I watched great fields of wheat recede to squares of green and gold in a patchwork quilt, the runway becoming a stripe, then a thread strewn through the land. I imagined men and women similarly shrinking to barely visible specks, blurbs of flesh. The knowledge of my own insignificant size in the eyes of God, whom I then considered the Eye behind the clouds, depressed me. Yet in my seat in the plane, my own hand before me retained its size and its concrete shape. People below disappeared, but cutting the heavens in the bullet of a plane, I was yet large enough to myself to demand notice. To say, "I am here."

Like color and like time, size is relative. It is forever changing with proximity and perception. A man on the horizon is small until he crosses the field to stand, fully grown, beside you. I am small in this universe, infinitesimal inside infinity. But size is never the measure of worth. Each of my cells is its own singing Andromeda. For Christ my body is a temple. My beating heart and thinking brain and running legs: throne, altar, pillar. Loved, every inch. And I am a Father's princess, beloved, shot through with holiness. I carry on my shoulders a burden of glory and on my head a crown of life, light as the hairline gold halos of the painted quattrocento madonnas.

Faith, like beauty, is complicated by the eye. To find both, I had to learn to see with something more. Jesus said that with faith, you can move mountains. Whenever I return to that little town in Pennsylvania, I drive through the hills winking one eye, then the other. I watch the horizon jump to the right, to the left, to the right. By closing the eye, I move mountains.

ACKNOWLEDGMENTS

Thank you, Mrs. Powell, for reading the first fledgling chapter of my novel when I was in the tenth grade and for thereafter addressing me as the next great American novelist.

Thank you to Kay Sloan for telling me I had what it takes and to David Schloss for convincing me to stay at Miami University and complete a masters degree in creative writing. Much gratitude to Kowalski, JJ Miller, Ted Brengle, Squance—my favorite road-trip conversationalist—Kärstin my Other Half, Bill "breaking-boards" Green, and the other esteemed members of the MU Creative Writing Workshops of 2004-06 for their criticism, praise, and friendship. Bryan Roley, thank you for keeping your office door open, and thank you Tim Melley for drilling plot into my brain.

To the Kofenya coffee shop and its workers for keeping graduate students afloat on a steady stream of caffeine and music, and for providing us with a bright, cheerful place where we can at least pretend we are being social when writing for looming deadlines.

Mom and Dad, thank you for raising me with an appreciation for the creations of God and of the imagination. Thanks, David, for sitting an entire day in your lawn chair during a family camping trip to read the first finished edition of the novel, and thank you Grandma for never doubting that I will one day be on the Oprah Winfrey show. Christy, you're forever a fino sister; I love you more than all the bread in the grocery store. Jillian, talking with you kept this story grounded in reality during its final revisions.

Thanks to my copyeditor LB Norton for saving me from several embarrassments with her thorough inspection of the novel before it went to print.

And most of all, I am indebted to my editor, Andy McGuire, for giving my book a chance and for making a sixteen-year-old girl's dream of being a real-live author come true.

ISBN: 0-8024-4084-3
ISBN-13: 978-0-8024-4084-6

Opposites.

Ellen, the daughter of an esteemed family counselor, finds old love notes between her father and her English teacher while trespassing in her teacher's home. Caught in the crosshairs of reckless criminals and power hungry church members, Reverend Clayton and his daughter must now face down both danger and accusations—together.

by Cliff Coon

ISBN: 0-8024-8982-6
ISBN-13: 978-0-8024-8982-1

Nowhere to go.

With their newly built church turned into a smoldering pile of ashes, six teenagers on a mission trip are forced into the Indonesian jungle. A religious conflict that has been brewing on the island for years is now a deadly reality. Their ensuing struggle for emotional stability and spiritual answers proves just as difficult as the physical journey home.

by Lisa McKay

Find it now at your favorite local or online bookstore.

www.MoodyPublishers.com